HOW
TO *EARN*

NECK

& SAVE A WRECK

D.N. BRYN

HOW TO
BARE YOUR NECK
AND SAVE A WRECK

Guides for Dating Vampires
Book Three

D.N. BRYN

Printed in the United States of America
First Printing, 2024

Print (paperback) 978-1-958051-61-0
Print (hardcover) 978-1-958051-60-3
Ebook 978-1-958051-59-7

For information about purchasing and permissions, contact D.N. Bryn at dnbryn@gmail.com

www.DNBryn.com

Cover design by ThistleArts.
Cover and spine typography by Houda Belgharbi.
Page Breaks by Panji Habiburahman on vecteezy.com.
Published with The Kraken Collective.

This work is fictitious and any resemblance to real life persons or places is purely coincidental. No vampires were harmed in the making of this story.

This book contains a major instance of nonconsensual blood drawing by way of vampire bites and phlebotomy needles, perpetrated solely by villainous characters, as well as extensive descriptions of PTSD and complex explorations of consent and boundaries.

For more details, see the back of the book.

To those whose bodies are still fighting to protect them from the pain others inflicted upon them in the past. Healing does not have a deadline.

And to my editor, Asha Hartland, for convincing me to pick the objectively correct title.

With special thanks to Max Coffey-Brittain for helping me better represent Shane's diabetes.

1

Shane

Shane dreamed of him again that night: his vampire.

His. That was how Shane had been referring to the mysterious fanged stranger who'd kissed him at Vitalis-Barron Pharmaceutical's masquerade gala. *His,* like that single press of lips made Shane entitled. It had felt that way at the time, like a declaration.

A claiming.

Shane swore he could still conjure the vampire's touch as they'd danced beneath the shimmering chandeliers, and the prick of the vampire's fangs on his finger. And that kiss... Shane's vampire had paused his flight from security just long enough to steal it before vanishing back into the night, turning himself from a glorious monster into a sentimental memory.

And Shane couldn't stop remembering.

It had been five months since that fateful October night, but his lips tingled even now, curled in the bed that he hadn't shared with anyone in years. If he focused on that sensation, maybe he could fade into the dream again, the hazy realm of sleep letting his fantasies run wild.

But Shane had a vampire he actually knew, who'd agreed to send him the location of her black market blood dealer later today. It had taken a week of buttering her up, promising extensively that he wouldn't say who'd given him the scoop—and that, yes, yes, he was taking his own life into his hands, he knew how dangerous it was to go tromping through a vampire's lair, even a temporary one, especially with the recent uptick in aggression the local hunters were displaying. But he wouldn't be tromping, exactly. He just wanted an interview, and it wasn't like they'd kill him for asking questions. He couldn't chicken out now; this was the make-or-break point of his *War on Blood* article.

Shane rubbed his eyes, scowling at the clock.

1:07 pm.

Before his mysterious gala vampire had crawled into his dreams and made a home there, he would never have been caught in bed past noon on a workday. But who was counting, really? No one. Mostly because there was no one in his life right now who knew him well enough to notice.

He rolled out of bed, clumsily kicking off the sheet, which seemed determined to cling to his calf. One glance at his glucose monitoring app confirmed that he'd slept in longer than he should have.

"Gross," he grumbled, and opened his bedside table, only to remember that he'd used up his last cartridge. The new ones were in the fridge. "Extra gross."

He slumped his way toward the bathroom.

The trek should not have been so hard, considering the abysmally small square footage of his studio apartment. As he forced his way across, he compulsively rated everything he passed: the desk chair and coffee table hit the middle of the list, as necessary furnishings that were not yet *entirely* overridden by dishes and clothes, but the laundry basket that had tipped over at some point last week was a zero out of ten, and the pile of stuff in the corner got negative points. He'd been meaning to donate it for so long that any day now it might acquire sentience. The whole trek felt like a quest, complete with the near-death experience of his cat trying to maul his leg. The skinny black fiend shrieked and dove back under the couch after.

"I'm docking a whole star for that, you nasty trash gremlin," Shane called after her, and made a mental note to pick up more treats that weekend.

And then clean.

He had been meaning to clean—wanting things to *be* clean, if for no other reason than that he knew he worked better in a tidy environment—it just never seemed to get done. There was always something slightly more important. Like his groaning bladder.

The toilet paper had run out, but he stretched for the last tissue in the box by the sink and quickly washed his hands after. He gave the dirty-blonde stubble around his mouth a little glare and untangled the waves of his hair with his fingers before banishing most of it to a high ponytail. A shower was probably in order later. In all fairness, a shower had been in order two days ago but who was counting? Again: no one.

Still, it was a good thing his *Shane Rates Stuff* series didn't include past, present, and future selves...

At least *this* self had a *proper* article to write.

The bathroom door caught on the jacket he'd draped over its handle. He pulled it loose, but something else came free, a few of its white feathers fluttering slowly to the ground. His mask from the gala.

Another feather broke off as he ran a finger over it, and he boosted one knee onto the bathroom counter to delicately loop its tie over the edge of his mirror. It hung gracefully, gently swaying back and forth against the glass.

The rest of his costume for the Vitalis-Barron gala had been a last-minute compilation of a white shawl over white clothing. He hadn't thought much of it as he'd donned it— he'd arrived at that gala expecting a dull night of dragging gossip from the rich attendees as he drearily snapped their pictures for ChatterDash's online celebrity column—but one smile from his vampire had changed that.

"*Cygnus, is it?*" Shane's vampire had mused, the heat in his gaze so strong, even behind his mask of blood-red whirls, that Shane could remember it long after the other few details he'd seen of his vampire's face had slipped from his mind. His vampire's perfect Dracula costume should have given him away then and there, yet the confidence with which he wore it swept over Shane. *"You're certainly lovely enough to be placed among the stars."*

Shane had felt like a prize then, a beautiful thing crowned in constellations and hunted across the night sky. He extended his hand toward the hanging mask and gave the little bow he should have offered back when his vampire asked him to dance. The encircling of his vampire's arms then had been a wonder and a comfort, his mouth so near. Now that Shane knew real fangs had hidden within it, the memory sent a lovely shudder up his spine.

He pressed his fingers to his own lips, watching the way they parted in the mirror and wondering if his vampire had felt that same parting as they kissed, the same soft gust of his breath. Whether his vampire might still remember it.

Even if Shane *had* been forgotten, he regretted nothing. It had brought him here, after all, to his vampire fixation and his first prestigious, paid article since college.

Moving to his kitchenette, he worked out his insulin with far less attention than he knew he should have, over-estimating to keep from having to poke himself again immediately after he ate. He jabbed his pen into a pinch of his stomach skin. His body was made for needles, he'd told his endocrinologist early into his transition. When he couldn't remember a time in his life before diabetes, it kind of had to be. The prick made him think of fangs though, graced by smirking lips beneath a dark half-mask.

Grabbing the last everything bagel and a full glass of water, he plopped down at his desk. His brain wanted nothing more than to drown in his *War on Blood* article. It wasn't technically an article *yet*, just a chaotic outline of notes and questions, and he had nothing useful to do with them without that blood dealer interview.

But he'd gotten this far on determination and courage, and he would make it the rest of the way or die trying.

Since his first real encounter with one of the most stigmatized and sexualized nonhumans that night at the gala, he'd been slowly working himself into the hidden sub-community of vampires that existed within San Salud's inner city. It had taken months of searching just to determine what exactly he was looking for in the first place, but the last few weeks he'd gone all in, running down rumors that took him into back allies and odd little sex and magic shops, frequenting the new vampire-centered blood bank in Ala Santa, and even paying a visit to a freelance metal-worker who accepted commissions from nonhumans. The backyard smith had refused to tell Shane anything beyond *"my customers' privacy is a sacred thing"* and *"maybe you should leave now"* and *"if you don't get out you'll be learning a hell of a lot more about vampires real soon."*

Learning a hell of a lot more about vampires was one of Shane's only two hobbies—all right, yes, obsessions—but he was fairly sure the smith would have just called the cops.

Fuck though, if this lead panned out and he could meet the blood dealer who illegally supplied most of San Salud's vampires, that would throw his investigation wide open. For the article, of course. Not because maybe, possibly, if he hung around vampire haunts long enough, he might run back into his vampire.

His *vampire.*

It had taken the whole night to reveal that the monster was more than a mask—that he, in fact, *was* his mask, a fanged creature of the night in the flesh. He'd taken Shane's breath away, catching him in the darkness, a baring of fangs and a prick of a finger so unlike those he'd grown accustomed to over a life of glucose monitoring.

"You're not planning to eat me, are you?"

"I admit that would be very nice, if you were offering," his vampire had replied, and then, as though he could see the way Shane's fear and intrigue fought, *"Do you think me a monster?"*

"Aren't you?" Shane had taunted. *"Cornering swans in the dark."*

But as alluring as his vampire was, he was far from the only one sneaking through the shadowed corners of the city.

If Shane did well with his article, the Star might hire him full time, and he could be *the* journalist for vampire-related topics. Topics like the cause for the decreasing vampire population in San Salud and why a random board member from Vitalis-Barron Pharmaceutical had admitted to her part in it. Shane could find no evidence linking her to anything shadier than a typical country club, but the more he got his name out there, the more doors he could break down in search of the skeletons within. He had already wormed onto the media list for Vitalis-Barron's Met Galainspired party that took place in a little over a month, hoping that a few well-placed questions to the right people might earn him a lead, or else a beautiful criminal preparing to sink in his fangs.

As things stood though, it was still ChatterDash's excruciating fluff bits that provided Shane's insurance, which knocked the price of his insulin down enough that it would have almost been reasonable, were it an occasional lavish splurge and not the unending cost of the thing literally keeping him alive. He turned to the meme-littered column of regurgitated celebrity gossip he'd been assigned the morning prior, trying to pretend it wasn't the tenth one he'd churned out that week. At least back when they'd been paying him for his rating lists, he could slip in some thoughtful commentary here and there.

His mind was nearly sludge by the time his laptop's chat app started dinging.

Nat1
San Salud.
LARP.
Con.

Of course it was Nat—no one else on his list had talked to him in months. Apparently there was only one way to make friends as a neurodivergent adult: you both had a socially unacceptable obsession with vampires and were just lonely enough to talk about them with a near stranger at a comic shop. Even if Nat's obsession was based in trauma, while Shane's was… less complicated.

Shane-anigans
Explanation please.

Nat1
Are you coming to LARPcon or not?

Shane-anigans
I've already planned a Shane Rates Things for it :)

Nat1
Loser /affectionate

Though not the "official" tone indicator for affection—that, Shane was pretty sure, was a shorter /aff—Nat's spelled out versions made it easier for them both to create and decipher what they needed in the moment.

Nat1
Though tbf the only other person I know who's into anything nerdy is my cousin and they're a miserable overachiever who will drop a grand on a cosplay to make everyone else look bad.
Honestly THAT'S more pathetic than any video content you could make.

Shane-anigans

So now I know just how much I mean to you. /jokes

What about your scientist boyfriend? I thought you'd said you were going to invite him?

Nat1

Idk tbh. He's been acting weird since I got myself fired. Like, overprotective weird. Which, yes, fine, leading up to that I let my grief get the better of me in a bad way, scared off the few people I thought were my friends and dragged my coworkers into a stupid confrontation I knew deep down was misdirected, ate an unfortunate amount of ice cream, that whole drill. But still it's some shoddy energy to try bringing to an event that's meant to be fun.

Also, and sorry if this is tmi, but I think he's still sad that the guy he's been thirsting over at work got laid off for being a vamp.

Like babe, he wasn't into you??? I don't understand why he's so hung up. I mean just go fuck a cute blonde with fangs and get it out of your system already it's annoying.

(He could also be fucking me, I'm RIGHT HERE, but no, he's got to be protective and mopey instead.)

I swear one of these days I'm going to catch a pretty vampire twink and deliver him right to my bf's doorstep.

There was a lot to unpack there, starting with, oh em gee, Nat was telling him personal details about her relationship, which was definitely a Stage Two friendship thing to do, and ending with the fact that he'd just used oh em gee in his head like it was a reasonable expression. He had to take a break from those damn ChatterDash columns.

Nat1
(Sorry did I scare you off.)

Shane-anigans
(No no, I was just getting some typing in on this vapid excuse for a ChatterDash article.)
This sounds like quite the conundrum with QUITE the solution, especially for you.
Are you sure you'd be ready to let another vampire get that close?

Shane didn't know the details of Nat's past—it seemed rude to poke at an open wound—but she'd admitted soon after they'd met that much of what she'd learned about vampires had come from her mentor, who'd done some kind of security and investigative work that put him in contact with them regularly. He'd been murdered five months ago, by a vampire with a record of forcing his fangs on sleeping victims. It had clearly fucked Nat up a bit, including instilling some ideas in her head that weren't particularly kind to vampires as a community. But if they had been put there by an external force, then Shane wanted to believe that with some guidance, she could move past them. This seemed like a good sign: her fear and bitterness wearing off enough that she wasn't acting like any vampire on the street might become the next murderer.

Nat1

Probably not, but I'm trying to be more open. I know, in my head, that not all vampires are like the one who killed my mentor. (And let's be real here, I've kind of let my anger over that consume me to such an unhealthy degree that I had to get fired and meet you to realize it.)

But it's still hard, you know? I've been so obsessed with protecting myself against them, that I forgot it's not just about the fangs, it's about what they do with those fangs. Literally but also, like, metaphorically.

Shane doubted Nat would approve of the way his own vampire used his fangs.

It had been luck that Shane saw that use happen, peering through the glass of the balcony door into the room where his vampire had cornered one of the Vitalis-Barron board members at the end of the night.

"*You are the monsters,*" he'd growled, "*wearing our faces at your ghoulish party while your company feasts on our flesh.*"

When she'd admitted to it—admitted her people were abducting vampires off the streets of San Salud—Shane's vampire had sunk his fangs into her neck, drinking from her until she'd collapsed. That had scared Shane. It scared him so thoroughly that when his vampire turned toward him beyond the glass door—toward his only exit—Shane had wrapped both hands around the outside knob.

"Is this where Phaethon dies?" his vampire had asked, casting himself as the lover that the swan constellation, Cygnus, mourned for. And Shane had known that if it were true, his grief would indeed throw him into the stars in one way or another.

So he'd opened the door.

He'd set his vampire loose.

And as his vampire had run into the night, the valiant monster had turned back once, pressing his lips so gently to Shane's. Though Shane's right mind had warred against it, his heart had yearned in that moment to be swept off his feet and whisked away like the old lore. Which was ridiculous— he knew how those biased stories ended, and it was not with happily ever after.

But he swore he could still feel his vampire's kiss lingering like starlight on his lips, and if he left all rational thought behind, he could believe the ultimate mythical tragedy would be worth another chance at that.

Shane swallowed and tried to roll away the tingling of his lips. It was the middle of the day now—or the middle of his day, at least, even if the night had technically already fallen— and he certainly didn't need those fantasies wrecking him yet. God, he needed a distraction or else he was going to spiral from this, end up curled on his floor with a box of gingersnaps as big as his head, hunting through pictures from the gala for a glimpse of his vampire in the background, for confirmation that he was real and any clue he could follow back to him again, even just a glimpse of the mouth Shane could eternally feel pressed to his own but couldn't quite picture in his mind any longer. He knew from experience that the backlash of that would decimate his mental health, and when the lead he was hoping for came in tonight, he needed every bit of his brain functional.

That meant turning his attention to special interest number two. He swore he had a half-outlined *Shane Rates Things* for the Fishnettery's aesthetic somewhere around here. And there was always half a chance that if he hung around the place enough he'd find a cute person to fantasize about in his vampire's place.

Shane turned in his ChatterDash articles for the day, and with a much-needed shower and a less hurriedly calculated dose of insulin, he headed out into the night.

2

ANDRES

Andres had decided to stop having dreams, since Maul was slowly taking them all away from him.

"We need that blood now," Maul said, his gravelly voice made rougher by their terrible phone connection. Knowing the vampire, he was probably in a basement somewhere setting up for the night's sales. Or, more likely, barking at the poor employees he'd roped into doing the work for him. "Andres, Andres, you know how this business functions. We can't survive off a few stolen bags here and a few stolen bags there. I need you to steal two hundred pints by tomorrow if we're going to compete with that damn blood charity—Hey! Table goes on the left, we have to fit the cart in here still!"

Andres held the speaker away from his ear with a cringe, pacing beside his kitchen counter as he waited for his boss to finish shouting. He tried to sound unemotional but decisive—Maul was more likely to respect that. "A few bags here and there will all add up once I've planted my people in enough of the human's blood banks, but I can't *do* that in the first place when the blood banks are on high alert because we

15

keep wiping out their entire supply every time they lower their guard enough for someone from my team to slip in."

My team, he said, when he really meant *your* team. The only members Maul hadn't forced upon him were so hard fought for that sometimes Andres wondered if Maul was doing it just to annoy him.

Andres ran his fingers through his hair. He could hear Maul in his head, snorting and telling him he was going to go bald if he kept doing that. Ironic, coming from a man who would have trouble competing with an egg, much less Andres's thick, dark locks. And the incessant motion saved him on gel. He sighed, dropping his hand to the counter. "A big heist is riskier than a long-term plant, too."

"That's why I've got you to *run* the heist." Maul paused, his tone twisting. "Unless you don't think you're up to it?"

That was not a question Andres had the luxury of answering no to, not unless he wanted to see Maul replace him with someone less conscientious. And there was the house to consider. And the paychecks. "I'm not worried about our safety on the heist, but the fallout that happens after it. You know how the media runs with these things. They pick it up like wildfire, and every other blood bank in the city will be on their guard by evening. Donations will dip and they'll double the police presence around the better sites, and when our stores are low again next month, we'll be in the same position, but up a river with no paddle."

"Can't handle a police presence suddenly? And here I thought you were the one who talked his way into—"

Andres cut Maul off before his boss could describe one of the many cons he'd run over the last decade. "No, no, that's not a problem for me."

He wrung his hair again. How was he supposed to explain to someone like Frederick Maul, who watered down and marked up the blood he sold despite the hardship it put on his own community, that Andres's problem was that very hardship? Renewed attention would make Andres's own work more difficult, but more than that, he cared about the vampires they'd arrest just for walking by a blood bank and the hatred which would stir throughout the city as the news cycled back to the theft over and over again, dramatizing it as though the vampires involved had sucked the stolen blood straight from dying children.

It was a dangerous short-term solution for everyone.

"We wouldn't have this issue if our best customers weren't getting snapped up by Vitalis-Barron hunters for their pharma experiments, while the rest scurry down to that damned blood charity." Maul grunted. "If Jose's is raking in the stuff, why don't you try your plant idea there? They can't possibly miss a few bags a night."

Andres felt sick at the thought. While he'd never been to it himself, Jose's Blood Bank had made life much easier for the most impoverished of his community, and that was enough to endear it to him. It was doing something that he could not so long as his life and business were under the thumb of Frederick Maul. So he tried to snag his boss's attention back with a half-truth. "We shouldn't have to. I think I'm closing in on Vitalis-Barron."

Closing in was an overstatement—by the time his current lead panned out, he'd probably already have taken advantage of the pharmaceutical company's annual onsite party next month to sneak into the corporate offices above their research labs and strip them of whatever information he could. But Maul still took the bait with an excited hum. "You bring me whatever evidence you find the moment you do. You know how sensitive this is. If we're going to hit them where it hurts, we can't be letting our guard down."

"Of course."

"And Andres? Send your team in at midnight." Maul didn't ask. He didn't have to; it didn't matter how good Andres was at talking and sneaking and sidestepping his way into places that no one wanted a vampire to go, Frederick Maul was the only one who'd take on a felon-turned-vampire, much less rent them decent living quarters.

"Make it one-thirty." Andres said, just to wrestle back a sliver of control. It wasn't as satisfying as he'd have liked, his worry and anger still roiling deep in his belly. "You have a van for me to transport them in?"

"I'm bringing in the black one we used for Burning Man last year."

Big festivals were prime places for phony donation centers that lured high and drunk attendees into dark tents long enough to fill a bag or two—most of them never even realized what happened. "I thought the fridge in that one was faulty? What's wrong with our usual rides?"

"There's been a human poking around their storage lot."

Andres feigned a scoff, because it was what Maul would expect from him. "You're afraid of a nosey human?"

"I'm not afraid; I'm cautious. This man says he's some kind of journalist. He's been sticking his head into vamp lairs all over the city for weeks, hounding my customers and banging down doors." Any vampire had a right to fear that, but the way Maul explained it, Andres could tell all too well who the predator was. "Don't worry, though," he continued. "Next time he pokes his head out, I'll take care of him."

Andres couldn't help the shudder that ran down his spine. He dragged his fingers through his hair, trying in vain to relieve the uncomfortable sensation. Take *care* of him. That could mean two things. One of them wasn't so bad, he told himself. One of them had made Andres what he was, after all.

He almost missed Maul's next statement over the thrum of his own heart. "Take the Burning Man van. And check in when it's done."

"I always do," Andres scrambled to reply, his final word meeting the buzz of a dead line. He leaned against the counter, covering his head with his hands, and breathed out. It didn't clear the slimy sensation of Maul's voice from the back of his mind.

Calls to the team members he'd be taking on this heist didn't help either, one of them acting like he needed Maul to personally confirm every step of the plan and the other's voice going audibly distressed when Maul's name was mentioned. Andres worried about her. She said she was fine, though. That she was dedicated. He wasn't quite sure why those two things went together, though occasionally Maul made a fuss over the latter, so perhaps that was it.

If anyone knew what it felt like to be berated and coerced by their boss, it was Andres, but at least *he* had learned how to conceal his emotions from his voice, or to find other outlets. He was a proper vampire—no matter how much some of his conversations with Maul made him feel like a will-ridden drone from the human's monster legends—and he could prove that. With four hours before he needed to be at his team's meetup point, he had the time for it.

There was more than one way to steal blood in this city, after all.

Besides, he'd been hounded that week by the sort of craving that only something warm and fresh and tasty could satisfy... something straight from the veins of an attractive human with a sharp smile and a fierce intellect. The image that thought conjured—dirty blonde waves tucked behind a feathered mask; hazel eyes that had flashed with such an enticing, breathless combination of fear and intrigue; a perfect, delicate neck scattered in soft freckles—made him sway. Andres hadn't thought of that night in days—weeks?

After he'd first broken down and used the author name listed on Shane Cowley's ChatterDash gala article to stalk like a cyber predator through his socials, Andres had sworn he was done fantasizing. But no matter how many times he put away his gala mask, it always managed to return to him.

It hung now from the mannequin bodice, atop the cape he'd worn that night, which he'd since embellished with a patchwork of black lace flowers and deep red satin that turned it into a beautiful, billowing wrap. It struck Andres as the wrong size and style for him, perfect for someone smaller, fairer. Someone who'd worn a swishing shawl when they'd met, whose slim lines and long limbs would glow beneath the darkness of the fabric. That was a ridiculous thought, though. He would never see Shane again. With Maul's presence still leering over his life from a distance, he wasn't sure it was right to pull any human into that.

Andres lifted his hand to his hair, then forced it back down. His insides felt wrong, a slight burn at the back of his eyes.

Perhaps he was more stressed by Maul's nonsense than he'd assumed.

Or he simply needed the release of having a human beneath his fangs. That was it, probably. It was certainly why he was now envisioning the moment he'd first caught his little swan, clothed in white and already flushing beneath his touch.

Andres swore his heart had stopped.

He hadn't meant to keep coming back throughout the party, to lead Shane on, but each flirtatious tease pulled at him, and the eagerness with which Shane fell for his every charm was intoxicating. When his swan had trembled as

Andres finally bared his fangs, it had ruined him, like that single moment of vulnerability was carved into his soul. Andres had called him Cygnus teasingly, but by the end of the night, he thought perhaps Shane really was his constellation. The last time they'd made eye contact, Andres had turned back to steal a final kiss goodbye, as half a taunt and half a gift—something to remember him by, for better or for worse.

The soft graze had lingered on his lips for hours, then weeks.

But Shane Cowley wasn't his, and he never would be.

Andres tried to ignore the way that knowledge sunk into him like claws, hitting all the same places that Maul had already felt the need to maim. He'd just have to find another release. There were other humans in this city who'd tremble under the pressure of his fangs.

He threw on one of the three leather coats he'd customized during a series of sewing tutorials on his channel—the black one with so many cutouts of lace roses that it was hardly a jacket at all—over a scarlet button-down opened to the middle of his chest and a black gem necklace to match the large studs currently in his ears and the shimmering black of his nail polish. He checked the look in his foyer mirror with a hum. It held a certain masculine draw, while still feeling very *him*—very not-quite-gendered—like the *he/they* pronouns he'd added to his business card at the start of the year. He'd wondered at first why the change hadn't prompted any rearranging of his own thoughts; even if his heart soared when others referred to him with his secondary pronouns and danced when he heard the singular *they* on the streets, he still felt himself gravitate toward *he* and *him* in his mind; the words Cygnus's lover would have used when he proclaimed who he was, who he loved. And that didn't mean Andres was any less non-binary, he'd finally decided. Any less *they*.

He figured that he was making a bigger deal of it all than he needed to—but it felt like a big deal, felt like his heart and his bones and his soul trying to come into alignment after nearly three decades apart, bloody and torn and working little by little to heal back into place.

He had one baby cousin, at least—his Hellbeast, the other black sheep of the family, the two of them practically raising each other despite their seven-year age gap—who never failed to make him feel whole. He snapped a quick mirror pic and sent it to her, with the caption *am I breaking gender yet?*

She replied with a line of middle fingers, followed by *you're not as hot as you think, you fuckfaced themboy.* With a sparkling *killing it* sticker.

He laughed and returned her insults with his own middle finger emoji, but the joy didn't stick, the discomfort Maul had left him with returning beside a creeping loneliness that felt like a layer of grime on his skin.

Killing, perhaps not, but stealing a lot of blood from a bank and perhaps a little directly from the veins of a gorgeous human? That, he'd become a professional at.

Regardless of how he felt now, he was going to make this night a good one.

The Fishnettery was already bustling by the time Andres walked in.

With its colorful fairy lights strung behind draping fishnets, the glitter that seemed to occupy every free space, the overpriced rainbow shots and the happy hour deep-fried cocktail shrimp, the place looked like a fancy crab shack had collided with a gaggle of twinks. It was slowly losing its reputation as the last genuinely queer bar—or bar-adjacent alcohol-serving spot—in San Salud as the cishets wormed their way in like it was a friendly tourist spot, and not a place deliberately curated to be free of their unwanted attention, but it was still far gayer and brighter—and as safe as one could get for a gender-not-normal sort—than any other establishment in town. And the calamari was delicious.

Andres ordered an Old Fashioned at the central square bar that sat beneath a fishnet canopy and strolled through the adjoining rooms with their arched wood ceilings and colorful underwater theming, keeping an eye out for the red pin that covertly signaled that the wearer was happy to be bitten. Such humans were rare these days, and always sure to have their pick of the single vampires. Everyone wanted a safe neck to nibble on. But any harbor would do in a storm, and plenty of humans were open to a bite, so long as it came with an orgasm in the bathroom and they didn't have to risk leaving the building with the fanged monster after.

Andres meandered through the space, letting his gaze slip from human to human—gender wasn't important for this. While it were always men who stirred his heart and left him daydreaming months later, his physical needs were less picky. Right now, he just wanted someone who could hold his attention long enough for him to forget the way caving to Maul's demands made his bones itch and his stomach turn. There was someone else it seemed he needed to forget first though.

Every time Andres caught a mildly enjoyable blood scent, his brain jumped to the smell of Shane, bright and sun-kissed, like breathing in the earth after it had baked for hours. It made Andres think of the last time he'd been able to properly lay out on a summer afternoon, nine years ago. He'd spent months picking that scent apart: a little spicy, with a depth like umami, a tinge burnt, and something shockingly sweet at the end. It tingled Andres's nose now with such luscious veracity that he could have sworn, over and over, that the man was somewhere in the next room.

It was as if the universe was reminding him just how little control he had over his life at that moment. He knew how to display just the sensual aspects of the tall, handsome, dark-haired vampire of myths, to use those parts of himself like a weapon, but between thoughts of Shane and Maul's lingering domination, it seemed even that had been stolen from him. He dragged his hands through his hair, reminding himself that he had power over his own body. His own emotions.

He could push through this.

Still, his lungs refused to open all the way, as though Maul himself were squeezing the life out of them. Andres finished off his alcohol, but all that achieved was a burning sensation behind his eyes that produced a film at the back of his throat.

He did not want whatever pointless breakdown his body was trying to force upon him.

Another drink would help. If he made it a double, maybe it would drown his agitation enough that he'd be able to put thoughts of Shane aside and convince himself—and a random human—that he was still the vampire he so decisively showed the world; one who didn't need to please Maul the way some of his subordinates did, or quake beneath him like the rest.

Shane's scent still haunted him at every turn, though. His second glass was barely in hand when the tightness between his head and his heart turned painful. His eyes had to be moistening, because one of his contacts slipped awkwardly out of alignment, and when he tried to correct it, he only managed to pop it out of his eye entirely. It vanished onto the bar floor.

Fuck, this was stupid. He was stupid.

He yanked out the second one with a pathetic growl.

He shouldn't have come. This could have been a decent night, curled up on his couch exchanging texts with his cousin—perhaps even hanging out with her for the first time all year and pretending he wasn't still afraid she'd figure out what he was after all this time. Pretending that the one person he loved wasn't also so estranged. That he still knew what their relationship was about, even if they could no longer be the chaos children of their youth, breaking into hotels just to soak in the spa and making blood-drenched comedy-horror home videos with the thousand ketchup packets they'd smuggled out of fast-food restaurants.

He could still just go home, sit alone in his kitchen and watch Shane rate things through a phone screen, and wish they'd never met. His mind shouted to flee—to get to the car before the tidal wave of emotions rising inside him finally broke. With his contacts gone, and his eyes already tearing up, his poor vision couldn't keep up with the dim lights and the pounding in his head. As he struggled to pull out his emergency glasses from his jacket pocket with one hand, he stumbled over a lip in the flooring, falling directly into another Fishnettery patron.

The man yelped as Andres's new drink splashed, dousing his fingers and the front of the man's jeans. Bitter alcohol dripped to the floor. Someone to his right laughed.

The lump in Andres's throat broke, his entire persona cracking with it. He wiped back tears with the side of his arm, and shook his head, his brain sending up a series of curse words like alarms. Danger, danger, emotional collapse incoming. And he could still smell Shane as though his little swan was standing in front of him. "Fuck."

"Shit, I'm so sorry," the man he'd crashed into was saying.

Except it wasn't just *any* man saying it.

Andres was hearing things.

He pushed his glasses on.

Andres was *seeing* things too. Specifically, he was seeing Shane, standing with a hand still on Andres's arm. In the dim fluorescence, his dirty-blonde waves were turned to a light brown and his scattered freckles washed out, but his pink lips were as lush as ever and he had a softness to his features that provided him a masculine beauty. He wore an impeccably matched flannel, tattered coat, and hazy scarf situation, in greens and browns like he was some forest druid come straight from hibernation.

The sight of him broke Andres, a fresh flood of tears spilling over as a sound left him like a blubber. Shane was here, and Shane was seeing *him*; was seeing the mysterious and majestic vampire who'd kissed him at a gala so many months ago, now without the mask that had held their act together, alone at a queer bar crying like an idiot over a spilled drink.

Andres's little swan, his Cygnus, his perfect constellation, was here finally in front of him again, and the only thing he could wish for was to go back to being unseen.

3

SHANE

Filming in a public space always meant plenty of retakes, but this was the first time Shane was going to have to redo a shot because someone had literally run into him. It was fine, he told himself. He hadn't been convinced that the clear-topped jellyfish tables outranked the not-so-subtle tentacle theming of the left room's back corner, anyway. It just didn't have the same artistic flair.

Shane shut his phone camera off—his text app showed nothing from his vampire contact yet, dammit—before sliding it away entirely. He could take the shot again, it was fine. After he dealt with the drunk fool in front of him.

The drunk, *handsome* fool, with his dark hair slicked back and his nails painted and—was that lace worked into his leather jacket? And those lips…

Shane shook his head, forcing his brain to recalibrate. He hadn't come here to flirt, or to think about how every pretty man's mouth reminded him of his vampire's, or how every smile brought back memories of those ones that had been given only for him, like seductive inside jokes that had dug their hooks into Shane's chest. How every casual movement made him think of his vampire leaning in for the brush of lips that had claimed the number one spot on Shane's kiss list, the night he'd forever be comparing every other dalliance to. And regardless of his pretty face and fitted fashion and adorable glasses-nerd vibes, this person could hardly top *that* chart.

"Fuck," the stranger whispered, staring at Shane like a deer caught in the headlights.

God, this was uncomfortable. "I'm so sorry, that was my bad. Do you need..." Oh, shit—*tears*. Was this person *crying*? Shane's gut twisted. "Are you okay?"

That had clearly been the wrong question, because the stranger's pale and panicked expression worsened. He wavered, his drink sloshing again.

Shane grabbed his arm out of instinct. His gaze lingered on the stranger's lips. They parted with an intake of breath, a single tear sliding over them.

"Do you know me?" the stranger asked.

Do I know you? That wasn't an unusual question here, where the same regulars might pass each other five or six times before finally colliding—in this case literally. There was an instance where Shane wanted to say yes, if only for the subtle brightening in his chest that whispered he *would* know this beautiful fool someday, and that maybe that meant he always had, for better or worse. It was romantic fantasy though, and the reality was probably simpler: that they'd bumped into each other one of the times Shane had

31

managed to drag himself here last month, and Shane's inability to catalog faces for more than a week meant he couldn't place the stranger.

The longer he said nothing, the weaker the stranger looked, like the noise and neon of the bar was swallowing him up.

"No, I don't think so," Shane replied. "But I've got you now. Come on, let's sit you down."

He led the stranger to an empty booth where the wavey designs within the decorative sand dollars looked a bit like genitalia—he'd rated this one low for minimal effort and an overall lack of creativity, but as he helped the person sit, he wondered if he should have added a star for availability in times of crisis. He was almost surprised to find the stranger still there when he returned with a glass of water.

"Drink this."

The stranger made a sound, weak and hollow, but he took the cup with only a single tremor, his gaze steady. Was he actually drunk or was he just *that* sad? The second one seemed worse somehow.

"Are you good?" Shane asked. "Do you need me to get someone?"

He paused from drinking to shake his head. "No."

Shane noticed that he hadn't wiped at the fresh streaks running down his cheeks and had the oddest impulse to do it for him. But cheek touching, Shane was pretty sure, sat squarely at the top-most level of the friendship ladder, and whether or not the two of them had run into each other before and Shane just couldn't recall his face, he didn't actually *know* this person. "No, you're not good or no, you don't need someone?"

"I believe in this case I'm not good precisely because I *do* need someone." His voice was so soft, so broken, even when raised above the music. It tickled something at the back of Shane's mind, but he couldn't place it.

His gaze went mindlessly to those lips again, a second tear now cresting them, but he looked away before his attention could settle. Whatever this poor person—this human, if he was anything like 99% of San Salud's population—was going through, he did not need Shane's misplaced desires for a specific vampire on top of whatever had caused his public emotional breakdown.

"It's pathetic."

"I didn't say that," Shane objected.

"You're thinking it."

He hadn't been thinking it in those *exact* words. "I *was* thinking that I'd rate tear-streaked mascara a three out of ten on the fashion trend scale, due to the inherent effort required in crying every time you want to wear it." It had felt like a joke in his head but the stranger only winced, finally lifting a hand to his face. Shane watched him wipe uselessly at the tear stains with a growing look of misery, and added, "I hear it's therapeutic to trauma dump on strangers at bars, if you want to give that a shot?"

The stranger laughed at that, wet and choked. "Is it now?" He looked skeptical. "There's not much to tell, truthfully. I'm pathetic and a bit miserable, and tonight I couldn't manage to convince myself otherwise."

"We all have our bad days." Shane had no right to judge. He was pulling himself out of a few bad *years*—or trying to anyway.

The stranger glanced away again, taking another sip of his drink. "You were filming when I interrupted."

"I have a video channel," Shane replied. "But it's not very large. You probably haven't heard of it."

He seemed to hesitate, running one hand through his hair. "You're Shane and you rate stuff?"

"Oh my god." Shane wanted to cover his face in his hands suddenly. "Yes, that's me. How embarrassing."

"Don't be. Your videos are very... introspective."

That was not the word Shane had assumed most people would go for, even if it was the truth—or at least, the truth as far as Shane tried to make it. But then the stranger *kept* talking.

"Do you ever worry that judging things means you're imposing negative value on something that already feels bad enough about itself?" He wiped back another tear as he said it, but the question seemed thoughtful, like he wasn't sure what his own opinion on it was.

Shane hummed. "I suppose the real question would be: can restaurant tables feel bad about themselves?"

"Of course they can." *That* he did seem certain of, or perhaps it was just the slight relief that was slowly creeping across his features. Maybe this distraction was good for him.

"Ah, is that why chairs squeak at us when we sit down sometimes?"

"No, no—chairs are masochists. They like to be judged. But there are people watching these videos, and you could be affecting their opinions on things. Asking them to view one thing as better than another, when they'd have otherwise not thought to compare the two." He said it so bluntly, like he wasn't worried about offending Shane. Or, more accurately, that he didn't think he would.

And he was right. "I suppose I probably am. But am I responsible for other people's decisions?" It was a serious question, one he didn't think even he had the answer to all the time. "If the burrito place I rate lowest in San Salud goes out of business, is that my fault, the fault of the customers who listened to me, or of the people making the unfortunate burrito?"

The stranger nodded slowly, wiping at his face once more. "Perhaps we're all equally responsible for the world we create, and how that world affects those around us." Then, as though they weren't trading philosophical dilemmas in a vaguely sexual sand dollar-themed booth, he added, "Though if the octopus in booth ten has an emotional breakdown after you rate him poorly, I will legally back the cephalopod in court."

That brought a smile to Shane's face, the first one since talking with Nat earlier that day. He huffed comedically. "You assume I'd ever rate an octopus lower than a seven without very good reason."

The stranger's brows lifted. "What counts as a good reason?"

With his expression entirely serious, Shane replied, "He murdered my great aunt."

"Defamation!"

Shane leaned in, lowering his voice. "And he's not even particularly great in bed."

"Now I *know* you're lying." The stranger was smiling now too, a soft, timid expression on his teary face. Even with the redness of his puffy eyes and the smears in his mascara, he was lovely. If Shane didn't have an article to write, and his vampire to find along the way, his heart already tied up in someone with fangs and the softest of lips...

As though to drive that point home, his phone vibrated.

He pulled it out, the only notification popping up automatically. A text from his lead. Just an address, nothing more.

Shane's heart fluttered with anticipation, his head a little light but his hands surer than ever as he opened the location in his mapping app. It gave him a point in the inner city, a few side streets off the main road, where the tired, weathered apartment buildings always seemed to form a maze around the little gravesites that San Salud was known for. The spot held none of the charm or safety of the other places Shane had tracked vampires back to, not the gothic brick elegance of the touristy areas, nor the quaint creativity of the south end, or even the homely appeal that the oldest neighborhoods like Ala Santa boasted. This place was one of the few truly menacing parts of town; perfect for selling black market blood without anyone batting an eye.

Which also made it the perfect place to abduct a lonely, diabetic journalist and beat the shit out of him.

The flutter in Shane's chest dropped into his stomach. Despite all the effort he'd had to go through to reach this point, he'd still assumed that this interview would be akin to the others he'd instigated: decent people, who happened to have fangs, just trying to get by. Some had been annoyed with him, sure, others outright scared, all more likely to run from his questions than turn to violence. He'd never felt any more unsafe than previous jobs.

His worry now was ridiculous—and biased—making a rash judgment as to the blood seller's morals based purely on location. And Shane needed this interview. Danger or no, if he wanted the Star to publish him, he didn't have a choice.

Shane put back his phone and—the stranger, shit.

He'd taken to swirling the remaining alcohol in his glass around, now that his water was gone, and he gave a half-hearted smile when Shane stood. "Leaving?" He sounded genuinely disappointed. But then, he'd just gone from sobbing over a spilled drink to looking like he was almost enjoying himself, and here Shane was, abandoning him without explanation. It couldn't be helped, not this time.

"Yes, sorry. Do you... want to trade numbers?" Shane asked. That sad look turned to something almost like hope, and he immediately backpedaled into, "I don't have enough friends." Or friends, plural.

And friends was all he would ever likely be with this odd stranger; all he wanted, until he knew for certain that the kiss he'd been given at the gala four months ago was the last he was going to receive from his vampire.

But he *did* want to see this stranger again, like a soft nudge at the doors of his heart. If the childish excitement he felt over his new friendship with Nat was proof of anything, it was that he desperately needed to talk to people he wasn't trying to interview.

The stranger's expression was hard to parse through the tear-stains and the dim lighting, but he nodded. "Yes—please."

When Shane offered over his phone, he took it delicately, his painted nails tapping against the screen with every click. *Andres Serrano,* Shane read over his shoulder, followed by *he/they.* The sight of those pronouns relaxed something in Shane's chest that he hadn't realized he was holding onto: that permanent, instinctive worry that, queer or not, any stranger's opinion of him could shift radically once they realized he was trans. In its place burst a sparkle of joy—of understanding and kinship.

As Shane took the phone back, Andres's gaze met his again for that one breathless second, then darted away. It left an odd cascade of butterflies in his stomach. He tried to ignore them as he left, but the only way to quench the sensation was to think of the interview ahead of him.

That sparked an entirely different feeling. He tried to tell himself that none of it was fear, and failed.

The location Shane's lead sent him to was exactly as he'd imagined it: gray walls, tight alleys, and micro-cemeteries bare of plants and flowers, their trashed picket fences and headstones looking as though they hadn't been upkept since the city first decided to turn their grave-site problem into a tourist trap in the 70s. He was pretty sure the woman who hissed at him from a half-caved overhang was a vampire with her fangs tucked in, or else a human high enough to believe she was.

Shane tried not to let it rattle him. This didn't have to be any different from his previous encounters with vampires. Still, part of him couldn't help but wish he'd brought some sort of a weapon—he swore somewhere in the back of a disorganized drawer he still had a can of mace given to him by his mother pre-transition.

But he couldn't turn back now. And he had no real reason to yet; none but the darkness of the night, and the way his nerves tingled every time a streetlamp flickered.

The empty alley his map finally led him into was wide enough for a car to pass down and cleaner than most, at least from what his phone light could reveal. He skimmed along the doorways, past a break between two buildings, a rusty shed, then there—the chalk drawing of a droplet that signified the blood dealer's setup. Despite his fear, a little bundle of giddiness welled inside him. He was here. He was doing this.

His article would be exceptional.

Shane knocked. As he waited for an answer, the muffled sound of soft commotion came to him from the end of the alley. His heart skipped. It was probably nothing—possibly the very people he wanted to talk to. He forced himself to creep closer, peeking cautiously around the corner. A van was wedged into the space, its back open as two people unloaded a black container, handing it off to a third who stood at the building's back door.

"This is all for now," the person said, so soft Shane could barely make it out. "We're restocking tonight though, so if you run out we can have another batch brought around—"

Behind Shane, someone called to him, "Hey? You knocked?"

The three at the van turned toward him. He aimed his light at them instinctively, and in unison, their lips lifted. Fangs.

Well, at least he'd come to the right place. "Yes, sorry, I'm here to speak with a man—a vampire—a Mr. Frederick Maul?"

"He's human," one of the vamps from the van transfer hissed, and Shane almost thought they were referring to Mr. Maul until another echoed him.

"Human?"

"Smells too good to be anything else." It sounded almost flirtatious; almost, but for the edge that sent ice down Shane's spine.

Fuck. Maybe this *had* been a mistake.

"Someone's looking for me?" A bald, white vampire slipped from the chalk-marked doorway, wiping his hands on a rag. Apart from the fangs peeking out over his incisors and the dark gleam in his eye, he looked like any middle-aged professional Shane might pass on the street, well dressed but unassuming. He squinted through Shane's phone light, and his expression tightened. "Ah, you're the one." His chin lifted. "Grab him."

Shane didn't have time to piece together what that meant before two of the vamps latched onto his arms from behind. A third yanked his phone from his hand. Their bodies moved like blurs in the darkness, their heightened strength obvious from the moment they grabbed him.

The panic finally hit Shane. He opened his mouth to shout, but a hand clamped over it, muffling the sound down to its barest bones. They dragged him forward so fast that he struggled to keep his legs under him. His heart pounded, blood rushing through his ears and the world spun, black on black on black.

A door slammed—he was inside, then—fuck. The light clicked on, too dim for him to make out more than silhouettes. Shane fought to think rationally over the terror. They might simply throw him in a chair, bare their fangs and threaten to find him if he ever said a word; he could walk out of here with nothing but fear and promises. He'd probably even agree to their terms in the moment, with his stomach in his throat and his limbs trembling like this. If he could just tell them…

But the hand stayed clamped over his mouth.

They seemed to close in on him, body and sweat and breath polluting his space, fingers gripping into him hungrily. The one on his right grabbed his hair. Their nails bit into his scalp as another forced up the sleeve-cuff of his flannel, laughing as they seized his wrist and began playing with his fingers. The contact made his skin crawl and he struggled helplessly against their hold.

Shane tried to scream again, but the hand over his mouth pinched his nostrils closed. He choked, his useless gasp turning to a sob. The air smarted along his face, refusing to creep through the seal of skin on skin that locked off his lungs, trapping them in their panic, forcing him smaller and smaller inside himself. Every touch felt painful, his own body a claustrophobic thing straining and bowing under the weight of the oxygen it couldn't reach. His vision wavered, the silhouettes of the vampires around him filling with stars.

"You'll fuck up the taste," one of them complained, her voice rattling in Shane's head like a waterfall, and then the hand fell from his mouth.

He gasped. His throat burned as they yanked his head back, his lungs still fighting to replenish. Fangs punctured his neck.

Shane knew, distantly, what this was supposed to feel like—the blissful little rush of venom that had accompanied the prick of his vampire's fangs at the gala—but all he felt now was the pain and the fear, the stab of the bite sinking in again and again and the cry of his mind as he felt the blood leave him. His chin was shoved to the side, his face pressed to the greasy hair of the vampire feeding on him as the second of them bit down on his shoulder.

A third pinch of fangs at his wrist made his fingers numb. He whimpered, the sound trying desperately to turn to a cry but unable to fully manifest with the twist and tip of his throat.

"All right, enough," Maul's voice boomed.

Immediately, the vampires let him go, their tongues dragging roughly across the wounds. The chill of their saliva sent an uncomfortable shudder over him. They didn't release him, but he was sure his legs would have fallen out from under him if they had.

That was it—that was the end. They had scared him— dear god, they'd scared him—and now, now they'd stop. They'd let him go back to writing fluff pieces and dreaming of his vampire. He'd—he'd be okay.

But Maul made a sound, almost animalistic in its low, gravelly tones, and drew a phlebotomist's needle from a box, setting it delicately on an empty platter. "I want the rest in bags."

Oh.

Shane felt numb as they moved him to a chair, holding him there by his hair and his upturned wrists. One of them returned with a blood donation kit—a single needle, with far too many blood bags. Oh. His limbs tingled. His mouth felt dry, so dry that when he tried to speak, it came out hoarse and hollow.

"Please..." He managed. "I didn't mean any harm. I'm not a cop."

"No," Maul answered. He squatted beside Shane's chair and drew out a small pocketknife.

Shane tried to tug away, but Maul's goons held him in place as the vampire calmly tugged open the shoved cuff of his flannel and began cutting further upwards until Shane's arm was revealed from mid-bicep down. He could have just rolled the fabric, a slightly hysterical part of Shane's mind objected. If he intended Shane to ever need this shirt—any shirt—again, maybe he would have.

"You're the journalist who's been poking around my territory," Maul continued, "And see, I've been poking around about you, and it turns out you're what the people who hunt us would call a perfect target."

The people who hunt us. So Maul knew about whatever it was that Shane's vampire had been investigating back at the gala—but Shane was too trapped by his words and the goons literally holding him in place to interrupt with a question.

"You have no friends, no family in the area, all your work is remote, all your hobbies solitary." Maul kept moving as he spoke, wrapping the tourniquet with steady motions, cleaning the crook of Shane's elbow, and extending his arm out. The veins bulged. "Which means it will take a while for anyone to miss you."

"What do you want?" Shane tried not to sound desperate. Tried, and failed. "I'll help you, I'll write whatever you tell me to. Or I'll stop writing. I'll move to San Diego and you won't even know I exist."

"I'd like to believe that." Maul shook his head. "I'd like to, but I don't." Holding tight to Shane's elbow, he slipped the needle into Shane's vein with a single prick of discomfort. "Relax," he murmured. "It'll be painless."

Relaxed was the furthest thing from what Shane felt as the first hanging bag began to fill. The first bag in a long, long line.

4

ANDRES

Andres swore this night had been the worst ordeal of his life.

Not the heist, of course—that ran without a hitch. The lock of the window in the back room had been left open by Andres's informant and the cameras immediately disabled, the blood carried out in large black containers and stacked into the back of the freezer van. His driver had set off with it half an hour ago, leaving Andres to do the cover-up.

He tore out the security cameras, wrecked the entry, lobbed a brick through the window, haphazardly spilled a couple blood bags too old for safe consumption, caught the nearest of the two security guards and handed them off to be drained to unconsciousness by a trio of vampires he'd carefully selected for the improbability that they would ever be tracked down or connected to each other—anything to make it look like the theft had been the opportunistic rampage of starving vampires instead of a preconceived plot by a group of professionals. It was the best Andres could do on such short notice.

And he hated it. He hated that the media would cover it as though the vampires were dangerous monsters overwhelmed by blood lust. He hated that it would inspire outrage from the blood banks his community desperately needed to maintain their undercover access to. He hated it.

But it still wasn't the worst thing he'd done that night.

That had been, hands down, meeting Shane again.

Or, more specifically, having a full-blown emotional breakdown just *as* he was meeting Shane, and not having the courage to explain that he had been the one beneath the mask all those months ago. Shane had been so kind and smart—so much the man who'd caught Andres's attention back at that gala. But he hadn't been enthralled with Andres. He'd gone from annoyance to pity, and finally to a mild interest... in friendship.

Was it because of how they'd met, with Andres blubbering over nothing? Or was it the absence of the anonymity they'd shared at the party, the sparkling lights and beautiful masks so conducive to breathless wonder? A lot of the first, a little of the second, Andres thought. But either way, it meant that Shane—his Shane—didn't actually want him.

Andres couldn't blame him. Even his team had given his swollen eyes odd looks, only relaxing once he'd made a show of rubbing them while complaining that his new brand of contacts were fucking him up.

But what did it matter? Shane had likely taken his number as a mere courtesy. Andres would never see his little swan again, and that was how it should have been all along.

He ran both hands through his hair, scowling as he turned into the alley. He had to get the man out of his mind, at least until he'd checked in with Maul and confirmed that all the blood had been stashed in the proper warehouses.

There were no customers outside the droplet-marked door—a shocking abnormality when two months ago would have boasted a line halfway down the alley. He knocked, waiting just long enough to wonder if he should have gone around the back before one of Maul's staff opened it. She let him in without question. Maul was finishing a transaction with a gangly young vampire who licked his fangs as he watched Maul count the money.

"Three hundred?" Maul growled. "I said five twenty-five."

"It's everything I have." The young vampire wrung his hands, looking like he wanted to snatch the bills right back.

"I can give you half."

"Half of five-twenty-five, that's two-sixty... two-sixty-two?"

"Half for three hundred."

The vampire flinched. He swallowed.

Andres couldn't stand the way Maul took advantage like this—making his own community pay more for being the poor, disadvantaged group the humans had forced most of them to be. This vampire probably didn't have a permanent job or home, didn't have the luxury of coming up with another three hundred dollars in the five days it would take him to go through that single half pint—seven, if he stretched it the way it appeared he had been, leaving him constantly brain fogged and hungry.

"Let's say three hundred now for this half pint," Andres said, crossing the room, "and two twenty-five for the other half when he comes for it next week. We appreciate our long-time customers." He clamped the vampire on the shoulder, giving him a smile with as much flattery as edge.

Maul scowled, but he didn't discipline Andres the way he would have had Andres contradicted him five years ago. "As long as you *come* next week. Or else the price goes up."

"Thank you, yes, thank you." The young vampire dipped his whole torso as he said it, almost a bow. He hurried out with the blood like he was scared they'd take it back should he linger.

Managing to twist even that little bit of justice into Maul's schemes tempered the frustrated edge that still lingered after Andres's breakdown—always lingered in Maul's presence, breakdown or not. Maul certainly did his best to keep anyone around him from feeling comfortable.

Maul didn't stop scowling, even after the door was locked behind their exiting customer. "The van just parked at warehouse four," he said. "Everything should be unloaded by the turn of the hour."

But Andres wasn't listening. He was breathing, a long, deep breath, the back of his mind tingling as he swore he could smell something familiar. It had been haunting him all evening, an illusion of sunshine and the burnt edge of jam-topped toast.

It couldn't be *here* though—not here. Shane had no reason to have come to this place. His scent was a figment. Another memory. Shane had just lodged himself so thoroughly into Andres's soul with one chance meeting that Andres was transporting the ghost of him now.

His body carried him past Maul's table, though, like a cord at his center was pulling him forward, to where a curtain had been erected to hide their insulated cases of blood from view. In the dimness, Andres's sight had shifted mostly to the greyscale of his vampiric night vision, the world tunneled by the effect of his human-made contacts, but through the fabric, he swore he could make out the silhouette of a body in a chair. His heart thrummed in his ears.

He could smell Shane still, smell him *stronger* now, bright and wonderful and terrible.

This was a dream—or a nightmare. What else could it be, when his arm felt numb, his fingers barely sensing the curtain's rough material as he slowly pushed it back?

"My god." His throat caught.

Shane—*his* Shane—sat there—bound there—limbs limp and head lolling, a slow stream of scarlet sliding through the tube implanted in his vein. On a rocker below him lay full bags of blood. Too many.

Andres could feel each one of them like a punch to the chest, the rest of the world spinning down to that deep red that should have pumped Shane's life through his body.

Shane, who was left with so little that he'd lost consciousness. Shane, who was still *being* drained.

"My *god*." Andres moved in a haze, knocking into Shane's feet as he stepped around to his side. The man barely groaned, his lashes fluttering without opening.

Maul grabbed his arm. "He's the fucking journalist who's been poking around our territory. We checked and he has no one, we're safe."

The journalist Maul had said he'd *take care of* on the phone. So he'd chosen this: the certain death.

The worst outcome.

"You're killing him." Andres couldn't tell how his own voice sounded through the shock. Hollow, probably. It was how he felt, gnawed open and carved out, like he was trying to embody too many emotions at once and his soul was still deciding which ones it could reasonably fit.

"He stuck his neck into our business—he should have expected we'd bite." Maul narrowed his eyes. "I didn't think you'd care."

Andres shouldn't have cared, not *this* much, not about someone who had such potential to harm their clandestine community already fighting to survive. Someone who'd all but rejected him earlier that night. But Shane... his Cygnus.

Andres could still feel the breath he'd held at the end of the Vitalis-Barron gala, after Shane had watched him threaten and bite a woman with more right to call herself a monster than he did, waiting to see if his little swan would let him leave without protest. His heart had pounded with each moment Shane's hands had lingered over the handle of the door, but at his core, he'd known what his little swan's answer would be.

Shane had earned that kiss.

There was no fucking way Andres would let him die now.

He just had to make Maul feel the same. Maul, whose predominant state in life was to take advantage and wrest control at every point imaginable, and who currently had all the power. But Andres had been slapped by the hand that fed him enough times to know how to work around that.

He exhaled, slipping his face into something almost like his usual expression, aloof and sensual and perhaps just a little devious. Hopefully by now, the puffiness around his eyes had faded too much for Maul to notice. "Normally I wouldn't care about someone like him," Andres said. "But I tasted this one months ago and nothing has compared since. It's devastating to see so much potential blood go to waste."

Maul raised his brow. "I'll put aside some bags for you."

"Oh, but you know how much better it is when you sink your fangs into the throat of a pretty human, when they're warm beneath you and their breath quickens?" How many bags *had* Shane lost already? God, Andres had to do this faster. "Besides, if you kill him now, you'll get 7 pints, if you're lucky, perhaps 9 if you can exsanguinate the rest quickly enough to stay fresh after his heart stops beating. But if he's alive, being bitten regularly, he'll produce that in a few months. You cut my parasite gig on that blood bank short, let me at least try it on a single human; I bet I can keep him bleeding for me for a year, at least. Who knows, this could be the next big thing in blood collection." He should not have said that, fuck, he was going to be putting ideas into Maul's head.

But by the way the vampire's eyes gleamed, one edge of his lips crawling upward, it was clearly working. "A long-term supply, huh." He nodded slowly, eyeing Shane. "But he'll be your responsibility. And you're not just taking him for free. If you think you can get blood from him for a year, then he'll cost you the same as a year's blood."

Shit. Maul charged him less for his bags than the average vampire—one perk of running the side of the business that would have let him skim off the top, had he been willfully stupid enough to try—but that was still...

"Round it down to ten grand and you have a deal?"

"Fair enough."

"I'll have the money for you by the morning."

Andres could almost not believe the words coming out of his own mouth. Ten grand was the better part of his savings from the last few years, the safety net he'd been building for when his old Mazda finally bit the bullet. But then his gaze slipped back to Shane like he was the other end of a magnet. Like he was Andres's. Ten grand, for the life of someone he hadn't been able to get out of his mind for months; someone who hadn't even remembered him. Ten grand, for his constellation.

Shane was more than worth it.

A knock broke through the quiet. Maul grunted. Pulling a smartphone off a side table, he handed it to Andres. "This was his. Do what you want with him." He pulled the curtain closed and through it Andres could hear him greeting the newest customer—it sounded like a line was finally forming.

Andres forced himself into action. Tucking Shane's phone away, he knelt beside the chair and withdrew the catheter from Shane's arm. The man's blood continued to ooze, and the scent overwhelmed Andres like a gust of heat from an oven. He cradled Shane's arm and lifted the little wound to his mouth. That small taste of him was unparalleled, savory and sharp and a hint of sweet all wrapped into one haunting flavor that felt like a long afternoon in the sun as a human. If Andres had truly been buying him for his blood, ten thousand would have been far too cheap for such a delicacy.

Shane moaned, his whole body flinching away from Andres's touch with a feeble twitch that seemed more instinctual than conscious.

"My poor little swan, what have they done to you?" Andres muttered.

Andres held him still, pressing his fangs into Shane's skin slowly and gently to push a dose of the blood-regenerating vampire venom into his body. This time the sound Shane made was sweeter, addled by the momentary intoxicant. It passed as soon as Andres's fangs had left him.

He'd need more before the night was over, but that would be enough to keep him alive.

Andres scooped up Shane's legs first, lifting the man's knees until his lashes fluttered. His eyes didn't quite open, but he pulled from Andres's touch with more certainty. Andres's chest hurt. He followed the retreat, drawing his thumb up the side of Shane's arm along the rip Maul had cut in his sleeve.

"It's all right, Cygnus, it's me," he murmured, his voice dripping with the flirtatious darkness he'd employed on Shane at the gala, hoping that the sound and touch—devoid of tears and clumsiness and all the pathetic qualities Shane had first seen in him at the bar—might awaken the memories buried in Shane's subconscious. If only his little swan had held on to their kiss with a tenth of the spark that Andres had. "I'm here for you."

Shane went so still that a tight panic began welling in Andres's chest—if Shane didn't recognize him, or simply couldn't find some level of safety in him after whatever hell Maul had put him through—

Then Shane's breath released. He eased into Andres's touch, his whole being leaning toward Andres's side of the chair, toward his presence or his scent or whatever the man could sense of him in his current state. "It's you..."

"It's me," Andres whispered back. "I'm picking you up now, all right?"

Shane made a sound in response, his eyes still closed, but Andres thought it was affirmative. He slipped Shane's arm over his shoulder and cupped him behind the back, arm still beneath his knees, and lifted him bridal-style. It was so easy with his vampiric strength, but by the looks of Shane—lean and small and a little bony—he wouldn't have been hard to carry regardless.

His head lolled backward, and he groaned. Andres shifted his hold, helping Shane rest his temple on Andres's shoulder. Shane's pained noises turned softer, and he tucked himself close like he was going to sleep there. It was… strangely perfect. Shane so vulnerable in his arms, so trusting, so entirely *his*—this man that he didn't even truly know, but whose blood now belonged to Andres. He could still taste Shane, the last remnants of that sunshine scent singing on his tongue.

He avoided the now-busy front room, taking Shane down the hall and out the back, using the far alley to reach his car. If Shane had driven his own vehicle there, someone would have to come back for it later. As he leaned to open his passenger door, Shane muttered in his arms, his words slurring together.

"How did you find me?" His breath tickled Andres's skin.

"I think you found *me*, my Cygnus."

"I've been looking…"

That did something odd and lovely to Andres's chest. Shane had been looking for *him*? Had that been what the investigating was for? Because Shane had wanted him, had wanted more of their time at the gala, more of whatever *this* was.

He hadn't known Andres at the bar, but it seemed that was truly because of the circumstance—because of Andres's breakdown, his hoarse voice, the utter lack of flirtation and touch and mystery. Part of him feared that the moment Shane woke properly, saw who Andres was beneath the bravado, he'd realize he really didn't want anything more from Andres but friendship. Perhaps, though, Andres could do something about that...

He lowered Shane into the seat and put on his belt before climbing into the driver's side.

Fuck, where did Shane live?

"Cygnus?" He asked, but with his legs down again, his little swan had passed out, head dropped to one side to expose the length of his beautiful neck.

Andres could feel what remained of Shane's blood struggling to pump through the veins that ran beneath the skin. Andres could feel, too, the venom filling his fangs at the thought of another taste. But right now, what he needed was to get Shane lying down again and give him enough venom for his blood to replenish.

Andres had a vision of Shane in the luxurious king-sized bed he'd treated himself to last year, swaddled in silken sheets and sheer fabric, brought home and kept close the way Maul surely thought Andres would. The idea sent a shudder through him and he tried to burn it from his mind as soon as it appeared, but it left a residue behind: the thought of

Shane in a little collar of precious metal with a chain to tug on and a gap for Andres's fangs to sink in. It was delicious and it was monstrous and he could *not* let it get the better of him.

Horrors such as those were reserved for the vampires in the media, most of whom died when the human's destined lover burst in.

Andres slid his hand under Shane's limp, delicate fingers and laid his index on the print-reader of his phone, hoping either it or the face recognition was enabled. The device unlocked, and at the top of Shane's map app was the favorite place labeled 'home'. Andres was almost—*almost*—disappointed.

5

SHANE

Shane was dead.

He was *pretty* sure he was dead, anyway, or at least near to it, because for some glorious, terrible reason, his mind had conjured him the sultry voice of his vampire, with strong hands and a gentle touch. Lace and leather pressed against his cheek, and his forehead brushed skin. He snuggled deeper into the sensation, and a soft, floral scent greeted him.

"We're almost home," his vampire whispered.

A light sprung on, faint and distant beyond his eyelids, and someone's fingers intruded into his pocket—fuck? No, that was just his vampire, that was all right then. Keys rattled. Everything dimmed again at the sound of a door closing.

"My god, you live like this, my little swan?" his vampire muttered.

"Been... distracted." Shane had been, hadn't he? Distracted trying to find someone, someone who was now here. Which meant it had worked. Except he'd have much preferred it to work in reality and not whatever half-dead state of delirium he'd fallen into. "I keep meaning to—to—"

What were they talking about again? It didn't seem terribly important anymore.

A soft, flat surface met his back, and the warmth of his vampire pulled away. "No," Shane whimpered—whimpered—god, what was wrong with him? Blood loss, probably. Dying. Losing his mind. He felt his shoes tugged off, and for a moment he swore the faintest brush of fingers rested against the hem of his shirt where it had ridden up to the lip of his jeans.

"Can you sleep like this?"

Shane could sleep like anything right now. It was taking everything in him not to. A thought at the back of his mind grabbed for him, a floundering thing in the dark. Oh, right. "Insulin," he muttered.

"Where? I'll get it."

"End table." He forced himself onto his side, blinking his eyes open. He could make out the dim light from his studio window and a cloud of black stars that bubbled and shone, trying to drown him back into unconsciousness. He lost the battle, he was pretty sure, because what felt like an instant later his vampire was gently shaking him, asking a question.

"Cygnus, I need to know how much. It's the long acting one—I think that's right?"

A video was playing in the background, a single bright spot against his eyelids as a feminine voice explained something about needles.

"Glucose app," he muttered. He should have been checking for potential adjustments throughout the night, probably…

What felt like an instant later, his vampire read him off the number, and he tried to nod, replying with his most common nightly dosage. It would be close enough.

Soft fingers drew up the hem of his shirt, grazing his skin gently before pinching it. He barely felt the needle. What he did feel was the way his vampire's touch lingered, one thumb gliding gently across his abdomen. A part of him tried very hard to flash some absurd warning—this was weird, wasn't it?—but he couldn't fathom why. This wasn't *real*. Or it was real but it wasn't… it wasn't…

"I have to give you a little venom," his vampire was murmuring, "to help your blood replenish."

Shane didn't have time to respond before his hand was lifted, flipped over, and the next thing he felt was a pinch of pain, then a high. It lifted him up, pulled him out of consciousness in a whole new way, leaving his body loose and light after it had passed. His vampire let him go. Shane reached for him, instinctively, "Don't leave..."

His breath appeared first, the presence of him close and heavy. His voice sent a thrill down Shane's spine. "You're mine now, Cygnus. You won't lose me again."

Lips brushed his fingers, then his palm, and finally his wrist. Another prick.

The last thing Shane remembered was bliss.

6

Despite everything, Andres had never felt this alive.

He'd wanted to be sure that Shane was on his way to recovery, keeping an eye on his glucose levels as he took a crash course of videos on diabetes management, and by the time he'd slipped out of his apartment it was late morning, the sun blazing like a warning signal in the sky. It had taken nearly the entire drive home for its delayed poisoning to finally hit him. The intense aches and pains felt like his body was dying one cell at a time—probably was, for all he knew— but at least he'd always been immune to the shakes it imposed upon other vampires, letting him grit through the agony as he slowly worked on his upcoming sewing video.

All the while he thought of Shane.

Twelve hours ago, his little swan had been a haunting fantasy. Now, he'd put Shane's number in his phone, and bought a year's worth of his blood.

Andres could not stop wondering if he'd taken too many liberties in saving Shane, if maybe he should have found Shane his car, deposited him there, and left without a word, without a touch, without basking in Shane's exquisite helplessness and pushing that opening as far as he dared. But then that memory would backpedal him into questioning whether he'd done this all wrong in the exact opposite way, if letting Shane out of his sight for even a moment was a mistake. He could have come home with his little swan still. No collar, perhaps, but he could have slept beside Shane and made him breakfast, could have asked Shane to be *his* breakfast, if only for a little taste.

He shoved back the thought with a groan.

His cat merped at him.

Andres scowled at her. "Yes, princess?"

Her Imperial Majesty Queen Camilla Lestat Varney Augustus Tepes twitched her fluffy white tail from her perch at the top of her cat tree overlooking Andres's sewing setup.

With a sigh, he leaned over to pet her. When she gave his fingers an extra sniff, he chuckled. "You smell his little black devil, don't you? They're feisty. I bet even you couldn't boss them around."

Camilla took that as a sign to rub her face all over his hand. He let her until she grew bored and tucked her head back into her bed. Andres's thoughts immediately returned to Shane. Even if he could never morally justify his fantasies, Andres was still going to need to feed—and if he came to Maul for blood now, his boss would ask questions Andres didn't want to answer. Questions like what he'd done with Shane's body, where *I tucked him into bed with a kiss and let him keep living his dangerous journalist life* wouldn't be an acceptable answer. Besides, Andres had wiped out his savings.

And Shane kind of owed him.

Based on his reactions that night, Andres thought that his Cygnus wouldn't be entirely opposed to the idea of fangs in his neck—fangs and perhaps lips, an arm tight around his middle and the dark, sensual gala voice Andres had used as he'd rescued Shane. Andres just had to make sure that was the only version of him Shane saw. No tear stains, no broken complaints, no frazzled attempts at humor.

Andres had to be Shane's vampire from the gala.

As he stared across the living room, to the mannequin that displayed his reforged cloak from that night, his gaze caught on the mask still hanging from one side, and he smirked. Shane would get his gala Dracula all right: all teeth and flirtation and felonies.

7

SHANE

Shane woke groggy and slow, a slight pounding in his head and the back of his throat so dry he could barely swallow.

My god, the last time he'd felt this awful had been the hangover after his twenty-fifth birthday, which hadn't been the least bit worth it since he'd done most of that drinking alone. He swore even his bones ached. His blood sugar was probably a mess. He groaned, rolling onto his back. His flannel pulled awkwardly across his chest. Fuck, why was he still wearing his clothes? What the hell had—

Maul.

Maul had tried to kill him. He could feel the pain of the vampires' bites with such clarity that he had to rub his neck with both hands to convince himself the wounds were gone. The crook of his elbow felt raw and sensitive, and he wanted nothing more than to pinch it closed and tuck it against his chest and—and cry—god, was he *crying*?

Shane wiped a few hot tears from the corner of his eye before they could fall and pulled his knees to his chest. He'd almost died last night, and then… and then…

His vampire…

His vampire had found him. Had rescued him. Had brought him home and whispered sweet nothings to him, had removed his shoes and helped him with his insulin. That same vampire had let his fingers linger over Shane's skin, the memory of his touch a tingling, uncomfortable thing in the morning—or possibly afternoon—light. Shane's mouth felt like cotton, and he had to force himself to swallow. Something buzzed in his veins despite it though. The shiver that ran through him was half fear and half exhilaration.

He didn't know what to make of it, so he forced himself to sit up instead.

Black spots and hollow edges assaulted his vision, but he breathed through it, squinting across his tiny, single-room apartment. It looked different. It was like everything had been shifted just slightly to the left, and it took him a moment to realize what it was: the place had been *tidied*. His laundry baskets were righted and tucked to the corner, the stack for Goodwill piled so neatly that it looked half the original size, his dirty plates and collection of cups removed from the desk and coffee table. Even the cat's bowls had been cleaned and filled, the beast herself happily stretched across the couch. He couldn't see the kitchenette from around its half-walls, but he had a suspicion of what he'd find in the sink.

He felt… he didn't know. Violated and appreciated, annoyed and relieved all at once. His vampire—this relative stranger—had touched him, and touched his things, and yet he'd not only saved Shane's life, but gone out of his way to clean for him, and god, this was so confusing. He didn't know what to do with it. Fitting a phantom into his life had been easy—obsessions always were. This, however? This could ruin him, in the best way or the worst one, and he wasn't sure he'd know which it would be until it was too late.

On his coffee table sat his phone beside a cup of water, his apartment key, and a note.

Don't you fly too far, my little swan.
Love,
Your vampire

Shane stared at the final line, stared so long that his cat shoved her face into his fingers, purring. He scratched his void monster's head absentmindedly with one hand. *Your vampire.*

His vampire.

By the afternoon, Shane felt remarkably better.

Whether it was the venom he vaguely recalled his vampire murmuring about, or the fact that he'd corralled his glucose levels back into range—*without* having to ask his endocrinologist how to adjust his dosages after being nearly *exsanguinated*, thank god—or the result of his body's own natural regenerative properties, he didn't know. The tidier apartment helped, too.

All that time didn't lead him to any stronger conclusions about his vampire though. He still only knew that his insides turned light and fluttery every time he thought of his vampire's arms around him, and that he was absolutely terrified of it happening again—terrified that it wouldn't be the same next time, and terrified that it would. At about five in the evening, Shane had given up worrying about it. If his vampire came back for him, he'd deal with his feelings then. Instead, he turned his mind to the other fang-related problem: Frederick Maul.

Frederick Maul had tried to kill him.

The more times Shane repeated that, the angrier he grew. There was a vampire in his city with the power and influence to have a human he didn't like drained to death. That was worthy of a story all on its own. The people of San Salud had the right to know about it.

His near-death experience still made him feel nauseous at the thought of seeing Maul again, but it had hardened something in him too. This was real, and it was big, and he was a part of it. Maul might have started it, made it worse by trying to have Shane drained instead of simply offering him useless information and platitudes, but Shane was going to finish it: with a front-page headline. *The War on Blood* was right; his own blood had become part of it.

If Shane was going to keep pressing in on a group clearly fine with disposing of him, he was going to have to take some precautions. Not the police, obviously—he didn't want them fucking with everything until he was done with it, and knowing the way they reacted to all vampires as though they were Maul, they would only be learning of this when he had clear evidence of who was in the wrong and who was just an innocent bystander. And where his own vampire lay in that.

The events of the night were fuzzy, but he could recall his vampire's stunned voice: *"You're killing him."*

Maul had given a reason as he'd pressed the needle into Shane's vein. The crook of his arm tingled even through the thick fabric of the long sleeve shirt he'd donned, and he didn't want to think too hard about why. *"No family, no friends. It will take a while for anyone to miss you."*

No one to miss him?

Well, Shane could fix that. For the sake of this article, he could make himself a friend. He threw on his boots, a loose coat, and the fashionably ratty green scarf and shot off a text as he charged out the door.

Shane-anigans
Hey, weird question but can we voice chat?

Nat1
Sure? What's up?

Shane-anigans

Just trying not to die. You?

"I want to come with you!" Nat shouted, loud enough that Shane had to turn down the single wireless earpiece he was using to chat with her.

It was a little odd hearing her voice when they'd been strictly messaging since their first meeting, but the fervor with which she'd listened to his vague explanation and jumped to his defense without a question as to his truthfulness or sanity made him happy. Not that he had told her the truth—or the whole truth, anyway—only that the black market blood dealer he'd wanted to interview had threatened to kill him but he'd gotten away with a friendly vampire's help. No good would come from her knowing that help had involved carrying his nearly unconscious body away from an attempted murder.

His new friend was angry enough as it was.

"I'm just here to look around. No interviews, no blood bags." Shane ignored that last thought, folding his arms across his chest at the uncomfortable tingling in the crook of his elbow. He gave his car a once over as he passed it, still parked on the street where he'd left it the night before, and kept walking. "Even if I was looking for vampires, I'm not putting you in danger like that."

"I know a lot more about fighting them than you do."

"Because you were a corporate security officer? Are vampires that into espionage?"

The line went silent, Nat clearly seething on the other end. If Shane were being fair, she probably did know quite a bit more than him just by having been a part of a security team. His fighting ability began and ended with the knowledge that the thumb belonged outside the fist. But he wasn't planning to fight anyone.

"If you came, it would defeat the point. They could get rid of you and we're back to square one."

"At least I have someone who would come looking for me," Nat grumbled.

"Rude."

"But accurate. Backslash apologetic."

"Oh my god, that does not work the same way out loud." Shane glanced at the map on his phone. He was a block away from the place he'd been taken. His nerves were alight like firecrackers, but otherwise he felt oddly dead inside. "You have my location. If something terrible happens, you are free to come after me, preferably with back up."

"If a vampire kills you, I won't need backup." She sounded like she meant it, the determination in her voice so strong he was momentarily worried for Maul instead of himself.

But then he turned into the alley, and all his anxiety slammed into him like it had been waiting for that moment. He forced himself to breathe, to keep walking, arms crossed tight to his chest. His bus had been fifteen minutes late, made later over the course of the trip, but he'd still managed to get there before the twilight quite set in, and he could see down the gloomy cement path well enough without his phone. Empty.

Maul wouldn't be here anymore—that was how this worked: set up for a night, vanish for two, emerge somewhere else. It made it easy to serve a larger territory while simultaneously hiding their tracks from the people they didn't want to find them. But just because they had moved shop didn't mean there was nothing left to learn. And it was the only lead he had right now.

The chalk mark had been washed from the door.

"You dead yet?" Nat asked. "You should know I'm sharpening my stakes as we speak. I'm thinking black roses for your grave? That's adequately dramatic, right?"

"I'm not dead," Shane grumbled, but as he did, a noise came from behind him. Nothing. His skin prickled. No matter how he turned, it seemed as though eyes followed his back. He pinched closed his arm and rubbed his neck with a palm. Carefully, he tested the door's handle.

He'd brought a lock picking kit that he'd been learning to use since the Vitalis-Barron gala, but the door swung open with ease. The place was dark—too dark, a creeping, engulfing blackness that seemed to seep into Shane's lungs like the clamping hand of Maul's goon. He flinched. Behind him, the noise came again.

Shane whirled around, but he wasn't quite fast enough. Arms circled his waist and shoulders, a presence at his back. He screamed. The hold on him tightened, solid but not painful.

"Quiet yourself, Cygnus, it's only me," murmured a familiar voice, dark and sensual, so close to Shane's ear that the warmth of his vampire's breath tickled.

Shane went weak in the knees. The fight didn't drain out of him but it transformed, his nerves tingling while his adrenaline coursed a path like fire up his spine. "Oh," was all he managed. He was excruciatingly aware of his vampire's hands on him suddenly, one palm cupping his hip and the other on the crook of his shoulder. Every impulse told him to turn, to behold his captor, but his body must have given it away because his vampire chuckled softly.

"Now, now, did I *say* you could move?"

A shudder rolled across Shane's skin like goosebumps. So this was how it was going to be. Whatever had happened between them the previous night had clearly convinced his vampire that he had a right to Shane. The thought slid through him in a hot tremble, tightening his lungs and settling in his pelvis. His heart beat faster, echoing through his skull like the voices of the vampires who'd attacked him.

Through his earpiece, Nat seemed to be having a similar crisis. "Fuck, Shane, who is that?" She sounded genuinely panicked. "Talk to me, dammit."

As she spoke, the vampire swept his fingers over Shane's temple, brushing back his hair. Gently, he plucked out the earpiece. "What's this?"

Shane looked over his shoulder, catching a flash of gala mask before his vampire moved to the other side. His breath came warm against Shane's neck, and for a moment Shane felt pinned, surrounded, suffocating like the night before. But this was just one vampire—just *his* vampire—his guiding touch on Shane's back so light that it could have been a breeze. Shane swallowed and tried not to sound like his soul was about to leave his body. "If you'd please hand that back, that call is my life insurance." He held his palm flat, arms still mostly wrapped against his chest.

"Huh."

In the twilight, he could vaguely see his vampire twirling the device out of the corner of his eye, a pale hand and darkly painted nails.

"Smart. Not smart enough, if you think you're coming here for Maul. But smart." His vampire ignored Shane's outstretched hand, brushing back his hair once more to tenderly press the earpiece in place. Despite the fear still coursing through him, Shane swore it was the most sensual thing anyone had ever done with a piece of technology in his life. And he even owned one of those vibrators that linked to his phone. If his last boyfriend had known how to use it with half this finesse and confidence, Shane might have still been dating the man. Though why the hell he was thinking of that now of all times—

Nat shouted through the returned earpiece, "Shane, my god, if you're dying—"

"It's fine, everything's fine," he interrupted her. "I'm just being *terrorized* by the vampire who saved me last night." He let a little snark sink into his voice, leaning back swiftly enough to bump his tormentor's chest.

The vampire laughed. "You might want to hang up. Or don't. Perhaps you like a little exhibitionism."

Shane's muscles tensed. Their kiss from months back still lingered on his lips and the memory of his vampire's fingers on his skin last night made him tingle, but his stomach twisted at the thought of his vampire pushing for more, without being granted it first—of his nails digging into Shane's scalp and his fangs forced through flesh the way Maul's goons had, no slow buildup or soothing venom, his roving hands finding places Shane wasn't ready for him to touch…

His vampire made a little broken noise of distressed embarrassment that sounded strangely familiar. "I'm just going to bite you, my little swan, tender as your lovely neck deserves," he said, his tone somehow equally as seductive as it was reassuring. "I only take what's owed me."

What's *owed* him. "Why would I owe *you* anything?"

"Phone first," he replied.

Shane hesitated. How much did he trust his vampire? Not at all and, after the care he'd shown last night, also entirely. He would only discover which of those feelings was correct if he stayed. Hesitantly, he held up his phone. His vampire's fingers slid over his.

"Hello, Shane's friend," the vampire said, chin tucked against Shane's temple on the earpiece's side. "I promise that I will return him to you shortly."

"It's all right. He can protect me," Shane added with a confidence he didn't quite feel. "I'll call you back when we're finished."

The line went quiet for the moment, before Nat hissed, "Oh my god, Shane, don't tell me you're going to *fuck* this creep?"

How the hell she'd picked up on the very erotic way Shane's entire body was reacting right now *over the phone*, Shane could not fathom, but at least he was fairly certain she couldn't magically make out the flush burning in his cheeks as he answered. "I'm *not*."

She didn't sound like she believed him. "You're just as bad as my boyfriend."

God, he had to get off this call. "Talk to you soon."

"Sooner than him," she grumbled.

Shane pressed the end call button. His vampire immediately let him take back the phone.

Shane released a breath. His nerves lingered, tickling along his skin and highlighting each brush of his vampire's hands against him, but giving in—and being rewarded for his trust with the immediate return of his phone—released much of his fear. It shouldn't have, he knew. It was the same positive reinforcement that turned feral animals into pets.

But he could reason to himself that if his trust had paid off once, it would pay off again. "You said I owe you blood?"

He tried to turn, but his vampire moved behind him once more, too fast for his eyes to catch in the dimness. As he did, he drew fingers across Shane's shoulder that sent another shudder through him... one not altogether unpleasant. "I thought I implied you were to keep still," his vampire chided, teasingly. "Are you so disinclined to do as you're told?"

"When I don't know why I'm being told to do so, yes, very much," Shane retorted, though he had the sinking suspicion perhaps that was a lie. Whatever they were doing now seemed to have set his every nerve on fire as though his body was made for it.

"You'll obey because you're mine," his vampire whispered into his ear, a single finger tracing along the collar of Shane's jacket. "Bought and paid for, as of this morning. I traded Maul ten thousand dollars for all the blood your body will ever produce. I own that which gives you life."

Shane's heart sank. "That's why you saved me. So you have a meal."

"No." The reply came fast, soft, his vampire's tone so changed that he almost sounded like a person—sounded strangely like... But then his mouth brushed Shane's ear, a tremble running through the vampire so strong that Shane could feel it in the hand he'd rested on Shane's bicep, and all Shane could think about was lips pressing to his on that gala balcony and firm arms carrying him home last night. "I saved you because I didn't want you to die. Maul had no fucking right to drain you." Now he sounded dark, but in a new way, black as vengeance and the void. "I needed you to live, and this was all I could think to do, all Maul would respect. If I was anyone else, asking anything else, he probably wouldn't have even allowed this."

"Why would he accept it from *you*?"

"I bring him his blood, so he gives me leniency over what happens to it."

He was Maul's business partner—a central piece of the black market. Shane could have laughed or cried. He'd come to Maul looking for a source for his *War on Blood* article, and while Maul had tried to kill him for it, here was a vampire just as invested in the black market. This was the in Shane needed; if only he could lure his vampire into a strong enough sense of trust to take it.

But for the moment Shane's vampire seemed more keen on taking *him*. His voice hadn't lost the edge, but it had gone sultry again, sliding up Shane's spine and nestling deep within his chest. "I saved you because I couldn't watch you die. But I need blood to live, and I paid all I have for yours. So you're going to deliver. That's only fair, isn't it?"

"For you, but not for me. You paid for my blood, but I wasn't the one who sold it," Shane challenged. "Can something be truly fair if it's unequal?" As he asked it, he found that he didn't want to prove a point, but simply to know what his vampire thought. He didn't want to be caved to; he wanted to be understood.

"Perhaps not." His vampire hummed thoughtfully, and his fingers drew little circles against Shane's shoulders. He was warm, and he smelled lightly floral, like a gentle lavender perfume. "It's not fair to force humans to give their blood up, but neither is it fair that vampires must pay and fight and steal for something they need just to survive the week. Perhaps fair is what you can wrangle back from the world, and nothing more."

"So you'll take my blood whether I agree to this or not?" It was a terrifying thought, but it didn't *scare* him, exactly, and Shane couldn't make sense of that dissonance.

The fingers at his shoulder transformed into a gentle squeeze, the lines of his vampire's hands feeling along Shane's collarbones and wrapping toward the back of his neck. His voice dropped into a growl. "Don't ask questions that you don't want the answer to."

A chill rolled through Shane, but it only fueled the fire burning deep within him. Goddamn this vampire. *His* vampire, who was being a damned prick but in the best way possible. "Why not? Will my not knowing the truth change it?"

He laughed, gliding his fingers against Shane's hair, so light that it was barely a touch. "Perhaps if it's Schrödinger's truth."

"A truth that only takes form once we know it," Shane mused. "What a concept." He could feel his vampire's attention like the warmth of the sun, and he had the inane desire to lean into him. Then he was doing it, his back brushing a strong, sturdy torso. His vampire's chest rose against him in a sharp intake, then fell with the slow release.

"Perhaps this truly is a kind of a Schrödinger's truth, because I don't know it yet myself. What if I won't know what I'll do *until* you push me?" The darkness of his voice conjured visions in Shane's mind, a vampire's palm clamped against his mouth, lungs screaming, teeth in his neck as he struggled.

His stomach twisted, his desire turning to ash. Yet a part of him felt safer leaning into his vampire's touch, his grip near Shane's neck a comfort rather than a cage, like the imagined monster could never be him. Shane desperately hoped that was the case, for his own sake. "Is *that* the truth?"

"It's *a* truth." His hands followed the base of Shane's neck, fingers forming a loose collar. "Push me if you must. I can promise you that there are lines I will never cross, but not where they lie."

For once, Shane didn't have a response to that.

He still held his arms pinned against his chest, but his vampire wrapped a little tighter around him to take hold of one of them—the one Maul had pressed the needle into. Shane's instinct told him to hold it tight, keep the vulnerable skin tucked closed where no one could hurt it. But it seemed his vampire had other ideas. Gentle but firm, he nudged against Shane's arm. His mouth fluttered over the back of Shane's earlobe. "Let me have what's mine."

It was part demand—Shane couldn't have ignored that if he'd tried—but it was part offer too, and perhaps just a little bit of a plea.

"Push me if you must," his vampire had said, and Shane couldn't bring himself to do so. Next time, perhaps. Next time, he wouldn't cave so easily, wouldn't let the slightest hint of gentleness and the smallest of rewards sway his courage. Next time, he'd get answers to all his questions.

But this time, Shane gave in. A chill washed over him, his fear building even as he forced himself to trust. It was dark now, the sky purple and the nearest lights too far down the wide alley to penetrate, and he could barely see the drag of his vampire's hand down his arm as he stretched it out, but he could feel the pressure of it so blindingly that little else was worth his focus. His vampire pushed a thumb against the place where Shane's pulse ran.

A whimper worked free of him, unbidden. He was embarrassed immediately—what the fuck had Maul done to him that he was overwhelmed merely by being touched inside of his elbow through a sturdy jacket? But the response seemed to please his vampire, the little instinctive tugging back of Shane's arm making him tighten his own grip for just a moment before shifting it to press his palm against the vulnerable spot. Like a shield, Shane realized, as the sensation appeased some of his nerves.

"Does it hurt?" his vampire whispered.

"It's the memory."

"My poor Cygnus." He let go, softly guiding Shane's arm back into place, tucked once more against his chest. His hand remained, tracing the jacket fabric around Shane's elbow. "I could bite you there, give you a new memory?"

Shane didn't answer—he was too busy imagining it ten different ways, all of them gentle but not necessarily soft. It could be a tender offer, his vampire willing to take his time to help him acclimate, sitting with him in a place of safety, tracing the spot with his lips, waiting for Shane to tell him it was all right. Or it could be a protective demand. He could almost feel the way his vampire would tug his jacket off, teasing the skin with his nails while Shane shuddered, cooing *"you're mine, little swan,"* in that voice of his that could have declothed emperors in another time. And what terrified him, more than needles or fangs, was that he didn't know which of those outcomes he wanted more.

Or he did know, suddenly—knew he wanted to be laid bare, unfolded at his vampire's whims in ways that turned him weak and helpless.

Merely imagining it made him yearn, made his knees wobble and his breath catch. The horror of that realization nearly doused the fire building in his pelvis. He *shouldn't* want that. It would mean that his vampire—this stranger, whose right to anything of Shane's was already hazy at best— was willfully taking advantage of him. He should *not* want to be taken advantage of—god, what was wrong with him?

From one thought to the next, his body had tensed so hard that at the roar of a nearby sports car, his flinch nearly jerked him out of his vampire's arms. The sound continued rumbling as the vehicle slowed in front of the alley, turning towards it like they planned to drive down the center. With Shane and his vampire standing in the open door of the building, he doubted the owner had seen them yet. But they would soon.

"Fuck," his vampire growled, and let him go with a little shove that pushed Shane properly inside.

He spun around. This time, his vampire didn't tell him not to look. Not that Shane could see much in the darkness, just his silhouette: black leggings and calf-high boots, a lighter, lacy shirt under a long, tailored coat, all of it outlined by the sideways stream of headlights. His gala mask covered the upper portions of his face. A reminder of their last time together, perhaps? Or a sign that as much as he was asking Shane to trust him, his trust in Shane was so limited that he had gone for total anonymity, as though Shane might call the cops the moment he had a proper description.

His mask didn't quite reach his mouth though, and the white of his teeth shone in the darkness as his lips pulled back, fangs already extended. "We're about to have company."

ANDRES

The mask had been a good idea.

The mask, the stealth, the whispering in his little swan's ear while never quite letting him get a proper look—Andres could feel the way Shane's body responded to it all, his breath quick and his senses honed. His posture screamed prey-thing, so attuned to the knowledge that Andres was a vampire that he doubted Shane could have mistaken him for the crying fool at the Fishnettery even without half of his face covered.

And, if Andres was honest with himself, he'd been loving every moment of this. The feeling of Shane shuddering against him, his verbal sparring followed by his physical submission, the way he'd let Andres spread out his arm and rub at the defenseless crook he seemed so bent on hiding. And he'd *whimpered*. His vulnerability quickened something in Andres's chest.

He vowed to treasure it. To protect it. His little swan was his now, after all.

"So you'll take my blood whether I agree to this or not?"

Andres would never dare—he'd told Shane there were lines he wouldn't cross, and that was one of them. Just as he'd never truly consider stealing Shane—his or not—back to his bed and setting him up like a king in chains, even if for the last twelve hours he had been unable to stop *picturing* it. He'd drawn his fingertips along the base of his beautiful Cygnus's neck and envisioned how his pet swan might look with a collar, how he might whimper and melt and slowly yield beneath tender kisses.

They were *just* fantasies.

Andres would never dare. He was not the kind of monster who did such things. Only, it seemed, the kind who thought they were sensual in the first place.

He had already felt the tension return to Shane, like his little swan was feeding off Andres's own guilt and doubts, when Maul's familiar orange Mustang rolled into the front of the alley. Andres had always badgered him for driving something so outrageous when their jobs were built on secrecy, but now he thanked the universe for making his boss such a prick, because he recognized the vehicle quickly enough to push Shane into the building before the headlights could turn toward them.

There was no time to get Shane out of the building unnoticed.

"Into the closet, my little swan," Andres ordered, gentle and hushed but a demand nonetheless.

Shane didn't immediately move, and Andres pressed a hand to the back of his neck, directing him across the room.

It must have been too dark for his human eyes because he fumbled, missing the knob entirely. Andres opened it for him. The small nook smelt of mold and rot, and Shane stiffened against his guiding. Outside, the roar of Maul's engine shut off, then his headlights.

"Go," Andres growled as forcefully as he could manage without cruelty.

Shane breathed out and, slowly, stepped into the closet.

Andres rewarded him with a quick kiss on the temple, just a gentle brush of lips as he cupped the back of his Cygnus's head, and murmured, "Stay quiet. I'll retrieve you when it's safe." When Shane still didn't respond, Andres tipped his chin up, "Do you understand, pet?"

"Yes," he whispered.

Andres closed the door on him.

Light spilled from the crack between it and the floor—Shane's phone screen—and Andres' heart stuttered. He could be texting his friend to confirm he was safe, or just as easily dialing for help, freeing himself from Andres permanently. Then the closet went dark once more. Everything was quiet; no car engine, no 911 operator, not even the gentle sound of Shane's breath.

From down the alley came Maul's footsteps.

Andres felt his skin chill at the sound of Maul's distinctive stride, and he tugged off his mask, slipping it beneath his jacket and into the back of his waistband like a secret weapon.

Maul's brow barely rose as he entered, taking in Andres for half a moment before his eyes narrowed. "What brings *you* here?"

"I was wondering the same of you," Andres countered. He shifted his voice instinctively, just as dark as the sensual predator who'd slipped in behind his little swan, but with a dry edge in place of the sultry. Still the persona of a vampire, just with a slightly different intent, the feigned dominance hiding any morsel of weakness Maul might chip away at, even as he monitored every word to keep from overstepping to the point of angering his boss. "I thought you were making a point not to bring that flashy monster to a sales spot twice in a row."

The resurrection of the long-standing argument made Maul huff, but the suspicion didn't leave his gaze. "Max spotted a human who looked like the blood bag you bought off me last night, and you haven't been answering your phone."

Fuck, he'd put Maul's number on mute to get a few hours of peace last night and clearly hadn't remembered to turn his notifications back on. At least Maul had decided not to come down on him for it. Andres shrugged. "I was going to poke around his place, see if I can't stage it to look like he up and left, but he lost his keys somewhere here. I have him contained, though, never fear. Clearly Max can't tell petite blonds apart." Petite blonds with scattered freckles and bowed lips and thick lashes, whose waves of hair brushed against his long neck like a veil and soft skin trembled under Andres's touch.

Dammit, even with Shane tucked out of sight and Maul scowling a few yards away, riling his nerves and frustrating his senses, Andres's mind still couldn't let go of his little swan.

He tried to wipe the thoughts aside for later, but Maul's next question just stirred them into a frenzy instead.

"Contained? You're sure you locked the cage when you left?"

"Chains are more my style." Specifically collars, if Andres's incessant fantasies were to be trusted. "He's wilted across my bed right now. Probably still half-conscious." He swore he heard a *sound* from the closet at that, though Maul seemed not to notice. Still, Andres should probably not have been getting quite so descriptive. He didn't want to scare Shane into making that 911 call after all.

The fictional display of power must have contented Maul though, because he switched topics. "What progress are you making with the Vitalis-Barron investigation? I thought something would have come of that by now."

This was worse, somehow. At least salaciously fictionalizing his little swan's captivity had its perks—mainly that his mind had free rein to imagine just what a life with Shane chained to his bedpost would be like—but he had no interest in sharing how few developments he'd made on the Vitalis-Barron front, especially when a negative update always led to Maul swinging his sights back toward their other competition: the new Jose's Blood Bank.

Andres settled on a calm but forceful, "I'm working on it." He *had* found the name of a vampire rumored to have escaped Vitalis-Barron's laboratory and the diabolical experiments they'd surely been doing on her there, but try as he might, he couldn't seem to locate her now.

"Work faster," Maul grumbled, then, right on cue, "Something has to change soon. If it's not Vitalis-Barron, then we need to switch our attention to that damn blood bank."

Andres chose not to respond to that, running a hand through his hair instead. There was only so much he could argue without it pissing them both off, and the more pissed Maul grew, the meaner and less pliable he became, and the harder a time Andres had controlling himself or his emotions in turn. "Well, in the meantime, you feel like helping me hunt for a pair of keys?"

Ever true to form, Maul made a disinterested sound and took a step back. "I have actual business to see to. You can pick locks, so why bother."

"I can't pick them closed again. There's an entire mystery sub-genre called locked door murders for a reason."

"Right." Maul clearly didn't actually care about any of this, and somehow it only made Andres more annoyed and a little nauseated.

I'd like to see you do my part of the job, he wished he could snap.

Instead he straightened his shoulders, chin high and lips in the half-smirk that made his jawline sharp and highlighted his fangs. He was glad suddenly that he hadn't chosen to wear any of the leather he'd inserted lace cutouts into and that he'd traded his glasses for contacts, despite the odd blur they placed on the edges of his vision. Maul could dismiss him all he wanted, but these days they were clearly equals in strength, if not in power.

Andres bared his teeth. "Have a good night, Maul."

Maul's lips peeled back. "You as well."

He left without another word, the slam of his Mustang's door followed by the rev of its engine. It sped by in a blur. Only as the sound of it faded into the distance did something ease in Andres's chest, his frustration fading to a lingering discomfort.

Andres stood there, staring into the darkness of the alley and breathing through his mouth, before he suddenly remembered—*Shane.*

He forced his mind off Maul and tugged his mask back on, moving toward the closet door. He slowed as he neared, listening. It was cruel not to let Shane out immediately, now that the threat had passed. But a part of him wanted to see: he had told his little swan to stay until he was retrieved. How long would he actually wait? One heartbeat, then another.

Not a sound came from anywhere in the abandoned building, not even the creaks of settling wood or the tiny scurries of mouse feet. The quiet broke Andres's chest in two. Oh, fuck him. Shane had obeyed; he did not deserve to be tested like this. Andres forced some level of composure onto his expression and opened the door.

His Cygnus stood there, visibly shaking, arms tucked tightly around himself and one hand cupping the side of his neck, fingers drawn across skin like he was protecting himself from a bite. Ah, double fuck. Not only had Andres been talking about chaining Shane to his bed, but he'd been describing it to the vampire who had almost killed him— *would* have killed him, had Andres not done something dramatic. And here Shane had been, having an anxiety attack alone in the closet.

"He's gone?" Shane whispered.

"He's gone." Andres reached into the small space, and when Shane flinched, he didn't let it deter him, gently folding a hand around his arm and drawing him out. "But we shouldn't linger. He's paying more attention to us than I'd assumed."

For a moment, Shane's anxiety seemed to grow, but then it eased out of him instead, the tight pinch of his expression loosening as he released a breath. He didn't pull away from Andres's touch. "I could hear you in there," he said, tipping up his chin. "What do you and Maul want from Vitalis-Barron? How are they connected to the black market blood trade?"

"That is not your business, my little swan." He hoped that would be the end of it, that Shane might submit to him in this as easily as he had to Andres's other demands, but he knew, too, that anyone intelligently curious and unwavering enough to catch Andres's attention and refuse to let it go for so many months wouldn't leave such a mystery alone.

"This is very much my business!" Shane replied. "If they're impacting the flow of blood through the city—or the existence of vampires within it—then it's important to me, and to the work I'm doing."

That brought Andres up short. He paused just within the entrance, pulling Shane to a halt. Shane was smart enough to understand the black market, stubborn enough to track it down, but when all his other endeavors were gossip columns and quirky rating videos, Andres had just assumed... "You really *are* writing an article on us?"

"Of course I am!" Shane's brow tightened, and his tone went stony. "The blood trade, the existence of healthy consensual feedings, even the little vampire charity work that's been done, has all existed in the dark for so long—"

"No." Andres felt a kind of panicked hysteria rising in his chest at the mere thought. *Danger*, his every cell screamed. He fought to morph it into anger, to turn the bladed emotion outward instead of letting it weaken him, but just keeping his voice the dark, sultry version he'd been using throughout the night was growing harder. "The trauma this could cause for the vampiric community... if you draw the humans' attention to us, to just how much of their blood we're consuming and how many of us live in their streets, it's not us they'll be siding with."

"You don't know that," Shane countered. "This isn't Schrödinger's trust. Vampires need this blood and hiding that fact doesn't change it. Showing the ways the current system has failed you—maybe that can."

"Who do you think *made* this system? You want to air out all our pain, our greatest vulnerabilities, in front of the people who put us here—for them to see how weak we are? You can't." Andres fought the urge to run his hands through his hair. "Besides, if Maul realizes what you're trying to publish, he won't let it happen. And I won't be able to protect you."

"That's part of the problem." Shane touched his neck again, his throat bobbing, and his palm slid flat against the skin, protective. A shield. "Maul wanted to profit off my death by selling my blood to destitute vampires who can't even question where it came from because if they don't accept what he offers, it'll be *their* death, and I'm only alive still because you were forced to *buy* me like a blood slave."

Blood slave. Andres had never used that word—would never have dared—even if the image it conjured held a tantalizing beauty: gothic castles and golden collars and utter satisfaction. He tried to feel disgusted at himself, mortified even, but his only emotion was a quickly-growing sense of the conversation slipping away from him. He could feel his breathing quickening, his confidence wavering.

He needed it back, needed, somehow, to regain the power he'd had at the start of their meeting.

Andres reached out, past the flinch that Shane gave, placing his hand over the one Shane had wrapped protectively around his neck. With gentle nudges and tugs, he pulled it away, letting his fingertips trail across his little swan's pulse as he withdrew. "I bought you because I couldn't watch you die. I won't apologize for that, nor for taking what I paid for."

The intake of breath that trembled out of Shane was nearly as delicious as his blood smelled. He lowered his chin but he did not try to back away. "Don't you see my point, though? The system that the humans of this city—this whole fucking country and most of the western world with it—have put in place made *purchasing* me look to Maul like a reasonable option, and means that for you the follow-through is a necessity. Because you can't afford to buy blood now that you've spent your money on me, can you?"

"That's not strictly true." Andres had been able to buy a sufficient bagged supply on his current paycheck; the problem would come when his car went out, or he had an accident his increased resilience couldn't fix, or Maul raised the price of his rent with inflation again, and he had no buffer in his bank account to keep him above water. "Though you're not wrong either," he admitted, quieter, a little hollow. It felt too much like the Andres he'd been at the bar—the person he tried so hard to hide from others. He buried that person back down. Without tightening his grip on Shane's fingers, he tugged at him, teasing him closer.

Shane could have let his arm extend, but instead he stepped forward with a little inhale and a backward lean. "I could pay you back," he said, weakly.

"Do I act as though this situation burdens me, my little swan?" Andres growled, tender and fierce all at once. "I don't regret that you're mine. Your bared neck brings me far more delight than a thousand chilled bags. And," he added, harsher, "whether you're indebted to me or not, I will care whether this article you're trying to write inspires you to keep poking your neck places that will put it in range of Maul's fangs. He will kill you, Cygnus."

Shane closed his eyes. "I don't want that either, but I need to do *something*." It sounded so much like a plea, small and helpless and delightful. "If you're still investigating whatever nefarious plot was happening with Vitalis-Barron back in October, let me help you with that. Please, I can't just sit here on the edges of all this and pretend it's okay. I already have a media pass for their onsite gala next month—I can be useful outside of Maul's domain."

Andres wanted to give Shane everything in that moment: not just free rein in a world without Maul, but the world itself, every joy and pleasure it had to offer. That was not their reality though, not the reality of any vampire. "I had planned to find a way into that gala when the time came, so I won't say no to the help, but I doubt there's anything you could do for me right *now*. Vampires have been disappearing, and that woman I cornered at the gala is just one cog in a much larger machine that works within Vitalis-Barron. I'm looking for one specific vampire, who vanished almost a year ago and was rescued from within the Vitalis-Barron complex in October. If I can find her, I can find the people who broke her out—people who must know more than I do."

"*Vitalis-Barron* is the one abducting vampires?"

"Something like that."

Shane sighed. "If you tell me the truth, I promise I won't publish anything recklessly. I've seen the ways the media will turn something into a shitshow of needless debates and illogical objections instead of focusing on the real harm that's happening right before their eyes. I want us to have the best chance of doing what we can from the shadows before then."

His Cygnus was sincere about that—Andres could tell by the way he said it, each word deliberate and fiery, like he was speaking it to life. And Andres... Andres wanted to trust him.

So he did.

"As far as we can tell, Vitalis-Barron has been experimenting on vampires in secret for a number of decades. They collect their victims in part by offering blood or money or research opportunities to volunteers they know can vanish without causing too much of a stir—which, for vampires, is most of them—and when that isn't enough, they send their personal hunters out to compensate."

More and more of those hunters lurked the streets these days, but Andres was just as disgusted and enraged by the research board's leadership—people like the woman he'd cornered at the gala six months earlier, happy to sit back and reap the benefits of their heinously unethical research without ever dirtying their hands.

"Vitalis-Barron operates under the knowledge that it's, in the most technical terms, still not illegal to coerce vampires into dangerous scientific testing when all laws around research ethics were written for humans. If we can prove what they're doing to the public, though, it's possible for a court case to change that legality—to force them to stop their experiments." The darkness had turned Andres's vision monochromatic, and between the tunneling effect of his contacts and the literal blinders of his mask, he wasn't sure what Shane's expression meant. "Do *you* believe me?"

The little huff Shane gave would have been precious, were it not for the genuine annoyance in his expression. "I'm diabetic. I know very well that these big pharmaceutical companies will let people die if it makes them a profit." He lifted his brow. "So, what have you been doing about it?"

"I can keep singling out Vitalis-Barron employees as I did at their October gala, but confessions given under duress are useless at this point." He needed to go deeper. To get inside… or find someone who had. "I've heard reports of a vampire who escaped from Vitalis-Barron, and while they're still hiding—and likely don't know much themself—every rumor includes the detail that *someone* set them free. It's a wild goose chase that might lead nowhere, but finding them is the best lead I have right now."

Shane nodded along, looking more and more grave as Andres explained. "Tell me about this rescued vampire?"

"First name Tara, but I couldn't get a surname. She's Black, uses both she and they pronouns"—it made Andres happy just saying it, remembering them and their dual pronouns weren't alone in the world, though that joy was immediately doused by the knowledge that she might no longer be living in this world at all, if his inability to find her again was any sign—"and last summer she had a very distinctive afro in pastel pink and blue."

"Tara Williams? They drew cartoons outside the bars sometime in the summer?" Shane's lips quirked. "They were buying candles at a twenty-four seven magic shop near the boardwalk last week. They refused to let me interview them, but we had a very nice conversation about the effects of lighting on mood. Apparently they do staging and hospitality for a mysterious interactive-style theater event that I assume caters to vampires, likely one that serves blood if they're so secretive. I never figured out the name or location though."

Andres just stared at him. "How the hell do you know all that?"

Shane snorted. "I'm not an incompetent investigative journalist, just, it seems, an undesirable one." He appeared completely oblivious of how magnificent he was, and it left a pang in Andres's chest. "If you can find this secret club where Tara works, I imagine we can go speak with them."

We. Andres and his swan—his constellation—tackling this threat *together*. It felt like a light had been turned on within his rib cage, aiming a high-beam onto an emotion that suddenly seemed an awful lot like loneliness. He wanted to cry. He wanted to break apart like he had at the Fishnettery, but this time not from sadness—not entirely. The sadness was there, but so was relief, hope, fear, desperation.

He boxed in the fluttering of his heart and merely purred a sultry, "Perhaps. We shall see." He stepped forward and slipped around Shane, angling himself once more over his little swan's shoulder. "Right now, stay away from other vampires—stay safe. Your attention belongs to no one but me."

The way Shane shivered beneath his touch was a pure delight.

And perhaps that he enjoyed it should have worried him. But he could feel that guilt later. For the moment, he was going to drink, and drink deep. "And you, my little swan, still owe me a piece of yourself."

9

SHANE

Shane hated this.

He hated, specifically, that he kept thinking about that fiction his vampire had painted: Shane wilted across his bed, chains at his wrists and two fresh bite marks in his neck. Despite the fear and confliction that had already been coursing through him, when he'd heard it, his heart had done *something*—something indescribable and terrible. It left him hot and his neck strangely tender, so tender that Maul's voice had felt like bruises beneath the skin and his own vampire's like a gentle caress. Even through their talks of Vitalis-Barron and the merits of his article, Shane could not quite dislodge the feeling.

It roiled in him as his vampire whispered in his ear and pressed at his arms and hips, smoothly nudging him against the frame of the door. He was pinned, he knew, but he didn't feel it, because his vampire's grip continued to be soft, the tugs and grasps more like questions than demands. Still, when his vampire tucked back his hair, and his hot breath brushed over Shane's bare neck, it wasn't tenderness or chains his body remembered, but the unwanted clamping of fangs deep into his skin, the suffocating grasp of a hand on his mouth, the complete disregard for his terror and his pain.

Shane flinched, the way he'd been instinctively flinching at every remembered horror all evening. Each time so far, his vampire had pushed gently past his guard, soothed him with a touch so light it could never have come from anyone else. Shane waited for it—anticipated it so much that when his vampire's fingertips slid along his neck, his nerves lit, not in fear but in relief.

"Did Maul hurt you here as well?" He sounded miserable, as miserable as thinly-contained rage could be.

"Yes." It wasn't the literal truth, but the one Shane felt when he thought of Maul, watching from the darkness, only interrupting for his own profit.

"Damn him." It was grumbled so low that Shane didn't know if he was meant to hear it at all, but when his protector—monster—spoke again, his voice was as silky and sensual as ever. "Squeeze my fingers if it's too much, Cygnus."

"Thank you." It wasn't the right response, a gratitude signifier as though what his vampire was offering was anything beyond the bare minimum, but *of course* felt too casual and to say nothing seemed like it would give the wrong impression—the impression that this wasn't meaningful to Shane. He slid his hand through his vampire's, trying in vain to loosen the muscles in his shoulder. This wouldn't be like the bites Maul had set on him, but like the little pinch of venom from the October gala, amplified. He hoped.

"I never want to hurt you," his vampire whispered.

And Shane believed him.

As fangs pricked his neck, Shane expected the same fear, the returning memories of that night as Maul's goons had held him in place, but he felt himself melt instead, like his whole body was exhaling the panic that had been building in him since he'd first met the blood dealer. The venom burst that followed felt lush and full, enough to make him swoon against the doorway. He was pretty sure that he would have agreed to anything in that moment, would have sold himself to his vampire in blood and body and heart and life just to have this again.

His vampire held him, an arm around his waist and mouth tenderly working at his neck. It was not the harsh *bite, bite, bite* of Maul's goons from the previous night, but a soothing pressure, ending with a lick that seemed to make all the venom already in Shane's system light up.

Shane drew the tips of his fingers back and forth over his vampire's hand with a sigh. "Thank you," he repeated, and this time it felt right.

"Precious little swan," his vampire replied. "You are mine, now. Don't forget that." With a final drag of his tongue that left Shane hot and weak and trembling, he pulled away.

Shane fought the impulse to reach for him. To turn for him, to find those lips that had pressed so softly to his what felt like yesterday and a lifetime ago. When he finally did, there was no one.

"You're mine now."

It should have scared him.

And yet…

And yet.

"I'm here, I'm alive, everything's fine."

"God dammit, Shane!" From the sound of Nat's voice in his car's speaker, she sounded like she was across a room from her mic. With some banging, her voice returned to normal. "Fuck you. I've been here for half an hour trying not to have a panic attack wondering whether my only real friend is getting eaten out or just plain *eaten* by a vampire." Her only real friend.

He had a friend. They were friends. "I'm eternally sorry. Thank you for watching out for me."

"Geez. Well. Whatever." She made a disgusted noise. "What happened? Is that creep finally gone? Did you actually fuck him?"

"I did not, as I was never *planning* to fuck him." Shane pulled away from the curb. "He's gone, at least for now. We just talked for a while and then he bit me." He could not admit that at one point the bastard who'd almost had him killed came back, and even then Shane hadn't called for help. He'd been safe, he reasoned. And bringing in outside help *might* have managed to take Maul down without ruining Shane's entire investigation, but it also might have taken Shane's vampire down instead.

"He fucking *bit* you? My god, are you okay?"

"Relax, it was nice. He was…" Sweet wasn't quite right, and compassionate implied far more than he'd given. Shane finally settled on the word that kept coming back to him, that comforted him even when everything else should have made him flee in terror. "He was gentle."

He had been so very gentle, ever since they'd met, soft hands and flirtatious comments layered over a witty intellect and that genuine desire to know what Shane was thinking. No matter how sharp his fangs were or how willing he was to use them as a threat against the woman he cornered at the gala last fall, he had always been so very gentle with Shane.

"Huh. Well, he sounds like a melodramatic ass," Nat said. "I still think we should stake him. Just in case." It *sounded* like a joke.

"You're not allowed to stake him so long as he's being sweet to me. He's also looking out for me. You're on the same side."

"I still don't trust him."

"Overprotective much?" Shane grumbled, but he felt lighter, happier. He had someone in his life to worry over him—he had Nat. Nat and his vampire. He wasn't alone after all. "Thank you, by the way. It means a lot to me."

"Oh, get off the phone before you start crying," Nat snapped, but she added, quieter, "You're welcome. Anytime. I mean it." before hanging up.

Shane Cowley had a friend.

He beamed to himself. It wasn't quite the full social life he'd had in college, but it meant a lot more now, somehow. And it didn't have to end with Nat. There were other relationships out there for him—platonic ones, without fangs. Ones, perhaps, like his acquaintance with Andres Serrano.

The last twenty-four hours had wiped Andres completely from Shane's mind, but the memory he did have of them was a fond one, a little quirk coming into his lips at the recollection. Shane had his vampire—or his vampire had *him*, anyway—and the mere thought of wanting someone else felt oddly like a betrayal.

But he'd only asked Andres for friendship.

And if Shane finally had one friend again, perhaps he could have two.

10

Andres

Shane still didn't know who he was.

It left a giddy, anxious bubble in Andres's chest, something so conflicted that he wasn't sure what to do with it. He knew this was the right choice. The way his little swan had relaxed, breathless and eager—Andres doubted that would last once he realized the dark and sexy vampire who owned his blood was the same person who'd stumbled into him, sobbing, at the Fishnettery.

And he both loved and hated that. As much as he thrived on the dramatics and the mystery of the mask, a part of him was beginning to despise the fact that it had turned out this way. There was no world where they'd flirted at the Fishnettery instead, just as there wasn't one where Shane lay, bare and lovely, on Andres's bed, a little gilded collar around his neck and bite marks branding every prominent vein. It was no use dreaming about things he would never have.

Anyway, Shane had given him enough to fantasize about as it was. The thought of his Cygnus pressed to the doorframe—melting beneath his bite, making that *sound*—

Andres tried to force the memory aside as he pulled into the little garage beneath his townhouse and entered through the remodeled kitchen—granite counters and second-hand stainless steel appliances, a few of which he'd stolen from a particularly awful neighbor and had no regrets about—past the otherwise modern living room with an ancient sewing machine stashed in the corner, the shelf at its side filled with leather scraps and lace that he was hoping to incorporate into a pair of pants.

His princess merped at him from her hammock on the landing, and he gave her a quick pet.

His phone chimed.

Hell Creature Extraordinaire
Hey dork bitch, send me cat pics.

His cousin had incredible timing. He sighed.

Cat Mom
Give me one good reason, demon child.

Not that she was technically a child any longer, but no matter how far they drifted, she would always be that hilarious, chaotic kid he'd spent his teenage years bandaging up.

Hell Creature Extraordinaire
I'm nice to you?

Cat Mom

You literally just proved the contrary.

Hell Creature Extraordinaire

I affirm your gender.

Cat Mom

That's the bare minimum for anyone.

Hell Creature Extraordinaire

I'll send you spider gifs until you cave.

Andres grimaced at the thought. Over the course of their lives, he and his cousin had learned the hard way that his abhorrence of spiders was rivaled only by her own love for them. He knew her too well to cave to such a hollow threat though, and he'd worked under Maul's constant fear tactics long enough that hers hardly fazed him.

Cat Mom

Intimidation won't save you. You have to actually *earn* pictures of the princess.

Hell Creature Extraordinaire

Well FINE how about this:

It's 7:30pm on a Tuesday and I'm drunk and unemployed and my boyfriend is nowhere to be seen. Send me the fucking cat pics you miserable asshole.

Andres paused, rereading the text with a sinking stomach. They never really talked about important life details anymore—he knew she'd lost her job recently, but he couldn't actually remember if she'd mentioned where or how. Their conversations, including that one, were all dramatics and memes and goofy insults, and that had felt deep, because the two of them had been deep, once, but standing alone in his home, imagining the baby cousin he'd cherished as a teenager—picked on and loved on in obsessive intervals—grown into a sad, lonely adult broke his heart.

They could hang out again, he reminded himself. He could sweep her into his arms and tell her he'd always love her even when no one else did. They'd managed it on and off since he'd turned nearly a decade before, and she still hadn't realized what he was yet. But she'd been so outspoken against vampires lately that he worried…

In the end, Andres replied with the single word *fine*, then a stream of his most recent pictures of Camilla, her little pink toe beans surrounded by fluffs of white fur.

Hell Creature Extraordinaire
She deserves better.

Cat Mom
You're right: there is no one good enough for her, and we both know it.

He closed the thread and, after a final kiss to Camilla's head, he forced his thoughts elsewhere.

It wasn't hard, not with Shane still lurking at the back of his mind.

The rest of his body followed that rabbit trail, and this time he didn't bother fighting it. The thought of Shane settled so low and steady, a pounding need Andres had little reason to ignore. This was his day off, and he had no further obligations now that he'd seen Shane. Touched Shane. Sunk his fangs into his little swan's neck and felt him shiver.

He left his coat draped over his desk and his leggings on the floor, settling into bed with the kind of sigh that only a massive mattress and a hoard of pillows could bring. He felt like a goddamned queen against the luxury, a beautiful creature of the night, genderless but feminine and perfectly himself. The bed could have easily fit Shane beside him, spread out and clothed in a similar red silk to his sheets, but embroidered and sheer, chains at his wrist and a—

Fucking hell, he was not supposed to be thinking about *that*.

As he tried to refocus on more realistic thoughts of Shane, though, his phone chimed. He would have left it alone—whatever it was could wait fifteen minutes—but he made the mistake of glancing at the screen as he prepared to toss it across the bed. His blood went hot and cold, his heart leaped into his throat.

Unknown Number

Hey Andres! This is Shane Cowley from the bar.
If this is weird, you can just ignore me, but I thought maybe we could get friendly drinks sometime? And not spill yours everywhere.

Oh, was all his brain seemed capable of for a moment, then a sputtering of joy and another bubble of fear. Because he wanted this: wanted to go sit with Shane at the bar and laugh and joke and tease in all the ways he couldn't behind a mask and a sultry voice. But the more Shane witnessed him as Andres—Andres, whom he clearly didn't want anything more than friendship with—the more likely it was that he'd put two and two together.

Andres

I'm kind of busy with work at the moment, but if you don't mind friendly texting instead, I believe that has a pretty low risk of spilled drinks?

That sounded casual, right? It was direct, but considerate, returned Shane's implied request that this be platonic, and included a joke. Andres folded his legs in and stared at the screen. Surely his pulse was not meant to feel like this, loud and rough like his blood was trying to burst out of his body. Shane was already in his life, for better or worse. Whether he replied to the fool he'd met at the bar didn't actually matter.

It didn't.

But when the text came in, Andres's stomach still fluttered.

Shane

I think you underestimate my abilities. I have spilled plenty a drink during a precarious texting conversation ;)

Andres

Oh have you now? And how would you rate our spill, compared to those.

Shane

Nine out of ten, easy. It was comedic, but no one's outfit or technology was ruined, and it made me a friend.

Fuck, he was adorable.

Andres

And the star you took off?

Shane

Do you think I'd just hand out the secret to a perfect drink spill? Not a chance.

You'll just have to test other variations on me
someday ;)

That was a *second* winking face. A second winking face,
right after an explicit description of their relationship as
friends. Andres pressed the phone to his forehead with a
groan. He had to stop overthinking this. This version of
himself could never accept anything more real from Shane
than texts as long as he wanted to keep what they'd started
in the alley. It was better to just enjoy whatever they did have.

Shane

So, what's this work that's getting in the way of
your normal drink-sloshing activities?

Andres

I'm in project management and acquisitions. Our
supply chain is fickle right now and an upshoot has
been closing in on our customers. My boss is so
stressed, I think one of these days he's going to
tear my throat out. I feel worse for his less-
important employees though; at least I have job
security.
And you're a journalist, right?

Shane

Damn, that sounds rough.
A journalist of a kind, anyway. I'm trying to move
out of the content mill and into something that
gives me space to write what I care about. There's

so much I want to say, so much that *deserves* to be said and revealed and acknowledged, you know?

Andres

I'm sure you will impart some very great exposés upon the world someday :)

Have you considered attaching ratings to the secrets you expose? I think there's an untapped market for that.

(I am the untapped market. The untapped market is me.)

Shane

Watergate would normally get a 6 out of 10, but the fact that his administration was already wiretapping each other and themselves gives it an extra star.

But then, I'm biased in that I don't really like political journalism on its own. I care more about uncovering the effect that the government is having on its people than any individual scumbags.

Andres

Oh thank god, I guess I can keep my own wiretaps in place then.

You know, the ones that tell me when there's a renowned stuff-rater filming at a bar where I can accidentally run into him ;)

Shane

If that was a setup, then I applaud your commitment to the bit.

Andres

Getting my mascara to run like that is a talent, I assure you.

Shane

I take back my original rating of that look. It was a 15 out of 10. Truly spectacular. I think you might set a new trend tbh.

Andres curled onto his side with a smile, stuffing a pillow under his chin, and kept typing.

It took a force of nature to pull him out of bed—one in the form of a princess with the vocals of an entire opera house and the desire for a can of wet food immediately—but he carried his phone with him, replying to Shane between scavenging for snacks and sewing research and rewatches of *Shane Rates Stuff* episodes, all of which he live-messaged to Shane.

They hadn't stopped texting for more than ten consecutive minutes by the time Andres flopped back onto his bed, his gaze bleary but his heart far too filled with anticipation to sleep. When Shane's texts finally stopped coming, the clock read 4:46am. It felt like too soon, even if the dry, gritty sensation of staring at his phone through his disposable daily contacts warned that it was probably high time Andres let himself rest too.

He dragged them out and dropped them into the trash, closing his eyes as he finally slipped a hand between his legs. He was half asleep as he finished, his mind filled with thoughts of Shane's skin and the tiny sound he'd made when Andres had pierced his flesh.

11

Shane

Andres was easy to talk to.

Shane swore he spent just as much time over the next week messaging them as he did waiting impatiently for his vampire's nightly visits. It was like Andres's conversation with him at the Fishnettery had never stopped, their engaging mix of relaxed banter and thoughtful analyses dragging Shane in like a moth to the light. He found himself going deeper than he had with anyone in years—not that the bar there was particularly high.

As he splayed across his couch in the late afternoon, the feline heathen lounging between his legs, he casually explained his hopes for his future as a journalist and his fears that after so long in the content mill, no one would ever see him as such.

Andres
Tell me something then. Something journalistic.

Shane

If you're not more specific, I hope you're prepared for the sheer chaos you're likely to get.

Andres

I'm happy for whatever you throw at me.

Shane

Really? Well then, did you know that statistically speaking, nonbinary people are more likely to be cooler, smarter, and hotter than your average human? This research is based on a data pool of one, though, so it may be flawed.

Andres

Oh, very funny.

They sent a gif of falling pink, blue, and white sparkles afterwards though, which made Shane's grin even wider.

Andres

Tell me something beautiful, then. Something that worms its way into your soul and makes it a little bit brighter.

Shane

That's harder, huh.

Okay, how about this:

Sometimes I have weird thoughts about death. And I don't mean like intrusive thoughts or existential dread, but strangely the opposite? When I die someday (hopefully someday very far in the future, mind you), it won't be simply a tragedy, but an honor too. We all came from stardust and it's kind of wonderful that we'll all return to it someday, the molecules in our bodies remade into new life a thousand times over between now and then.

It made him think of Cygnus—not simply the pet name his vampire had chosen for him, but the constellation and the mythology behind it, the mourner having been transformed into a swan and placed in the heavens by the gods after the death of his lover, Phaethon, made him inconsolable. Though the tragedy of the young lovers was far from enviable, Shane thought there was a symbolic beauty in the idea; Cygnus going on to light the nights of other couples for an eternity after, lost but never gone.

Shane

I want to be here for as long as I can, but after that I want to be the breath in someone's lungs, and the crisp water they drink on a hot afternoon, the iron that pumps through their veins. I hope the words I write will have a direct, positive impact while I'm here, but once I'm not, my very body will have that impact instead.

Unless someone sticks me in a coffin, in which case I'll just be dead forever.

Did I scare you off?

(Sorry.)

Shane attempted to shift his position on the couch without disrupting his obtrusive cat and forced down the flutter of unease in his gut as Andres continued to leave him on read. They'd been open to all his wild thoughts so far, but he knew that most people didn't take well to talk of death, much less having that tragedy presented as a thing of beauty. Even the ways he could already offer parts of himself for the fueling of someone else's life while he still lived weren't viewed in the most positive light. His blood could be let willingly in his vampire's mouth every night, a treasure that would pound through his vampire's heart, but most people saw that not as a gift, but a vulgarity.

Perhaps Andres was the same.

Shane tapped the side of his phone as their typing bubbles finally appeared, forcing himself not to cut in by dismissing his own thoughts. If this was enough to scare Andres off, then Shane told himself he didn't need their friendship. Just the thought of losing their messages made him feel sick inside, though.

Andres

(Sorry, I'm back!)

No, that was wonderful. Thank you <3 I've never thought of death like that before, but it seems rather lovely the way you described it.

It was the little heart that Shane got caught on, those two unassuming characters that seemed to beat in his own chest.

Andres

I think it's safe to say that your words are already having a positive impact on someone <3

And another one.

It didn't hit Shane any less potently, a warm ache settling inside him. *Your words are already having a positive impact on someone.* He hadn't known just how much he needed that. Leaning against his elbow onto his chair's armrest, he pressed his palm to his cheek. His whole body felt light, and his heart large.

He'd had enough crushes to know what that meant.

The realization settled into his stomach like a cloud of butterflies. This wasn't simply the little spark of chemistry he'd had with Andres when they'd met, or the platonic joy of having someone to talk to—it was bigger, a breath-catching thing that offered to eat Shane alive if he let it.

Which he absolutely couldn't. He *had* someone, even if that someone was a vampire who'd claimed him only for his blood, who still refused to show Shane his face or tell him his name even as he appeared to torment Shane on a nightly basis.

But Andres was currently just a friend; Shane had been clear on that when they'd first started texting, and after Andres's original rejection to meet up, Shane had felt too awkward to ask if they wanted to try getting together again. Andres had never broached the topic.

Whatever Shane was starting to feel, this wouldn't go anywhere—not anywhere outside his chest, anyway.

So when Andres texted the next day, *tell me something limitless or something liminal,* Shane broke down and spoke of ghosts, of souls and memory and the worth of a thing regardless of whether or not it was forgotten. He did not say that every sweet and considerate message Andres sent back made him smile uncontrollably.

Through every new exchange of existential musings, Andres was so thoughtful and curious and caring. When they finally moved the conversation from whimsical discussions to something more personal, the question they sent left Shane with an ache in his chest. He paused from the ChatterDash meme spread he'd been working on, turning his full attention to Andres's text.

Andres
Do you ever feel like you've lost track of who you are on the inside?

It seemed odd, coming from someone as warm and open as Andres.

But Shane could not respond that he felt like he knew the person inside Andres already; that they were kind enough to not simply put up with him, but to revel in his absurdities, with their little old-school heart emojis and their unending pensive questions and their gentle responses that proved they were genuinely dwelling on the often ridiculous and long-winded answers Shane gave. Despite all the words in him, he didn't know how to say any of that without sounding like he was a little bit in love with Andres. So he answered the question instead, just as he'd done with all of Andres's others.

Shane

I think I know who I am? (I say that with hesitation only because while I did have to do a lot of self-reflection in all areas to get to this point in my gender and neurodiversity journey, I also don't believe we're just stagnant beings). But sometimes I also think the person I am—not the journalist persona or the me that random strangers get, but my full self—might be someone who not very many people actually like, so I kind of know what you mean. Like, who I'm putting out in casual settings isn't the person underneath it all, and while that's okay and normal, it's left that unseen me within to languish. Is the person we are beneath the layers of formality real if no one gets to know them?

Andres

Am I getting to know him?

Shane

Yes <3

The heart emoji slipped out before he could help it; the same simple, keyboard formed one that Andres used. Shane held his breath, hoping they wouldn't notice. Wouldn't take it the way he had, all sparkling nerves and blooming crushes.

Andres
Then he's real now.
I'm sorry about whatever deeper me you're having to discover here, they're a little dusty.
Sometimes I think I've come so far, and then other times I still feel like I'm just the quiet, weird kid who spent freshman summer locked in their room sewing a cosplay for a con they forgot to buy the tickets to.

Shane
You're wonderful, don't worry.

Fuck, he was losing it. He had to backtrack before it was too late.

Shane
But.
Oh. My. God. Baby Andres made their own cosplay?!
Who were you going as?

Andres
Do you know Howl from Howl's Moving Castle?

Shane

You think I *wouldn't* know what Howl's Moving Castle is? I'm truly offended. /jokes

For real, it was my favorite as a kid. I thought I wanted to *be* Howl for a lot of years, but in the end his gender wasn't masculine enough for me (even if his fashion sense is absolutely killing it) and my personality was always more of a Sophie anyways.

Andres

So I take it you're tidy?

Shane scoffed out loud, grinning against his fingers. He'd sworn to himself that he'd use his vampire's intrusive cleaning to help him stay at least a little neater, but in the ten days since then his apartment had somehow fallen into complete shambles again. It took him some brain-racking to remember when he'd first used half the dishes on his desk, much less left them there…

Shane

Tidy is the one trait I don't share with Sophie, unfortunately.

More like bossy and single-minded?

Andres

Her other good traits then. Noted ;)

Shane

Oh, fuck off ;) /affectionate

But Shane did not want Andres to fuck off.

As painful as it was to suppress his growing crush, he wanted more of them in his life. He thought, not for the first time, that a relationship with them would be honest and appropriate and healthy—nothing like the connection he had with his vampire.

He didn't want his vampire to fuck off either though, and that was the problem. It seemed Shane was always thinking about one of the two. With Andres, those daydreams were soft and fluttery, a giddiness he hadn't felt for someone in years, but with his vampire... the fire those fantasies set ablaze was one Shane had never felt before.

And, god, he really had to stop envisioning himself chained up for his vampire's pleasure.

Even all these days later, he could not get out of his head the exact way his vampire had spelled out that fabrication of Shane in bed, like it was such an easy thing to imagine. It haunted Shane, choked him in the night, made him burn between his legs. He'd find himself tracing his own throat, like part of his subconscious expected to discover metal there.

There was something wrong with him, surely.

The way he'd accepted all this—his vampire's ownership of his blood, his demands and his pet names—was already putting into question Shane's sanity. No one should have been able to waltz into Shane's life and force that on him. But with his vampire, he didn't feel forced. He felt guided, gently manipulated by protective arms, a cage that was also a shield and blanket.

He could not stop alternating between giddy texts with Andres and hot anticipation of the moments when he'd be in front of his apartment after dusk and he'd feel a breath on his neck, a hand fluttering down his arm. Every time, his heart leapt and his legs turned to putty, his breath catching in his chest as his vampire whispered a greeting into his ear, possessive and dark. They didn't talk nearly as much as they had that first meeting that Maul had interrupted, but his vampire would always respond to him with the same intense fascination and joy that he had so many months ago at the October gala, continuing conversations from their prior meetings without missing a beat. He still wore his mask for every encounter, though between the darkness and his tendency to creep up behind Shane, a monster amongst shadows, it seemed more for the drama of it than anything else—the same reason he'd given no name yet, forcing Shane to think of him only as *his* vampire.

Over a week after their night in the alley, Shane knew the drill, knew to stand outside in the shadows near his regular parking spot along the street—he'd stopped going any farther from his house after sunset, the quiet fear of running into Maul at the grocery store or walking along the boardwalk always lingering in the back of his mind.

He twirled a finger through his hair as he finished a message to Andres. The longer their relationship—*friendship*—progressed, the more obvious it was that he knew Andres—this person he hadn't seen or touched since their first meeting—far better than the vampire who pressed his mouth to Shane's neck every night. Though he supposed they both had masks of their own, even if Shane had seen Andres's face before they'd vanished behind a wall of text.

The moment Shane slipped his phone away, he was pushed against the side of his car with a pressure so soft it was barely there, the murmur of his vampire's greeting behind him. Always behind him.

It was lovely, and it was empty too, somehow.

Before his vampire could get too far—could distract him from all thoughts of relationships with his overwhelming touch, Shane asked, "I'm not just a thing you take pleasure in, am I?"

"Well, I certainly do take pleasure in you," his vampire replied, chest brushing Shane's back. "Do you think there's anything so wrong with that? Do you wish that I'd find you less lovely, or that you'd taste of ash on my tongue? Would you prefer to be treated like a ball and chain and not a delicacy?" As he spoke, he gently drew Shane's hair behind his ear, each touch like fire.

Shane couldn't help but bask in that flame even as he tried to keep his mind centered. "If I did taste of ash, would you still have paid so much to save me?"

"You'd have to unravel time with that question," his vampire replied, running two fingers along the side of Shane's neck. "If you tasted any differently, you would not be yourself, and I wouldn't have seen you that night at the gala and known that my world would stop dead if I didn't dance with you. And if we hadn't danced, you would never have realized what I was. Perhaps you'd never have come looking for vampires at all."

Shane felt his whole body tremble at the brush of his vampire's mouth on his neck. "Imagine I had. Imagine I was dying behind that curtain, but you found no pleasure in the thought of me."

"We all want to believe we're the kind of person who'd sacrifice for a stranger, don't we?" His fingers tightened into Shane's hair, but it didn't hurt, just held him there, held his soul aloft. "Yet I don't think most of us truly would."

"That's a hopeless outlook."

"It's realistic." He nuzzled his nose against the back of Shane's ear. The edge of his mask pressed against Shane's temple. "If there was any reality where I'd left you to die, then I would have been a fool and a monster."

Shane wanted to melt into him at those words, to defy every possible warning sign and be consumed. Instead he whispered, "You don't know me."

The hesitation—the tension—that radiated from his vampire in that moment could have cut like a blade. "I sink my teeth into your flesh and I taste your life," he finally breathed. "I know you better than you might think, my little swan. Now, give me your lovely neck."

Shane tipped his head back, leaning into his vampire's touch, but he continued thinking of those words long after the pain of the bite had faded into bliss.

The twinge it left behind made him feel like he knew his vampire far more than he realized.

12

ANDRES

Juggling both relationships with Shane became easy strangely fast. Every time he slipped up behind Shane on the way to his car in the evening or as Shane lingered with a drink on the dark porch in front of his apartment, Andres could be his favorite parts of his vampiric presence: sensual and in control and just a little bit demanding, and with the Shane he spoke to over text, he could bare the deepest parts of his soul, switching seamlessly between the two; soft smiles for one and dark smirks for the other.

But Shane would never truly belong to either version of Andres in the way he wanted, not while his mask was necessary.

He was accepting of Andres's bite. He never fought, never asked Andres to stop, merely trembled, his lashes fluttering and his breath quickening. As much as Andres enjoyed that vulnerability—that fear—he worried more with each passing meeting that he'd played their first encounter too mysterious. He had thought, vaguely, that Shane would either grow comfortable with him, or else push back if he didn't. Instead he kept quivering and wilting and finally submitting.

Andres couldn't stop his doubts from creeping in, slow and sure.

He had the lingering taste of his little swan's blood in his mouth as he paced his living room and racked his brain for any way he might bring up vampires with Shane through text, in the hopes that Shane might reveal his true feelings to the wreck he'd met at the Fishnettery like he had with so many other things. Each typed and retyped question about monsters and bites seemed more obvious than the last, though. He pressed the phone to his forehead with a growl.

Its sudden call vibration nearly launched Andres out of his skin. Goddamn Frederick Maul. At least this was better than being ordered to a physical meeting.

Running his fingers through his hair, he begrudgingly answered the phone.

Three minutes of Maul's incessant plotting later, and Andres wished he'd pretended he was busy. "I can't do it, it's too risky."

"If you're not capable—"

"Let me rephrase that." Andres cupped his arm over the side of his head, slumping against the wall like it might give him the strength to weather this conversation. "If we go after that blood while the robbery from two weeks ago is so fresh in their minds, we will set ourselves up for failure. There's difficult and then there's ignorant. I warned you this would happen."

"I want to ramp up our Coachella presence next week, then."

Andres had driven the hour and half back and forth from the event all that weekend, helping smooth over his deceptive connections and ensure Maul's faux blood-donation vans and underhanded backroom setups could collect and transport their bags without getting caught. "We're pushing our luck there as it is."

"You can't keep telling me *no*, Andres."

"I don't know what else to tell you when you ask for impossible things."

"Excuses—"

Andres tipped the phone away from his ear in preparation for the incoming tirade, but Maul's grumbling was cut off by one of his subordinates nervously explaining that one of the storage fridges had risen above acceptable levels.

"Can no one do their goddamned jobs?" Maul hissed under his breath. "If you have to be spending all this free time not stealing me blood, your investigation into Vitalis-Barron had better be making progress finally."

"I have a lead now. Be patient."

The shop where Tara had met Shane had given Andres nothing, and neither had relentlessly walking the surrounding area, poking his head around until he had memorized every neighborhood micro-cemetery and gentrified coffee shop—of which there were nearly equal numbers now; enough coffee to support the tourists who came to see the American city with the most cemeteries. With flowers blooming along the sides of the walkways and the air warm enough to make boating pleasant, they were slowly funneling back in.

It was a habitual tourist from San Diego who had finally helped him, claiming to have a friend who commuted to San Salud to attend Tara's work on the regular. Andres kept reminding himself that there were still plenty of ways for this lead to fall through. If it did, then at least they were only a few weeks from the Vitalis-Barron Met-inspired gala. That *had* to pan out, because he would be squeezing something useful from it even if it meant tearing through the offices of every executive on their staff.

"Just a *lead*." Maul huffed. "Sometimes I wonder why I let you live."

Not out of the goodness of his heart, Andres was certain of that. "We'll have enough blood to get through, don't worry."

"*You'll* certainly have enough." It sounded half an accusation. "How is that living blood bag of yours faring? Not causing too much trouble, is he?"

Andres didn't think Shane could be any less trouble if he'd tried. For some god-awful reason, Andres's mind went straight from that to the image of his little swan on silken sheets, the picture he'd painted for Maul two weeks before coming to life behind his eyelids. He blinked it away. "He understands his place in this... arrangement."

"Maybe that's the future," Maul began to say, and the icy chill of those words was still sliding down Andres's spine when his boss switched targets again at the shouting of a subordinate on the other end of the phone. "Bring her here!" The sharp edge of his voice made Andres flinch irrationally, his heart rate kicking up. He ran one hand through his hair.

Over the line, someone apologized, her words becoming clearer as she neared the mic on the other end. "I swear, it won't happen again."

"No, it won't," Maul agreed, his tone so terrible that Andres moved to end the call. His fingers slid over the screen, not quite hitting the red button before his boss continued, "Hold her down."

When the line went dead, Andres wasn't sure which of them had disconnected.

He leaned against the arm of the couch, forcing himself to draw in long, slow breaths, and waited for the numb chill to subside.

He hadn't thought Maul was still doing that shit. But then, he'd been having as many of his interactions with Maul over the phone as he could since he'd been trusted with the position as his boss's practical right hand, manager of everything blood collection-related while Maul handled the distribution end. The thought of what that poor vampire was likely suffering at this moment made him sick.

He tried to put it out of his mind—what other option did he have? If he left, there would be no one else with the confidence to say no to Maul when it mattered most. And he had no doubts that Maul would simply make another of him: a weaker, more malleable version. Regardless of how great his life was now, he could not put another person through that. Maul's next victim would not have Andres's luck of coming out unscathed.

Andres would just have to quiet Maul's temper with fresh dirt on Vitalis-Barron; give him something else to fight that wasn't his own employees. When his phone chimed with a text from his lead ten minutes later, he tried to relax. Then he read the message. He stared at it for so long that his contacts felt dry when he finally forced himself to blink. The vision of Shane returned the moment he closed his eyes.

He could almost convince himself not to act on the information. It was too perfect—too much like it had crawled into his mind and curled up in the darkest, filthiest parts of himself. But it *was* so perfect, down to the smallest details.

And it would be for his investigation, after all. Not just to see a piece of his deepest desires played out in front of him. It didn't make him a monster—not if his little swan agreed to everything.

Still, when he wrote a note to slip under Shane's door, he could not seem to find an explanation that didn't tug every inch of his gastrointestinal tract into knots. So he kept it vague. Vague and demanding.

Be outside tonight an hour after dusk.

We're going shopping.

Your vampire

(PS: I found Tara.)

13

SHANE

Shane's vampire still wore his mask, only the fine edge of his jaw and the elegant line of his lips visible below it. He smiled as Shane slipped into his passenger seat. His fangs gleamed in the low light.

He had on a long leather jacket over a lacey red button-up that showed off the lines of his musculature beneath, and Shane fought very hard not to admire him *too* much in it. It looked custom-made for him, the same exquisite mix of feminine and masculine, the red and black matching the polish of his nails and the dark liner around his eyes. He was, undeniably, far too beautiful for his own good—and his own good seemed to be other people's morally ambiguous.

Yet Shane couldn't dislike him for it.

If anything, his possessiveness was thrilling. The desire and the sensuality of it left Shane's heart pounding and his knees weak and a deep, unconquerable ache between his legs that no vibrator could sate for long. That *this* was apparently what his sex life had been lacking all these years should have left him far more uncomfortable than it did.

The fifteen-minute-old unanswered text from Andres felt more shameful by far. Shane should have been running headlong after his new friend. They were the safe crush: a simple, kind human, a little tired and lonely but genuine and lovely. They were the option Shane should have been letting himself fall head over heels for, would have been flirting with far more were he not still feeling the brush of his vampire's lips from months past.

As warm and giddy as new messages from Andres always left Shane, even the most sensual imagining of them—their appearance now a blur of tear-stained make up and dark lashes in Shane's memory—couldn't stoke the kind of yearning that Shane's body seemed determined to build for a vampire whose face he'd never seen at all; who pressed up against Shane's boundaries and so possessively demanded his skin and blood and submission. And for all that he should have been battling those feelings down, instead Shane was beginning to hope that his vampire might take even more… might take his mouth, as gentle and forceful as he'd taken over Shane's life.

He pushed back the intrusive vision and tried to focus on where they were and whatever the hell they were here for. *Shopping*, his vampire had said. Well, this did not look like any kind of shopping he'd ever experienced.

As they drove toward the edge of the city, the tight blocks of the artsy districts turned to hilly suburbs where each house looked as if it were built in a different era. They pulled up at a picturesque single-story home with no fence around it, a hedge separating it from the next lot on one side and a patch of forest on the other. It looked familiar.

"This way," his vampire said, leading him around the back.

"Please tell me we're invading someone's private property for a reason." Shane grumbled the words under his breath, feeling self-conscious at the light on in the kitchen window, spotlighting a young teenager obliviously doing her homework. At least *his vampire* had a mask on.

"We're not invading. We have an appointment." The path around the back split toward a patio overlooking a scrubby grass lawn, but his vampire continued walking deeper into the yard, past a line of trees and toward another tall, barnlike building. He paused at the wide rolling door and knocked.

"Now will you tell me what we're here for?" Shane leaned closer, trying, just a little, to get in the way.

His vampire had the gall to shush him, and his hands were somehow shifting Shane back, moving him with barely a touch. He knocked again to no answer.

"Hello?" He gripped the handle on the sliding door, starting to drag it open.

"Careful!" came a shout from behind them. A broad middle-aged man with brown skin jogged through the tree line, waving. "I'd closed up for the night before you called. Don't want to set anything off," he explained, as he typed something into his phone. A faint buzz sounded. He put the device away. "That should be better. Now, where were we?"

Shane's vampire slid an arm around his shoulder, a light touch that never quite settled. "This is my—this is the human I mentioned." He twirled a lock of Shane's hair between his fingers in a way that felt just a little bit possessive, tipping his face toward Shane's ear to add, breath hot and voice husky, "Mercer occasionally works with vampires on special projects. Like what we'll need for Tara's work access, and... other things."

So they needed something from him to reach Tara—a lock picking tool or a faked ID badge, perhaps, if the issue was access—but why he had Shane here for it was unclear. Unless Shane wasn't here for *that*.

"And other things," his vampire had said. But what kind of other things...

Mercer didn't look the least bit fazed by any of this—not even the mask Shane's vampire was still adamant about wearing. He held out a hand, and in the small porchlight above the shed, Shane finally recognized him as the person who'd ordered him off this very property in the daylight after refusing to answer questions about his vampiric customers.

Mercer seemed to register it at the same time. "You're the journalist who came poking around here a couple months ago."

"That wasn't my finest moment," Shane admitted, though *technically*, he still didn't regret it. He moved through the motions, taking Mercer's hand and trying not to cringe.

Mercer shook with a firm grip, calluses spread across his strong fingers. "Seems you found yourself a vampire without my help."

"He found me," Shane admitted.

Mercer said nothing to that. His biceps strained beneath his tight t-shirt as he shoved open the sliding door like it weighed a ton—perhaps literally—revealing a darkened interior.

"Please don't hate me," Shane's vampire whispered, lips brushing Shane's ear.

"How comforting." Shane almost wished he did hate his vampire—or even just feared him properly. That, at least, would make so much more sense.

Mercer flipped a switch on the shed's wall.

Bright white lights illuminated the wide space, revealing a series of tables and instruments, hanging tools along one wall and supplies of metal and wood and gems in cases against another. Something that Shane could only describe as a furnace had been built out of the back, open windows on all sides. And the shop was most certainly in use. A dozen different projects lay about, spaced perfectly into tape-designated workspaces or laying atop velvet cushions, each unique and lovely and at least partially metal.

Shane pressed his fingers to his lips. Whatever his vampire was intent on ordering here, it would certainly be beautiful. He glanced at Mercer and motioned to the tables. "May I?"

The smith nodded. "Just don't touch anything."

"Go on," his vampire added, like Shane needed his permission. Or perhaps just as an encouragement. Fuck, with that voice of his, so smooth and sultry like he was a moment away from kissing Shane's throat or commanding his complete submission, Shane couldn't tell.

He dipped his head and stepped between the tables. His gaze swept across the smith's creations, jewelry and figurines, armor and weapons. A little sculpted wizard boasted an opal as the top of her staff. A set of the most delicate knives were halfway through having silver vinery worked up their hilts. Beside them lay a silver rocket-shaped piece with textured ridges and an elegantly fashioned base that was so ornate it took Shane a moment to realize its purpose, though not much longer than that to imagine it. He felt his cheeks warm and avoided his vampire's gaze.

Oddly, his second impulse was to tell Andres how he'd rate them all, ordered by practicality—what use were knives that dainty, really?—and beauty—why put so much detail into something that would be hidden in a toy box when it wasn't pressed into the dark, tight space it was made for? It felt rude to pull his phone out, but he memorized everything as he moved. He'd text it all to Andres in delicious detail later. Right before losing himself to very specific fantasies involving a few of these objects and a bed that wasn't his.

Behind him, his vampire and Mercer spoke in casual tones.

"You'd mentioned on the phone," the smith was saying, "that you wanted openings for your fangs. Were you thinking little custom-sized tooth gaps, or a segment large enough for your full mouth?"

Fang gaps.

A tremble ran down Shane's spine. Even after so many of his vampire's blissful bites, with a stranger in the room his mind suddenly jumped to the claustrophobic feeling of being held in place while Maul's goons sunk their teeth into him. But he trusted that his vampire wouldn't let anyone else bite him. Custom-sized sounded incredibly specific. Whatever he was having the smith build, if it was *for* Shane, then it was meant for his vampire's personal feeding.

A shiver ran up Shane's spine and suddenly he could feel the pulse of his own blood through his neck like a heartbeat. This couldn't possibly be about Tara Williams. Perhaps Shane's vampire had also been thinking too long and hard on the state he'd told Maul he was holding Shane in. Perhaps he'd decided to act on that.

Shane thought of chains and his body rushed hot and cold. He slipped a hand against the edge of the table to keep himself standing. His vampire had brought him here, introduced him to the very person who would be constructing these. That couldn't be standard procedure for *suddenly locking up your human.* And now, after so many days? None of that added up—it just didn't. But he couldn't get the thought out of his head, the way it settled between his legs and tingled up his spine and fluttered, unwarranted, in his stomach.

And all the while, his vampire and the smith were still plotting.

"What's the difference, practically speaking?" Shane's vampire asked.

"Well, let's put it this way: is it just the act of sinking fangs into your human that you want—whether you're both after the pain or the envenomation or a combination of the two—or is it the full feeding experience? Some couples find the custom-sized fang openings attribute a stronger sense of ownership, especially if this is the only skin your human's showing with optimal vein-contact, but as you can imagine, a mouth full of metal isn't practical to actually feed through."

Ownership.

"Yes, right, that makes sense," his vampire replied.

Wait, some *couples?* Shane's mind snapped back to their introduction. *Oh.* Did Mercer think they were *together?* It wasn't an entirely incorrect assumption. Shane had bundled up all the feelings his near-constant texting with Andres had been trying so aggressively to spark in him for the sole reason that he *was* already claimed, if in the oddest, least socially acceptable way possible.

And now the vampire who'd claimed him was buying him something with *fang gaps.*

"I'd like to still be able to take a full meal from him, so the larger spaces would be preferable." His vampire glanced back at Shane, his lips tight and thoughtful.

"Alrighty." Mercer jotted in a notebook. "You were thinking five pieces, so I assume you want a gap for each traditional vein access point? I'll need measurements too if…" His gaze shifted to Shane, brows lifting.

"Come to me." His vampire uttered it like a command, dark and sweet in a way that brushed across Shane's skin and fluttered deep in his chest.

He should have been put off by it—his vampire, ordering him around in front of people, like he owned Shane's whole being instead of just the blood he'd bought without Shane's consent—but goddamn him for wearing that sheer lace beneath his long coat and looking at Shane through the slits in his mask of blood-red whirls with such a wreckage of desire and admiration and confidence. Shane found his feet moving, his head dipping obediently. His cheeks burned.

He shot his vampire a scowl as he stopped in front of him and grumbled, "I'm here." Shane *was* here. For better or worse, it seemed.

His vampire maneuvered him using a few gentle nudges, positioning Shane's back to his chest as they'd done so many times before, not quite touching, but so close that it felt like a promise pricking along Shane's skin. "Thank you, my pet," he murmured in a voice that poured like molten gold through Shane's chest. His breath hovered over Shane's pulse. His fingers seemed unsure whether to start tipping Shane's chin or fiddling with his hair. Finally he murmured, "Lay your head back for me."

Shane was pointedly aware of the smith watching them, looking so professional with his notepad and pen. He'd caved to his vampire in every one of their clandestine meetings, but having an onlooker changed the dynamic, or perhaps just sharpened it. Made it real.

Shane breathed out and tipped back his head.

The very tips of his vampire's fangs pressed against his neck. From the edge of his vision Shane could see the smith leaning toward the spot with a flexible measuring tape. His muscles went stiff, something sharp and aggrieved rising up in his chest at the sight of someone—someone not his vampire—coming toward his throat, but his vampire's fingers slid beneath Shane's and his anxiety eased. Mercer was just human, just taking simple measurements that required barely the softest brush of the tape against Shane's vulnerable throat. And Shane's vampire wouldn't let anyone hurt him.

Shane didn't have to be told that. He'd lived it.

The smith must have still picked up on his insecurity, though, because he shifted back, instructing Shane's vampire on how to take the measurements along Shane's neck instead. For that alone, Shane wanted to trust him. To trust them both, despite the obfuscation and the power plays. Between his vampire's touch and his soothing commands and Mercer's professional scrutiny, Shane felt both appreciated and dominated. The sensation curled like a happy little fire through his torso and rested, tingling, between his legs. It only grew with his mounting suspicion of what they were appraising him for.

His breath caught and he could feel his blush deepening, burning across his cheeks and down his neck. His head was still tipped back, his vampire's fingers on his neck. As he flinched instinctively, his vampire slid into a gentle grip behind his jaw, steadying him.

"Just one more, my swan," he whispered, his mouth pressed so deep into Shane's hair that it could have been a kiss.

Shane's body betrayed him, relaxing into his vampire's chest like he belonged there—belonged to him—and he let himself be measured for the collar.

He was in shock—that had to be it. It would hit him soon, just how *wrong* this all was, how much danger it surely meant he was in. Then, Shane would be afraid. Then, he'd run.

It hadn't happened yet when his vampire nudged his head back up, helping straighten and turn it for a final measurement as he and Mercer discussed mobility and weight—"He has such a lovely neck, I wouldn't want to clutter it."

Mercer stepped back, motioning to Shane's wrist with a casual, "May I?"

Shane stared at him, his whole body strangely alight. Shock. This was just shock.

"Can he measure your wrist, my swan?" his vampire murmured, hands running up and down Shane's shoulders without really touching him. But he *needed* to be touched. God, he needed to be touched.

Shane grabbed his vampire's arm, trying to tug his hand closer, to show him he was allowed this. With a sound so deep it seemed a sob, his vampire yanked free. The shock of it—the speed and strength—left a flutter of genuine fear in Shane's chest for the first time that evening.

But then his vampire whispered again, this time pleadingly, "Cygnus?" He sounded so hesitant. So much like... someone else. "I'll take your hand."

Shane couldn't put a face to that voice, though. He found himself nodding limply, offering over his wrist.

The smith looked questioning, pausing for a moment longer before beginning measurements for the cuff. These were quicker, culminating in an awkward amount of Shane's vampire and the smith deciding just how far up Shane's forearm the cuff should run and whether to include loops to his fingers. When Mercer commented on a bondage addition that could let his vampire pin those fingers to Shane's palm, both Shane and his vampire responded with such definitive overlapping 'no's that it defused the tension that had been building between them. Mercer finished recording his notes on Shane's wrist manacles—"ornamental cuffs," he called them.

Chains then, but not *restraints*. Whatever this was, his vampire expected Shane to accept and obey willingly.

Shane felt too many types of fire at once, the heat of his vampire's gaze even behind the mask and the ache that went straight into his core, the indignation that his vampire was painting them as co-conspirators in this and the hunger to keep being his regardless, to hear his vampire say *you're mine* in a way that rewrote his existence without trampling his agency.

Shane wanted this, he realized with a chill so sharp and pure it felt like an orgasm. He wanted this, he was just pretty sure he didn't want it quite *like this*. That it was all happening around him without his initial agreement held a slimy aftertaste, the moment of waking from a nightmare to find he'd enjoyed something about the experience. And he didn't want *that*, dammit.

Mercer cleared his throat. "You had mentioned something delicate to highlight the medium basilic vein—that's the one inside the elbow."

Fuck.

That vulnerable patch of skin was not something his vampire had demanded access to again. Shane's flesh began to crawl there, the memory of the way he'd gone weak in the alley when his vampire had asked for it warring with the desire to tuck his arm tighter and crawl into himself. He started to do it too, his hands curling upward, and he hid the motion by pressing his palms to his face. His cheeks were beginning to burn, and he could already feel the way Andres would draw him apart for it, pull his trauma into little glittering pieces and build him something new from its ashes.

And *that*, he wanted, too.

As much as he hated himself for it, as much as he knew the knowledge that he'd given in would cling like grime to him later, Shane wanted, more than anything, to be undone.

14

ANDRES

Andres was tearing Shane apart.

He was a monster; he could feel the guilt and horror already lodging in his chest so thoroughly that he nearly told Mercer no then and there. They didn't need this final piece. They didn't need any of them, truthfully. They could wait outside the place Tara worked and catch her as she left, or they could break in through a window, grab her out of a dressing room, follow her home even—anything that didn't involve going through the front doors.

He'd just wanted to dress Shane up and pretend his little swan really belonged to him for a night, wanted it so badly that he'd convinced himself to ignore his growing fear that Shane was simply putting up with his nightly feeding because he didn't know how to deny him.

But now Shane had gone paler and paler, his breathing shallow and his body stiff, clearly afraid in a way he'd condensed into tiny trembles and whimpers before now, and as much as Andres loved him vulnerable, he did not love *this*. He hated this, in fact.

He'd never meant to hurt Shane. Andres had added that last piece in—despite the growing cost—because he'd thought it might give Shane something new to bear in place of the old memory. Something to prove that his life didn't belong to Maul, or to any of the vampires who'd tried to take it. Except that instead, Andres supposed, it just seemed like he was putting even more claim on Shane himself.

And Shane clearly didn't want that.

Andres wrapped his arms across his stomach, taking a slight step back. "We, uh, we don't need this one, it's fine." He was sounding like unsexy Andres, like the dork who spent an entire night testing out different kinds of nail polish just to miss the closure of the bar he'd been planning to wear it to. "We'll stick with the first three we measured for. The wrists, at least. Perhaps we'll hold off on the choker if—"

"No."

It took Andres a moment to truly internalize Shane's objection, and a moment longer to answer with a parroted, "No?"

Shane's throat bobbed, and despite everything, Andres couldn't help tracking the movement with his gaze, his attention settling on the pulse that he'd pressed his fangs into so many times already. His little swan trembled once, glancing down. And that should have been Andres's cue to back off. To listen to the rational, ethical side of his brain screaming at him that what he was doing to Shane had been a mistake long before his little swan's face had gone pale and his tension mounted.

Instead he found himself sliding his fingers ever so delicately around the center of Shane's neck, slowly closing them, giving no pressure, only the barest sensation of skin on skin. He waited for the quiet inhale, the tiny tremble, but then came what he did not expect: Shane leaned against him, his eyes closing, and very slowly, he tipped his head back.

His voice so rough it was barely his own, Andres amended, "We'll take the choker after all."

Despite the relative peace that wrapped up their meeting, Shane walked like he was trying to outpace a monster far faster than Andres, his jacket bundled against his chest and his arms tight. "You make me go through all those measurements and then don't even let me *see* the design after?" he complained. "I have a right to veto what I don't like!"

Beneath his grumbling, he seemed to be masking something as closely as Andres concealed his own face, and Andres fought down the lingering suspicion that perhaps he had frightened Shane more than he was willing to let on. He'd said yes to the collar to appease Andres, obviously, though whether he was doing so out of affection or fear, Andres couldn't tell. With the way he was still shuddering— so gloriously, but shuddering nonetheless—beneath

Andres's touch, Andres was growing worried it might have been the second. "As though I would ever pick you something that didn't compliment your loveliness perfectly," he replied, opening the driver's door. "Besides, is this *not* how presents normally work?"

Shane scowled and slid into the passenger's seat.

It was hard to tell whether the rust on his cheeks was a blush, with the greyscale of Andres's vampiric night vision fighting the dim lighting from the porch. And his contacts were annoying him again. He tried not to rub the edges of his eyes beneath the mask as he climbed into the car.

The engine felt a little too loud in their silence. Andres had already turned onto the next street when Shane finally asked, his voice small and hard, like he was fighting to hold it in place, "Do you expect me to wear them all the time?"

"Wear—*what*?" The wheel suddenly felt slick in Andres's grip. *All the time.* Wear them. Oh fuck. No wonder Shane was on edge.

The guilt that bloomed in Andres's gut came almost as fast as a vision of just that: Shane lounging in his bed in nothing but the chains, laughing in his kitchen with the ornate pieces sparkling against his lounge-wear, having them hidden beneath his clothes as he shopped, feeling the constant reminder that he belonged to Andres. But *he* didn't—it was just his blood Andres had bought, and that hadn't even come with consent.

"They're for infiltrating Tara's work," he clarified. God, he really was a monster. "I told you that?"

Shane made a sound that was impossible to pinpoint, flat and hollow and a little something else. Relief? Annoyance? Discomfort? "But you said—" He swallowed the words, breathing in and out, and started again. "You said that Mercer is making what we'll need to access Tara's work, *and* other things. And then you measured me for a *collar*. I assumed..."

"Ah." Andres groaned. "In my defense, that was an accurate and literal description. Mercer *does* make things besides the jewelry we'll need for Tara's work. Though, I, um, apologize for scaring you. It was not my intent."

"I see." Shane stared out the windshield, his gaze unfocused. "Do tell, where the fuck are we going that you need me in a collar and cuffs to get in?"

Andres had the impulse to drag a hand through his hair, but the cords of his mask were still wrapped around the back. "It's kind of embarrassing." He laughed bitterly. "And you're going to hate it."

"Try me?" This time, Shane seemed *almost* as curious as he was horrified.

Well, Andres was about to change that. "So, ah, apparently at this underground theatre-dining experience where Tara Williams works, the vampire attendees dress their humans in fancy chains like blood slaves and feed on them as though they're the old gothic predators from the movies. It seems to be more or less a consensual ordeal, though how eager any of these humans could truly be, or how honorable the vampires, I don't know."

155

Sure enough, Shane's hollow tone returned. "Well… fuck."

It made Andres want to reach across the center console and pull him close, to tell him that he was safe, safe from anything he didn't want to do or any act he wasn't willing to give. But it was already a lie, wasn't it? Andres had broken that for his own desires multiple times—perhaps every night, every night he asked for Shane's neck and let him bear it while shuddering, still too afraid to admit that if Shane told him to stop, he would do so in a heartbeat. "You don't have to…"

"No, I can—" Shane paused, his throat bobbing, and he started again. "I want to talk to Tara. If this is how we do it, then we do it."

"I'll be gentle." He could promise that, at least. "Whatever we have to do, I'll be gentle with you."

"I know," was all Shane responded with, his gaze out the front window, arms curled against his chest.

Andres wanted, desperately, to change the subject, but he struggled to find a conversation starter that Shane hadn't already told the Andres from the Fishnettery over text. There were so many things that he wanted to ask, too, so much depth he wanted to build off. But the masked him had none of that friendship with Shane, only poetic musings and the ability to make him wilt.

And, apparently, to put him in chains.

It was Shane who finally bridged the gap, asking about the only thing he could know they had in common. "How is Maul?"

Andres ran a hand through his hair. "He asks about you every few days, but your lying low has helped; none of his goons have spotted you out and about. Hopefully they'll ease off soon."

"And then?"

"And then I don't have to worry about you constantly." He knew Shane would want a different answer, one that gave him the green light to keep writing about the black market blood trade, but as long as Maul was a fixture in his life—in the lives of so many of San Salud's vampires—he didn't know what other answer he could give. "Let's focus on Vitalis-Barron. We find out enough about that, and you could probably even write an article on it."

Shane grumbled under his breath, but his sullenness seemed more feather-ruffling than full on rejection.

"Maul is already pissed that our sales are plummeting. If I don't do something, he will, and his target won't be the big pharma researchers, it'll be that little charity blood bank that's giving away free bags in Ala Santa." That, and his own employees. The ones who weren't Andres, anyway.

"Sincerely, fuck Maul. Jose's is such a wonderful place. I got the sense they're really trying to do good there."

"You've been?" Andres wasn't sure why he was surprised. Shane had wormed himself into the vampire community's cracks with a vengeance.

"I donated when they first opened—I'm not allowed to at regular blood banks, but they have vamps on staff there in case I got too low, and I had my insulin handy. I was going to return when I hit the 56-day mark. Though with you biting me regularly, I suppose I don't have to wait for my blood to replenish the regular way?" He said it almost hesitantly, like he was waiting for Andres to object.

And a part of Andres wanted to—not in order to stop him, just to say the words: *your blood is mine and mine alone.* But if Shane could help another vampire, one not so well off or long established as himself, then Andres would always support that. "If you want to keep donating, I'm fine with that. While my venom's good, though, it's not magic. You could probably go no more than every week or two—start with two, to be safe. And tell me when you do. I'll take good care of you that night."

"You'll take *care* of me, hmm?" It was soft and low, and so smooth that Andres couldn't quite pinpoint the emotion behind it, but when he glanced over, the little tip of Shane's mouth could have been a smirk.

"I..." Andres swallowed.

"That was my street," Shane said.

Andres swerved before realizing he was far too deep into the intersection to turn.

Shane lifted a brow at him. "If you're intending to chain me up in your bedroom after all, then you should know that I have a very disturbed cat and two entire human friends, one of whom will certainly come for you with a stake."

Andres made a sound between a laugh and a snort. "Ah, yes, a vampire's two worst fears: angry cat and pointy stick." As he turned at the next light, though, he couldn't dislodge the sinking feeling in his gut. He had wanted that. Had wanted it, not like a joke or an excuse but a deep, burning desire, black and ugly, and dear god, he could never let Shane know. He pulled up in front of the apartment, and Shane popped the door open but continued just to sit there, glancing between the keys in the still-running engine and Andres.

"This is your apartment, isn't it?" Andres asked, confused.

Shane scowled. "So you put me through all of that and you're going to just drop me off and drive away?"

"I'm sorry?" Andres blinked. Did he want his room tidied again? Andres supposed that was an understandable retribution for making him sit through a collar fitting without being sure exactly what it was for.

"Well, are you going to feed on me, or do you secretly have another human you've spent ten thousand dollars on?"

"I've been seeing you so consistently that I can skip a night or two," Andres said. Besides, Shane was literally covering all the normal places Andres would have fed from. It made Andres want all the more to unfurl him, to make his little swan loosen for his fangs one shuddering muscle at a time. But it was beginning to genuinely terrify him that by doing so, he was hurting this brilliant, sharp, intimidating human who'd consumed his life like a raging comet. "I figure after everything I put you through tonight, you'd enjoy a break."

"Why would I enjoy that?"

"Why wouldn't you enjoy…?" It hit him finally like a sledgehammer. "Are you saying you *want* me to bite you?"

Shane groaned, leaning both elbows against the car console, his head bowed and his palms cupping his neck. "My god, yes."

Andres's heart beat a little faster, hungrier. "But you've still been acting so on edge every time I do?"

If his doubts were wrong and Shane's trembling, his whimpering, his quiet submission, were all signs of desire and not fear…

"Have you never been afraid to want something before?" Shane whispered, still cupping his neck as he leaned closer.

Andres's skin felt as though it caught fire. "Every time I look at you," he breathed.

"Then look at me." Shane watched him as he said it, moving forward another inch. It felt like a thousand miles, like a star burning toward Andres at the speed of light. His own Cygnus constellation, dark eyes and lips outlined in the glow of the lamps and the passing cars. Shane still cupped his neck, arms tight and breath held.

Andres felt alive like never before. Gently, he drew two fingers along the back of Shane's wrist. He slipped them between skin and fabric, nudging at Shane's pulse. "Give me your hand, my little swan."

The shudder that ran through Shane was immaculate. He obeyed, sliding his wrist into Andres's grip, letting Andres pull his arm across the console, making him stretch and bow until he was forced to look up to see Andres. Even then, Shane held Andres's gaze, afraid, clearly... but not of him.

Andres laced his fingers over the backs of Shane's and held it to his heart, bringing their pulses as close as they could come, imagining he could feel them settling into the same rhythm. He could hear Shane's, beating through his neck in a soft but rapid thud-thud, calling to him. He grinned. "Your other hand, too."

Shane made an indignant sound, but he peeled his fingers off his neck, holding them out almost sullenly. He was the most beautiful creature Andres had ever seen, in his simple burgundy shirt with the split in the collar unbuttoned, his hair half up, and his lips quavering, his gaze so fixed on Andres that he seemed enraptured, enthralled, owned. He was Andres's, if only for that moment.

Andres drew Shane's other hand away from his body as well. He lifted it to his lips, kissing his fingers gently, one side then the other. With each turn he slid a fang just a hair into the flesh, presenting Shane with a burst of venom, building it with every new love nip. Shane's tightness eased away in a series of hums and whines, and he sprawled across the center console, resting his head on the steering wheel as he gazed up.

Andres flipped his wrist over, pressing his nose to the soft underside. Sunshine. Of all the ways he could describe it, even held to his mouth, Shane's scent was still best summed up by that single word, the feeling of basking in a warmth beyond oneself, beautiful and loving and reckless all at once. "You are an impeccable mystery," he whispered.

Shane responded with an almost delirious, "Uh-huh."

When Andres sank in his fangs and took his first, perfect taste of Shane's blood that night, Shane moaned like he'd been, not just fearing this moment, but waiting for it. Wanting it. Andres hadn't hurt him after all.

The thought made his heart soar and plummet all at once. He could keep this up, this and this alone. No fantasies of chains or demands of obedience, not once their excursion to Tara's work was complete. He could be content with just this—just his fangs in Shane's flesh, and the little happy sounds Shane was making.

Andres licked the wound closed, but he couldn't bring himself to let go, cupping Shane's wrist gently. Shane reached for him, sliding a hand along his jaw. Andres didn't pull away, not until Shane slipped two fingers under his mask and tried to lift.

"No," he said, slow and gentle.

Shane stilled, lounging against the wheel with the lamplight on his face as he stared up into Andres's darkness searchingly. He glided his thumb over Andres's cheek. "This isn't just for the drama," he concluded, so awfully brilliant and terribly genuine. "Do you not trust me to see you? After I've obeyed you in everything... do you still think I'd turn you in?"

"If you wished to be free of me, I could never have stopped you." He saw on Shane's face the truth that his swan had always known that, and felt for a moment, a little lighter, a little free. Then the feeling collapsed into reality. "But I still don't want you to look under the mask. I'm afraid you won't feel the same about the person beneath as you do with me."

"So this is permanent?" For all the vague and empty tones Shane had taken that night, Andres could hear the displeasure in this one with a certainty that scared him.

"Be patient, my little swan."

Until when, he didn't know. How quickly would this all fall apart once he revealed to Shane that the vampire making him shudder was his harmless disaster of a friend after all? He still wanted—*needed*—that thrill and tension, all the more now that he had confirmation that his little swan wanted the gentle coercion and the venom that Andres was giving.

But the way Shane's attention went to his phone as soon as he was out of the car made Andres's heart leap once, then again at the little buzz of his own cell after.

It was such a lovely contrast to the unread melodramatic message from Maul that sat below it, and despite everything he'd just told Shane, a part of him forgot he couldn't simply text him *please be safe* and *see you soon <3* as Shane unlocked his apartment door; forgot so thoroughly that he was halfway through typing the message before he realized what he'd done.

His chest ached with each backspace.

15

SHANE

Shane could still feel the lingering tingles of venom in his fingers and the curves they'd traced of his vampire's face, like the slope of his bones had tried to imprint themselves there. It didn't matter to him that the car had been so dark he could barely make out his vampire against the shadows. He wanted to see beneath the mask, to see the person who'd been making him come undone, who'd convinced his body it was safe and persuaded his heart to stay despite the danger. The anonymity had felt thrilling in the beginning, but he wanted depth now.

Still, his vampire wasn't comfortable enough with the idea.

"I'm afraid you won't feel the same about the person beneath as you do with me."

What the fuck did that mean? Did he think Shane would find him visually undesirable? Did his appearance not fit what he thought a tall, menacing and sensual vampire's should?

The final option was the only one that gave Shane the slightest bit of hesitation: maybe his vampire didn't want Shane to see who he was, because Shane already knew him, and disliked him. A celebrity he'd interviewed in the past, perhaps. An old coworker he'd forgotten. Someone he'd run into at a bar...

Sometimes, when his voice slipped out of its sultry growl for a moment, Shane thought it sounded weirdly familiar. He'd make a rated list later. Andres would get a kick out of that—and it was probably time he shared the existence of his vampire with more than just Nat, for his own safety, if nothing else.

Before he'd pulled away, his vampire had asked for Shane's clothing measurements, and Shane's mind had flashed through a strange array of fantasies, then to thoughts of the upcoming Vitalis-Barron gala, before realizing he was probably ordering them outfits for Tara's work. At least he hadn't demanded to take the measurements himself. *At least,* or *if only*? Shane couldn't decide as he drew the measuring tape across his body, envisioning his vampire's fingers skimming the same places.

Shane wrote his results down, slipped the paper beneath the doormat, and returned to his computer to record what little he'd learned tonight—most of it theories about kink in the vampire community. Even if he wasn't writing the *War on Blood* article yet, he wanted to record as much information on the vampiric existence as he could. No matter how strongly his vampire believed that what was happening with Vitalis-Barron could be viewed as a singular event, its existence was interconnected with the rest of vampire society. Shane would prove that, even if that meant finishing the damn article and shoving it in his vampire's face.

In the meantime, he accepted a new set of obnoxious review pieces for ChatterDash, one of which had a grammatical error in the keyword phrase they mandated he include in it, then checked his glucose levels and took his nightly insulin. He'd have to pick up more soon—another trip to the pharmacy, another payment he wished he could have been spending on anything else. He wondered if he tasted any different to his vampire with the rising and falling of his blood sugar.

Rate your human's blood based on how long it has been since he took his insulin sounded boring for a video that would probably play like a porno: bite after bite after bite.

Shane shuddered at the thought, and the tremble went straight between his legs, settling there warm and tender. Fuck. He hadn't even been *kissed* again; he could not run away with himself yet. Though at the rate they were moving, it seemed like Shane might have to be the one to run away with them both if he wanted anyone to.

His phone pinged as he was climbing into bed. He hoped to see Andres's name, or if not him, then at least Nat, but instead the text came from an unknown number.

Hi Shane, this is Mercer. I hope this is not intruding. I dug up the old business card you'd given me, so perhaps it's the wrong number now. Anyway, I wanted to check that you're all right. The vampire you were with has always been perfectly nice in all our interactions but I've worked with a lot of kink couples over the years and you both seemed unusually tense. If I'm overstepping, I apologize immensely. I just wanted to offer help if you need it, and if not then I wish you both the very best.

Oh, fuck. The back of Shane's throat felt dry suddenly. They *had* been tense—but that was, in part, because they weren't a couple. Or they were, perhaps, just not in the way Mercer assumed, not two dating lovebirds who called each other partner, but a human and the vampire who'd bought him. And together or not, they weren't into kink.

Not that Shane had anything *against* kink—or what little he knew of it; restraints and leather and sex dungeons. While bondage wasn't his thing and he didn't want a dominatrix to tell him he'd been a bad boy, he could still respect that it worked for some people. Collars though…

He'd assumed those for kink were all dark and heavy with little metal hooks and thought nothing of them, but something beautiful and delicate—a gilded piece that made him not a pet but a *prize*…

Shane rubbed the side of his neck, the heat between his legs undeniable. There would be little gilded chains too, his vampire had said. Little chains that could be tugged on, pulling Shane close, his vampire asking him, sultry and possessive, to tip his head, revealing where his racing heart pounded through his exposed pulse. That was still just a bite. Still just the same thing—the same wonderful thing—they'd been doing this entire time. And yet dressed up like that…

Was *that* kink? Fuck, Shane didn't know, and in that moment he was too afraid to google; to be told in definitive terms that this version of it was just as unhealthy and harmful as he'd suspected. He'd been letting his vampire coerce him, control him, scare him even—that couldn't be right.

He couldn't bring himself to stop it though. No matter how much he'd grown to long for every text he received from Andres, he didn't know how to go back to a world where that simplicity was all he craved. Where it wasn't his vampire he wanted most.

That was far too much to tell the poor smith, though.

Shane-anigans
Thank you for checking, but I'm fine. You just caught us on a bad day.

He clicked send before his weaker self could tag on a question about vampires and kink, and flipped over to his chatting app.

Shane-anigans
So is it weird how into this vampire I am?

Nat1

Dude it's 2am

Shane-anigans

Dude you're the one responding to me.

Nat1

Fine.

All right. I want to say immediately UM YES HE'S A VAMPIRE; maybe he really is a great person after all but if it turns out he ISN'T, you're putting yourself in a lot of unnecessary danger. But also, I guess it depends on *why* you're this into him? /curious don't hate me

"*Don't hate me,*" his vampire had said. And Shane was sure there were plenty of humans who would have, in his place, but somehow Shane was still here, still begging for more.

Shane-anigans

No it definitely is weird, I don't know why I even asked.

Nat1

I'm not going to shame you for your preferences but be careful, please. Keep one foot out the door and if you get even the slightest vibe that maybe he isn't as heroic as you think he is, run.

Shane-anigans

He's not going to kill me.

Nat1

You super can't know that.

The one that killed my mentor didn't look capable of it either.

I just can't lose my only friend too, okay.

And take it from me, it's better not to risk falling for someone you know you shouldn't. (Because otherwise when you realize maybe you should end things, it'll be so late that you'll know it'll kill you, so you don't, even when the sex isn't good anymore and he's talking about other humans more than he's talking to you, and you've already said you're fine with him fucking around but you don't want that to mean he treats you less like you're his world in the process.)

Shane-anigans

So have you told your boyfriend all this?

Nat1

What if he breaks up with me.

Shane could more than acknowledge her fear—he could feel it himself. *What if:* What if she was right, and this ended in heartbreak? There were so many things he didn't know and so many ways it could all crumble down.

And that didn't mean it wasn't all worth it.

But it meant *something*.

Shane-anigans

Then you can come eat ice cream on my couch and we'll get really drunk and I'll tell you how I would totally fuck you if you had fangs... By which I mean, I'm so sorry, you deserve better than this.
Whatever you choose to do, I'm here for you.

Nat1

You're incredible and I love you. /platonic
And I might take you up on that night sometime ;)
Did you want to talk about your problem?

Shane-anigans

It's really not a big deal lol
And honestly, you've given me a lot to think about. /grateful

And she had. He just wasn't sure what he was going to do about it.

A new text came through, flaring across the top of his screen like a light at the end of a tunnel. It left him giddy regardless of how many others he'd gotten that day already.

Andres

The truth: do you ever think two people were destined to meet? (Not to be together, necessarily, just to fall into each other, as many times as it takes.)

Shane couldn't help the instinctive smile that loosened his face. The warmth that had been flaring low in his pelvis was replaced by a bright, joyous blaze in his chest. It turned quickly to a knot. This was the relationship he needed. Something real, and normal, and healthy. His memories of Andres were buried in dim colors and loud music, but he could still recall that they'd looked so lovely even with their makeup running, an intensity to their gaze and a softness to their lips.

They had both fallen into each other, hadn't they?

And if Shane hadn't felt what it was like to have his vampire's breath on his neck and his whispers of *you're mine*, he was certain he would be letting himself fall fully for Andres too.

Shane

With all the free-will-ruining implications of destiny, I'm not sure how firmly I can trust in it.

But if you want a truth, here's this: occasionally, when a truly wonderful coincidence happens, I wonder if perhaps God is real, and she created the world ten seconds before just so she could experience that moment with me.

Andres
What if you don't recognize the coincidence when
it happens?

Shane
If a tree falls in the forest, does it make a sound?

If a vampire wore a mask, did he have a face? Shane
would find out. Sooner or later, one way or another.
Coincidence or not.

16

ANDRES

Andres hadn't gotten a full night's sleep since they'd visited Mercer's metal shop, and he was beginning to feel it. Between his hours of sewing—and taking videos of his progress to put up on his channel, which he was thankful Shane had not connected to him yet, probably because it never showed his face—and starting a new infiltration project for Maul despite better Coachella results than expected, he'd been texting with the friend-version of Shane nearly constantly. He devoured Shane's hopes and fears and poetic wonderings with the same passion that he drank his little swan's blood.

With what time that left, Andres tossed and turned, his sleeping mind unable to decide whether roping Shane into this upcoming part of the investigation was a dream or a nightmare. In either one, he still felt a little like a monster. A monster who'd designed two impeccable outfits.

The rush orders from Mercer had been worth it, too, the jewelry matching perfectly to the clothing he'd designed. He would have paid every penny again, and the ten thousand on top of it, just to see Shane in them a single time, to run a fingertip along the upper edge of his collar and feel him tremble...

Andres clung to that imagery as he came up behind Shane in the dim alley. The chaos and joy of the boardwalk echoed from two streets over, just loud enough to hide his soft footsteps, but not the inhale that Shane took as Andres traced three fingertips over his shoulder. "Shall we?"

Shane settled with a sigh, but when he spoke, his voice had that odd hollow ring he'd adopted at Mercer's. Fear, annoyance, displeasure—Andres still couldn't pinpoint it. "I think the theme of this night is that you give me orders, not options."

"You're always free to disobey." He meant that, but with the way it came out in the sultry, deepened layers of his fictitious vampire voice, he wasn't sure it sounded as such.

They walked around the side of the building, following a series of chalk-marked symbols to a simple wooden door. Andres knocked. The door cracked open, an androgynous person in an old-fashioned butler's outfit peeking out. At the confident flash of Andres's fangs, they were led inside, where an antique desk sat in an otherwise bare room with a curtain at one end, candles twinkling from sconces on the plain walls. Shane stiffened, halting in his tracks.

A rush of predictions spiraled through Andres's mind— he wasn't as accepting of this arrangement as he seemed, he couldn't bear to go through with it, he'd realized that even pretending to belong to Andres in public was too despicable—before realizing just how many similarities this entrance space shared with the room Maul had nearly drained Shane dry in.

Gently, he pressed his palm to Shane's back, rubbing his thumb up and down. *I'm here for you*, Andres wanted to say, *and so long as that's true, nothing will ever hurt you.*

Shane released an audible breath. They approached the desk together.

Their host opened an elegant notebook, raising one brow. When they smiled, their fangs slipped out. "Names?"

"This is Cygnus and I'm his vampire." He curled a finger through Shane's hair as he said it, adding a little growl beneath his voice. From what he'd been able to learn of the place, they didn't seem to be actively forcing the humans to participate, but he knew the kind of thoughts that had led him to crave this scenario, and he could imagine just what monsters lay behind the curtain.

The host scanned their notebook and frowned. They took a second look at Andres's mask. "I don't have you on my list. Did you put any other names with that?" As they spoke, they withdrew a tablet from inside the top drawer, the technology breaking their otherwise faux-historic surroundings. They tilted its screen out of view, but seemed to be flicking through another registry.

Andres had expected this. "Were we meant to fill something out before arrival? I was recommended here by a friend who said she'd put in a booking for us. She didn't mention anything else."

The host's other brow raised then too. "Which friend is this?"

"Tara Williams. She works here." He said it with a confidence and poise that could outplay honesty. "I could call her, but I know she has duties tonight."

"Oh, right, they're on the floor I believe," the host muttered, and Andres's heart lifted at the casual use of Tara's second set of pronouns. "Well, you won't be as integrated as if you'd filled out our story forms, but tonight's all free-play anyway. I'll still need a few signatures for the non-disclosure and consent agreements."

That was how they did it, then. They got their humans to sign things—things that were unlikely to hold up, should the club be taken to court—but which might convince someone unversed in the law or unable to find or afford a decent lawyer that they were trapped into this system of obedience and blood-letting. At least no one had asked for their legal names yet. Or Andres's face.

"And I'll need that mask off."

Well, damn. He fiddled with Shane's hair again, curling half his mouth up, a fang bared. "It's part of our game, you see..."

"Just while you sign." The host sighed, shuffling up two small stacks of forms. "Your identity is sacred to us, I assure you, but so is that of every person who's already walked through these doors. We have nothing against masks, only those who have to hide beneath them from their own people."

It was well said, Andres had to admit. He tried not to look at Shane, whose face had already tipped toward his, gaze searching like a spotlight. If he found out now, how much would that ruin? Everything, perhaps. Nothing, maybe. If Shane already didn't want to be here, would he accept it more or less if he knew he had come with the silly, emotional fool he'd been platonically trading ridiculous musings with for weeks? He would shudder less, Andres was certain. And god, despite how much of a monster it made him, he didn't want to lose that. Didn't want to lose the way Shane had started looking at his lips, like he was remembering their kiss, or the tiny, whimpered moan that left him every time Andres's fangs sunk in.

Shane glanced down, a soft heat in his cheeks. "Is there somewhere else I can sign mine instead?"

"Of course," the host answered immediately, handing Shane one of the stacks and a pen. "If you go through the curtain there, you'll find the dressing room."

Something hot and wet burned behind Andres's eyes, but the most he could do to thank Shane was press his lips to the top of Shane's head. "I'll be in shortly."

The way Shane startled at the kiss could have been everything or nothing. Andres watched him leave, unable to tear his gaze away until the curtain had re-settled behind him. He took a quick glance around the room, trying to spot any cameras they might have hidden in the corners, but the attempt only slid his contacts slightly off-center. The tunneling effect they had on his non-human eyes made him nauseous at that angle and rolled the red of the colored iris he'd chosen for the night directly into his vision. Oh well; if they really were providing a space for a bunch of vampires with morally-questionable preferences, then they were probably locking up that information tight.

He removed his mask long enough to squeeze an eyedrop into both eyes, then signed the forms after an attempt to look like he'd skimmed them, planting a fake name on the print line and hoping Shane had the forethought to do the same. Andres felt terrible just for asking him to put any mark on something like this. They could be waiting at the back door for Tara to emerge later, or stealing their employee records to hunt them back to their house or—

"Thank you very much. You may proceed whenever you're ready. If you wish to return for future events, stop by before the end of the night and I can provide you with a code to our pre-event forms."

And that was it.

Andres slipped his mask back into position and pushed into the hall-space behind the curtain. Shane's scent had already taken over the space, turning the air bright and bold and a little sharp to Andres's nose. A bench and three ornate dressing mirrors had been arranged inside, electric candles hidden in bundles of fake flowers along a counter. He hung their outfits from an elegant metal rack and plopped the bag on a stool. Shane was still staring at his form, his brow tight and his focus unmoored. He startled, then signed before tucking the papers farther onto the counter.

Andres felt sick. *He* was going to enjoy this evening—he'd put so much work into making sure it happened—but god, he wished Shane could do the same.

He tried to be gentle as he set Shane's ornaments on the counter and showed him the pieces of his outfit, not quite relishing these particular flinches and swallows as Shane brushed his fingers over the silk and refused to meet Andres's gaze. He'd be sure their outfits to Vitalis-Barron's gala looked nothing like this.

Andres turned away to let Shane change. Flashes of skin still caught his attention through the surrounding mirrors: a graceful shoulder blade, a pale hipbone, an ankle with a line of ink. He forced himself not to look.

His own outfit was coordinated to match Shane's in an *opposites attract* fashion. Black lace gloves ended halfway down his fingers, and his high-waisted black pants were tucked into his tall boots, an elegant belt holding in the deep red shirt he'd unbuttoned nearly to his navel to show off more lace in the form of an undershirt. He kept his long dark coat over it—a new one, thrifted two days ago, which he'd augmented with frills of lace. His dangling earrings of black and maroon gemstones matched a brand-new necklace that he slid on delicately. It hung down the front of his chest, a rose gold chain ending in a large maroon gem at the base of his sternum. It all came together nicely with the spiraling red of his gala mask and the scarlet of his colored contacts.

He looked good. He looked *great*; like he'd drawn his soul into the fabric and formed it to fit. It was the kind of outfit he felt seen in, regardless of whether anyone was looking, but especially when they did. And if they had a problem with it, then, well, he had the strength and the teeth now to make that a problem for *them.*

But his looks were less important than—

"A little help?" Shane asked, his voice low.

Andres's knees went weak at the sight of him, but he cleared his throat, stepping in to button the back of the rose gold outfit. Every faint brush of his fingers on Shane's back was like being reborn, the world started afresh just for him, the first ever touch of skin on skin. Shane was so soft, so elegant, from the long curve of his neck to the graceful slopes of his shoulders, scattered in constellations of freckles, and down his back, his spine a defined ridge.

With a few quick twirls and tugs, Andres fastened the stray waves of Shane's hair with bobby-pins studded in pearls and little red stones. Finally, he took up the collar. It felt so much lighter in his grasp than everything it could represent. He slipped it around Shane's throat with the utmost tenderness, basking in the way his swan trembled as he drew his fingertips along the sides of his neck.

His tension accumulated into a visible shudder as the jewelry clicked shut.

"You can remove it whenever you'd like," Andres whispered, taking Shane's hand to glide it over the latch.

Shane fiddled with it for barely a moment, but he kept his fingers in Andres's far longer, staring at himself in the mirror like he was trying to see inside the being that stared back.

Shane was a vision. His pale silk shimmered pearlescent in the low light. The fabric started at his shoulders, wrapping in an x across his chest before turning to a jumpsuit that appeared as a skirt at first glance. It made up for how little of his torso it covered by pooling in waves off his shoulders, turning fine and translucent and filled with twinkling white gems—a star to Andres's black hole. A puff of the same material fluttered around Shane's arms, veiling the little white glucose monitor on his triceps, and tucked into his wrist cuffs.

On its own, the outfit would have been spectacular, but Mercer's work exalted it. Each polished rose gold piece contained flat segments of elegant etching connected by delicate chain linkage, with a red stone suspended against Shane's pulse on the cuff's undersides, and a dangling series of them in the gap where Andres preferred to sink his fangs into Shane's neck. He knew the little clip beside each would unlock them, giving him unrestricted access—though in truth the metal hardly covered enough to prevent a bite. Like the loop of delicate chain that draped down the front of Shane's chest, waiting to be tugged on, it was for the show of the thing. The message it sent.

Shane belonged to Andres.

For tonight, at least.

Shane seemed to be coming to the same conclusion, his throat bobbing against the collar. He shifted, swaying first to the right, then the left experimentally. A pair of sneakers poked from beneath the swirling fabric around his feet. Andres knelt before him, wordlessly pulling them off to replace them with the jeweled sandals he'd altered to match the rest of the ornamentation Shane now wore.

"There's one more piece," he said, withdrawing the simple sleeve from his pocket. "Give me your arm, my pet."

Shane drew in a breath, hesitating for a deliciously long moment, but slowly he let it out, and as he did, he uncurled the arm that Maul had tried to drain him from. No trace of the vampire's work remained, but Andres could still see the invisible scars of that night in the way Shane moved, his arms always tucked in close—closer the more tense he grew. It was wrong of Andres to enjoy that tension, wrong of him to love how it gave him the chance to peel his Cygnus apart.

He wondered, absently, if Shane ever held himself so tight while texting the Andres he'd met at the Fishnettery.

A quaver rolled through him as Andres took hold of his wrist. Still on one knee, Andres gently slid the six-inch sleeve up until it covered the crook of Shane's elbow, remaining still when Shane twitched and letting him slowly ease into the touch. As soon as the fabric was in place, he seemed to relax, just a little. It fit perfectly.

Andres let his gaze travel up Shane with what he hoped came across as tender adoration even from behind the mask. His attention caught on a pair of scars that Shane's outfit didn't quite cover; small, light things with a hint of a crook around one of his ribs where a tattooed flower had been inked as though it was splitting from the irregular tissue.

Oh. *Oh*. The thought was small and bright and it settled quickly into a contented warmth. His little swan had searched and found himself, the same way Andres had, and there was a beauty and bond in that Andres could find nowhere else. He was a wonder, a monument to his own godhood. Andres wanted him all the more for it.

"I..." Shane started, then flushed, turning his face away.

"My Cygnus," Andres breathed. He lifted his hands to the scars, slow enough that when Shane flinched back, he could move like a wave with the motion, steady but gentle. The tips of his fingers drew over the sliver of the line he could see, then his thumb followed as he cupped Shane's sides, staring up at him once again. "You're magnificent."

Shane's eyes gleamed. His lower lip quivered.

"So very magnificent," Andres repeated, because it was true. But if Shane was like him—if he'd strived for so long to find the styles that showed his soul and not merely his body—Andres worried. He'd picked what he'd known would look good on Shane, taking inspiration from the thin, loose scarves and flowing cardigans he commonly wore in his videos, but Andres had never actually *asked*. "Did I overstep with the design? If this makes you feel too feminine—"

"No," Shane interjected. "It's princely, truly. I feel like me."

Andres stood, and as he did, Shane—his magnificent, starlit Cygnus—leaned into him, wrapping both arms around Andres with a tender sound.

"Thank you."

Andres was too shocked to reply. His arms knew better than his brain, though, because they drew naturally around Shane, holding him close like he was meant to be there. "You're mine," he finally managed.

Shane trembled at that, and Andres swore—swore—he held tighter.

From beyond the curtain came the vague sounds of new arrivals, and the butler lifting their voice. "Let me check if the couple before you has finished yet."

"I think that means we should go in," Shane whispered, like they were criminals up to mischief.

Andres supposed this *was* a type of con, after all, if only because their target seemed determined not to let them approach in any other way. He brushed his fingers over the delicate chain that hung down Shane's chest. "If you're overwhelmed or uncomfortable, tell me. We can always—"

The laugh that Shane cut him off with was so sharp and frazzled it grated. "I'll be fine, don't worry."

Andres tried not to as they handed off their regular clothing to the host and were directed to the double doors at the far side of the hall. It felt like so much more was riding on this night than just a conversation with a Vitalis-Barron escapee, every one of his terrible fantasies begging him either to take the leap or let go forever.

185

His breath caught as he pushed the doors open.

The lighting was dim still, electric candles hidden behind wall chalices and set into candelabras. Across the ceiling hung strings of tiny fairy lights, arranged in what Andres swore were real constellations, even if the only ones he personally knew were Orion and now Cygnus. They gave a sophistication and sensuality to the already gorgeous array of old-fashioned lounge furniture: sofas and loveseats, chairs draped in silks and little end-tables filled with bundled flowers and tiny discarded appetizer plates. The room sprawled, its seating clearly arranged to inspire close connections, with paper and wooden screens and potted plants artfully assembled to create the feeling of rooms in a space where it seemed the only truly separate chambers were a series of doors along two walls. Curtains shimmered over a half a dozen of those entrances, revealing glimpses of private, shadowy spaces, while further down it seemed their doors opened to more intimate parlor settings like those in the main space, blocked by silk ribbons that likely signified reservations.

It was a brilliant design, mobile enough for the constant moving that kept them secret, but with plenty of solid and detailed pieces to make the place feel truly grounded in its own ethereal way: a gothic castle, not pulled from time but from fantasy. Though Andres suspected it would have been far less a sight without the people occupying it.

The space was already full of low, sensual talk and sharp laughter. A few more vampires dressed like butlers walked with platters of bite-sized appetizers, while six humans in the same dark velvet—though noticeably less of it—moved behind them, filling tiny shot glass-sized goblets with a splash of dark red liquid. With the aroma of so many tapped veins already wafting through the room, it took Andres a moment to spot the tube the human servers were pouring from... how it slipped beneath the band on their wrists and vanished.

Their own blood, offered to the vampiric participants like a taste test.

A terrible, selfish part of him leapt at the concept, not for want of it—not while he had the blood source he desired most already standing at his side—but at the idea of having the necessity he'd spent his adult life lying and stealing and charming for presented on demand, like a gift. But it probably wasn't a gift, he reminded himself. Even if the humans smiled as they offered it, laughed at the languid touches some of the vampires gave their hands and seemed to bask beneath the obvious looks their bared skin received.

As Andres scanned the room of suits and dresses, frills and lace and overwhelming jewelry, he found nearly half of the two-dozen vampiric occupants had a human of their own, lounging at their feet or curled obediently in their lap. Most wore even gauzier, more revealing pieces than Shane's, with their own collars or cuffs—though few as lovely, Andres noted with a bizarre burst of pride. Bizarre and mildly unwarranted, considering that Shane had only come with him for the chance to talk to Tara.

And Andres shouldn't have *wanted* to compare himself to these people anyway. Not their smirks or their possessive touches or the way their humans melted against them, submissive and vulnerable and so obviously *theirs*. He should have been checking on Shane, who could only be far more aghast at all of this than Andres.

But when Shane's hand slid against Andres's, it wasn't with fear or trembling, but a thoughtful pressure. He glowed beneath the lights, a quirk to his lips and his eyes wide and alive. His fingers drew up and down Andres's wrist in an absentminded motion, steadier than Andres and just as eager.

For the life of him, Andres couldn't figure out *why*.

He didn't have much time to think on it, because a blonde, pale-skinned vampire in a suit of blue flowers with full blooms spilling off his jacket collar meandered over from a group that was clearly appraising Andres and his human. Despite how young he looked, Andres was certain he had to be at least forty, a depth to his eyes and a few laugh lines around his lips.

"New to my home, are you?" he asked with a purr. "It's a pleasure to have you here; I'm Master Valentine."

Valentine. Andres almost snorted. That had to be some kind of stage-name. "Pleasure," he replied.

Valentine's gaze meandered over Shane, half-veiled behind lashes that sparkled with gold mascara. "You've brought someone delicious with you, I see."

The obvious attention made a sharp heat stir in Andres's chest. He wrapped an arm along Shane's back, barely touching him, but sending a signal all the same. "He is. And he's rather special to me."

"Now I'm just more intrigued!" Valentine made a show of licking one of his fangs, like he was thinking of Shane on his tongue, in his *mouth*, and Andres had the urge to knock the pointed tooth right out.

He could feel Shane's breath catch.

The other vampire laughed, and the barest flush sprang to his pale cheeks, gentling his haughty expression. "Relax, I don't take what's not offered to me. Though I must say, he looks born out of pure starlight…"

As he spoke, he reached for Shane, his long gold-tipped nails stretching eagerly toward the locks that dangled around Shane's cheekbones, as though he might tuck them back. Andres could sense the tension that came over Shane like it was pounding in his ears. For all the times he had relished in Shane's vulnerable flinches, this he could not stand.

He caught Valentine's wrist, his grip tight and rough, and he lowered his voice beyond even the dark, sensual tones he'd been using, cascading into something truly menacing. "I will split open your skull if you touch him."

Fear flashed in the other vampire's eyes, and he flinched so hard his fangs retracted partway, the color draining right back out of his face. Andres was proud of that. Proud, at least, until it was echoed in Shane's surprised yelp.

"Let him go, please," Shane said, reaching for Andres's wrist—reaching, like he might grab—

Andres instinctively yanked away. Shane's fingertips barely brushed the back of his hand, the touch searing up Andres's spine and tightening like claws into his lungs.

That was fine. He was fine.

Andres stretched his fingers, breathing in, then out. Fuck, how long had it been since someone's mere grasping had triggered a panic response? How long since someone had tried to touch him like that to begin with... Had dared. He tried not to think about it.

"Give us a moment, Master Valentine," Shane murmured.

Andres took the hint, stepping back with the barest of nods.

So did Valentine, his brow tight as he bowed to them. "Of course."

He hurried across the room, toward a tall man cloaked in sheer blue and cuffed with silver, his bare chest defined despite the white beginning to pepper his dark hair. The human—Valentine's human, Andres assumed—didn't tremble or grovel, but wrapped an arm around him like an old friend, their heads close as they spoke. It was such an odd sight that it took Andres an extra moment to realize how imprudently he'd acted. He should never have let himself react with such obvious aggression. If he'd turned the place's owner against them before they'd even spotted Tara...

But he knew, too, that if their success required him to let another vampire touch Shane without consent, he would have rather failed a thousand times over.

Except Shane seemed convinced that *Andres* was the one in the wrong here. His Cygnus stared at him with narrowed eyes, whispering through his teeth, "Did you not read the packet?"

"The *what?*"

"The forms we signed!"

Andres suddenly worried they'd stated that the master of the house—who was still talking in low tones to his human—was allowed to partake in any blood brought on the premises. "I didn't put my real name," he admitted, "so it seemed irrelevant."

"You're a terrible journalist," Shane grumbled.

"That's probably because I'm a thief and a con-artist, but go on." Andres could tell they were disrupting the flow of the event, standing in the open and having a hissed argument like an old married couple. Valentine's human kept glancing their way. "Your insubordination is attracting attention," Andres muttered, curving his lips into a smirk. He pinned one palm against Shane's lower back, and gracefully fiddled with the chain on Shane's collar with his other hand, giving him the softest tug.

Shane huffed, but as he leaned away with his shoulders, his hips came forward, brushing Andres's. Andres could feel the thrum running through him, less like fear and more like… anticipation? "That's not what they care about, master," Shane breathed, tipping up his chin. "It's a game."

Did he just call Andres his… Andres knew his heart shouldn't have leaped with such abandon, and it caught in his throat when the rest of Shane's comment sunk in. "A *game*?"

"Yes, a game." Shane didn't sound annoyed, but rather alight, his enthusiasm growing with each word. "It's like a sensual form of LARPing. My contract was full of all the rules—lines we're not allowed to cross, and safe words to communicate consent and refusal, ways to inform staff if we need intervention and how the staff themselves need to be treated. When the event host—Valentine—referenced starlight, he was letting us know that he understood he was pushing a boundary and if we objected he would back off. And then you did object, by sincerely threatening to murder him." Shane gave Andres an adorable glare that melted as his gaze swept the room. "It's all so… safe. And look how much everyone is *enjoying* it."

Andres's heart pounded in his ears. His knees felt weak, suddenly. It wasn't possible—Shane had to have misunderstood somehow. Of course the vampires would be basking in their own manipulative control, but their humans couldn't be *pleased* with this.

He scanned the room again, searching for evidence that proved him right; he'd seen it when they'd first entered, he was sure of it. And the humans *were* certainly wearing less, preening and submitting and bleeding on command, but when he looked closer, he found one of them swooning as she was fed chocolates by her vampire, another giggling in their own lover's lap as the vampire whispered in their ear. A man in the corner of their own parlor section looked nearly orgasmic every time his vampire kissed his wrist with their fangs.

They... were happy.

Somehow, Shane was *right*.

Andres had painted these vampires as monsters in his mind, but everyone here seemed to be genuinely eager. Because they found joy in this, he realized, and perhaps because they wanted to be sure the people participating with them would find joy as well. And if what Shane said was true, and they were being protected by the rules of the establishment, giving them a safe place to act out their submission, without their blood being literally bought by a vampire who made a point of sneaking up behind them in the dark and turning their forced obedience into a fantasy...

Standing among them, Andres felt small and exposed. He rubbed his cheek beneath his mask, like that might dim the heat rushing through his face, and wished he could bury himself in the ground. He was right in thinking these people weren't like him. They weren't.

They were so much *better*.

Shane's fingers trailed along his arm. "Are you all right? We can sit down?"

Andres shifted just out of reach. "No, I'm... I'm good. This is good." His voice was too weak, as pathetic as it had been the night they'd met at the Fishnettery.

Shane watched him. As he did, his hand drifted up, towards Andres's face. It detoured away at the last moment, coming to fiddle with the edge of his collar.

A sudden thought hit Andres. "Do you wish I *hadn't* objected to Valentine touching you?"

Pink blossomed beneath Shane's freckles, and he pressed his hand to his neck, just above the metal. "I would have accepted whatever you asked of me," he said, so softly that the emotion behind it was muddled. "You just didn't have to scare him. I think he was testing the waters, trying to feel out what we're into."

Whatever you asked of me. Because of their mission. So they could talk to Tara. *Not* because Shane was his little swan who lived to please Andres. Even if he *was* Andres's, even if he *had* always obeyed of his own free will...

Andres swallowed, the laughter of the party ringing in his ears. Here were people who'd taken that pretense and made it—what had Shane called it? *Safe.* At least for a predetermined period of time. Perhaps there were ordinary couples beneath the costumes, but for this one evening they got to be something else entirely, and they reveled in it, vampires and humans alike.

Andres was not sure what to do with the lightness forming in his chest.

One of the human servers took note of his and Shane's weird little huddle and moseyed up to them. She was lovely, with flawless brown skin and long dark lashes, and the personal jewelry she'd added to the customary velvet server's outfit looked like it had come from a Bollywood movie. Andres could smell her, a faint shimmer of blossom and a deep oaky scent that reminded him of red wine, and while he doubted he could ever fall in love with her the way he was quickly feeling himself tumble head over heels for Shane, he knew that—before meeting Shane, anyway—he would have been able to lose himself easily in her blood and body.

Her bright smile outshone the room's flickering lights, and when she bowed her head to Andres, it seemed both sincerely submissive and exquisitely eager. "Master vampire, I see you have a delicacy of your own, but if you would like a taste of me, I'm happy to oblige…"

Shane stiffened, glancing up at Andres, his expression went so hard that he looked like he was contemplating murder based on Andres's response.

The sight made Andres giddy. He coiled a finger through Shane's hair, drawing the tips of his nails gently down the side of his little swan's neck until he reached his collar, relishing in the way it birthed a tremble so strong it tore through Shane's indignation for a moment. "What do you think, pet? Should I indulge?"

Shane leaned into his touch and turned a sharp smile on the woman. "He'll have nothing from you, temptress," he snapped, then flushed, his voice turning to an apologetic whisper. "Sorry; you're wonderful. I don't know what I'm doing."

"What you're doing is great," the server assured him, waggling a hand at him with a smile. "You both have a lovely evening." The quirk of her lips grew playfully sly. "But do tell me if you change your mind…"

As she wandered off to the next couple, Andres wrapped his arm around Shane. "I'll have *nothing*?" he purred. "Is that so?"

"*I'm* your human. If you want to go biting other people, you have to drain me first."

It took Andres a moment to register the words in relation to his tone—sharp and serious with only a hint of a tease at the end—and then another moment to convince himself they'd actually come from Shane. His Shane. Who was claiming Andres, and not only claiming him, but claiming a sole spot as his human. It felt wonderful, right and warm, and it filled Andres with overwhelming pride. Shane wanted to be *his*, or something very *like* his, at least—even if it wouldn't last beyond the moment Andres removed his mask.

Unless this was all just for the show of the thing? But the show here was obedience, and Shane was very obviously breaking that. It seemed then only right that Andres put him back in his place, made him quaver and swoon and turn his sharp edges to puddy. For the sake of the game.

He *tsk*ed, flashing Shane a loose smirk. "Bossy little pet. And overdramatic, too." He eased his hand down Shane's shoulder, pressing his fingers into the slits of his transparent sleeves to touch him, skin to skin. "If I *did* want to drain you, you know where I'd go for?"

Shane stiffened as he kept moving, drawing his way down Shane's arm toward the vein inside his elbow. He didn't pull away, though, trembling meekly under the touch. Each soft brush of skin still sent a rush through Andres, the thrum of Shane's pulse and the rise and fall of his chest such fascinating things that Andres would have been happy to bask in them forever.

At the last moment, Andres diverted away from the vulnerable inner elbow that hid beneath Shane's shielding fabric and scooped his hand around the back of Shane's arm to lift it, sweeping Shane's wrist towards his mouth. He kissed the tender skin there. Shane breathed out and leaned against him. It felt so natural, to let him linger there, to share his release in the most physical way possible. Weeks ago in that alley Andres had basked in this with a hunger, but now what he felt went deeper than desire. It sparkled like the laughter around them, stable as a safe word and warm as fresh blood.

From across the room came the clatter of falling plates, and Shane jerked, stumbling. Andres caught him with an arm around his waist. "Be gentle with yourself, my swan," he muttered, trying not to laugh.

Shane straightened with a flush, but his lips lifted. "Isn't that your job, master?"

"Is it a master's job to treat that which they own in any particular way?" Andres countered teasingly, baring his teeth.

"Perhaps not, but *my* master has always been good to me, and his hands and mouth are soft... even if his teeth are sharp." He touched Andres's mouth as he said it, his thumb brushing Andres's top lip with such tenderness that Andres was caught between adoration and disbelief.

He wanted to live in that moment forever, to take up permanent residence there. But across the room, where Valentine and his human had been standing, he spotted a vampire he'd heard described so many times that even with their cloud of cotton candy hair dyed all in deep blue streaks, he still recognized them.

He brushed Shane's fingertips as he whispered, "I think I've found our target. Would you like to pay Tara Williams a visit with me?"

SHANE

What Shane knew for certain was that he was in love—in love with this place. The fashion, the role play, the way the swirling of his outfit let him shine with his own kind of glorious masculinity that always seemed unwanted in the larger world and the metal around his throat made him feel like a trophy—all of it. If the Starlight Club was on his rating list, not a single aspect would have lost a star. He'd read the consent agreement quicker than he'd have liked, but what he had taken in set a longing in his chest. This was what he'd been craving, what he'd been hating himself for wanting. Or the healthier, better version of it, anyway.

If he were worried the exhilarating effect of submitting to his vampire would be at all diminished by the knowledge that it was a game, he'd have been so wrong. His gaze shifted between those lips that had tenderly brushed his what felt like a hundred years ago and the fangs that pressed into his skin nearly every night, and the feeling that rolled through him in rushes and flutters was just as bright and bold as fear with none of its sharp edges; all the anticipation and desire alone.

Perhaps *this* was what he'd wanted all along—this thing that could be so very normal. So very good. Could even, someday, be love, the way it was supposed to exist, not merely as the intoxicating drive for the rush and the bite, but a deeper, selfless thing.

And it made him think, oddly, of his relationship with Andres; their long, thoughtful conversations and the trust that the baring of their souls had forged.

But then Tara William's name slipped from his vampire's mouth, and Shane's mind returned to their purpose here.

Tara's attention skimmed away from the women she was chatting with, over Shane and his vampire, past them, and into one of the private parlors. She gave a cursory farewell and headed for it.

Shane followed her. He could feel his vampire at his back, one hand resting protectively against the spot between his shoulder blades. The room had filled a little more since they'd arrived, but they wound their way through the portioned-off spaces and around the silk barrier without causing too much of a stir. They slipped into the private room just in time to catch Tara fleeing out of its far exit.

Valentine sat in front of her, a glass of wine in one hand and his fangs retracted. "It seems you've come to my home uninvited…"

The door closed behind them, cutting off the sound of revelry from the main room. Shane spun toward it, finding Valentine's human there, even taller and more muscular up close.

Shane's vampire stepped threateningly forward, fangs bared, but the human slipped something out of his cuff—a piece of silver, slim and edged. The moment it was exposed, a shift came over Shane's vampire. He jerked back, bringing one of his arms up to shield his face, like the metal was a tiny sun stirring an instant draft of poison in his blood.

Shane had heard of this while scouting the vampire's hangouts: the fabled holy silver, sometimes called Roman silver by the rare few who'd survived within the oldest generation. The immediacy of its effects was terrifying to behold, the pain and fear that seemed to tear through Shane's vampire also lodging itself in Shane's own chest. He caught his vampire from behind, guiding him away from the terrible metal until he could stumble into the nearest seat. Shane hovered over him, half in his lap with his back to his vampire's chest like his own body was a shield, and prepared to fight the man and his friend off with his teeth if he had to.

Valentine's human grunted, his monolidded eyes narrowing skeptically. He slid the metal into his cuff once more and glanced at Valentine. "Well, at least he's real."

"What the fuck?" Shane demanded.

His vampire echoed the curse.

Shane shifted off him, giving him as much attention as he felt comfortable sparing. "Are you all right?" he whispered. "Would my blood help?" He knew it was rumored to be good for sun-poisoning, but not whether that held up with holy silver.

His vampire seemed already to be pulling himself back together, though, his grip tight on the arms of the chair and every muscle tensed to pounce. "I'm fine," he growled. "That was nothing." His attention didn't leave Valentine's human, even as he blinked within his mask like he was having trouble focusing.

Valentine approached, shaking his head. "Why does this shit always happen on my night? I'm quitting, Maddox, I swear. I'll go back to being our full-time house-spouse."

"You'll be lonely with the kids gone," Maddox objected.

"Or, I'll be eating cheese and wine in the bath like Diego's probably doing while we deal with *this*."

Shane's vampire rose, slow but menacing, his jaw tight and one hand on Shane's shoulder. "We'd much prefer *not* to be dealt with if it's all the same to you. If this is about my protectiveness earlier..."

"*This* is about the fact that you told my front staff that one of my employees invited you here, yet that employee has no recollection of ever doing so."

"You can hardly blame us, when you make it near impossible to find this place," Shane's vampire replied. "Even if our invite did not come directly from her, my human *has* met Tara before. Call her back in. I'm sure she'll remember him now."

Both Valentine and Maddox hesitated, but the statement was so confident that it seemed to slowly take hold of them.

Shane needed to talk with Tara, and this was one way to make that happen. But it seemed cruel to carry on their dishonesty now that they'd been confronted with these people, both of whom were only worried for this beautiful place, one where they provided joy and freedom for a group whose relationships were deemed taboo by much of society. "We should tell them the truth. They'll be just as affected by everything we're trying to accomplish," Shane said.

"Pet," his vampire started, but then he sighed, rubbing the side of his face. "You're right. Of course you're right," he grumbled. His gaze shifted back to Valentine and Maddox, his tone stiffening. "If we can have a civil conversation…"

"Yes please." Valentine sounded hopeful, while Maddox only crossed his arms.

Slowly, Shane's vampire sat back down like he was buckling in for a long conversation. "What has Tara told you about Vitalis-Barron?"

"Unfortunate things," Valentine replied.

Maddox had none of his hesitation, fiddling with the secret chamber of his cuff as he added, "They're experimenting on vampires beneath their research complex at the north end of the city and killing them when they're done. What do *you* know of it?"

"Not much more than that," Shane's vampire said. "Which is why we're here. We'd like to talk to Tara about it."

"How do we know we can trust you?" Maddox asked, and it was clear from the way he stared at Shane's vampire that it was, in part, the mask that bothered him, like it had bothered the staff member at their front desk.

Shane expected more rebuttals, more poised reasonings for why he needed it on, but his vampire quietly slipped his hand around Shane's wrist. Gently, he tugged Shane into his lap. His hands were soft, his presence warm and solid, and while the demand confused Shane, submitting to it felt comfortable. Safe. He understood what was meant by it the moment before he was asked.

His vampire was not hiding from the world, only from one particular person in it.

Shane expected that conformation to hurt or scare him, but it was sadness he felt, a deep longing between his ribs to know why his vampire was so worried that Shane would reject the person he was underneath the mystery. Shane could always narrow down the suspects or pull off the mask, but what good would that do, if his vampire wasn't ready to move forward?

So when the command came to close his eyes, Shane obeyed. He slid between his vampire's legs until his thighs pressed around Shane's, and relaxed against his vampire's chest, feeling each strong breath like it was his own. He turned his head, burying the top of his face into the base of his vampire's jaw and the softness of his throat. Without his sight to taunt him, the arms wrapping around him and the rise and fall of the chest at his back were Shane's entire world. The rustle of the mask coming off felt distant and blurred.

"Thank you, my little swan," his vampire murmured, his voice thick with affection.

This meant something to him, clearly, even if Shane couldn't understand why. He could not put the secrecy and denial aside forever. But for now, he would do what would make his vampire comfortable, because that was worth it to him.

"You may have heard of me in concept, though not by name. I'm the primary blood supplier for Frederick Maul," Shane's vampire said. "I've been searching for some way to stop the hunting Vitalis-Barron has been doing in our community, in part because Maul is upset that his customers keep vanishing, but mostly for myself. We've lost so much, suffered so much. What they're doing to us is unacceptable."

"Agreed," Valentine replied.

"Tara's memories from her time with them are traumatic," Maddox added. "I'd ask you not to question her unless you have no other options."

"I only need to know about the person who helped her escape." Shane's vampire fiddled with his hair as he spoke, soothing and gentle, and brushed his thumb along the ridge of Shane's jaw as he seemed to contemplate. "My—Shane is an investigative journalist, though. He would probably like to ask her more. And if she's all right with that, it might help everyone in the end."

Shane's heart did a little leap, and he barely caught the urge to open his eyes from excitement in time to keep the world a hazy blur of his vampire's skin. "You'll support this?" he asked his vampire, softly.

"*This*, yes."

Not the *War on Blood* article, then. But at least having his vampire's encouragement in one area was a start. "I'll only interview her if she's willing and able," Shane added. "We can meet now or later, here or anywhere she's comfortable. She can share as much or as little as she chooses. All I ask is that she be allowed to consider it."

Valentine gave a soft, "Are you sure?" and then at what must have been a nod from Maddox, replied more firmly, "I'll ask her." Then, "You can both wait here."

Shane listened as his footsteps retreated, then Maddox's as well, the side door opening and shutting. His vampire traced the line of his jaw, then his ear, quiet with what seemed like thought. Shane was suddenly keenly aware that he was still sitting in his vampire's lap, lounging against him like he was genuinely a pet… or a lover. He could still feel the gentle motion of his vampire's chest, and as they stayed like that, in silent contemplation, his vampire running gentle lines and circles along Shane's skin, he recognized, too, how their breathing had synced. They felt so much closer now than they had just a few days ago, like stepping into this place—this place where parts of who and what they were could be a safe, joyous thing—had given both of them a sense of peace and security with each other.

A foundation that might turn into something more; something like the emotional vulnerability and trust he felt with Andres, but with all the sensual exhilaration of his vampire.

The door opened again then, and Shane's vampire finally scooted him forward with a soft nudge and a, "You can open your eyes, my pet."

He'd slipped the mask back into place.

Shane tried not to be disappointed. He turned his attention instead to the dark-skinned vampire who'd entered with Valentine. Her natural curls made a cloud around her face, and the blue dye throughout them matched her brilliant eyeshadow.

Her gaze shifted nervously between Shane and his vampire. "You wanted to speak with me?"

Like they had all the time in the world, Shane's vampire kissed the side of his head, gently teasing the stray locks around his temple. "I did my part; it's your turn now."

Warmth flushed through him, not as hot or sharp as the heat that so much of this night had built, but steadier and fuller and settling easily behind his ribs. His vampire trusted him. Not with the face behind his mask, perhaps, but with this larger, life-altering thing; this future. "Thank you."

The smile he received in return was so small and soft that it made Shane's mind flash to another mouth, another smile, one his brain couldn't seem to properly identify.

He shook the thought away and stood, offering his hand to Tara. "I'm Shane."

After a moment's hesitation, she took it. She followed his lead, taking a seat across from him like they were old friends out for a coffee who just happened to have a masked vampire lurking in the shadows behind them. The occasional laugh still resounded through the walls, but their private space and its low lights felt intimate in a haunting, melancholic way.

"As Valentine might have told you, I'm an investigative journalist, but I'm also—well, you've met my vampire." Shane quirked a smile, finding his fingers drifting along his collar subconsciously. "I've been thinking for a while that the way the media portrays and highlights the existence of vampires within our city, and most others, is an awful, bigoted misrepresentation, and the more I see of your world, the more I want to set the story straight. That starts with exposing Vitalis-Barron."

Tara had perched on the edge of her seat, and she wavered, rubbing at her wrists. "I'm not sure…"

"I understand," Shane reassured her. "How about we begin with something else? Something easy." He waited for a subtle nod of acceptance before opening the recorder on his phone, showing it to her with a quick *for my own recollections,* before setting it between them. "How do you like working here?"

"This is on record?"

"If you'd like it to be. I'll keep you and this place anonymous, for your safety."

Tara nodded with more confidence. "I love it here. I know that might seem egotistical considering the event we're running right now, but we do versions of these where the humans are in charge, or where the grouping is mixed, or the power play is minimal."

Shane found himself less attracted to the other varieties of play the club put on, but he still thought it delightful that they catered to a range of desires. "If I might ask, as a vampire who's been traumatically deprived of your power in the past, how *does* it feel to work in this particular event? And know that I hold no judgement. Your emotions are appropriate, whatever they may be."

"I guess…" Tara trailed off, rubbing at her wrists again, but her expression turned soft and genuine. "This might seem weird, but it makes me feel cherished? Vitalis-Barron stripped the value in my vampirism down to what it could do for humans, and being here, with humans who will do anything for their vampires—it's helping me love myself regardless of what I am and how I've been used. There's something very special about this version of power play, I think. It's nice to imagine for a night that we aren't the subjugated, and reclaim the legends used against us in a way that brings pleasure to both parties."

"You feel safe here, then?"

"Absolutely," Tara replied. "Since I've come back, I've struggled to… to exist with humans in a place where I can't predict whether they'll be indifferent or hate me or—well, it's hard. It's really hard. But the owners of Starlight are paying for my therapy and providing me with blood. They helped me find housing and they connected me with one of their customers who was a physician before she turned. I don't think I could make myself walk into a medical facility even if I knew they'd actually see me, but this doctor is helping me so much more than I could ever repay."

That stung in a place Shane couldn't pinpoint, deep and hot and not guilty, exactly, but guilt's furious neighbor. For all his annoyance with his routine doctors' appointments and needle sticks and the overwhelming costs that had come with them since long before he'd been the one shelling out that money, he'd never considered what it would have been like had those doctors refused to help him in the first place. He knew the vampiric turning process could stop a type 2 diabetic's slow pancreatic failure and insulin resistance from progressing—for all the myths of vampires being undead, they were sometimes more alive than humans in the most literal sense—but his own body was already entirely reliant on insulin injections, not to mention hormone replacement therapy and surgery. Had he fangs among his teeth, would he have been able to transition the way he wanted?

He'd have to ask his vampire about it later.

Shane gave Tara a soft smile. "I'm sorry if this is intrusive, but are you implying that you've needed regular medical visits since your escape?"

She glanced away, her arms snaking around her torso in a version of the motion Shane had done himself so many times over the last few weeks. It made the crook of his elbow feel uncomfortably tender, and he was glad for the little fabric sleeve his vampire had given him. "Whatever those fucking—whatever they did to me, it hasn't been fully reversible," Tara said. "I think I'm the only one who's survived this long. The others I escaped with all turned up dead within the month or vanished. Maybe they're just hiding, like me, or maybe Vitalis-Barron—" The words ended in an anguished growl. "I hope they're dead, instead of back in that lab. I'd rather die out here then have to relive…" She dragged in a breath and seemed to force herself back to something easier. "Starlight lets me take all the breaks I need. If it's a bad day, I'll sit at the front desk and someone will help me do check-ins. I know I sound like a broken record, but this place has given me a community I didn't think I could ever have."

Shane's vampire lurked behind Shane's chair, fingertips brushing the nape of Shane's neck, and he made the faintest distressed sound. He'd used that same word for the vampires of San Salud before: a community. But from what Shane knew of the blood trade, that community was nothing like *this*.

"Why did you not believe you could have this? Did you feel separated from other vampires before?" Shane asked. "Or were they not helping you the way Starlight has?"

"I knew other vampires, sure, and some of them were my friends, but before this—before, you know—I was barely able to buy blood. I'd do freelance ad stuff online, and draw for people on the streets, and pick up gigs when I could, but it was never enough to cover three bags a month and rent. Since I've started here, though, I haven't once gone hungry or slept outside, even if it's someone's couch or one of the humans letting me take a few sips before work. But Starlight's reach is only so big. They make more than most vampire-serving establishments because they have a few vampiric members willing to offer a private service that rich humans will pay good money for." She grimaced. "That should probably be off the record."

"I'll ask Valentine and Maddox before I include it."

Tara nodded. "They have some money, is what I'm saying, and they put it all back into this community."

Before Shane could respond, his vampire wrapped a gentle hand around his throat, fitting it just above the collar. His thumb graced Shane's lips, sending a slight shudder through him. He went quiet, letting his vampire ask in his place, "What would you have liked to see from the vampires you knew before?"

"I don't know. Most of them were just as badly off as me, and I don't blame them, really. What could they have done?" Tara shrugged, though her expression was the furthest thing from noncommittal, her brow tight with thought. "But then I hear someplace like Ala Santa took in a bunch of unhoused vamps when they were having hunter problems a couple months ago, and now they have that blood bank charity, right there in the poorest part of town. But we can't bus in vampires from around the city to one single blood bank. We need more neighborhoods who work together like that, and more businesses that take care of their members the way

Starlight does... And fewer places preying on us, like Vitalis-Barron."

Or the blood dealers, Shane wanted to point out. But as his vampire withdrew his hand, pressing a soft kiss to the top of Shane's head like a seal of permission, it seemed the wrong time to throw the thing his vampire had committed his life to under the bus, even if he didn't get along with its greed-driven leader. That was another thing they'd have to talk about later...

Instead Shane went with, "May I ask how you ended up in their labs?"

"A woman of theirs found me at the beginning of the fall, when tourist season was coming to an end and my caricature revenue was drying up. My rent had just gone up, and the price of blood, too, and I didn't want to be back on the street again. It was so hard to pull out of that last time, and I—"

"It's not your fault, Tara," Shane said, as gently as he could.

She nodded, rubbing a hand under her eyes. "They offered to pay me, just for a few tests, the woman said. It would be three hours a night for a couple weeks. When I arrived, things felt... weird. But I signed their papers and answered their questions, and then they brought me down an elevator, and everything..."

"You don't have to tell me about that if you're not ready."

"It was hell," Tara settled on. Her hands trembled as she tucked them closer against her sides. "I thought I was dead sometimes, and the rest of the time I wished I was. We were so starving, we'd drink any human blood they gave us, regardless of what they put in it. They were always taking samples, or putting us through experiments; medical scans and shocks and injections and hooking stuff into us. We were lab rats—lab rats shaped like people—but because our bodies didn't work like theirs they couldn't see that we *were* people. Or they didn't care."

Shane could hear his vampire pacing behind him, as physically restless and unmoored as the heart in Shane's chest. He couldn't think too hard about the horrors Tara had been through—not yet. They needed to finish before it hurt Tara any further. "On your last night there, someone broke you out?"

"I don't remember it well; I was so hungry. I think I killed a lab tech—we all did. I probably would have killed our rescuer too, if he hadn't run."

"He wasn't a vampire?"

"No. But he had one with him—his partner, though I don't think they were together at the time."

Shane's vampire gripped the back of his chair, leaning forward over his head. "So you know them? Where are they now?"

"We were able to connect recently, through a mutual friend who helps them host vampires who need a temporary place to live." Tara pulled out her phone. Her hands still shook. "They're good people, but that's all I know. I don't want to give out their information without their permission, but I have their number still—I can ask if they'll meet with you?"

"That would be great, thank you." Shane retrieved his own cell from between them, stopping the recording. "Please explain to them what we're trying to do, and that we'd just like to ask them some questions—off the books, if they prefer that. And give them my number." He pulled it up, letting her add it into her contacts.

"Right," she said. "I... hope what you're doing works."

"So do we all," Shane replied. He smiled, wishing he could give her something more substantial—even just a hug. But he had the feeling she needed to receive that from someone closer to her, Valentine or Maddox or another from her tight-knit Starlight community. He and his vampire would just have to repay her with Vitalis-Barron's blood. "Thank you for everything, Tara. We'll let you get back to work."

She gave a little bow that looked perfectly in place with her butler's outfit, and departed through the main door, leaving it half-open behind her. Sounds of joy and pleasure refilled the room like it was lighting the place up, driving out the ghosts and lifting Shane's heart. They had found what they'd come for with minimal fuss, and they had the whole night ahead of them.

At least, if Shane's vampire wanted that.

He was still behind Shane, fiddling gently with Shane's neck like he was thinking of his fangs sliding between the space in Shane's collar. Or perhaps that was just Shane's imagination, his mind running away with him in a happy shudder and an intake of breath. He could almost feel the way his vampire might hold him for it, a gentle cage, secure and protective, pressing first his lips, then his teeth...

His breath rustled Shane's hair when he finally spoke. "You were rather good at that."

"*Rather*?"

"Very," he amended, his voice dark and teasing. "You were magnificent, my little swan."

"I'd hope so. It's all I want to do with my life, to learn how the world affects people, and then use that to affect the world myself." That *had* been all he'd wanted, but now he found he wanted this just as much: this thrill of being kept at his vampire's mercy, pushed to his limits, to be ordered to his knees and picked back up again, his obedience rewarded with the tenderest of care.

He was certainly being pushed now, his vampire tracing his way across Shane's shoulder to fiddle with the fabric that bunched there. His voice was darker still, lips brushing Shane's ear as he spoke. "That was more information than you needed for just the Vitalis-Barron article."

"You didn't stop me," Shane breathed, the warmth in his chest settling lower with each heartbeat.

"Would you have listened if I had?"

Even if the article was an entirely different matter from the slow relinquishing of his body to his vampire's hands and fangs, with how gently his vampire was pressing his fingers under the fabric on Shane's shoulder, he couldn't help but answer, "Have I not obeyed you thus far?"

"Repetition makes a habit, not a rule." He pressed Shane's strap aside, slipping it off his shoulder entirely. As it fell, so did the rest of his outfit, crookedly slipping lower.

It was such a little thing, a tiny unmaking of himself, but it burned through Shane like a wildfire, drawing a delicate sound from between his lips. It turned to a groan as his vampire kissed his shoulder, one soft, purposeful press of mouth to skin. He put the fabric back like it had been nothing, taken nothing out of him despite the longing it sent cascading through Shane.

With a little tug on the chain at Shane's collar, he murmured, "Come, pet. You have been taunting me too long."

Shane couldn't have suppressed the exhilarated shudder that ran through him even if he'd wanted to. He let himself be drawn up, guided by a hand between his shoulder blades and another playing with his chain. The atmosphere of the main room had shifted; the front half had brightened to a pleasant social level as groups split off to chat and drink—both from glassed beverages and the veins of their humans. Shane spotted a few card games in session, and something that might have been charades.

His vampire paused for barely a moment before leading them deeper into the space, where half the electric candles had been turned off, leaving softly flickering glows between dim chairs and dark corners. Conversation was muted here, sweet words spoken in ears and growled through fangs and released like moans. As Shane's eyes adjusted, he made out the couples' bodies beyond their outlines and his heart skipped. He wasn't sure what burned more, the flush in his cheeks or the space between his legs.

At least everyone here was *mostly* clothed.

Shane's vampire seemed to notice a moment later than he did, slowing uncertainly. "We can go back?" he asked, his mouth to Shane's ear.

"No, this is fine." A third of the couples were only engaged in feeding, their fondling kept to publicly acceptable places. "You can just bite me."

He wanted to offer more, to offer all of himself to whoever lay behind that mask, but despite his fantasies and how thoroughly this place's existence had seemed to slip into his bones, turning guilt and fear into hope and faith, he still needed something more from his vampire before he felt fully comfortable being taken like that. And there was the fact that having sex with him was not the same as most men, and even if his vampire had reveled in the scars that had slowly shaped him into who he was meant to be, that didn't mean he'd know what to do with the rest of Shane without some guidance.

His vampire certainly knew what to do with the parts of Shane he *had* been granted, though, maneuvering him right past the couches and lounge chairs to a low, cushioned bench up against the corner. Instead of sitting Shane down, he leaned him back, pressing him to the cold, hard surface of the wall, one hand clutching his hair and keeping his head from knocking while he caged Shane in with the other. It sent a chill through him, his heart thrumming with the feeling of being cornered.

"I can hear your pulse rising," his vampire purred. He slipped a knee onto the bench, fitting Shane between his legs, not touching him—not quite—just there, all consuming, all demanding.

There was nowhere else that Shane would have rather been.

"Give me your neck, pet."

He obeyed without protest or hesitation, a thrill trembling through him as he tipped his head to the side, lifting his chin. His vampire's fingers slid along his collar, and the cold of the gems that covered Shane's pulse fell away. It didn't matter that he'd spent his life walking the world with his neck on display or that his vampire had bitten him there a dozen times already; the release was like being exposed, laid bare in a new and beautiful way.

"My little swan, aren't you magnificent…"

"I'm yours," Shane whispered, low enough that he wasn't sure his vampire would hear—wasn't sure he wanted him to, not when Shane himself didn't know what that meant yet; couldn't know, until he finally met the stranger behind the mask.

But the little inhale, the slight but sure pressure of his vampire's body against his, a defined presence between his vampire's legs that did wild things to Shane's imagination—

they all said otherwise. "Bought and paid for," his vampire replied, so dark and sweet that it made Shane's aching turn white hot.

He wanted to roll his hips, to grab his vampire by the neck and press those beautiful fangs deep into himself. But he hadn't been asked to do that. And he would wait... he would wait.

Wait, as his vampire's lips brushed his skin and a shiver rolled through him. Then a flick of tongue, rough and wet, sending goosebumps up his arm. Finally, soft and slow, the press of two sharp points, perfectly spaced between the collar's metal plates. Shane felt taut as a stretched band, strung out in the darkness. As the gentle puncturing of his skin made him whimper, his eyes threatened to roll from the sheer pressure building inside him. Then the venom hit. His lashes fluttered and his knees went weak, but his vampire caught him, tucking one leg beneath his thighs and placing a hand on his hip, pressing him to the wall.

Shane relaxed into the bite, letting himself be consumed.

ANDRES

Shane was consuming him, mind, body, and soul.

When they'd first arrived, Andres had thought that perhaps the Starlight Club would make what he had with Shane look better by comparison, show all the ways that he had been less monstrous to Shane than other vampires with the same inclinations, but this place—this bizarre and beautiful place—had done the opposite. It had beamed a spotlight on their cracks and gaps and the grime between. And then it had offered to clean them out and fill them with gold. To make them into something beautiful.

And with each new step they'd taken, he could feel that gilding setting a foundation.

Shane was here not because Andres had manipulated him, or pressured him, or even because they needed this to get to Tara, but because he wanted it. Wanted *this*.

The way he'd shivered from the pressure of Andres's body, and whimpered from the touch of his mouth, and melted under his bite—it was eating Andres alive in the best way possible, building an ache so deep within him that it took a steady intention not to follow the lead of the couples around them and see how many noises he could get out of Shane before he licked the wound closed. But it was more than just the sensuality of it all. It was the way Shane had crashed between himself and Maddox to block out the holy silver, the way he'd listened when Andres had asked him to let his face remain a mystery, and the way he'd spoken with Tara, so calm and thoughtful and poised.

If all their texting hadn't already convinced Andres that he wanted so much more than just a vampire-prey relationship, then tonight certainly would have. And maybe... maybe that *could* happen. There were so many couples here, so many *partners* who—like Valentine and Maddox and their Diego back home—had to see each other as perfectly equal and normal people every day, and still feel the fire of the game's power and submission. Perhaps none of them had met their human while having an emotional breakdown, nor confirmed a hundred different ways over text that they were just friends, but...

Maybe he and Shane could still work even without the mask.

Or maybe he wasn't enough like the vampires around him, his weaknesses too apparent, the person beneath the mask too emotionally feeble to maintain a proper relationship to begin with. He knew what had happened when he'd kept a committed partner in the past. His *body* was stronger now, sure, his nails long enough to flaunt the polish that made him feel like the *they* in his pronouns and his fangs sharp enough that adding a little gloriously feminine lace to a coat wouldn't end with a black eye in an alley, but was *he*? Would he be someone Shane could still respect and obey?

This curated, masked version of himself was, at least— that much he knew.

Shane moaned beneath his bite, letting himself be pressed to the wall, neck bared so gracefully for Andres's pleasure. Each exhilarated shudder his little swan gave was so much better than his fearful ones, every whimper sharpened by the knowledge of just what Shane was begging for: more, not less. As Andres fed, savoring each slow drag of sunlight blood, Shane grew more confident.

His hands caressed Andres's sides and up his back, sending sparks across Andres's skin even through the layers of leather and satin. Shane held him, held him like Andres was his protection and his comfort, playing soothingly with the hair that fell around the nape of Andres's neck. Gradually, his fingers eased higher. They met with the strap that held Andres's mask in place.

Andres paused, every muscle tightening. He forced himself to breathe, to keep his fangs inside Shane, and slowly, he began to feed again. He wanted to be at peace with whatever Shane chose. He wanted to believe that if the couples around him could be more to their humans than fanged creatures of the dark and still feel everything that experience provided, then he could too. He *wanted* to.

But when Shane toyed with the strap, combing the hair beneath it, he forgot how to breathe. His pulse hammered. Slowly, so slowly that Andres could have stopped him with ease, Shane began to pull.

Andres's mind screamed: *No, not yet, not—*

Then suddenly Shane let go, jerking in Andres's grasp so hard that Andres could only pull back, barely managing to brush his tongue over the bite pricks to stop their bleeding.

Andres's mask wobbled, but it stayed in place, unlike his heart, which seemed to collide recklessly into his ribcage. Shane was still holding him, clutched now to the front of his jacket as he stared over Andres's shoulder. A tremble ran through him.

His voice came out weak. "I could be wrong—I'm bad with faces—"

Oh god.

Then he continued, "But I've stared at her picture so often, and I swear there's a woman in the brighter parlor who looks a lot like the one you threatened at Vitalis-Barron."

That chilled Andres in a whole new way, a lower, deeper panic fueled not by guilt but by rage. He turned, casually wrapping his arm around Shane like he was going to sit them both onto the bench, and as he did, he scanned the room beyond their darkened corner. He spotted Margaret Lane quickly. She wore a simple fabric choker, clipped in the front by a brooch, her high-necked black dress slit at the knees. In a room full of half-dressed humans in jewelry and chains, she looked awkward and underwhelming. Afraid, even.

Andres scowled. "Find Valentine or Maddox. Tell them we might need to empty this place soon."

"What are you—"

"I'm dealing with her."

In the haze of Andres's monochrome night vision, tunneled by his human-made contacts, he could have sworn he was dreaming as Shane quickly kissed the edge of his jaw. Shane was across the room in a flash, leaving only an imprint of the pressure behind.

Andres forced himself to suppress his fluttering heart and followed Shane at a more casual pace, turning to trail after his prey instead as she meandered anxiously. Maybe this time he'd actually finish the job.

"Margaret, is it?" he growled, slipping one hand around her waist, and the other over her throat.

She made a sound of surprise, then another of horror. Her body tensed, as still as a deer caught in the headlights. "W-what do you want?"

"A word."

He guided her into the nearby privacy space, through the curtains of the small, dark room. The couple already occupying the sea of floor cushions scrambled up, cursing. The human must have realized the severity of the situation, though, because he grabbed their things so fast he nearly knocked over the basket of fresh sheets. On their way out, Andres caught a flash of his face, and he swore the man looked just like the pictures of his cousin's boyfriend, same undercut and crooked mouth, his long hair pulled back into a messy bun. But he was gone in a flash, and Andres had other things to worry about than whether his cousin's open relationship secretly involved vampires.

He shoved Margaret against the wall, his fangs bared in a way the soft red glow from the fairy lights would turn monstrous. "Did Vitalis-Barron send you here?"

"Why would you think that?" Margaret snapped back, her voice fierce despite the fear in it. Andres couldn't tell if she remembered him, but she certainly remembered *this*, the nearness of a predator, the rush of adrenaline and the prick of the bite from when his fangs drove into her neck at the gala. She swallowed. "I'm here as a guest."

"Lies." And they were—they had to be—but they also weren't entirely.

As she trembled there, her gaze on the other side of the room and her heart pounding through the vein in her neck, her chin tipped and turned, so slight a gesture it had to be subconscious. Whatever she had come for, however much she clearly feared and despised the vampires she'd worked so hard to sacrifice in Vitalis-Barron's labs, a part of her yearned for the prick of fangs. The flood of venom. The rush and the bliss and the submission.

"If you want so badly to bleed for a vampire, I can arrange that," Andres murmured, dark and sensual in an entirely different way from the tone he took with Shane. Not a vampire's voice, but a monster's. "Or, you can tell me the truth."

Margaret whimpered as he caught her hair, tugging her head to the side. Andres could hear a buzz coming from just beside her temple. There—a little black earpiece. How he hated being right sometimes. He snatched it up, holding it to his own ear.

"Lane," a voice spoke through it. "We're sending our people in now. Just hold out a few more—"

Margaret wrenched herself toward the main space, yowling as her hair ripped in Andres's hold. He let her go. She was expendable to Vitalis-Barron. There was nothing else like this place for San Salud's vampiric community, and it currently held so, so many vampires they'd lose if it went down.

"Lane!" the Vitalis-Barron rep shouted, then gave a lower, obviously annoyed, "I think we lost her."

"Do you not even weep for your own?" Andres spat into the device. He dropped it and ran.

Maddox and Valentine met him halfway across the room, Shane just behind them.

"We locked the front as a precaution, and we have eyes on the back," Maddox stated.

Andres nodded. "We have to get everyone out of here, now."

"And funnel them into the alley all at once?" Valentine shook his head. "They'll be snatched up."

"What if we move them across from the roof to the buildings east of us and drop down onto the busier main street beside the boardwalk?" Andres asked.

"You make that sound so simple."

"I saw your upper stories coming in. I think I could *make* it simple—simple enough for vampires."

They stared at him, Shane included.

He shrugged. "I sneak into places I'm unwanted for a living. Sometimes the front door method doesn't work both ways."

Maddox pointed toward the private room they'd talked in earlier. "Go with Valentine. I'll send the other vamps up to you."

"I can help," Shane offered. His softness, his vulnerability and obedience, all of that had been bundled up beneath a fire that seemed to solidify him.

Still, Andres's heart cried out. It was too dangerous; he was human, which meant if Vitalis-Barron touched him, they would face legal retribution, so they wouldn't go after him purposefully, but that wouldn't stop him from getting caught in the crossfire. And worse, what if this wasn't a usual hunt for lab subjects; what if they weren't taking pre-selected vampires, chosen for the fact that they could disappear without a trace? Whatever their original purpose here had been, they could have easily decided that the risk of burning everyone to the ground—destroying the community that was keeping vampires out of their reach—served them better than collecting new specimens.

Shane must have seen Andres's worry, because he restated, "I *have* to help."

"Then please be safe," Andres replied. He slipped off his long jacket and slid it onto Shane, barely realizing that he was unfolding Shane's arms, gliding fresh fabric up the crook of his elbow, all without Shane shying away even once. Andres's throat felt tight, a lump forming at the base. "In case you end up outside," he explained belatedly.

Then, all hell broke loose.

Something crashed through a window near the front of the building, and Valentine grabbed Andres, pulling him along. They ran like vampires, speed and agility throwing them forward so fast that Andres's unfortunate eyes could barely keep up with his body, only Valentine's grip stopping him from crashing into things. They barged into the private space they'd talked in earlier and through the side door, down a hallway and up two flights of stairs. Andres could hear the pounding of feet behind him, other vampires running as well.

When they reached the top floor, Andres redirected Valentine, leading the way to the back, eastern-most side of the building. He passed one window with a cursory glance, then another, and another, until—there, the ledge he'd seen from the alleyway. "Get it open."

Valentine and another vampire burst forward to oblige, while Andres removed his lace gloves and mask, tucking the latter in the back of his pants when it wouldn't fit in his pocket. He slid out his contacts after, retrieving his glasses from his jacket. It hurt to trade away the impeccable, elegant façade for the practical frames, but he needed the better vision.

As soon as the window was open, he swung himself out, scaling down the ledge one, two, three steps. It would have been better if they had something to mount into the wall—it would have been *best* with a rope, technically—but this would have to do. The next building wasn't more than ten feet away, the roof of one of the lowest of its tiered levels a slight drop from them. Any vampire could make that, with enough courage.

Drawing a breath, he flung himself across the gap. He cleared it by twice what was needed, just to make whoever watched feel like it was possible. When he turned back, Valentine had already helped the first vampire out after him. Andres perched on the edge, extending his arms.

The vampire jumped to him.

Below, the Vitalis-Barron humans continued to crash through the lower levels as, one after the next, the vampires from the club escaped the building, more than half carrying their humans across with them. Andres only had to catch a few, including Valentine, who crashed into him so hard they both nearly stumbled over the ledge. Andres clutched his shoulders, sensing the tremble that worked through him, so like Shane's particular brand of fear that it made Andres feel protective.

"You good?"

"Yes," Valentine replied, but his gaze went down to the alley. Not the height, Andres realized, but the people they'd left to bar the way. Their humans.

"You have a person back home, right?" Andres asked.

Valentine replied instantly, "Our spouse, Diego."

"Go to them," Andres instructed. He waved a hand toward the group that had broken into their new building but were awkwardly waiting for further instruction. "And take some of these fools with you."

Valentine managed a nod. He seemed to have to drag himself every step, but he did it.

There were only a few vampires left: three, then two, then—Tara.

Andres had watched her stand beside the window, taking note of every time she stepped back to let someone else jump. And it wasn't chivalry, he realized. It was terror.

As she pulled herself onto the ledge, she shook her head. Her legs trembled visibly. "I—I'm too weak. Everything Vitalis-Barron did to me—they—" Her words died in her throat as she swayed, glancing back at the window.

Andres could make out motion inside, accompanied by shouts and a scream. He thought back to Tara's interview, not the horrified recounting of what she'd suffered, but the way she'd spoken about the vampires at the Starlight Club. Her community. His community too.

"Ah, fuck," he muttered.

He gave himself half a second to judge the sheer stupidity of his decision, but not long enough to rethink it, before taking five steps back and running at the gap between the buildings. Distance wasn't a problem, but he was jumping from low to high now, and he had to grab for the ledge Tara was standing on as his body slammed into the building's side. The air left his lungs. His fingers slipped, his long nails scratching against the brick.

A strong hand latched onto his arm. He grabbed back, leveraging himself up to find Maddox, panting, a literal sword in one hand. There was something very much like blood on it.

"We should go," Maddox insisted. The door inside bulged against its lock.

There was no one else. No Shane.

Don't think about that, he told himself, *not yet.* He swept Tara into his arms on one side, and linked his hand with Maddox on the other, and hoped to god or the universe or whatever nonsense had prompted the evolution of vampires that this worked. As the door burst open behind him, he launched them all across the alley.

They tumbled as they hit the rooftop, and Andres let Maddox go, wrapping Tara in his arms. He helped her up immediately, finding Maddox already on his feet, his sword miraculously still present.

"Shane?" Andres asked.

A bullet whizzed by his head, sending a bolt of fear down his spine.

He wrapped an arm around Tara and ran for the building. Each step felt like tearing off a piece of himself. The moment they were behind shelter, he grabbed Maddox by the shoulder, repeating his question with a growl. "Where's Shane?"

"I think he went out the back." Maddox pulled his phone free with one hand as he jogged across the room, a limp in his step. Andres was pretty sure the graze bleeding on his bicep was from a bullet. Yet he seemed so calm as he continued, barely pausing for Tara to lick the cut closed. "They captured one of our vampiric employees, and there's a few injured humans. I'm calling an ambulance. Where's Valentine?"

"Safe," Andres replied. "On ahead, with the others."

"Thank you." Maddox nodded. He found the stairs, taking them two at a time with Tara on his arm. Andres could hear the roll of loud music from below—one of the bars along the main street, probably. They could slip out the front, blend into the sidewalk traffic; or if not blend in, then at least use it like a shield, the human bystanders offering a certain amount of security against being bagged and dragged off. Vampires might have been easy prey under their country's loose laws, where people could argue the protections included only those without fangs, but an obvious kidnapping was still generally considered illegal.

Andres let Maddox and Tara go, watching from a distance to be sure they got safely to Maddox's motorcycle, but his heart, mind, and body were still focused on Shane, his worry consuming more and more of him by the minute. Andres couldn't just walk around to the alley. He'd transformed his outfit by buttoning up his shirt to the collar and pulling his pant legs down over his high boots, the coat, gloves, and mask he'd worn all evening already long gone and his sturdy black frames on in place of the night's colored contacts, but he still had an air of ostentation and a plethora of red, gold, and black eye makeup that might have been suitable for any number of boardwalk clubs but not a backstreet full of an unknown number of Vitalis-Barron employees. And Maddox had called an ambulance there anyway; Andres could hear it pulling in now.

His phone buzzed.

He'd forgotten it so completely that the vibration startled him. But he'd constructed a pocket into Shane's outfit to let him carry one himself, so—

Andres scrambled to pull out the device. He had to flip away from a stack of grumbling messages from Maul in his scramble to open the thread he wanted.

Shane

I just had the weirdest night, and I kind of need someone to know I'm alive right now.

Oh thank fuck. Andres could cry. He *was* crying, mist forming at the corners of his eyes. He tried his best to wipe beneath his glasses without smearing his makeup. This wasn't *his* Shane, he reminded himself. Not the vampire's Shane, but the one belonging to his friendly neighborhood emotional wreckage.

Andres

Are you all right? Where are you?

Are you alone?

Do you need help?

/I care

Shane

You are such a mom friend, and you know that's not how you use the backslash /affectionate

Yes, I'm fine, just shaken. I got separated from my partner, but I'm not really alone if I'm talking to you? ;)

(There's also plenty of strangers around now, if I need help.)

Wait, *partner*? Andres's heart skipped a beat, trying to settle somewhere between an overjoyed *we're dating now* and the icy knowledge that they could never have a real relationship so long as he still hid his identity. Then a selfie loaded with the message *proof of life*. Shane had Andres's black coat wrapped tightly around him, and he must have removed his collar, because one side of Andres's hastily-closed bite mark peeked out, a red dot surrounded by a bruise. The background was so dark that it took Andres a moment to recognize it: the lake. Shane was at the boardwalk.

Phone still clutched in his hand, Andres ran.

When they'd entered the Starlight Club, it had been late in the evening, the Saturday night crowds in full swing, but now they were starting to tamper off, the sidewalk hordes lessening to a scattering of couples enjoying the mild spring night and a tipsy brides-person party in rainbow tiaras tottering on their heels from laughter, the Fishnettery aglow behind them. The lake had emptied of all but a single boat, far across the water.

And there stood Shane. Arms clutched tight to his chest, his cheeks pink and his hair a mess, the scent of him, savory, a little burnt and a little sweet and so, so warm, mixing with the tang of the breeze off the lake. He was the most beautiful thing Andres had ever seen—whole and uninjured and waiting for Andres.

But that wasn't right; Shane wasn't waiting for Andres. He was waiting for his vampire.

Andres's heart caught and his hand went to the back of his pants where he'd stashed his mask. He found nothing— lost during the escape. He took a step back, but his moment of hesitation allowed Shane's gaze to latch onto him in the darkness.

No horror or anger followed, Shane's brows simply tightening as he squinted. He lifted a hand to wave without really tugging it away from his chest, and asked, "Do you know me?"

"Oh. Um, yes, hello." Andres was crying again, tears too big and full to miss. Shane still didn't know. He was safe and he was alive, and he didn't belong to any version of Andres that could be here right now. "I'm sorry," he muttered, wiping his eyes as he closed the gap between them.

Something like recognition crossed Shane's face, but his confusion only deepened. "Andres?"

His name on Shane's lips was immaculate, and yet it sounded just like the beginning of the end. "I promise I'm not always like this."

"It's all right." Shane looked unsure of what to do with himself, like he wanted to offer a hug but didn't know where they stood on physical touch. Andres's whole heart yearned for it, to wrap him up in his arms and just hold onto him until the chaos in his chest subsided, but for all the emotional intimacy they'd shared over text, they'd never really touched, not from Shane's perspective. And Shane kept watching him, his eyes pulling back across Andres's jawline, over his lips, along his earlobes to where the ends of his hair curled.

Andres pressed a hand to his mouth, looking down the boardwalk. "Can you not?" he muttered. "I feel enough like a fool."

He hadn't specified what he wanted stopping, but Shane turned slowly toward the lake, one hand on the railing. He cleared his throat. "Were you at the Fishnettery again?"

"No, just… a club." Andres had to stop talking. He had to stop *being* here. But he had to stop lying, too, or he was going to ruin this, dig himself deeper until it was a pit he couldn't climb out of without breaking both their necks in the process. He had already lied for so long…

Shane could choose to hate him for it.

The knowledge was still sinking in, pressing its slow, terrible hooks into Andres's heart. He'd been focusing so much on how Shane wouldn't be able to see him as the over-emotional friend and still tremble beneath his touch and melt in his arms, that he hadn't considered the option where Shane decided to no longer see him as either. Not lover or friend, but a monster.

Andres tried not to think about that. He tried to believe that if only he could knit the two halves of himself together strongly enough, they could still move forward. They could become one of the couples from the Starlight Club, mixing romanticized moments of power play into an ordinary life of extraordinary love. They could.

He just had to prove that.

Shane hadn't replied yet. Standing at the railing, a soft flush in the moonlight, he looked fragile suddenly. He held his arms against his chest, his brow tight as he gazed across the water. Beneath the worry and the pain, part of Andres longed to unwind him, to peel him apart, to see him quaver and melt and feel his pulse flutter. The more Shane bundled himself tighter, the more that impulse grew.

"Do you know what it feels like," Shane asked, "when you're so consumed by another person, so quickly and so completely, that when you lose them, even for a moment, it's like your whole being is in suspense, pulled out of time? You become a Schrödinger's person; whether you're alive or dead depends on them, but you won't know yet, not until they return." He dragged his fingernails against his neck, pressing them to the bruises where Andres had bitten. "Is that love, or is it obsession?"

"I think it's both, and it's neither." Andres stepped forward, soft, monstrous steps, coming up behind Shane like a creature of the darkness. "The feeling is the same, but it's the action you let it drive you towards that makes it one or the other."

Just keep loving, he'd been told by a stranger a few months ago, golden hair and fangs and so much of that singular emotion in his eyes that it had hurt to look at. Andres wondered where that vampire was now. If his loving had held him together or torn him apart.

Andres refused to keep letting his own obsession make that choice. So he'd have to try love and hope for the best.

Shane made a sound like a creature dying. Or one coming to life. "You know, I'm waiting for someone," he said, his voice shaky with a humorless laugh.

Andres took one last step, until he was hovering over his Cygnus, around him. "And you've been so patient for me." He whispered the words, leaning in. "But I think you've waited long enough, my pet."

19

SHANE

The pieces had come together for Shane slowly but surely, drenched in numbing denial.

"*Andres?*" he'd asked the person he could recognize only as the farthest thing from a stranger, a part of him expecting—hoping—to be corrected. A tremble ran up his spine, and he gripped the boardwalk railing as he repeated the name. "Andres?"

He tried to turn, but a hand pressed against the side of his head and another cupped his hip. The hot breath on his neck slid all his suspicions perfectly and painfully into place.

"Be still for me." Andres's lips brushed Shane's skin as he spoke. Shane couldn't find the strength to disobey, his knees so weak that only the vampire behind him and the railing before him held him up.

His vampire, Andres Serrano.

Andres, whom Shane had been harboring a small, guilty crush on for weeks now, smiling over every time his phone chimed, was his vampire. His vampire, who'd been so very good to him tonight, who'd gotten him the interview of his dreams and then pressed him to a wall and bitten him like he was precious. Two personas, who'd both worn masks, kept this secret, lied through their teeth just to trick him into— into *this*.

Whatever the hell *this* was.

Andres loosened Shane's tight arms, winding through them, wrapping him up. A panicked tremble in the back of his mind shouted through his shock, screaming at him to refuse. To fight—

"Give me your neck." Andres had it already, his mouth against it, but Shane knew what he was asking for: not just the flesh and the blood but the surrendering. Shane's submission, the way he'd given it to his vampire every night.

But this was not just *Shane's vampire* anymore.

"Your neck, my Cygnus." There was a little growl to his voice, so dark, so sensual and yet it was now unmistakably Andres's.

His presence felt smothering, claustrophobic, and Shane curled toward the wood, instinct pushing him away from Andres. As he did, Andres loosened again, and Shane could feel the tremor that ran through the vampire's chest. Two of his fingers slid beneath Shane's, just as he had done during their first bite in the alley: a kind of safe word.

"Cygnus?" Andres said, like a question. Or a warning. "I want you. Will you let me?"

Shane trusted his vampire—*had* trusted, until now, until *this*—but in that moment he feared the predator behind him, feared him properly for the first time. It was a terrible sensation, thick and ugly like a room with nothing but empty blood bags and a needle jabbed into his arm. It closed up his lungs and got into his chest, and he could not—could not—

"No!" He squeezed Andres's hand like he was trying to draw blood.

Andres let him go, his presence vanishing from Shane's back in an instant.

He could breathe again.

The boardwalk life echoed through his ears, distant laughter and muted music. Pain throbbed behind his jaw, building in the back of his throat. He sucked in air and let out anger.

"You fucking—" Shane spun as he shouted it, turning so fast that his shoulder rammed into Andres's chest. The vampire stumbled in surprise, eyes wide, and Shane took that as a sign to keep going. "Asshole. You *knew* I didn't recognize you from the bar. You knew, and you just left me in the dark? For weeks," he shouted, "you've strung me along. All the while, pretending you were my—my friend?!"

That's who he was pissed at—Andres, his *friend*. His vampire had been clear that there were hidden parts of himself; a literal mask to be removed. But Andres? Andres had presented like that was all they were, just a thoughtful human with big emotions who liked Shane's odd takes on life. They'd become a solid, sure part of Shane's everyday life. And all the while they'd known they owned Shane, had been whispering sweet nothings to him and demanding his neck in the darkness.

The bastard—

Shane pushed both palms against Andres's sturdy chest, enough to force them backward. "You fucking—" He shoved again, for good measure. "Manipulative—" And again. "Asshole!"

Andres's expression stiffened. "Shane…" They said, gentle, cautious, but as they did, they grabbed for Shane's arms.

"Don't touch me," Shane snarled. "I'm not done yet!"

He was so, so fucking done, though, done being deceived and coerced, done being stared down by those dark, tear-stained eyes of Andres's, just as deep and beautiful as his vampire's but twice as soft and so uncertain it hurt. When Andres tried to step toward him again, not reaching this time, just holding up their palms in a gentle onslaught, Shane grabbed them instead, locking around Andres's wrists like he could transfer the confusion and pain and fury in his chest into his vampire's flesh if he just held on tight enough.

Like he could keep his almost-lover and his traitorous friend there long enough to truly be done with them both.

But as Shane latched onto Andres, the motion send a visible shock through them. Their fangs slid out, and faster than Shane could track, they jerked from his reach with such force that it flung Shane backwards. Shane hit the boardwalk railing with a crack. Pain shot up his back. He whimpered, struggling to stand, that new fear creeping back in, harsh and debilitating and—

"Step away from him, bloodsucker!" The command came from down the boardwalk, far too near for comfort, though Shane wasn't sure there was any distance at which he'd find comfort in the police, especially not one already fondling the hilt of his gun. "Hands on your head."

Andres stepped away, lifted their palms to the side, their chest wide open. An easy target. They said nothing, but they looked weaker suddenly, looked like the tear-stains that had begun to form in their makeup.

Shane's heart squeezed.

"I said stop," the cop shouted, as though by retreating, Andres was secretly preparing to lunge for his neck. His grip tightened on his gun.

Everything else Shane felt toward Andres was nothing compared to the chilling rush that overtook him then. He was not done with Andres—he was not done with them at all. And he would sure as hell not be rid of them like this.

Shane stepped out, sliding himself neatly between the approaching cop and Andres, both his hands spread out from his body in a pacifying motion. "Please, officer, what's wrong?"

The cop gave him one look, then another, his gaze catching on Shane's neck. On the visible bite mark. "That creep been feeding on you?"

"Yes, but—I let them."

There was so much more Shane could have said: that he craved his vampire's bite, dreamed of his vampire's hot breath on his neck and the pressure of his tongue, yearned for the way he'd whisper in his ear: *you're mine.*

But the cop deserved none of that, so Shane told him the simple truth. "It was consensual."

"That didn't look consensual." He still had one palm on his gun.

Shane's vampire—his *Andres*—had pushed him, had held him in place, but they'd listened to him too, had let go when he'd asked. He didn't know what that meant. Didn't know if it could mean anything in this moment. "We were arguing," he pleaded, "that's all."

The cop hesitated. His gaze strayed behind Shane once more, and he shook his head. "There's been a disturbance involving vampires in this area. I'm sorry, I have to take him in."

The thought made Shane sick and angry; far angrier than he could ever have been at Andres. For Shane, a simple arrest would have been merely inconvenient now that all his legal documents had been fixed with his proper gender, but for a vampire... There was a reason they now built windows into holding cells, and it wasn't for the view.

From down the boardwalk, the cop's partner jogged toward them.

Shane could still sense Andres behind him, waiting uncertainly in their tear-stained makeup. He slipped his hand behind his back and made a shooing motion to them. Run, he wanted to shout. Run, dammit—*can't you see I'm not done with you yet?*

And Andres did.

The cop cursed, bolting after them as he drew his gun, but the split second he had to take to dodge around Shane was enough for Andres's vampiric speed to carry them across the boardwalk.

Shane watched long enough to see them cut down a path toward the main street and vanish between the buildings. Then he broke into a jog himself. Neither officer tried to stop him. That was worse somehow—worse being alone.

By the time Shane reached his car, he was shaking, trembling from head to toe. He was too afraid to check his glucose—there was nothing he could do about it now, except pick at the bag of emergency fruit gummies he kept in his glove box. Through the miserable, resentful bitterness in his mouth they tasted like sweetened wax. He drove in a daze, cycling between the same series of thoughts and emotions; anger at Andres's lies, fear of them and for them in equal measure, and a numbing uncertainty about what to do for any of it.

Somehow, he made it to his apartment, his heart pounding in his chest. He closed the front door behind him and when he couldn't push himself any further, he slumped against the wall there, pulling in his arms and sniffling.

He had to think about this rationally.

It could, technically, be a good thing: he was obsessed with his vampire, in love with the way their relationship made him feel, and Andres—Andres he'd been quietly crushing on nearly since they met. Rating-wise, this should have been a ten out of ten for love interest consolidation. But Andres had been *lying* to him.

Taking him for a fool.

The jacket his vampire had given him felt constricting suddenly, and Shane tugged violently out of it, his arms catching twice in the twisting sleeves before he managed to rip it free of his skin. The chill of his apartment immediately replaced its warmth and gentle floral scent. It felt like the way Andres had gone stiff when Shane had shoved him, the aggression with which he'd yanked from Shane's grasp. With a curse, Shane slid his coat back around his shoulders, hugging the sleeves to himself.

The vibration of Shane's phone startled his heart into a panicked rhythm once more. He scrambled for it, hating the way he needed to know.

It wasn't Andres.

He breathed out, and it felt like a sob.

Nat1
Hey fucker. /affectionate
Boyfriend is gone again tonight and I'm lonely.

Shane-anigans
Fuck him.

Nat1
Wishing that was literal lmao.
It's fine, I'm fine.

She finished it with two fire emojis and a dog.

Shane-anigans
You and me both.

What he thought were his two potential relationships was actually a single relationship set ablaze in the least sexy way possible, and he was the kind of fine that needed so many black-slash sarcasm tags.

His traitorous fingers automatically switched him over to his thread with Andres, swiping through motions he'd performed a thousand times that week. Their contact name still read *Anders Serrano he/they*, with a little sparkle emoji Shane had added a week into their texting. He hadn't known his vampire's pronouns, he realized.

His stomach turned, grief first, then anger, then grief again. *I'm not done yet*, he'd said. And he didn't feel done, still—he felt raw and empty, like a piece of himself had been ripped away.

When a text appeared at the bottom of their thread, he wasn't sure whether he wanted to hug the device or hurl it across the room.

Andres
Did you get home safely?

Shane
Yes

He didn't hesitate to answer; didn't even realize that letting Andres sit with their fear was an option until after he'd already pressed send, and despite the hurricane of emotions rushing through him, Shane couldn't dream of cruelly holding Andres in suspense like that.

Andres sent back a single heart, white and small and somehow so hopeful that it severed right through Shane. He slumped against the wall beside his door, light still off, his vampire's jacket around his shoulders. Dots appeared on Andres's end, then vanished. Appeared, then vanished. Shane wasn't sure he wanted to see what would finally come over. Maybe he wanted to jump the gun, get in his own accusations first? But he'd shouted enough of those on the boardwalk, and Andres had...

Andres had hurt him.

His back still felt bruised from the shove, but the jarring shock of it was as painful as any physical malady. The surprise and horror that had crossed Andres's face when it happened, like they were just as hurt as Shane had been...

Finally, Andres's text came through—not a long message after all, but four words that spoke louder than any essay.

Andres
Can I come over?

A chill ran down Shane's skin, disquieting and uncomfortable and yet still yearning. Always this goddamn wanting, like his body had tuned itself to his vampire that first night they'd met and with every bite since the thrall had grown. Anger or not, fear or not, part of Shane belonged to his vampire, not just for better, but for worse too. No matter what happened between them, a part of him always would.

But he still had to be rational. He had to.

Shane
I don't know.

He leaned against the wall, watching the text sit there. No response dots. No pressure.

He hated it.

A knock came at the door.

Shane jumped. He tried to steady himself, but he still shook, like the extra adrenaline was determined to course through his system in a terrible repetitive cycle. His fingers glided over the chain. Before he could second guess himself, he slid it into place. Calmly, he opened the door a crack.

"Shane," Andres started, pushing forward.

The chain caught, snapping the door to a stop.

Andres froze. The four inches of their face that Shane could see through the crack transformed, descending from confusion to horror to shame. They let go of the handle. "I see."

"I can't, not yet." Shane leaned against the wall beside the door, staring into the gap. Even now, he wanted so badly to reach through it. "I don't know how to say no to you otherwise."

"Oh." Andres's mouth moved through the sound, and seeing his face with it, makeup smeared and eyes puffy, was like an entirely new experience. "If you tell me to leave, then I'll leave. Otherwise I'm going to keep being here. You're… mine." He seemed to hesitate over the words, testing them out, tasting them. When he repeated them, they felt different from any time he'd said them before, not a claiming, but a revelation. "You're mine, Shane. I'll never see you again, if that's what you ask of me, but your safety, your joy, your passion, will always feel like they'd been mine to protect. You're mine, and I'm failing you."

"Of course I'm yours," Shane replied, because goddammit, it was still true. This night had, if anything, set that in stone. "But you are failing me. You lied to me. You twisted my feelings around your finger and I know two of you now but I don't feel like I know you at all."

"I'm sorry." It sounded sincere—so desperately sincere. "I did lie by omission; I tricked you—I wore the mask and made sure not to meet you as more than your vampire. But I never meant to manipulate your feelings. What I've shared with you has always been the truest parts of me. I've meant everything I've ever said to you, as your vampire and as your friend."

That stung, but the burn faded warm, bringing relief with it. The way Andres had made Shane feel—the fire of his gaze and the intimacy of their texts; that wasn't a lie, at least. Shane folded his arms tighter to his body. "You hurt me. On the boardwalk."

A flash of terror spread across his face, but it was gone as soon as it had come. "I didn't mean to react that way. It won't happen again. I would never... I promise to only ever be gentle with you."

That Andres meant always to be gentle was the truth; Shane had known it before he'd even known Andres, and while it hadn't stopped whatever came over him on the boardwalk, that aggression felt like the fluke, not the routine. Even flukes had reasons, of course, but if Andres claimed he was handling himself, then Shane would believe him until proven otherwise.

"Don't make me go." Andres watched Shane, his brow tight and his gaze soft yet hungry. "You can ask me anything you'd like. I'll answer truthfully. Or you can ask me nothing at all. Just let me be here. Lock me out if you must, but don't make me leave."

"Andres..."

"I know, Shane. And I'm sorry."

Shane couldn't find a way to say no to him, and as the adrenaline left his body, he found he didn't want to. His knees went weak. He slid down the wall, settling onto the floor.

Andres watched him, fingers on his lips, then running through his hair, before both hands clutched behind his neck. Slowly, like he was testing whether the weight of the floor would hold him, he settled there and slumped against the door. The light of the little apartment porch set shadows across his beautiful face. Two little fangs peeked out between his lips.

Shane didn't make him leave. He stared, and, quietly, he commanded, "Tell me something."

"Something true?"

"Something you."

Andres exhaled. He nodded, his gaze shifting into the middle distance. "I make my own clothing—or doctor up existing pieces—and I have a channel where I share what I've created. The videos do well. They get ugly comments on occasion, when the wrong person notices how masculine my hands are, but it inspires people too. I never tell anyone it exists, though. I'll get questions at the Fishnettery and I just shrug and pretend I can't remember where the jacket came from."

Shane fingered his rose gold fabric. "You made our outfits?"

"I'm a criminal and seamstress, and occasionally the two collide." It sounded like a confession. "Letting you believe I was two different people was exceptionally selfish of me, but I want you to know that in both cases you've gotten a version of myself that's the most *me* I've been in a long time. I've withheld things, but what I did give you has always been sincere. Always been me. I think you're the only one that's true for."

It helped, knowing that at least what they had in itself hadn't been a lie. But it didn't fix things. There were the obvious questions: why me, why this. Instead, Shane asked, "Who *are* you without me?"

"Without you, I'm no one," Andres whispered, fiddling with his long necklace—the one that matched Shane's collar.

Part of Shane wanted to let the dramatic words woo him into submission the way his vampire's possessive murmurings had been doing since they met. But they were supposed to be getting to the bottom of this. After weeks of dodging the truth in favor of the romance, Shane owed it to himself not to be led astray, because maybe—just maybe— then they could really have that romance they both seemed so desperately to want. "That doesn't seem healthy," Shane replied. "I can't make you real, Andres."

"No—I know," Andres admitted. He tipped his head back against the door, still gripping his necklace. "I suppose what I mean is that before I started texting with you, and before we decided to stand against Vitalis-Barron together, I'd grown incredibly shallow in how I presented myself. Not really an individual, but a caricature of a vampire; strong and dark and secretive and sensual, and I let no one see beneath that for so long that sometimes I wondered if there was a me there at all."

Shane could relate to that, in a way. He hadn't dimmed himself, but he had portioned out who he was where it felt appropriate, and the people who'd received the biggest and brightest versions of him—the ones where he hadn't buried his passions or limited his emotions—had all left one by one until his only friends were a woman nearly as obsessed with vampires as he was, and the vampire who was obsessed with *him.* "Why wear the literal mask with me, then? What was so terrible about the person I texted, that you were afraid for me to see them?"

"You're looking at them." Andres drew a breath that could have been a laugh or a sob and waved at his face, long lashes and dark eyes and tear-stains blurring his makeup. "I'm not a pleasant sight."

He was, in fact, gorgeous, and holding his gaze made Shane hot in all the right places, though Shane recognized neither of those things were the point. Gently, he stated, "I *had* seen you already, back at the Fishnettery."

"And you thought I was a wreck."

"True," Shane admitted. "But I'm also a wreck, and it doesn't seem to bother you much." He felt himself grinning a little at the thought of waking to find his apartment tidied that first morning. Andres had seen how far he'd been letting his life deteriorate and instead of judging him for it, he'd quietly committed to helping pick up the pieces. If Andres's life was a mess, too—and clearly it was, beneath the mask— then what other option did Shane have but to offer him the same compassion in return?

Andres stared through the crack in the door, brow tight and lips parted. "Well, you only wanted to be friends."

Shane snorted. A wreck, indeed. "I had a vampire who owned parts of me and pressed his mouth to my skin every night! How was I supposed to explain that on a third date? There's open relationships, and then there's *I'm in a toxic blood-bondage thing with a mask-wearing vampire criminal!*"

A twisted expression broke over Andre's face, and in the low light it took a moment for Shane to realize it was a shocked delight. "Us, *toxic*?" Andres scoffed, lips quirking. "I'm offended. I thought you liked my antics."

Shane snorted, but the little shiver that ran down his spine was blissful. "What gave you that impression?"

Andres's smile grew. He leaned toward the gap in the door, and his hand crept closer, brushing Shane's. Goddamn, how the one little touch could make all of Shane's body light up. He drew in his fingertips, forcing Andres to follow him.

His vampire did, lacing his fingers between Shane's, gently tugging them out. He encircled Shane's wrist with the barest of touches. "May I?"

Shame lifted a brow. "Are you asking or commanding?"

A growl came into Andres's voice as he responded, fangs bared. "Give me your arm, my pet."

Shane closed his eyes.

Andres tugged, and Shane loosened, letting his arm be drawn through the gap in the door. The vulnerability of it coiled in his gut and tingled along his skin, the jacket slipping off his shoulder to leave his arm bare but for the billowing strips of his outfit's sheer fabric and the small sleeve Andres had given him for the crook of his elbow. Beyond that, his brain sparked with the uncanny knowledge that he was trapped like this, his shoulder in the gap of the door and his arm stretched at an angle where one wrong push could snap it. It would be easy for someone with Andres's strength— would be just as easy to hold Shane in place and dig in fangs as he cried and struggled.

But all that fear felt muted by the brush of his vampire's fingers, like their quiet touch was slowly but surely calming Shane's demons.

Andres touched the edge of the tiny sleeve that protected Shane's inner elbow. "May I?"

"Yes," Shane breathed. As Andres tugged down the piece of fabric, he focused on his breathing and the gentle pressure of Andres's nails on his skin, so tender and thoughtful that it formed a lump in Shane's throat. All the pain he'd felt on the boardwalk and the longing he couldn't seem to extinguish came together, thick in his chest, and he whimpered.

"Look at me," his vampire whispered. Two fingers traced into the crook of Shane's arm, settling there with a pressure that trapped Shane's lungs. "Cygnus, look at me."

Never, not now, of course—a cascade of reactions flew through Shane's mind. This was his vampire *and* this was Andres, and they both wanted him, all of him, one a request, the other a demand. Shane's heart said *yes* and *yes* and *yes* again for good measure.

He pressed his forehead to the gap in the door and opened his eyes.

Andres held his gaze, strong and sure and wonderful. Slowly, they lifted Shane's arm, cradling it as they brought the crook of Shane's inner elbow to their mouth. They pressed a kiss to Shane's pulse.

Shane's world quavered, his heart pounding, but all he could feel was the softness of his vampire's lips and the giddy lightness in his chest and a warmth so pleasant that it seemed to form a film over the awful memories of Maul's vampire's bites. The pressure of the kiss retreated without a prick or a nip, and somehow that was perfect, because it left Shane with a wanting in place of his fear. A desire where apprehension had been.

His vampire smiled and laced their fingers through Shane's. "Hi, I think it's time I make your acquaintance," they said. "I'm Andres, your vampire. I'm a little bit obsessed with you, and I'd like to turn that into loving you instead. If you'll let me."

Shane groaned with relief. "God, fucking yes."

ANDRES

There was no better sound in the world than the chain unlocking from Shane's door.

Despite all the ways he had managed to push Shane— showing up on the mere chance he'd be let in, asking for his arm, for his eyes, for his heart—Andres still hesitated at the threshold. "May I?"

Shane grinned. "I happen to know vampires like you don't need to ask permission to enter their humans' house."

So he did, letting the motion carry him further, reaching for Shane and wrapping him up in a shaky hug. It wasn't sensual or erotic, more relief and hope and a flood of other emotions that welled in the backs of Andres's eyes, and when Shane returned the hug, Andres had to kiss the top of his head to hide how ridiculously he was blinking away the tears.

"Sit with me," he whispered as Shane withdrew, not a question or a command, but a plea. "I don't want to stop holding you."

"You're a sap." Shane laughed. He nudged his shoulder into Andres's. "It's very cute."

They moved to the couch, settling beside each other like it was the most natural thing in the world. It felt like it—felt right. It occurred to Andres that perhaps there were other questions they needed to answer now that everything was out in the open. And he found, oddly, that he wasn't afraid anymore. He had his Cygnus, not as a bought body or a play-acting human pet, but as a partner—as just Shane—and now that they were here, he found it was what he'd wanted most all along. "Do you prefer me sappy? I know I've been demanding, and—correct me if I'm wrong—you seem to enjoy that, but it's a role I enjoy playing, not the person I am underneath. I *can* stop it."

"Please don't stop it permanently." Shane pulled his legs onto the cushions and leaned against Andres, his knees resting on Andres's thighs. "I loved what we did at the Starlight Club. Like twelve out of ten, something I didn't know my life was missing until now. It was exhilarating, and so damn hot. And as long as we have rules, like they do, and we know when it's appropriate and when it isn't... then maybe we can have our sappy, equal partnership and when we're both in the mood, I can still be your blood slave?"

Blood slave. All his guilt and shame would have made him recoil from the phrase, if not for the hope on Shane's face. Andres's heart soared. He was *allowed* to want to take what his little swan was happy to offer. "So you'd like to go back, then? Have nights where we dress up and play the part someplace like the club?"

"Yes, but maybe not just those nights, and maybe not such a strict separation of the two?" He bit the inside of his lip, tucking his knees against his chest and cupping the sides of his neck, but as he did so, he leaned onto Andres's shoulder, looking up at him through soft lashes. "As I said, I really enjoy you taking control, *master.*"

Andres's little swan, his magnificent Cygnus, was curling himself up on purpose. The two of them weren't basking in the mysterious thrill of darkness and anonymity, or even the sensual pretense of the club, but sitting on the couch beside a coffee table stacked with used dishes, a cat giving them annoyed glances, as casual as any couple and bare as their hearts would allow. And Shane *still* wanted this.

It made Andres yearn, for more, for *him.*

"Is that so, my pet?" He took hold of Shane's thighs and hips, and, gentle as ever, nudged him forward, tugging Shane up and into his lap.

Shane let himself be unfurled, and when Andres pressed his legs apart, he whimpered beautifully. A part of Andres wanted to keep pushing him, to see what Shane would do if he slipped a hand beneath the fabric that pooled around Shane's navel, what noises he might make, how he might tremble then—but there would be time for that later. Instead, he pulled Shane flush to his hips with one arm wrapped around his back and the other cradling his neck.

"And if you do disobey me?" he whispered, fiercely holding Shane's gaze. "What should I do with a little swan who doesn't submit to his master?"

261

Shane's throat bobbed as he swallowed, his breath noticeably lighter. "I have no plans to be anything but perfectly and utterly submissive." He leaned closer, his breath on Andres's lips, cheeks pink. His fingers skimmed along the front of Andres's shirt. "But if I displease you, then you can punish me with your fangs or your touch, if you'd like."

Andres responded with a smirk and a growl, deep and low and sensual, but the swell of affection in his chest warmed it in a way he hadn't anticipated, and the sound turned to a laugh, fresh tears brimming along the corners of his eyes. "I'm sorry, I just—this is wonderful, Shane. *You* are wonderful. I spent so much time worrying that you wouldn't want this, and now here you're asking for it, because you have the freedom to do that, and I have the freedom to accept it, and—"

Shane kissed him.

It was so quick, a brush of lips as sudden and soft as the one Andres had given him on the balcony months ago. It caught in him like a blow to the chest, his mouth tingling long after Shane had pulled back.

A flush deepened in Shane's cheeks. He looked down. God, he was perfect, with his hair half fallen from its pins and the top of his outfit shifted out of place from being pulled onto Andres's lap, one of his chest scars still peeking out the side.

Andres caught a few of his stray hairs, tucking them gently back. He traced up the length of Shane's soft jaw and through his waves until he was cupping the back of Shane's head, and whispered, "Open your mouth for me, pet."

Shane looked at him again, finally. Without question, his lips parted.

Andres stole them. He pressed his tongue against Shane's and caught the next breath from his lungs, dragging forth a moan that he echoed himself, lower and more graveled. Shane returned his aggression with a hungry obedience, moving always with and never against, letting Andres tug and tease and lick. His fingers tightened into Andres's shirt and Andres could feel every tremble and shift, every whimper and groan.

He tasted like he smelled: like sunshine and all the brilliance and bitterness of living, and it made Andres hunger for him—not merely for his blood but for his essence and the wetness between his legs. The latter, he'd have to ask for, but there were parts of Shane's body he knew were his, not because he'd bought them, but because they'd been given freely.

Holding Shane's head firmly in place, he pressed his fangs into the soft skin inside Shane's lip. The sound his little swan made was transcendent, and Andres sucked; sucked and bit until Shane was putty in his arms, both their mouths faintly red. By the time he finally let go, his whole body was alight with a throbbing ache, caught somewhere between total satisfaction and eternal yearning.

Shane leaned into him, forehead resting against Andres's cheek. He breathed hard and his shoulders shook, but he seemed deliriously happy, spent in a way that was akin to orgasm. Andres ran a hand down his back and along his side, just holding him. His thumb brushed Shane's scar, and he let it linger there.

"Tell me about this?" he asked, "The surgery, the transition? I'd like to know. I'd like to know you."

"It was hard," Shane replied. "And beautiful, and ugly. Perfect and messy. It was so much. Transition is more complicated as a diabetic too—the hormones threw my blood sugar all out of whack—and it took a while to get to my top surgery, because of the extra risks. When I finally did start it all, I left a great internship at a newspaper in LA, and I couldn't bring myself to go back—to tell them all that I wasn't actually a woman like they thought and watch them struggle to change their perception of me or reject the new me altogether. I've grown a lot bolder since, a lot more ready to claim who I am. But it's still hard." His voice went small, his shoulders sinking. "I wonder, sometimes, if I ruined my career because of it. I should have been braver. I should have taken what I wanted regardless of what people thought of me."

Andres wanted to wrap him up, to press his lips into Shane's hair and tell him that he was magnificent, then as he was now, and he realized with a sudden wave of joy, that he could. So he did, cuddling his little swan and whispering tenderly, "You need more than just bravery in this life. You need safety too." He held Shane close, feeling his heart beat, his blood pump. Love, and life. "Everyone has always known there was something queer about me, but it's taken me a long time to actually tell my family about my nonbinary gender nonsense. They still don't know about the vampirism. I think they don't really know me at all, anymore, and it feels safer that way. Some people aren't worthy of certain parts of you, and that doesn't make you any less yourself."

"Very few people could possibly be worthy of you." Shane lifted his chin. Their lips brushed, not in a kiss, but a smile. "Because you, Andres, are magnificent."

Having the words Andres had used to describe Shane's transness earlier repeated back at him broke something inside him—or perhaps, it didn't break, but it mended; mended in a way that felt like being torn asunder, seen inside of for the first time in his whole goddamned life. "And you were always worthy of all of me. I made a mistake in ever worrying otherwise."

"I was," Shane agreed, staring at him so intently it was impossible to look away. "But how could you have known that?"

"I…"

"It was still a real fucked up thing to do, don't get me wrong. I think I understand now, though, and I forgive you. You *are* so magnificent," Shane repeated, running his thumbs over the skin of Andres's sternum. "And I'm so fucking obsessed with you. And I know we need work— goddamn, we need work. But I want to do that work *with* you, *for* you. For us." His brow lifted, and he pulled back enough that they could lock eyes properly. "We're an *us*, right?"

Andres felt like he owned the world. "I figure if I'm not allowed to bite any human but you, the romantic exclusivity is implied."

"Good." Shane kissed him softly, then relaxed against his chest, nuzzling into Andres's neck as though he were the vampire. His lips brushed skin and the touch shivered through Andres, landing pleasantly between his legs. Andres played with Shane's hair, and for a moment they just sat like that, entwined and contented, until Shane finally asked, "How old are you? I was just thinking how vampires don't always look like they're aging and you could be twenty-five or seventy and I might not be able to tell."

Andres laughed. "I'm thirty-four."

"Ah, yes, just as I predicted, you're ancient." Shane fiddled thoughtfully with the collar of Andres's shirt. "I'm only twenty-five. Is that a problem?"

"I think if *that's* dubious enough to be an issue, we're already fucked," Andres said. "We're both adults with jobs and a space of our own. I was a year younger than you when I was turned, and I went through a lot of growth in the few years after,"—he had Maul to thank for that, for better or worse—"but I don't think I've changed much mentally or emotionally since."

"How did it happen?"

"My vampirism?"

"Yeah."

Andres shifted a little, his muscles fidgeting like they were trying to shrug out of the conversation. Which was ridiculous, because he was fine. For all the ways his vampirism had hurt—still hurt—it was ultimately a good thing. He'd found stability through it. His few memories of its inception weren't even painful, just flat.

He was fine. He could talk about it.

He really did shrug then, almost accidently dislodging Shane's head from his shoulder in the process. "I was stupid, and significantly more reckless than I am now. I tried to con Maul. When he caught me, he had his subordinates do it while he watched."

Shane sat up. "He what?"

Andres saw his panic in the way he tucked his arms around his chest, fingers pressed to the sides of his neck so mechanically it seemed he didn't even know he was doing it. Shane had suffered something he felt was similar under Maul's hands, and it clearly lingered in his bones, haunting him. But Andres's turning had done the opposite for him. "He saw something in me that he thought he could use," he said. "And we both know I'm stronger now that I've turned. I'm not afraid of him."

"People *die* from the turning," Shane protested. His lower lip quivered.

"I didn't die." Nausea twisted in Andres's stomach, and he fought the urge to run his fingers through his own hair by playing with Shane's instead. He'd been doing that more and more lately, and it felt solid. Felt like existing.

"Andres…"

"I'm fine, I promise." He was done talking about this. He cupped Shane's chin and kissed him between his tight brows, then along the side of his nose, following the trail of his freckles across to his temples. Shane didn't unfurl himself, but he relaxed enough that Andres could fit his hands beneath Shane's and press them away from his neck. He bared his teeth, letting his fang graze down Shane's jaw, into the soft space just beneath. "And I'd much rather not be human if it means I can do this to you," he whispered, giving Shane's hair the softest tug on one side.

Shane trembled as he breathed out, and he went limp in Andres's grasp, allowing Andres to tip his head until his neck was laid bare, pale skin and light freckles and the small purpling bruises of his ill-closed bite at the club with the gentle pulsing of blood beneath. Andres kissed him just above the place he'd bitten last, then just below, circling the spot so gently that by the time he'd finished, Shane was shuddering against him, fingers gripping in his shirt like that was the only thing holding him to this plane.

"What a magnificent constellation you are, my pet." Andres left a little possessive growl in his voice. "I'm going to bite you now."

"Please," Shane muttered. "Please, take from me anything you desire."

The offer—the demand, for that was what it was, bundled in Shane's submission and his beautiful vulnerability—was everything Andres had ever wanted. Just before he sank in his fangs, he whispered back, "I desire all of you."

He drank Shane up, gentle and purposeful, and took him in, every soft sound and beautiful line and the intoxicating scent. Holding him close, knowing that he wanted this, not merely from a masked felon but from Andres, was intoxicating, euphoric. He swore he felt like himself, fully and utterly, vampiric and genderless and powerful, for the first time in… ever.

He took his time sealing the wound after, the knitting of Shane's skin with each tender kiss and press of tongue seeming to heal something in Andres too.

As he licked the last of the blood off his lips, he realized Shane tasted slightly different. Less sweet than usual. He didn't put the pieces together, though, until Shane nearly collapsed when he tried to stand up after, and Andres felt his life flash before his eyes. He helped lower him back down.

"Your glucose!" Andres's voice quavered, and for once, he didn't care.

Shane seemed far less worried. "I should have eaten something when I first got back," he grumbled, checking the glucose app on his phone. He scowled at the number it gave him. "Fuck."

"I'll get your juice," Andres said, and bolted for the kitchen.

He sat with Shane while he drank and half-carried him to the bathroom after, collecting his pajamas as Shane peed.

Andres had to argue him into brushing his teeth, but five minutes later, he was laying Shane into his bed with a kiss.

"You're such a mom," Shane complained.

"It's the gender nonsense," Andres replied.

Shane laughed.

As Andres tried to step back, though, Shane grabbed for his hand, giving it a soft squeeze. "Stay until I fall asleep."

"I wasn't going anywhere," Andres reassured him. He stole a pillow and blanket from the mound beside the twin-sized mattress, and—wishing sulkily for his massive bed back home, not to watch Shane writhe naked but to cuddle him up with his soft pajamas and tired smile—he settled on the ground, fingers still laced through Shane's.

Shane was his, for real now. If he could help it, now would last a very long time.

21

SHANE

Shane swore he was dreaming again.

He could smell his vampire's floral perfume and feel the delightful tingle of his kiss, as sure and strong as if it had happened that night. The warmth that pressed against Shane's side and fitted under his head rose and fell in slow, relaxing motions. Shane drew his fingers over silky clothes and found skin. He snuggled deeper.

As the haze of sleep began to dissipate, warm sunlight peeking through his eyelids, it didn't take his vampire's presence with it. The realization settled on him like a sigh, soft and sweet. Exactly how his life was meant to be.

They were together now: he and Andres.

They wanted the same things. Wanted to make space for both their shared kink and an equal and honest relationship. Wanted to turn the weird obsessive thing they'd started with into a lasting, healthy love. That was far more magnificent than anything Shane could have gotten out of a predator taking him from behind in the night... especially since he was pretty sure Andres would oblige that fantasy too, if Shane asked.

He grinned against his vampire's shoulder, and finally cracked his eyes open. They both lay on the floor, tangled in half of Shane's sheet and an old blanket. Morning light streamed across the mattress and cascaded over the coffee table that butted up against their other side, catching on Andres's hair and drawing a golden line across his face. He was so beautiful like that, sun-kissed and sleeping. But as Shane watched, he spotted the pinched areas of Andres's expression.

With a pained groan that sounded a little like a no, Andres rolled away from the sun. A shiver trembled through him, and he settled again, Shane in his arms and his body tense. He felt... warm. Warm like a fever.

Oh god.

The sun.

Fuck.

Shane scrambled out of his vampire's arms, diving across the bed for the blinds. He slammed them closed with such force that something in their cords snapped. The apartment's other window was smaller, looking out into the tight alley where the light barely reached, but he closed that one too before hurrying to Andres's side.

Andres, who still hadn't woken.

Oh god.

"Andres?" Shane brushed back his vampire's hair, his heart pounding so hard he could barely hear his own voice. "My love, please."

Shane shook him, panic fueling the motion.

In a blink, he was shoved against the coffee table, pain roaring through his back for the second time in twelve hours. Andres crouched before him, and while their legs were still tangled, he seemed so far away suddenly, his eyes wide and his chest heaving, fangs out. As his gaze settled properly on Shane, he cursed.

"I'm sorry. I forget my... my strength," he muttered and reached out a hand to Shane.

As Shane slipped his fingers into his, Andres flinched. Another little shudder went through him. Shane shifted closer. "Is it the sun? I didn't think to close the blinds until just now. I'm a terrible boyfriend."

"It's fine." Slowly, Andres straightened himself, pulling his body up to sit on the edge of the bed. He looked unsteady but when Shane reached to help him, he battered the offer away. "I mean it, I'm fine. I've had far worse."

You don't look fine, Shane wanted to say.

Andres must have picked up on his hesitation, because he smiled weakly. "I have a little pain, but look, no shaking." He held out his hand as though to demonstrate. "The aches have always been the worst part for me, but that's easy to work through."

"Blood helps, doesn't it?" Shane asked. "I feel great, if you want to feed?"

"Maybe after your breakfast and insulin."

"That will be fifteen minutes."

This time the quirk of Andres's lips looked more genuine. "I'm not dying, pet. And some food would do me good, too."

Shane grumbled all the way to the kitchen, but exactly sixteen and a half minutes later, he sat in Andres's lap, nibbling on a toaster waffle while his vampire lapped at his neck. It felt so normal that it caught in his chest, like just existing in that quiet domesticity was filling a place in his heart he hadn't realized had been empty. There were sexual pieces of their relationship that he'd missed in previous ones—and the way Andres could so casually slide fangs into Shane's neck first thing in the morning and trace the skin along the lip of his pajama pants in between bites of breakfast were certainly doing things for him—but he'd missed this too, this *comfort*. Not being made to feel like he needed to tone down who he was or quietly conduct his insulin routines out of sight. Hell, Andres would probably help him with his testosterone too.

And it wasn't that his vampire withheld all judgment— they were certainly side eyeing the general clutter Shane had let pile back up over the weeks—but it was as if each objectionable part of Shane only made Andres care for him more.

The blood must have helped, or perhaps Andres truly was as fine as they claimed, because as soon as Shane had finished eating, they licked his bite closed and pressed a red kiss to his temple, and, to Shane's delight, his vampire set about cleaning the apartment. Andres ignored the sunlight that still slipped in from between the closed blinds and save for an occasional wince that could have been about anything, and a momentary meltdown over a spider they forced Shane to remove from the premises while they hovered on tiptoes at a distance, they did seem fine.

Fine enough to start ordering Shane around.

Andres pointed to the pile of old stuff in the corner. "Why is this still here?"

"I was going to take it to the thrift shop down the street, but it just looked so sad at the thought of leaving me..."

"You're outrageous," Andres grumbled, pressing their lips to Shane's hair. They picked up the entire load in one arm and headed for the door.

"Andres, the *sun.*"

"It'll be five minutes," they replied, already twisting the handle.

"Andres!" Shane scolded. "I'm perfectly capable of taking it out."

"All right." But Andres didn't move from the door, staring Shane down like a predator on the hunt.

Shane groaned. He maneuvered to them, hopping over the cat's toys and a stack of unread books and a pile of trash Andres had collected, and accepted the over-full donations box. "Fuck you."

Andres kissed him properly, slipping one fang into Shane's lip just enough to deliver a blissful dose of venom that tingled like a caress between Shane's legs. They whispered against Shane's mouth after, "I'll do your laundry."

"Fuck *me*," Shane responded.

Andres grinned, gripping his chin possessively. "Oh, don't worry, my pet. I fully plan on taking over every little piece of you in time."

Somehow Shane made it to the thrift shop and back. When he returned, Andres was in the building's basement, doing Shane's laundry, so he started on one of the five useless clickbait articles he was supposed to finish that day, in between checking his phone for messages from Tara or their contact. Two-thirty in the afternoon, and still nothing.

"Aren't you worried?" he asked when Andres returned.

They shrugged. "It's only been sixteen hours. Give it another three. Then I'll be worried."

But Shane couldn't maintain that kind of calm. Between what Andres had told him of the vampires' valiant escape the night before, and Shane's stand with the humans, they figured the Starlight Club had come out with limited casualties—limited being an unfortunately non-zero number. But that didn't mean nothing else had followed the vampires home. And now more than ever, Tara's contacts should have been willing to speak up. They had no guarantees, though.

He tried to remind himself that even if this fell through, they still had the Vitalis-Barron spring gala coming up—the Met-inspired one. But the more they knew before attending, the better that night was bound to go. And if anything was going to change long term, they'd need all the help they could get.

With his thoughts constantly swarming back to Vitalis-Barron, Shane finally gave up the clickbait in favor of his vampire article, transcribing Tara's interview and bulking up his outline, sifting through the records of everyone he'd spoken to over the last few months to connect the dots and back up Tara's pain and fear and hope. He shot Andres questions in between, to no avail.

"What did you think of the Starlight Club?"

"You can figure that out yourself, pet."

"How does having a safe space for vampires to express themselves *as* vampires affect the overall community?"

"No comment."

"Does the secrecy necessary for the Starlight Club's survival detract from its advantages?"

"Shane, please." He looked up from the shelf he was re-organizing. Had there always been this much space in Shane's apartment? Andres was clearly some kind of dimensional wizard, with a side of cat-whisperer, The Heathen having curled up at his feet any time he stopped moving for more than three minutes. He had gone entirely still now, his expression dark. "You know what I think? That secrecy is paramount. That the more the human society knows about this, the harder it will be for us to hold onto it. It's one of the few good things we have. If they were on the lookout for the Starlight Club—god forbid, if they knew where it would be and when it would be there—they would come for us, like Vitalis-Barron is already doing. Maybe they wouldn't bring weapons, not at first. Maybe they'd just bring their hate, their insults, their statements of death. But words don't stay words for long."

"We have words too."

"And who will listen?"

"I will," he insisted. "And others like me."

A tragic twist came into Andres's lips. "I'm afraid there is no one else quite like you, pet."

Shane didn't know how to object to that. He leaned his forehead into a hand. "Well, how do you feel about Maul monopolizing the blood trade in this city in order to rip off his own community?"

"Don't ask me that," Andres snapped. "You're human—you don't *get* to ask me that."

The growl in his voice caught Shane off guard, sending a chill along his skin and lifting his hairs like he was a prey-thing. He *was* a prey-thing. But then Andres's brow tightened and guilt overwhelmed his features.

"I'm sorry," he said. "I didn't mean to scare you."

"I know." Shane smiled. "And I get that this is not entirely my place. It's *why* I'm asking questions. You know, you're not the only one whose life has been treated as expendable? My rights—rights to who *I* am as a trans man and the substance that keeps *me* alive as a diabetic—are also treated like things to be granted and taken away on the whims of governments and corporations and religions. And that doesn't make it appropriate for me to probe into your community's pain; I have my own privileges. But I know what I've experienced, and I want to know what you have too, because maybe we can be stronger together, if we understand each other."

Andres looked down at the drawer. His fingers moved, sifting through the same three objects he'd been failing to sort since they started this discussion. "Maul ripping off the vampiric community hurts," he whispered. "It *kills me* to know that there are vampires going hungry because of him, and it kills me even more because he wouldn't be able to do this at all if our larger, human-populated society didn't maintain the system he works under. The system *I* work under, too. But what else am I supposed to do?" He looked at Shane then, pleading.

Considering how many half-written clickbait articles he had to finish by tonight in order to keep his health insurance, Shane thought he understood that. But he didn't have an answer for it. He asked instead, "What else do you *want* to do?"

"I don't know."

"Would you leave his business? If there was a better place, or a better way, would you risk it all to reach that?" Shane asked. Andres's nails dug into the pack of expired batteries he was sorting, and it made Shane's heart hurt as though it were the center of his own chest that his vampire gripped. Gently, he added, "It's not just this city's impoverished vampires he's hurt, but you too."

Andres dropped the items in his hands, running his fingers through his hair in a motion so rushed it looked painful. He shook his head. "No more than anyone else who works for him. Less, even."

Somehow, Shane didn't think that was true.

The text finally came at nine-seventeen that night.

Unknown Number

Hey, Tara said you wanted to talk to my fiancé and I? There's not a lot we can tell you, but if you want to meet up, I can probably arrange that. Wesley works until six on weekdays, so maybe after his dinner? We can grab some horchata? That's safer than coming to our place. Let me know what you think.

By the way this is Vincent Barnes.

The black heart he sent after his final message made Shane like him instantly. They scheduled a meeting for the following night, and Andres went home to feed his cat and work on a few of the upcoming blood acquisition plans he'd promised Maul he'd get to. Shane almost volunteered to come with him, but the chaos he'd put his body through was finally taking a toll, and he still had a thousand words he was supposed to write about a product he was pretty sure was not made to massage *bananas*. He opted for a lingering kiss at the door instead, with promises that Andres would grab dinner with him before their meeting with Vincent and Wesley.

The bruises along his back hurt as he settled into his desk chair.

He'd startled Andres. That was all.

After his vampire had taken such care never to grab him with more than the lightest of touches, never to push or twist, even the prick of his fangs always coming with a rush of venom, the shoving wasn't like him. It had to have been an accident. Just an accident that had happened twice in twelve hours…

22

Andres could not keep his nerves together.

He wasn't normally like this—not before a con, or a theft, or even a seduction. The knowledge that they would be talking to their only lead into Vitalis-Barron soon, the one thread he'd followed so hard to get here, was wearing on him, certainly. But the thing that kept fluttering up his stomach and tightening his lungs was far simpler, and somehow even more important: their pre-meeting dinner was, technically, his first date with Shane.

They hadn't gone out together like this before, no mask, no pretenses, their goals for a future—a normal, healthy future—stated out loud. Things had felt easy and natural back at Shane's apartment, but they had both been preoccupied with their own tasks, delegating them to different spaces, physically if not mentally. But now...

Andres could no longer ignore how pathetically his body had been reacting to Shane's sudden touches—his grabbing on the boardwalk and his shaking of Andres yesterday. Even that little pressure had ignited in Andres's mind like agony, like anguish, all his vampiric strength rising at once to throw the feeling off. And it had hurt Shane in the process. Shane, who did not deserve that.

Andres would just have to contain himself better. Keep enough distance. But not too much distance.

Just *how much* distance was the right amount when out on a public first date with your bought-blood-turned-willing-role-play-slave who also wanted a normal relationship on the main?

Andres checked the time as he pulled into the lot for the little Mexican hole-in-the-wall he was supposed to meet Shane at. He was twenty-three minutes early. Huh. Better that than late, at least.

He opened his phone, shooting a quick *here early, let me know when you pull up* text to Shane before flipping to his thread with his only decent cousin.

Cat Mom

Going on a first date, can you believe it?

(Okay so technically we know each other already and we've kissed before but it's the first Real Date and I'm FREAKING OUT.)

Hell Creature Extraordinaire

Ugh, you suck. (Congrats bitch!)

What's he like? I need all the deets!

And more importantly, what are you wearing?

Cat Mom

He's brilliant and messy, adorable freckles, sharp as fuck but does as he's told (you know, in the sexy way.) And in the limited time I've known him, I already can't imagine life without him, so there's that.

I'm dressed like a fashion devil, obviously.

He sent a selfie after, the camera angled down at himself, still sitting behind the wheel in the leather and rose-lace jacket he'd had on during his run-in with Shane at the Fishnettery—now that he could finally wear it without giving himself away—over a sheer crop top, with his dangling necklace from the Starlight Club, and a pair of simple studs in his ears, black on one side and red on the other. His thick black leggings were mostly out of view, but they could not possibly have been tighter, filtering into lace around the calves, the muscles accentuated by the heel of his sandals. It was a more feminine look than he usually wore outside the security of his own home, but Shane had told him that he was magnificent, and Andres wanted to share this with him, this wonderful, beautiful, magnificent part of himself. As anxious as he was, he felt real in his own skin, like all the pieces of himself had come together for this.

Hell Creature Extraordinaire

You're such a NERD.

(I love it, though. I'd still kill for one of those jackets, you know.)

Cat Mom

Then people might realize I'm related to you!

Hell Creature Extraordinaire

I haven't seen you in person in like a fucking year, I don't think people even know we've ever met.

Honestly, I forgot what you looked like until that selfie.

Cat Mom

Way to guilt trip?

He meant it to be teasing, but there was a very real pang in his chest that told him otherwise. He missed her, regardless of his fear that she'd figure out what he was. And beneath that, he worried that perhaps there was another reason he'd pulled away, one that had nothing to do with her, and everything to do with him. This distance felt safer. Far fewer things could hurt him over text.

Cat Mom

Yes, fine, we can hang out soon. We'll see a movie or something, like the old days.

Hell Creature Extraordinaire

You know my parents still blame you for corrupting me. I think CPS now arrests teenage boy-appearing individuals who take their child cousin to R-rated shit just to watch her laugh at the blood.

Cat Mom

I needed the emotional support, okay. You were always braver.

(I miss spending time with you, though. I really do mean it when I say we should go out.)

Also I saw someone who looked like the pics of your newest boyfriend last night and it tripped me so hard.

Hell Creature Extraordinaire

Ha, maybe it WAS him. (The fucker.)

I know we're in an open relationship so it's not technically cheating, but god, it does kind of feel like cheating when he's all mysterious about where he's been and shit.

It's fine though, you know? It's just a rough spot.

When he looked up, Andres spotted Shane hovering around the entrance of the place with his phone, somehow making his simplistic green t-shirt and ragged brown scarf look like a fashion statement with half his dirty-blonde waves pulled up and his long lashes catching the streetlights. Andres couldn't help but smile. As he watched, the text came through: *Here! Just took my insulin so we should get onto the food <3 Hyped for this Cali Burrito.*

Cat Mom

My date's arrived, but I promise popcorn is on me next.

(Love you, Natalie.)

Hell Creature Extraordinaire
Love you too, you idiot.

He slid out of the car and jogged to the front of the shop, opening the door for Shane with a little bow. "My dear Cygnus."

"Thanks," Shane laughed. His gaze traveled down Andres's outfit, lingering on the tight lines and revealed skin. He sucked his lower lip into his mouth like it was an impulse and the softest flush bloomed on his cheeks. "You look magnificent."

"As do you," Andres replied.

And everything seemed all right—seemed normal.

Andres let Shane order and collect their food—a pair of medium horchatas, a California burrito, and the plain cheese quesadilla that Andres could reasonably assume had not a pinch of garlic in it—and waited for him to slide into one of the old red plastic booths that hugged the shop's tiny stall before sitting down across from him.

Shane handed over his phone. "This won't take long, I promise."

"I'm happy to watch you rate things all day."

"You're an enabler."

"I cleaned your apartment."

"A better life enabler, then."

"I am going to do incredible things to one specific part of your life, that's for certain." Andres grinned and purposefully licked the canine where his fang would normally sit.

He could almost feel the way Shane shuddered, the little inhale as his imagination surely ran as wild as Andres's. They hadn't planned on going home together tonight, but it would happen at some point. For now, Andres was thrilled just to edge Shane along, to play cat and mouse with him like they had all the time in the world. Andres wanted that stable future with Shane more than he'd ever wanted anything else: wanted to keep filming his *Rate Things* videos for him and watching the little flush build beneath his freckles and smirking as he ran the top of his foot along Shane's ankle beneath the table, binding them together with a casual touch. He turned the camera onto Shane and started filming.

Shane was a natural, his smile bright and his expression just a little cheeky. "We're at *Jaramillo's*, and this time I've got my incredible partner—that's the spicy kind, yes—behind the camera." He gave a little wave. "Say hello to the fine people back home?"

Andres grunted a *mmhmm* and zoomed in on Shane's lips, settling there long enough to catch the roll and shine of them and remember what it had felt like to pull the lower one into his own mouth, fangs sinking in. He hummed in satisfaction again.

"Or make a noise, I guess." Shane shrugged. "He's good at those, if you know what I mean. Breaks the scale for sounds that will make you—"

"Shane!" Andres snapped.

His little swan only smirked and began unwrapping the California burrito from its paper, before opening up the tortilla to get a close up at the contents within: French fries, steak, sour cream, guacamole, and a scattering of cheese. "Let's see how this bad boy compares to our last three attempts." Then, he began fishing out the fries and eating them solo.

Andres watched in wonder as his boyfriend gave a thoughtful sound.

"Crispy outside despite the burrito-fication, good internal temperature—a little grainy, though. It's picked up a sufficient amount of sour cream but the guac just isn't sticking. Look at that? You still need *some* clumping to successfully eat your guac with de-burritto'ed fries, but this is outrageous. I give it a six out of ten for French fries unstuffed from a burrito, with a bonus half a star for the crack in the shop's front window that looks weirdly like a bullet hole." He scooped up a few pieces of the meat from his open pile of pickings, placing it into his mouth with a sensual roll of his tongue and lick of his lips. "Mm, carne asada is good though. You know I do like myself some meat." With that, he *winked*.

Andres stifled a laughing snort as he shut off the video. "You're going to turn yourself into a thirst trap like that."

"Are you jealous?"

He shrugged. "Just don't let any of them bite you."

"I would never." Shane rewrapped his burrito and shoved a proper bite into his mouth.

Andres started on his quesadilla, cursing how common an ingredient garlic—even just the powered form—was in most modern cuisines. There was more than one reason he hadn't had a sit-down meal with either side of his primarily Mediterranean family since he'd turned. The fresh tortillas were fantastic though, and sitting there, watching Shane as they ate, was absolutely joyous.

"I do want to donate to that blood bank in Ala Santa again though," Shane said between bites. "I think you mentioned you'd ehem, *take care* of me afterward?"

"Your apartment will be *so* clean," Andres teased.

"Villain." Shane grinned, reaching across the table for one of Andres's hands.

Andres's lungs tightened and panic shot through him. He restrained himself enough to merely pull back, but the adrenaline remained, pounding like a war drum through his chest. Over something so slight, so ridiculous? His soul wanted to scream, and his body wanted to cry, one hand frantically pushing back his hair like it was part of someone else's arm. God, fuck, what was *wrong* with him?

Shane watched him in confusion, and Andres forced himself to reach out in his place, pushing through the pointless anxiety to draw his fingertips over the back of Shane's hand and encircle his wrist tenderly. He gave the softest squeeze. Shane didn't look quite satisfied, but the couple who'd been at the counter for the last few minutes interrupted them.

"Hey, um, if you're not Shane and Andres, this is going to be super weird," the man in front said, both thumbs looped into his jean pockets. He wore a shirt with a set of fangs and the phrase *Bite me baby!*, and his grin seemed to fill up his broad jaw like it was meant to be there. "I'm Wesley, this is my Vincent."

"His fiancé, named Vincent," his dark-haired companion clarified, like this was a common introduction mishap.

"Hi. I'm Shane, yeah."

Vincent blinked, fiddling with his fingerless glove. "Do I know you from somewhere?"

A hint of pink appeared in Shane's cheeks. "I post rating videos online?"

"I don't think that's it…"

"Maybe I just look like someone else?" Shane shrugged. "My memory for faces isn't the best though, I'll be honest."

"After the first time we met, he obsessed over me for months, and he still didn't recognize me when we ran into each other at a bar," Andres explained.

Wesley cackled, a bold, exuberant sound that was thoroughly joyous and seemed to light up his fiancé's face as well as his own. "Vincent had to hang out with one of our vamp friend's boyfriend *three times* before he realized the man had *literally* saved his life before."

Vincent groaned. "I'm never living that down, am I?"

"Never." But the way Wesley smiled at him was all affection and sunshine, like the blushing vampire was the one thing that held his world together, and his fiancé looked back at him with all the joy and adoration of someone who knew their partner inside and out and loved every last dusty corner and broken piece of hardware. It was so soft and sweet, so healthy, and Andres envied it. He and Shane would have that someday, he decided. He'd make it true, anxiety be dammed.

Vincent's brow shot up. "The library, last fall! You asked me about memes or something."

"What, really?" Shane laughed. "I do kind of remember that. I was pissed about the fluff piece I'd been assigned."

"Right, yeah, it was a vampire thing. You wanted to focus on the framing of vampirism in the media but they wouldn't let you." Vincent whistled. "Fuck, I guess you really are a journalist then."

"It's not like we were doubting or anything," Wesley clarified, in a way that sounded like they were *definitely* doubting. "And you want to know about—"

Vincent cut him off with a poke in the side. "Maybe not *here*."

"He's right," Andres said. "Can we walk?"

He finished up the last few bites of his burrito while Shane wrapped his for later, and together they headed outside, walking along the edge of the quiet strip mall. Vincent and Wesley passed their horchata back and forth between sips. The spring night air was still a shade chilly, but it didn't bother Andres the way it would have before his turning. Shane tucked his bare arms across his chest, though, fluffing up his scarf. Andres swore a little string of metal glimmered beneath the fabric around his neck, and his heart skipped before realizing it was a regular old necklace, not the rose gold of Shane's collar.

Andres slid his jacket off, wrapping it around Shane's shoulders without a word. He received the softest kiss in return, leaving his lips to tingle pleasantly and his heart beating to a new, happy thrum.

"Vitalis-Barron," Andres said, "tell me about it. What was the security like? How did you break in? Do they have records—proof of what they're up to? Photographic evidence? Anything?"

"The lab's in the lowest basement level, but there's a couple of security people in the building with the elevator that leads there—or there was when we entered. I don't know if they've increased that since. There's also the stairs we took out, but the doors only open one way." Wesley shrugged. "We didn't really *break* in exactly. I passed Vincent off as a vampire I'd caught for them, and after I was finished poking around for the info I wanted, I just kind of released the vampires they had imprisoned there."

Andres stopped alongside his brain, the whole system coming to a crashing halt of confusion and horror. "Fucking hell. That worked?"

"In hindsight, I think we just got like really, really lucky."

293

"You *think*." Andres rubbed a hand up his face, like that could ground himself to the stupidity of these amateurs. "Had you ever run a con like that before?"

Wesley lifted a brow. "That's considered a con? Does that mean Vinny and I are con artists now? I should put that on my resume."

"Clearly not," Andres grumbled. "Con artists have at least some skill in the trade."

"You're so offended, it's adorable." Shane wrapped his arm through Andres's, and Andres managed not to flinch under the suddenness of the motion.

It felt right once he'd settled there, though, not the threatening grip Andres's mind seemed determined to interpret it as. "This leaves the Vitalis-Barron Met-inspired gala as our best option still."

"We were already planning to go," Shane said.

"To generally poke around, yes. But without a plan or more thorough knowledge of the complex, it's unlikely I can get us anywhere useful."

"I know a vamp who used to work there," Wesley said. "Maybe he could help?"

Andres's heart did a little leap—a smaller, more hesitant one than it had when Tara had sent them here, and Shane had sent them to Tara before that.

Vincent nudged Wesley in the arm, and Wesley glared at him. A silent battle seemed to wage between them, then Wesley sighed, and Vincent turned back to Andres. "We did get something from Vitalis-Barron while we were there. It might not help you with your break in, but it could be useful for Shane."

Wesley grunted in the back of his throat. "It's a list of all the vampires they'd captured; test logs and death dates and everything. But the fact that I have it—that I haven't given it to anyone—is the only reason Vitalis-Barron hasn't come after us yet. We weren't exactly sneaky."

"Fucking hell," Andres repeated, because the situation kept calling for it. He really had to stop getting his hopes up just to crush them.

But Shane seemed to be taking the news with the opposite mentality. "Do you understand what logs like that could mean? If they got to the right people? If the whole city could look at the data and connect the dots? Saying Vitalis-Barron has an unethical lab hidden in their basement means nothing, but showing the whole city—the whole world— exactly what experiments they're running and who they're hurting would be substantial. It could make people stand up against them. It could stop them for good."

"Or, it could barely hinder them, with their money and lawyers backing their every move," Andres objected. "And we'd have ruined the lives of two innocent people, people from my—from our community."

"Look, if it was just me on the line, I'd happily go to jail in order to get the truth out there. But if they take Vincent..." Wesley shook his head. "You didn't see that place. It was..."

"Tara explained some," Shane said, his voice soft with sorrow.

Vincent tucked his face against his human's neck, kissing his skin softly, and Andres didn't know two people could look so sad and so happy at the same time outside of a Renaissance painting.

"We won't do anything that will hurt either of you," Andres promised. "We are not in the business of trading lives."

"What if we focus on Vincent's capture and escape as part of the article?" Shane asked. "Then at least if Vitalis-Barron comes for him, everyone will know who to blame. From what we've gathered, they've been purposefully taking vampires with limited connections—we connect Vincent to the whole city, and it'll be far harder for them to touch him and get away with it." He frowned, his focus shifting to Wesley. "I know this doesn't help you. If Vincent was just there as a prop, he could avoid charges, but they might still come after you for—"

"Fuck that." Wesley's words were sharp, his tone immovable. "I will suffer whatever comes, as long as it means this city's vampires can sleep safer at night. That *my* vampire can sleep safer."

Vincent wrapped an arm around him, pleading softly, "Wes, no…"

Wesley shook his head—shook from his core outward— not the way Shane did, from fear or exhilaration, but with a fierce, boiling rage. "We have to. I don't want you to lose me, even for a few months or years. I—" He broke off, drawing in a ragged breath. "I would hate that with everything in me.

You are my heart just as I'm your blood. But how many vampires have lost everything because of Vitalis-Barron?" He turned fully toward Vincent, cupping the side of his fiancé's face with such a perfect mix of tender affection and intense fire that it nearly masked the sadness in his voice. "We protected ourselves. We gave ourselves time, and it's been incredible—the best six months of our lives. But we can't be selfish forever."

"We could leave," Vincent protested. His eyes glistened.

"Babe." Wesley spoke the word like it was theirs and theirs only. "We both came back to San Salud because as much as it hurt, we didn't want to be anywhere else."

"I know." Vincent pressed his lips against Wesley's palm, just standing there, breathing him in. It seemed like a moment Andres and Shane shouldn't have been witnessing, but as Vincent muttered, "I hate this," he turned his attention back to them. Though his fire was colder than Wesley's, it burned every bit as strong. "You say you can get into the upcoming gala?"

"Yes," Andres answered, and he could feel Shane's tension and anticipation like it was his own.

Vincent breathed in, then back out. "Dr. Blood—Vitalis-Barron's head of research—is doing more than just the hideous work that's happening in their basement lab. She offered our friend a research position on a special project after he was fired. He turned it down but…"

"Now you want to know what it is," Andres finished for him.

Vincent nodded. His arms wrapped tighter around his fiancé, who leaned into him, neck exposed and eyes alight with something murderous. Wesley replied in his vampire's place. "It's a wild card, one that could take her down, or take us with it. It's not worth dying over. But if you were already prepared to go then, hell, let's see what we find."

Shane lifted his gaze to meet Andres's, a fierce grin on his face. "You up for a little investigative journalism?"

Andres kissed him, a soft brush of lips as he replied. "Only if you're down for a crime."

Shane sighed his acceptance.

"Regardless of what happens," Vincent cut in, "promise me one thing?"

"Of course," Shane replied, and Andres echoed him, his heart and mind in unison. Whatever the sacrifice, whatever the cost. If these two were risking their lives together to help the greater vampire community, then he could too.

His face still half buried in his fiancé's hair, Vincent's lips parted, his fangs slipping down in a baring so feral it would have sent shivers down Andres's spine before he'd turned. "Promise me you'll make those villains pay in the end."

23

SHANE

Make those villains pay.

Vincent's challenge had been lingering in Shane's mind, bobbing in and out like a tide along the shore. With it, it brought a determination for the inverse: to give back to the people those villains had hurt. Villains like Vitalis-Barron, but also Frederick Maul, and the entire city who'd made their vampiric population scrounge for blood in the shadows. Vengeance alone wasn't justice—even if Vitalis-Barron certainly had to be stopped. But there were things beyond their destruction that needed doing, and Shane was in the perfect position to step into one of them now, because, as it turned out, the vampire who'd worked at the pharmaceutical company until recently was the same one who ran Jose's Blood Bank.

A softly glowing *blood available* sign sat in the building's large, tinted and curtained front window, two little fangs poking from the bottoms of the *o*s.

They'd called ahead, to be sure that ex-Vitalis-Barron scientist Dr. Clementine Hughes would be there, but as

Andres was about to hang up, Shane had taken the phone on impulse. "Do you have a phlebotomist in at that time?" he'd asked, ignoring his sudden instinct to tuck his arm in close. "I'd like to donate again."

He was ready—ready to give back to the vampires of San Salud who'd already lost so many of their own. He had plenty of blood to spare, his glucose levels managed well enough that losing some wouldn't bother him, especially with Andres's venom to pick him back up. It was just a little needle prick.

The crook of Shane's arm still tingled uncomfortably as he skirted past the line of vampires waiting inside the blood bank. He tried to focus on the pressure of Andres's hand against his back, on his nearness. His protection. Nobody here would dream of trying to take Shane's blood without his permission, but if they did, he had someone ready to fight for him.

The phlebotomist met them at the front counter, escorting them both to a secluded donation chair in the farthest end of the large, portioned-off room. The arched wood ceiling crested over them and a display case of unusual salt and pepper shakers separated them from the next chair over. Shane's nerves roiled as he sat down. The phlebotomist crossed the room to collect supplies, and Shane focused on the eccentric display, comically rating the shakers in his head. Two stars for originality, two for creatively coordinating the salt versus the pepper, one for whether they reminded him of needles or blood bags. The air tasted a little stale. What the hell was taking the phlebotomist so long? She couldn't possibly have that many supplies to collect. It wasn't like they intended to bleed him dry.

Shane found himself tugging at his shirt collar, then running his fingers through the ends of his hair.

Andres hadn't bothered to put on his contacts that morning, and he watched Shane from behind his glass's sleek, boxy rims with a worried look. "Are you all right, my swan?"

"I'm fine," Shane responded automatically.

The lie didn't seem to placate his vampire. "You know," Andres said, gently, "they *will* want to access your veins somehow."

Shane huffed, like that would clear the tightness that was building in his lungs. "I've done this before, yes." He dragged his arms down, forming an ex of protection across his chest. He had asked for this. He was ready. Besides, the best way to keep riding was to get back on the metaphorical horse, wasn't it?

Andres looked like he was prepared to argue, but in the end he only pressed a kiss into Shane's hair. "May I?" he asked, touching Shane's hands with all the tenderness in the world.

The affection melted Shane, dimming the buzz of anxiety beneath his skin. "Please," he whispered.

Andres pressed his lips to one of Shane's knuckles before gripping gently onto his wrist. "Give me yourself, pet."

The demand felt like the sun's warmth, a stable, eternal heat that bloomed from the center of Shane's chest. He let Andres unfurl one of his arms, felt more than saw the pressure of his vampire's fingers drawing up his skin. His insides still squirmed as Andres's thumb pressed into the soft inner vein of his elbow, but he focused on Andres's face, on his ever possessive and protective presence. *I'm yours*, Shane thought.

And like they were connected, Andres murmured it, "You're mine."

Shane leaned back in his chair, one arm still folded against his chest, and dwelled on the sensation of Andres tracing up and down his vein. When the motion shifted upward and a gloved hand took the place of his vampire's fingertips, tightening the tourniquet and applying the sanitation wipe, Shane kept focusing on Andres's touch. He could do this. He was ready.

He just wouldn't look.

So he kept his eyes closed and thought of his vampire. He could not quite pretend the prick of the needle was anything but cold metal. A fresh flash of panic rolled through him, quelled only by Andres's voice, his breath hot on Shane's ear. "You're safe."

A few more seconds, and the worst part was over. Now just came the waiting.

This was good. The blood he was giving now was life-sustaining, and he would *not* think of Maul's needle, or the feeling of his goons' fangs sinking into his skin, or the slow panic of his consciousness slipping—slipping—slipping.

Shane made the mistake of opening his eyes, trying to find Andres's face again. Instead his gaze latched onto the machine his donated blood was rocking in, the sterile plastic and the slowly filling red. His mind went to another room, another night, the bags beside him filling and filling and filling, switched out again and again as he struggled and cried and eventually succumbed to the blackness.

"Shane," Andres murmured, worry in his voice. It latched onto Shane, grimy fangs lodging deep into his flesh. His very existence in this reality seemed to spin. And still his blood was pouring out of him, too much too fast. Like last time.

"Andres," Shane choked. His eyes were open—he'd opened them, he swore—but half his vision was dark spots like the world had been hollowed out, like his chest, like his veins. He suffocated on it, barely forcing out the words. "I can't—"

He'd hardly moved his lips when the catheter slipped free of his arm, a warm pressure replacing it. His vision slowly returned in flickers and crackles, the room coming back into focus around the phlebotomist dropping the used donation supplies into a red bin and Andres at his side, both hands gripping Shane's arm and a bead of red on his lips from where he must have quickly licked the wound closed instead of letting it be bandaged.

Both of them were speaking to him, gentle but worried.

"You're safe, Shane. Look at me, I've got you. You're safe here."

"How are you feeling? I'm going to lift the footrest and lean the chair back, all right? You're done now, just rest."

Shane felt numb, empty, tight and terrible. His world shifted again as his chair moved, and his senses returned in a proper flood. He gasped in air with a shudder, forcing himself to breathe out slowly. The panic didn't abate entirely, still tingling beneath his skin, his arms tight to his chest again, but the clearer his head grew, the more he could feel a very rational shame sinking in. He managed to force his gaze to his donated blood, hoping perhaps the whole ordeal had taken longer than he'd realized, but the bag had only filled a tenth of the way. It was barely enough to feed a small vampire for a day, and certainly less than Andres was drinking from Shane in a single bite. Not nearly enough to knock him out, even if they'd taken it directly from the vein in his neck.

The darkness had been all in his head.

Shane dragged in a breath, tearing his gaze away. "I didn't finish."

"That's fine, it happens sometimes," the phlebotomist reassured him, smiling. "We don't want anyone to force themselves into a position that makes them uncomfortable or unsafe. Just relax for now. I'm going to get you juice and a snack—does that sound all right?"

"Yes, thank you," Shane said, vacantly, briefly cataloging the insulin he'd need to take to adjust for her offer, though in his head he was still reeling too much to do the math.

He'd thought he was ready for this. He should have been ready. Trembles raced up and down his arms and through his rib cage and it took him a moment to realize that they where: shivers. He tucked his arms all the closer.

"Is it cold in here?" he asked Andres.

Andres responded by stripping off his jacket, draping it over Shane. "If that's not enough, I'm sure they have blankets."

"No, I think this is fine," Shane replied, weakly. Maybe it wasn't, but it smelled like Andres, softly floral, and it lay like a shield over his arms. A protection Shane shouldn't have needed still, a whole month after Maul's assault. "Fuck."

"Shane?" Andres sounded so scared and soft, and he knelt before Shane, a hand securely on Shane's leg. "You're safe. Everything's fine."

"I know," Shane snapped. "But that's the problem. I'm safe. I'm the fucking safest I could possibly be, and I still couldn't put up with a tiny needle prick and a little blood loss I'd have thought nothing of a couple months ago. It's pathetic."

"I don't think that's how this works? I'm certainly no therapist, but it does seem to me that your reactions are perfectly normal. You can't brute-force your body to accept something that's hurt it in the past."

"You did." Shane hadn't meant it like that, or perhaps just hadn't meant to say it out loud, and he felt a bit rude once he had. His own failures had nothing to do with Andres's ability to keep going after the traumatic event that had radically altered the rest of his life. Shane tried to soften his voice, smiling weakly. "I mean, you got over it, didn't you? You started working directly for Maul after he had you turned. And here I can't even engage with something that's barely related to him."

Andres looked confused for a moment. Confused, or... vacant. But then he blinked and his shoulders bobbed upward. He ran a hand through his hair. "Maybe I'm the one who's not normal."

The whole reaction certainly hit Shane as a bit irregular, though perhaps not in the way Andres meant it. It made him feel even worse than before. "I'm sorry. However you handled that trauma after doesn't make it any less potent in the moment."

"You could offer that advice to yourself, too," Andres replied, giving him a weak smile. "You have every right to be hurt. Maul is..." He swallowed and removed his other hand from Shane's thigh to run it through his hair as well. Partway through the motion, he seemed to rethink it, slowly reaching to fiddle with Shane's hair instead. The touch appeared to calm him the same way it did Shane. "He's a bastard. He's been cruel to far more people than me. Crueler to them, I know. I have a special use to him, so he lets me do what I want, rents me my house, even listens to me sometimes. He never really tried to kill me." Andres shrugged. "So it's fine. I'm fine. But you don't have to be."

Fine seemed the wrong word, wrong in ways Shane couldn't quite pinpoint, but that thought was derailed as the phlebotomist returned with a cup of juice and a collection of individually wrapped cookies and snack bars. She was followed by a golden-haired vampire dressed in a wool vest and slacks, a black turtleneck underneath. He wore a contemplative look with it, like he should have been stashed in the back of some dusty library musing on the meaning of life, or teaching Shakespeare to a room of posh graduate students instead of running a blood bank.

Shane felt his cheeks heat as the vampire approached, and he was suddenly conscious of how tightly he was holding his arms, still buried beneath Andres's jacket. He couldn't seem to let go, though. "I'm sorry. I'd donated before, I thought I'd be fine."

"It's all right, truly. That you were willing to try means more to us than the result." The owner—Clementine—didn't smile, but he seemed so sincere that it relaxed Shane. The gentle expression didn't diminish as his gaze fixed on Andres, but his brow lifted. "Oh."

Andres made a short, bemused noise. "First my work, now yours."

"We just can't get away from blood?" The other vampire suggested, as though he wasn't sure whether it was a joke or not.

"I take it your romantic dilemma sorted itself out?"

Clementine smiled in response. "And yours?"

Andres drew a hand through the stray lock around Shane's face, smirking. "Turns out, he remembered me after all."

Whatever they were on about seemed amusing, but Shane could ask his vampire about it later. "Vitalis-Barron?" Shane suggested, trying to shift the topic.

"Right." Clementine nodded. "So you're taking down my old boss together?" He smiled properly then, his fangs out. "How can I be of service?"

Their conversation turned into a three-hour analysis of Vitalis-Barron's security, layout, and employee population—in which it became clear that their security was extreme, their layout annoying, and their employees varied between those who knew the full scope of their villainy and the far larger set, who were only vaguely aware that some samples they received had come from vampires, but not that they might be taken under duress. Sometime around 2 a.m., Clementine's boyfriend appeared with a pizza, and an hour after that their flagrant flirtatious touching, which would have put the couples in the dark corners of the Starlight Club to shame, had grown to the point that Shane and Andres excused themselves.

From there, the planning progressed to a text thread, where the remaining pieces came together little by little.

Dr. Clementine Hughes

On second thought, your best bet is probably to go after Anthony. He's a bastard and a sociopath, but he also had the knowledge to fool Vitalis-Barron for years, and still—somehow—hasn't been fired. I believe I am currently the only person from there who knows he's been stealing from them, but I've decided to keep that information to myself because he still supplies a few nonhumans with medications they can find nowhere else, if only for his own selfish reasons. He's loyal to nothing but the science, so he might not even need much convincing to help you.

He hasn't missed this party since I started, so I imagine he'll be there again. I don't have any more specifics than that though, unfortunately. I've always avoided the biannual galas like the plague.

"We're really doing this," Andres muttered.

Shane glanced at them across the kitchen, catching their gaze for half a second as his vampire finished the dishes. He'd come to Andres's house for once: a place that was, so far as Shane had seen, just as tidy as he'd imagined. He was dying to explore the upstairs—and one particular room in it, his mind still haunted by the image Andres had given Maul nearly a month ago. Shane didn't care to be passed out or literally chained, but he burned at the thought of being laid bare and defenseless in Andres's bed, whimpering and trembling beneath his vampire's whims. If his vampire would make the next move already.

Shane had been imagining it all week—turning those musings into the best series of orgasms he'd ever had, in the bathtub, under the sheets, twice at his desk and even once in the kitchen. Yet Andres still had not tried to do more with him than kiss and nip, their mouth always agonizingly above his collarbone. Shane was about to be very annoyed, and an un-submissive level of demanding, if it continued.

At least he'd had enough else to occupy him, trying to track down the relatives and friends of those who Vitalis-Barron had kidnapped without putting himself in Maul's line of sight. He'd uncovered little enough in the beginning, but the more he searched—and the more of his assigned clickbait articles he ignored—the more he found situations where the murdered individual had people looking for them. He reached out to those he could, though he tried not to press them too hard, to turn up any more grief than he had to. Vitalis-Barron had caused enough pain without Shane adding salt to the wound.

As he worked, he kept coming back to the one oddity among the many, many names—one so-called patient of Vitalis-Barron whose identifier was left blank. They had no defining specifications—Dr. Blood had signed the patient's consent form herself. The study listed for them had only the signifiers *VR Study*. Shane had found ten other vampires enrolled in it, all entering it around the same time, and marked as dead in quick succession after. The mystery patient had no death date, though, vanishing along with the VR Study.

It was so odd—and like the special project Dr. Blood had tried to recruit Clementine onto, it could have been nothing. Or it could have been so much more.

Andres snapped Shane out of his mental wandering with a soft touch to his shoulder. "I should start on your ensemble for Vitalis-Barron's knock-off Met Gala today." They looked almost embarrassed. "What are you most into? I'm sorry I never asked when I designed the first outfit. You could be a suit guy, for all I'd know."

"I hate suits on myself, so you're safe."

It was the great tragedy of Shane's transmasculine life. They just weren't his style, even after transitioning. But then he'd donned the costume Andres had made him for the Starlight Club and felt like the world had aligned for him, letting him be suddenly perfectly beautiful and still perfectly a man; every aesthetic he'd wanted while yearning over Howl from the Ghibli movie and a dozen other beautiful animated boys, while no less the pinnacle of his version of masculinity.

"I love the flowing aspects of my Starlight Club outfit, and the sheer fabric, and the sparkles. I'm not into true dresses, but things that mimic the swirl of a dress when you spin? That's a ten out of ten on the list of mundane things that feel weirdly like magic." It was topped only by the very specific sensation he got from walking one foot after the other in the wind with his arms out, and the pressure of

Andres's fangs when they were just about to prick into his neck.

Andres was staring at that neck now. "And for skin? How much do you feel comfortable showing?"

"It depends on the setting. For the gala, I'd prefer more layers than I wore to the Starlight Club."

"Of course. Work and play are different situations..." Their voice dropped into a growl as they spoke, and they scooted closer, dipping down enough that their lips brushed the top of Shane's ear as they added, "When you're attending my pleasure, though, I get to show off however much of your skin I desire."

The shudder that rolled through Shane was so ecstatic it felt like its own kind of orgasm. "As you say, my love."

That seemed to please his vampire immensely, Andres's fingers coming to drag teasingly along Shane's sides. They settled against his scars, the thin ridges tingling beneath the fabric. "What about these? Do you want them exposed or hidden?"

The timid ecstasy of being touched there, not with hesitation but with affection and desire, tightened in the back of Shane's throat. It wasn't as though his past partners—the few he'd had since his transition—were anything but courteous with him. But they'd remained at an arm's length, people who Shane might, possibly, let touch him, but would never have laid beside his bed as he slept, never have thought of his needs first or treated him like he was something to be treasured. Some of them had fucked him, but not once had they made love.

None of them had made who he was feel like a treasure.

"Exposed," Shane replied, "but only when I'm with you."

"Oh," they said, and Shane thought it was a sound of understanding; of more than that—of recognition. A single trans person was a victim. A group of them was an army. Together, they could conquer, if not the world, then at least the anxiety the world had instilled in them.

One of Andres's hands slipped back down, sliding curiously under Shane's shirt. Shane felt as though his heart stopped, the world slowing to those five points of contact, fingertips drawing gently along his skin. It wasn't like they hadn't touched before, but Andres had never been this bold with him—this possessive—tracing each rib like they owned it. Shane relaxed under the pressure. He leaned back against his vampire's chest, letting Andres feel each tremble that ran through him.

Lingering in the sensation, having Andres experience it with him, felt so right, and safe, and beautiful. Now, if only Andres would push him just a little farther... if Shane could get that meandering hand to reach between his legs...

Instead, his vampire did the second-best thing.

"You know what else I get to do with your skin whenever I want?" Andres pressed their mouth to Shane's ear, letting one fang scrape harmlessly along the lobe.

Shane braced himself on the countertop, focusing on the feel of his palms on the cold granite to stop himself from fingering his own clit through his jean fabric. Oh—god, he'd have to tell Andres to order him to keep his hands off himself once they finally made it that far—he could already hear the growled commands in his head: *don't touch yourself until I tell you to. Don't come unless I say.*

Just the thought had him pressed up against the edge, a hungry pounding between his legs, the tender flesh around his slit hot and swollen and his clit greedy for pressure.

With their free hand, Andres fiddled with the collar of Shane's shirt, tracing the spot where his collarbones met. "What do I want from you, my pet?"

"All of me," Shane breathed.

"Then give it to me."

Shane did, closing his eyes and tipping his head back against Andres's shoulder. His whole neck felt unprotected, his exposed throat a fragile thing that could be torn through with a single rip. Andres traced the path of Shane's trachea, a soft pressure against him as he swallowed.

"Thank you, my magnificent little swan," they murmured, lush and hot on Shane's neck. The shivery delight of those words were still sinking in when Andres bit down.

A delicious pain sliced through Shane's mind, like hitting the head of his clit rough and fast, held down by the hips and pushed through it to the peak. The crest of the venom burst made him gasp, a whimpered sound that turned quickly to a moan. He could see only stars, bright and twinkling between his lashes, and feel the hold of his vampire's strong arms.

That they could do this while sitting in the kitchen, on a quiet, normal evening between work, and it could feel this fucking good—last month, Shane would not have been able to imagine it. He allowed himself a little smirk, basking in the joy of that, before the yearning caught back up with him.

He kept himself steady, curling his toes around the barstool's footrest. The little pleading moan he gave when Andres bit down harder was nearly feverish, escaping him before he'd even realized he was making it. His vampire shuddered against him in response. Andres's hand slipped down, thumb hooking into the belt of Shane's jeans.

Oh, *god*.

A chime clattered through the house, so loud and unexpected that it took Shane a split second to recognize it as a doorbell. Andres sputtered, yanking their fangs out with such speed that it widened the little pin-pricks, a pulse of pain making its hazy presence beneath the venom still coursing through Shane's body. Blood slid in dual rivulets along Shane's shoulder and dripped off his vampire's chin.

"Fuck, sorry," Andres muttered, quickly licking the wound shut as they pulled out their phone. They swiped a few times, and their expression darkened. They turned the screen towards Shane.

From the doorbell camera, the person's form was blurred and twisted, but Shane would have recognized him anywhere. Frederick Maul had come to call.

Andres

Maul was here—at his home. Maul knew the townhouse, of course; he'd first purchased it fifteen years before he'd begun renting to Andres. Andres just hadn't expected him to physically show up. He'd text and call and email, leave enough voicemails that it filled Andres's inbox, and ultimately demand that Andres come to him, but he'd always left the house be.

That Maul had decided to change that *now* chilled Andres to the bone.

As he showed the live video to Shane, the text Maul was clearly typing into his phone arrived.

Frederick Maul

I see your car is out front and the lights are on. If you don't open the fucking door soon, I will.

Shane paled, glancing between the bend that turned the living room into the entry space, and back. "I can hide."

"He'll smell you." Andres licked his lips. "I hadn't bitten you yet when he found us in the alley, but your blood scent is in the air now—will be for minutes yet."

Shane breathed in, then out. "This is fine. I'm supposed to be here."

"Yes, restrained to my bed."

"Do you—"

"No, I don't own *chains*." Andres could feel the panic rising in the back of his mind, a slow, monstrous creep that was surely building toward whatever disastrous nonsense his body had decided was now the proper reaction to anyone making the first move to touch him. Now it wanted to join him for this too. Goddammit.

He startled as the doorbell rang again, every nerve in his body seemingly shouting for attention at the same time. Banging followed, and the vibration of his phone.

"Fuck, he's calling."

Shane slipped off the barstool, snatching up a towel to clean his shoulder as he spoke. "You're letting me wander the house. I'm well trained, okay?" He said it with such calm certainty that it almost sounded reasonable.

Somehow, it was enough to snap Andres back into form. "Right. Good, yes." He nodded, and began tousling his own hair, unbuttoning his top two shirt buttons. "Just in case he comes in, put on that piece on the mannequin and take off as much as you can under it." The transformed gala cloak was loose, lengthened and layered by lace, and he'd

317

subconsciously fit it to Shane's basic proportions in the first place. It would fit. "If he comes in, act like I was just…"

"Ravishing me?" Shane suggested, a quirk to his lips despite the situation.

It steadied Andres. He layered his voice with a growl, letting it pull him into character—the character Maul knew, stronger and more aggressive and far less compassionate than the vampire underneath. "How much of you is mine?"

"All of me," Shane replied immediately.

The door rattled like it was about to cave in.

Andres ran for it. He untucked his silky rosé-colored shirt from his high-waisted black pants, fiddling with the belt area as he opened the door. "Goddammit, Maul—"

Maul barreled into him.

The shove caught Andres so off guard that his body took a moment to respond, but as the full force of his panic caught him, he reacted much as he had with Shane, lashing out with his vampiric strength like it was his last chance to defend himself. This time, at least, it might have even been true.

Maul crashed into the door frame with a yelp that was half snarl.

Andres growled right back despite the tightness of his chest and the tunneling of his vision, forcing himself to bare his teeth and stare Maul down. "What the hell?"

The other vampire scowled, fangs out. "You were at that fucking blood bank, talking to the fucking owner."

"Talking to him about Vitalis-Barron, you fool," Andres snapped. "Doing the job you fucking gave me!"

Maul's eyes narrowed. "What does he know about them?"

"He *worked* there for years before turning. He's one of the best resources I've found!"

Maul still looked skeptical. "That better mean you finally have something useful." He paused, his attention shifting. He sniffed. "That's the human I sold you."

"Yeah." Andres wiped his mouth with his hand. A smear of blood came off his chin. He scowled. "You have really great timing, you know that?"

Maul snorted, and he seemed almost back to his usual mundane assholery when something clearly clicked in his head. "You were with someone at Jose's," he accused. "I *thought* you were keeping him *contained*."

"In a manner. He's useful. And I spent my savings on him, so I might as well get my money's worth."

As Andres spoke, Maul maneuvered past him, continuing into the living room like he owned the place. Which, technically, he did. It was all Andres could do to keep up with him, slowed first by the lingering panic still threatening to take him over, then by the sight that met him.

Shane looked perfectly undone. His hair was mussed in the most majestic way possible, his cheeks lightly flushed. He'd wrapped Andres's long necklace of rose gold and ruby around his own neck so many times that it was nearly a collar of its own. The layers of black and red, silk and lace, fell from his shoulder on one side and flowed around his petite body in a way that did nothing to hide the curves and angles beneath. He'd buttoned it low against his chest, one leg slipped gorgeously out of the side slit and the other propped up, the fabric bunched around his thigh. The fifteen-year-old in Andres wondered if he angled his body enough, whether he could see right up—

No, fuck, as delicious as Shane looked, swathed in the robe Andres had made with his own hands and spread out like he'd been brought near the verge of coming and denied at the last moment, this was *not* the time for lust.

Shane sat up with a little whimper as Maul entered, pulling a pillow in front of him. The tension and fear that grew in him with each step Maul took was so real that Andres couldn't be sure his words weren't just as genuine. "Don't let him touch me, master. Please."

"Your money's worth, huh." Maul looked almost impressed, his gaze clearly roving Shane's body like he was seeing all the places Andres's hands had grabbed, imagining something Andres wanted no part in.

It made him sick. "He gives himself to me freely," Andres clarified. "He enjoys the way I... *care* for him. Don't you, my pet?"

Shane ripped his gaze away from Maul long enough to land on Andres with such submissive longing that Andres wanted to wrap him up and kiss him until he was breathless, make him whimper and squirm through more orgasms than he'd ever had in his life, and shower him with soft affection after.

"You can come to me now," Andres told him, a depth to his dark growl that it would never have had if they'd kept their relationship masked and mysterious.

Shane all but flung himself at Andres, his robe whisking around him in a dance of fabric and lace. It settled as he tucked himself against Andres's chest, pressing under his arm like that alone could hide him from Maul. Andres let him, holding him so tight he could feel the press of the little glucose monitor on the back of his arm, and kissing the top of his head.

Maul looked mildly disgusted. "You *do* actually care for him? How adorably pathetic."

"You wouldn't understand." Andres bared his fangs. "You've never loved anything with flesh and blood."

"Fair enough." He shrugged. "Enjoy him all you want, just don't come crying to me if he's your downfall. If he's *my* downfall though…"

"As I said, he does as he's told," Andres retorted. He steered Shane in front of him with gentle tugs and nudges. "Show him, my pet. Give me your neck."

Shane's obedience was immediate and flawless, his little sigh so immaculate even the best actor couldn't have mimicked it. He tipped back his head, and Andres angled it sharply to the side, making him stretch. Shane didn't protest, didn't so much as tense, letting Andres hold him in place with a thumb and finger pressed into the soft spots underneath his jaw. With slow precision, Andres pricked a single fang into Shane's skin.

Shane did tense then, but only for a second, loosening himself under what Andres hoped wasn't too terrible a discomfort as he dragged that fang up the length of Shane's neck, cutting a long, thin line through his skin. Blood began to bead from it. Andres licked it, sealing it as he lapped the blood.

A sound left Shane like he'd been shown something beautiful for the first time in his life, and once Andres had finished, Shane caved against him, his lashes fluttering.

Maul watched with growing fascination. The edge of his lips quirked. He took a step toward them, caressing one fang with his tongue. "If he listens to you so well, then tell him to let me bite him." He smiled. "Just a little taste."

The tremble that ran through Shane then was not the least bit sexy, and Andres could feel both their heart rates increase in tandem. And yet Shane didn't squeeze the hand he wrapped around Andres's. He would do this, Andres realized, love and horror intermingling. The mere thought of Maul still haunted Shane, but he'd suffer Maul's bite if it meant he and Andres could be safe here.

But there was no fucking way Andres was going to trade any part of Shane for that.

"Go to hell," he snapped. "Your fangs don't belong in him. He is mine now. If you wanted him so badly you shouldn't have sold him off."

Maul opened his mouth, but Andres cut him off.

"No." He scooted Shane behind himself, closing the final step between himself and Maul. "I think I've been insulted enough for one afternoon."

One more step and they'd be fighting.

He hoped it didn't come to that. God, if it did, could he win? Before this, he would have had a fair chance, but with the way his body had been reacting lately...

Maul watched, his lip curling. His fingers clenched. Then he laughed. "You really aren't that boy I turned," he said. There was no humor in his voice, only truth. "But you're still my subordinate. Do you have something on Vitalis-Barron, something concrete and useful, or not? Because if you don't, I'm sure I can find another little thief who wants my paycheck, a house, and a plaything."

Andres felt the threat like a kick to the gut. His fingers ached to run through his hair, curl his head down, pull back into the corner like it could protect him, even though he knew it couldn't; knew it like the grip of Maul's fingers into his collar when Andres's early jobs hadn't gone so well, the hiss through his boss's teeth as he'd shouted *why did I even turn you if you were just going to fuck everything up, huh?* Andres wasn't certain how far this particular threat expanded—whether Maul was prepared simply to fire him and kick him out of the house he technically owned, or to dispose of him the way Andres suspected he occasionally did with his less desirable underlings and create himself a new Andres, fangs and all. Either way, Andres couldn't push

Maul that far. He *would* follow through, if not this time, then next.

"Andres," Maul said, flat and deadly.

Andres swallowed. "I'll send you what I've found."

But his boss didn't budge. "Then send it."

Andres didn't have to ask whether he meant now. He withdrew his phone casually, like it wasn't killing him to hand over such delicate material, and tried not to flinch when Maul tipped the edge of his screen in order to see it. The sent message made his gut sink.

But Maul would learn all of this once Shane's article came out. He was an asshole, and a selfish bastard, and whatever he did with the information Wesley and Vincent had gathered, it would not be *for* the betterment of his community, but it would help them. It had to. Maul wanted vampires on the streets, if only so they could pay him.

Maul checked his phone, huffing as though only half-satisfied with the wealth of information Andres—and others—had risked so much for. He didn't bother with a farewell. Nothing slammed on his way out, only the subtle click of the door opening and closing.

Andres had to creep around the corner to check that he was truly gone. He slid the lock into place again. For all the good it would do them.

He leaned against the wall when he returned, breathing in and out. It felt as if his body had forgotten how. He ran his hands through his hair, finally, holding them atop his head as his chest heaved. "Fuck." But he hadn't taken the worst of it—he hadn't been the weakest or had the most to lose. His attention went to Shane, and his own worries didn't seem to matter as much. "Are you okay?"

Shane dropped onto the ottoman. He crossed his ankles, wrapping his arms around his stomach. For a moment it looked like he was going to curl up—to curl himself right out of existence—but his gaze met with Andres's and he nodded slowly. "I think so, now that he's gone."

"I'm so sorry—"

"There were nice parts of that, you know," Shane cut him off, gentle but determined. "If *he* hadn't been here…" He shifted, loosening a little. His robe fell off one shoulder again.

"I wish he hadn't been. The way he looked at you—threatened you?" Andres growled. "I should have done more than just stand up to him. If I could have done more…"

"You did plenty. You made me feel safe, so thank you," he said, as though Andres had done a damn thing other than order him around and force him to bleed.

It soothed him still, let the adrenaline slip away. He tucked his hair behind his ears and let his fingers drop to his sides. They *were* safe. Safe, and together. "I don't know what you have to thank me for. *You* carried the performance. You were magnificent."

"Only because I have someone worth being magnificent for." Shane unfolded more at that, leaning back on his elbows. His robe shifted a little farther off one shoulder.

Andres's gaze tracked over the bared skin, and—god, he was hungry still. He could taste the last traces of Shane's blood in his mouth, that complexity of umami with a burnt edge and a hint of sweetness, and with the tension broken, the fear over, he could envision every sweet sigh and eager tremble of Shane's submission anew. Just the thought made him feel stable again. "We *could* keep on what we were doing; no Maul, just us." He added, quickly, "If you're up for it. I don't want to push you into anything you aren't ready for."

The little smirk to Shane's lips made his heart swell. "Should I change out of your outfit first, or?"

"It's yours now." It had always been Shane's, if Andres was honest with himself. "You look absolutely incredible in it."

"I think I'll look just as fine out of it, too." As though his words weren't enough to ruin Andres, Shane leaned a little further back, and slowly, purposefully, he dragged one foot up the side of his other ankle, along his calf, and under his knee, holding Andres's gaze as the fabric that had covered his legs rose up, piling higher and higher before tumbling in a pile around the base of his thighs. From the wisp of tawny curls that peeked out, he'd taken Andres's instructions to de-clothe *very* seriously. "I hear if I give myself to my master, that he'll take care of me."

Never in his life could Andres recall having gone so hard, so fast.

"Will this be a level of activity I need to prep for?" Somehow Shane made glucose and insulin levels sound sexy.

"Don't worry, my pet. You're not going to be allowed to do anything but moan."

Andres drew himself off the wall, the lightness in his head stabilizing with his nerves. He approached Shane like a predator, fangs out, showing off his desire in the way he raked over Shane with his eyes. He propped one knee on the ottoman, then the other, placing Shane between his legs as he leaned forward.

"You're mine; my little swan." He brushed a few locks of Shane's hair back and tipped his chin up, closing in on him. "I'll do what I will with you." Lips brushing Shane's cheek and fingers wrapped around his neck, Andres whispered, "You will deny me nothing."

Shane's lashes fluttered, his muscles loose enough to be conformed to Andres's pleasure, awaiting him in the way Andres had learned to recognize over the weeks. He knew Shane was ready for this—knew, too, if he wasn't, that his partner had the words to stop it and the trust that they could always reroute. It came as no surprise when Shane confirmed, "Nothing."

As his mouth opened, Andres kissed him.

They'd kissed in so many soft ways since Shane had accepted him as Andres, easy and tender and perfectly wonderful, but this time Andres took Shane's mouth like he'd done during the first deep kiss that night on Shane's couch, like he truly owned Shane, pressing against his tongue, tugging at his lips, bloodying him with venom-filled nips until each ravishment was a battle between his feeding and the healing saliva he was rendering into Shane's mouth.

He wanted Shane to taste him. To drown in him. To know exactly who he belonged to.

Shane moaned and trembled, giving himself over like he'd never had another purpose in life. His whole body went weak for Andres, except the knee he settled against the front of Andres's pants, not pressing, but offering. Andres obliged, grinding into Shane's shin as hard as he could without unseating his little swan, relishing in the ungodly satisfaction it dragged out of his cock despite the layer of fabric between them.

The fact that it was Shane's shin and not a more sensual position was a thrill all its own, ripe with the knowledge that he could give to Shane by denying him, just as he was about to give to him directly, tenfold.

Andres slipped his arms around Shane, lifting him up without breaking the kiss. Shane made a sound of surprised delight, melting against him as Andres carried him to the stairs. He left a trail of pink nips along Shane's jaw and he didn't have to ask for his little swan's neck this time, Shane giving it the moment his mouth made contact. He sipped from Shane in short drags, one for each step, careful not to overwhelm him.

He flicked on the switch for the fairy lights that roped the room's ceiling corners and laid Shane in the middle of the bed, his little swan's head amidst the arrangement of fancy red and rose gold pillows. Shane smiled. He lounged immediately, his arms draping over his head and his foot rubbing once more up his legs. For every time Andres had imagined this, the reality was even better: the red of Shane's well-kissed mouth, the blood-marks of Andres's lips on his skin, no reaching hands to accidently trigger Andres's panic, only easy supplication, the strands of Andres's necklace wrapped around his neck—*that*, he decided, was staying.

Everything else, though…

"You think you can wear something this lovely and get away with it?" Andres growled, fiddling with the lower edge of Shane's robe—a lower edge that was not hanging particularly low at the moment.

Shane basked in the question like a cat in the sun. "I was only trying to please you, master."

"You will certainly please me." Andres slipped out of his jeans, leaving his underwear—floral patterned in maroons and pinks—and his rose gold socks on, his silken button-up hanging loose around his hips as he climbed over his little swan.

Shane quite clearly devoured him with his gaze, a fresh flush coming to his cheeks as his attention finally settled on the bulge between Andres's legs. Andres smirked at him. "Did I say you could look yet?"

"No," Shane breathed, and averted his gaze obediently.

"I hardly said you could look away, either. You should see what your future holds, my little swan." Andres perched on his knees between Shane's thighs and pressed his thumb into Shane's mouth to turn his head back towards him, and as he did, he repositioned himself, drawing up his cock until the tip nudged out the top of his underwear.

The little sound Shane made, desperate and timid, was pure perfection.

"Let me see what I'll be having from you, my pet." Andres drew his thumb out of Shane's mouth, trailing over his lower lip and down the front of his throat. The robe was held together with a few small ties and buttons, which he worked free as he moved down, slowly unveiling Shane from the center of his sternum to the little glucose monitor on the back of his arm. He outlined each rib as he had earlier, this time working downward, drawing his fingers along the soft curve of Shane's hips and into the line where his pelvis met his thighs, slowly peeling back the fabric that had bundled there.

Shane was as magnificent below as he was everywhere else, light brown curls neatly trimmed around his slit, and the spread of his legs already revealed the two-inch length of himself, ripe to be played with.

"This is fun." Andres swirled his fingers through his little swan's lower hair, gripping it ever so gently as he slid Shane's slit further open.

Shane trembled beneath the touch, his lip pulled into his mouth. He didn't budge, though, letting Andres admire him.

"Tell me," Andres purred, giving Shane a smirk that showed off his fangs. "What are you?"

Shane's muscles pulsed, the moisture inside him beading around his edges. "Yours."

"And what am I allowed to do to you?"

"Anything." It was a plea, one that shuddered through Shane as Andres pressed the tip of a finger into him, drawing his wetness up toward that little glorious clit-dick.

"*What* am I allowed to do?" he asked again, grasping it between his fingers, gentle but firm. He rubbed directly against the head.

Shane cried, soft and staggering, his hips giving a little buck, but he replied with purpose, "Anything! I'm yours. You can do whatever you wish to me."

Andres let him go. He drew his finger back down, massaging it into Shane's folds just to see where it would make him tense with pleasure. It was quickly obvious that Andres's nails were an ungodly length for it, though—even if *that* was also *just* the right length for trailing teasingly and gently scraping. But Andres had more than nails.

He stole a pillow from the head of the bed and slid it under Shane's ass, lifting him enough to breath against him, letting this muskier version of his swan's scent merge with that of the blood still lingering on his lips. He bared his fangs. A little quaver ran through Shane, but he didn't protest when Andres gripped his thighs, forcing them further apart and holding them in place.

Andres pressed his lips to Shane's tender flesh, then his tongue, roughly, and finally slipped in a fang. It was just a prick, the angles awkward for much else, and he didn't even bother trying to feed—blood wasn't the point. He'd had enough for one night—now he wanted to give back.

As his venom flowed into Shane, his little swan gasped, his brow tight and his lips parting so beautifully. A shudder rolled through him as he tightened and released. The sigh that slipped out of him came between fast and steady breaths of desire.

Andres licked the tiny prick closed, once, twice, and a third time just to see Shane squirm. The added pressure on the place his venom had just been released was clearly doing something for him. Andres ran his tongue over the fang. "How many of those do you figure it will take you to come?"

"Oh god," was Shane's response. He tipped his head back.

"Give me a number," Andres commanded. He slipped his fangs into the soft skin half an inch above his first placement, and let Shane have another dose of venom.

He whimpered, his toes curling, and his answer came out tight and desperate. "Fourteen?"

"Fourteen it is then." And Andres got to work.

Shane languished with pleasure beneath each administration, a sea of delicious sounds and tremors. By the seventh prick, he was curling his back, his arms tucking around his head and he lifted his gaze to the ceiling with the sound of a suppressed moan.

"Look at me, my pet," Andres ordered him. "You will look me in the eyes while you come apart."

Shane swallowed, and brow tight, lips parted, he stared back at Andres. The pink in his cheeks deepened, but he breathed, "Yes, love," and it sounded more like a promise of eternal submission than any utterance of master or mistresses ever could.

He broke at prick twelve, crying out as his body tightened. Andres didn't let up though, sliding the last and largest two doses directly into Shane's clit before he'd finished. As he lay limp and panting, his clit twitching and swollen and the robe splayed beneath him, Andres sat back up. He fiddled with the hair between Shane's legs, massaging two fingers along his folds to keep him gently quivering.

"I *am* going to fuck you, pet," he said, as dark and sultry as he ever had before. "You don't get to decide whether I do, only where I do it... here." He leaned forward as he said it, pressing the two fingers now musky with Shane's wetness into his mouth and dragging them once along Shane's tongue for emphasis. Shane swallowed after, his lashes fluttering in time to the bob of his throat. "Or here." Andres slid those same fingers against his little swan's front hole, coating them in a fresh layer of the slickness. He drew them further back. "...or here."

As he rubbed the rim of Shane's asshole, he felt the shudder that ran through his little swan like a physical ache of desire, so bright and hot and strong.

"*There* it is, then."

And Shane whimpered.

25

His vampire had told Shane to look him in the eyes while he was coming undone, but Shane couldn't seem to *stop* coming undone. His skin felt alive, heat and chills rushing through him, making everything tender, everything heightened. He could feel each envenomed inch between his legs, a bright, aching sensation that was half orgasmic on its own, so deep it felt like it was consuming him whole. When Andres had dragged his fingers over Shane's hole, he'd known it was over for him.

It was over, in the sense that it had just begun.

He almost didn't realize it when Andres climbed off the bed, the lingering sensation of his fingers and his voice—god, his voice—still haunting Shane, but he returned with a condom and a bottle, and the normality of it hit Shane in a giddy little rush. It didn't break his desire, nor did it shatter the role Andres had taken as master, merely curled inside him, warm and blissful. He was wanted, so incredibly wanted, and was about to be fucked within an inch of his life by the most beautiful person he'd ever seen, with the ridiculously solid-looking dick that was poking from the top of his lovely underwear, its tip already beaded with the pre-cum he'd be thrusting inside Shane soon, *and* this person also happened to be the vampire who cared deeply for Shane, emotionally and physically and now sexually as well.

As Andres made to tear open the condom, a realization hit Shane.

"I'm clean." Perhaps he should have felt silly for blurting it out like that, but the heat in his cheeks was all for the lusty gaze Andres raised to his. "In both senses," he clarified. "I've been tested, and I... prepared myself before I came. Just in case you wanted me."

Andres paused, the unopened condom still in hand, but a smile spread across his face. "You are the most obedient little pet." There was something almost like awe in his voice. "In that case, lie on your stomach for me, and pull your knees under you."

Shane felt the excitement and nervousness tremble through him, building a steady throb between his legs. As he turned over, his vampire helped position him, pulling him halfway to the foot of the bed and pressing a pillow beneath his chest. Andres paused to kiss Shane's temple, so delicate and affectionate amidst the rest of the domineering treatment.

"Vampires don't normally get pathogenic illnesses anyway," he said, soft and sweet, like it was a secret.

Shane could not have felt more loved, not then, and not when his vampire took hold of his ass, gently nudging it higher. Despite the difference in position, he felt just as exposed and unmoored as he had when Andres had made him hold eye-contact, the display of his holes and his total lack of knowledge for what was coming combining into a terrifying kind of pleasure, sharp and tender all at once. He expected a sudden pressure, then a thrust.

What he got, was another kiss. The gentle brush of lips to Shane's hole was followed by a dragging tongue, warm and wet, and he *moaned*. The sensation of it caught up his nerves, tingling through every envenomed cell, making him ache deliciously inside. Andres's soft chuckle, hot breath and the drag of his hands on Shane's ass cheeks nearly curled a second sound out of him. Andres licked him again. He explored, increasing the pressure, pushing into Shane the barest bit, and when Shane was certain he'd break under the agonizing edging, his vampire's fangs pricked him.

Every aching, yearning part of him came alive in a flush of tingling pleasure. He melted into the mattress, clutching at the pillow beneath his chest, and for a time there was only that: his lover's tongue and lips and bursts of intoxicant, swirling his world into a haze he never wanted to come out of. Unless coming out meant his vampire coming into him.

He barely noticed the transition until Andres had spoken, one pressure replaced with another, thicker and far more solid. "By the time I finish with you, I'll know with excruciating certainty just how much you belong to me."

"Yes," was all Shane could manage to get out before he was taken.

The first slide of Andres into him was like agony and ecstasy all wrapped into one, the fullness of him setting alight every nerve that had already been teased and taunted and a thousand more Shane hadn't even known he'd possessed. He cried out, quivering beneath the force. Then it came a second time.

"That's it, my pet. You're such a lovely thing." Andres's voice was a new kind of husky, the pleasure of this clearly hitting him similarly. "Keep still for me. Let me have you."

Shane bit into the pillow and took what he was given, each strong, blissfully debilitating stroke setting him on fire.

He hadn't even realized how tight he'd tucked in his hands until his vampire commanded him, "Lift up your arms above your head. I want to see you unfurled."

Shane could make no response but to whimper, slowly lifting up his arms as he was told. It lost him some of the leverage he had, the sense of permanence, left him up to Andres's mercy as his vampire fucked him like he was an owned thing, meant to give pleasure.

His wetness dripped down his legs, and he felt Andre's fingers sweep it up. They touched lightly to his clit. Shane's body tried in vain to grind into the pressure, but Andres held him back, forcing him to bear through the lightest of strokes as he growled, "Don't you come until I say."

"No," Shane whined, and he didn't mean it, didn't mean it one bit.

Andres growled, his grip on Shane's clit-dick tightening. "What did you say to me?"

"I'm yours." It was a cry, a plea. "Make me yours!"

"Then obey."

But god, it was hard, each painfully light caress of his vampire's fingers in time with the force of his thrusting made Shane delirious, quickly overwhelming any ability he had left to control himself. He arched and moaned, and his world came undone. The wash of bliss that followed was so blinding it took him over, turned him to starlight for long enough that he lost his sense of time, coming back to his insides pulsing around Andres and his clit tingling with release.

He could feel Andres slow, tentatively, still hard inside him—but he didn't want that, god, he wasn't ready to be done. "Punish me!" he whined. "I disobeyed you. I came too soon, make me come again when you say."

He wasn't sure if that would be enough explanation, but his vampire seemed to get it, pressing against Shane's clit with far more intensity as he resumed the ferocity of his thrusting. Shane's body jerked away from his fingers, sensitive in his post-orgasmic state, but Andres—blessed Andres—held him in place with both arms, forcing him to take his punishment head on. Shane shook, his body trembling from head to toe as his hips fought to escape, but between the white heat of the pain of it was something deeper and more powerful, a pleasure that burned low and long like a tsunami, preparing to rise back up.

"I will keep you like this until even your body submits. You *will* obey, my little swan," Andres growled, his voice thick with desire, each breath ragged. Only when he went tense against Shane with one last thrust, his hand on Shane's clit ragged and demanding, did he whisper, "Now, you may come."

And Shane screamed. He did come, this time in a flash of heaven, searing through him like a final flood of bliss before the shut-off switch. It left a single tremble in its wake, his muscles slack and even his bones somehow empty, like every store had been spent, nothing left of him but exhaustion and a subtle contentment.

He only really felt Andres pull out of him by the lack it left, then the gentle nudge of his vampire's hands as he was directed free of the position. He curled onto his side, wanting nothing more than to look at Andres, to memorize every line of his vampire's satisfaction. Even in his post-coital state though, Andres hadn't stopped caring for Shane, carefully beginning to clean, pausing every few moments to kiss Shane's head or caress his back or whisper something sweet to him.

"I'm sorry; I feel like I got far more out of that," Shane finally said, as his vampire slipped back into the gorgeous floral underwear Shane bet he'd made himself.

"Like *you* got far more?!" Andres laughed, stroking Shane's hair. "Ah, pet—*Shane*," he added, not like a correction, but an emphasis. "You just let me—" His voice broke with emotion and he cleared his throat, though the great depth of affection and awe remained. "What you let me do to you was perfect. You are perfect. And you made me feel like—like I'm all right. Like who I am is *good.*"

Shane reached for Andres, slow and obvious, sliding the backs of his fingers up his vampire's neck and caressing his cheek. "You *are* good, Andres. And you're magnificent, too."

"Well." Andres laughed, soft and wet, but his smile shone. "How about I start you a bath? You must be sore?"

"My clit feels fucking raw," Shane grumbled, but at the fear that crossed his vampire's face, he added, "I love it—it means you'll pamper me. And check my glucose." He lifted a brow. "You *will*, right?"

"For the rest of your life," Andres replied, and it didn't seem like a fiction or a stretch or a compensation or even an obsession. It felt like them.

SHANE

Shane held Andres to his word, making time throughout the week for his vampire to push him to his limits and pamper him senseless, but the closer they got to Saturday, the more their attention was—reasonably—redirected toward the upcoming gala.

Between Andres's confidence and Shane's legitimate ChatterDash celebrity and fashion media pass, getting them both into the pseudo Met Gala as journalists turned out to be easy. Shane didn't even feel bad that he planned to ignore the fluff article he was meant to be writing—he'd done enough of those that he could scrounge something together later. Their mission tonight was solely *Operation Dr. Blood's Office.* Though if he ever did a *Rates Things* video of his criminal activities, that title would be getting zero stars for a complete lack of originality.

At least they'd decided against any attempts to infiltrate the secret basement laboratory. With the sheer amount of security Vitalis-Barron had in position, Andres barely managed to slip them both unseen into the lobby bathroom to change from their standard media outfits into the more flamboyant ones they needed to pretend they were Vitalis-Barron guests.

Shane shoved his button-up and jeans into their bag, and slipped on his outfit with ease, the simple zip along the side holding all the majestic wrapping and overlapping folds into place. Andres had taken inspiration from the costume Shane had worn when they'd first met, but this version bore no resemblance to the hastily donned shawl and mask, the shimmering white one-piece a combination of a half-cloak and a robe and something out of pure imagination, the fabric flaring and folding in on itself in tiers. He'd worn it in various stages of creation, but as he stared at himself in the bathroom mirror, he couldn't help turning from side to side, watching the layered fabric swirl. The feathers pinned into his hair fluttered. He caressed the two smaller ones that hung from the center of his silk choker.

Shane had been a shameful imitation of Cygnus back in October, but now he truly was the swan himself, prepared to mourn his reckless lover for all eternity.

Carefully, he turned his choker until the feathers sat against the place Andres preferred to bite him. There. Now it was perfect.

As he waited for his vampire to finish changing, Shane pulled out his phone.

Nat1

Hey friend, what's up?

You've been quiet lately, I hope everything's okay.
/casually worried
Any updates on that vampire stalker of yours?

The messages sank like a weight in Shane's gut. He *had* been more quiet than usual, in part because he'd been busy, but just as much because he couldn't figure out how to tell her that the vampire stalker she'd been so certain he should get rid of was now his partner. He could give her *something* though.

Shane-anigans
Sorry, life's been wild (but in a good way, I promise.) I'm actually dating someone? I was waiting to tell you until we made it official, so ta-da, I have a partner now! (And yes, he makes me very happy.)

Nat1
Oh. My. God. No way????!! I'm so excited for you!!
But now you have to tell me everything!
What's he like? How'd you meet? Have you fucked? (How big is his dick. /joking but not)
(Tho I guess I shouldn't assume he *has* a dick at all. It just sounded more slutty than "how big is his preferred organ of penetration.")

She sent a little trans flag with an eggplant emoji afterward. God, Shane had missed her.

Shane-anigans

He's tall and handsome. We met in October at a
work thing and then ran into each other again last
month at the Fishnettery. Yes we've fucked and
he's incredible, like the he-makes-me-feel-things-I-
didn't-know-I-could kind of incredible. (His dick is
exactly the right size, you pervert. And he's non-
binary! Uses both he and they pronouns.)

These were all true things, things he loved about Andres,
but the omission that this person—his person—was the same
as the vampire who'd bought him from Maul left a foul taste
in Shane's mouth all the same. Maybe it *would* be fine if she
knew? She'd probably come around once she spoke with
Andres properly. Part of Shane still retreated from the
thought, though; of the work it would entail, the explanation
and convincing; the possibility that their relationship would
never be the same after.

It was the very thing Andres had done to him, Shane
realized: separated the two halves, the simple and acceptable
one from the dastardly vampire. For Shane, that had meant
something different than for Nat, but it was still a lie—a
perceived safety net, but one that would just end up harming
them both in the end.

Andres finally emerged from the bathroom and Shane
slid his phone away; he'd have to deal with Nat later.

His vampire looked incredible—the Phaethon to Shane's
Cygnus. Their top was sheer, the fabric as black as a

mourning gown and billowing around their arms before pulling tight at their wrists with a patch of white embroidery that looked just like a swan from the right angle, their lace gloves from their night at the Starlight Club beneath. In place of the necklace they'd matched to Shane's collar, they wore another equally long chain, two feathers bobbing at the end. Both their earrings were diamonds—or good imitations— one a simple stud while the other dangled majestically. Around their eyes, they'd painted layers of shimmering silver and gold.

To distract the cameras, they'd explained when they'd packed the makeup.

The glimmering distracted Shane as well, in all the right ways.

Andres quirked the side of their lips at Shane, looking like they were admiring far more than just their handiwork. Even with their fangs shut out of view, the baring of their teeth was enough to send a happy shiver through Shane.

Andres approached with a slow confidence, catching Shane's lips in the lightest kiss. It was reminiscent of their first one, back at a very different gala, but this one held a depth Shane could never have fathomed, left a warmth behind far more lovely than any obsessive memory. As Andres passed, they flicked their fingers gently against the feathers of Shane's choker, tapping his pulse in the process. They didn't have to say anything with the motion: Shane knew what it meant.

You are mine.

And Shane responded with his own actions—*I am yours*—sliding his hand into his vampire's palm, letting himself be grasped and led along.

For all his abhorrence of Vitalis-Barron, he had to admit their taste in party set-ups wasn't terrible. The event took up the entire top level of their main building. Rows of plants and canopies of lights transformed the massive central patio that looked up into the clear night sky. Live music played from a stage at one end, little standing tables were scattered throughout. Guests had arrived while Shane and Andres changed, meandering around the patio with little appetizer plates and drinks, some trailing into the surrounding lounge rooms or back to where a conference center had been turned into a silent auction.

It was all a little more preppy than Shane preferred, but that didn't stop him from humming along to the music while he scanned the patio. Clementine had given him a basic description of their target—brown hair, undercut, early 40s, a smile that made you want to run for the hills—but Andres was doing a far better job of searching simply by exuding the confidence they took to everything they did. Their expression a perfect mixture of calm and self-assured, they'd drift into a guest's space like they belonged there, asking if the person had seen Dr. Hilker yet as though the three of them were fast friends.

Every time, the guest's confusion would last only a moment, social courtesy stepping in to answer, *no,* they hadn't seen him. He was part of the lab, right? His team was hanging out near the food, perhaps try there. Oh, wasn't that him, over with his girlfriend? "She sure has nerve showing up with him after Vitalis-Barron fired her last—"

Shane drowned the rest out, searching across the patio to where the guest had pointed. Anthony Hilker was easy enough to spot, standing a bit away from the other party-goers at one of the high tables, the cocktail in his hands untouched. His brown hair was braided along the sides of his undercut, then wound into a bun. The bright purple scrunchie that held it together didn't quite match his aubergine suit, which didn't quite match his lavender tie, and yet it all came together in the slim, purple-patterned dress of the woman draped like a conspirator against his shoulder.

Andres stiffened beside Shane, their brow tightening, and beneath the sound of the live music, they gave the softest little, "Huh."

But Shane barely had time to register it, because the woman hanging off Anthony's shoulder turned toward him then, pushing back her long, dark hair and glowering like she was about to fling daggers at the nearest group of guests. He swore he recognized her—had stared at the icon of her contact on his phone so many times that even through his uncertainty, his feet were already carrying him across the patio, limbs numb and heart pounding. He could feel the worried smile in his voice when he spoke, so much hope and fear muddled together into something unfathomable.

"Nat?" he asked.

Their eyes met, and after a moment of confusion, her glowering dissipated, replaced by a soft, awkward grin and a laugh. "Oh my god, *Shane!*"

And behind him, Andres swore.

27

ANDRES

Andres's cousin was here.

His cousin was Anthony Hilker's girlfriend. His cousin, who was looking at Shane—*Andres's* Shane—like she knew him. More than knew him, by the way they both seemed to light up, Shane understandably more awkward given the situation, but still affectionate and eager, hugging Natalie like they were old friends.

Andres remembered the gossip of the guest who'd pointed them this way, how Anthony's girlfriend had been fired from Vitalis-Barron a few months before, which was around the time Natalie had told Andres her security career was over—she still had the brace on one knee from the crash that she claimed had gotten her laid off. In all her ranting, she'd never told him the name of the company, and Andres had never asked. But if Vitalis-Barron had been her employer, with how they collected and retained their vampiric victims, working "security" for them might have entailed so much more than he'd assumed.

The first jitters of panic tingled in the back of Andres's spine, not an attack, but a warning. There was a reason he hadn't told his family about his turning; a reason that circle of ignorance had included Natalie—his favorite, his hell beast, the kid he'd let trail around after him all their childhoods and come out to before anyone else—an impulse so deep he'd never questioned it.

Andres took a step back, the fear transforming into horror. He could feel the wave of his misery rising, threatening to crash. The feeling was pre-emptive, he told himself. She knew nothing of his fangs; to her, Andres was still the dorky but loving human she'd grown up with.

That much was obvious as Shane motioned behind himself, back to where Andres still stood, his words—*my partner*—ringing in Andres's ears, and Natalie's expression transformed again. The shock was there, but as it slid away, he could make out the love beneath, the enthusiasm of realizing that two people she cared deeply for also cared for each other.

She nudged Shane in the shoulder and winked. "He's a good one. I can tell."

Andres sighed. "Hey, Hellbeast."

"Hey, bitch," she replied, and threw herself at him.

He caught her on instinct, pulling his baby cousin close as he spun her around. He'd done so a thousand times before, but only now did he realize just how much of his vampiric strength he was putting into it. His chest tightened painfully, the panic taunting him again. As he set her down, he feigned a stumble, shaking out his arms. "You're not ten anymore," he grumbled.

Natalie scoffed and shoved her shoulder into his. "Yeah—when I was ten, you would *drop* me half the time."

The space beneath his sternum hurt all the worse. That was love, he figured, ripe and deep and now miserable at the thought of what she'd done and might still do. She was the only person he'd truly loved—the only person until Shane. His little swan watched them with a confused sort of happiness.

Andres gave him a soft smile. "So, um, how do you know my cousin again?"

"Nat's that friend I talk to online." He said it like a singularity, which Andres probably should have recognized with how Shane's chat app always seemed open to one specific DM. Shane's brow lifted. "Wait, she's your cousin. So you're *related*."

"That is usually how cousins work, yes."

He made an exasperated noise. "Is there only one family in all of San Salud who actually likes me?"

Andres couldn't help but laugh at that, regardless of all the less savory emotions still tormenting him, beating against the door of his heart. He tried his best to bar it closed.

"Not even a whole family," Nat replied. "We're just the weird ones. Though I still think if *he* hadn't practically *raised* me, I would've been normal."

Andres huffed. "You would have been boring."

"Normal *is* boring," Nat said, and stuck out her tongue at him.

Andres felt the urge to cry. He forced it down, nailing it to his spine where the tingling panic still threatened.

The miserable lurking fear was only made worse when Anthony finally chipped in. "I take it this is Andres?" He lifted a brow. "And Shane, was it?"

"So you *do* listen when I talk." Nat swatted her boyfriend in the arm, but beneath the grumpy act, Andres could tell she was beaming.

"Most of the time," Anthony responded and kissed her cheek.

It was so sweet. So sweet and so disastrous. They had based this little excursion on the hopes of persuading Anthony Hilker—with violence, if need be—to sneak them into Dr. Blood's office before they fled, strangers into the night. But they weren't strangers now, not with Natalie connecting them. And if Anthony even suspected what Andres was…

He tensed at the thought, his lungs fighting him for each inhale. He could not lose Natalie. He would not.

"Andres?" Shane's voice sounded hollow, too far away, and the hand that grabbed onto Andres's wrist felt worse than before—worse than ever—a cold, dead thing pulling him into Vitalis-Barron's depths.

Andres's body reacted like he had been hit by lightning, yanking him from Shane's grasp so hard he tripped over his own feet. He fell. The wind was knocked from his lungs as he hit the ground, but somehow his muscles kept moving, putting another foot between himself and the beautiful man he knew with all his heart and mind he had nothing to fear from.

Shane looked genuinely scared. He held his wrist to his chest, his breathing heavy, and Andres could practically feel his elevated pulse. The awful shame and horror of what he'd done—what he'd never wanted to do in the first place—hit Andres like a physical blow. The guests nearby turned their attention on him, pinning him down with their horrified curiosity. He was the one who was the actor, the one who could sway people to him with enough confidence and the right words, but he had no words now, nothing he could do to convince Natalie and Anthony he hadn't just thrown his own boyfriend off him in a panic, much less talk Shane out of having experienced it.

His magnificent Cygnus cleared his throat with a laugh, his voice shaky as he said, "Fuck, that thing was huge. How long had it been on your *sleeve*? Ew."

Natalie had saved Andres from enough spiders—bless her—that she seemed not to question it. "What? Oh my god, where did it go—I want to see!"

"I think Andres vaulted it into the stratosphere." Shane made a face. "We deserve a drink after that. We'll be right back?"

"Oh, sure." Nat's brow tightened, but their cover was saved by a guest who greeted her and Anthony with enough enthusiasm to drag her attention away, sweeping her and her boyfriend into a conversation about work gossip as the chatter around them returned.

Shane didn't reach for Andres—didn't so much as touch him, arms tight at his sides and his expression cordial. Andres climbed to his feet, shakily following him toward one of the bars. The moment they were past the nearest row of flowering plants, Shane veered to the side, tucking them out of view. He turned on Andres with such ferocity and pain that it took Andres like a blade to the heart.

"What the hell?" Shane snapped.

"I'm sorry." Andres's voice sounded so pathetic, his whole being slowly crumbling in on itself. His vision blurred and a tear slipped free from one of his eyes. He did his best to quickly wipe it away without upsetting his contacts.

The stony hurt of Shane's expression broke into gentle worry and he lifted his fingers like he might brush a hand over Andres's cheek, before stalling and retreating instead. Andres's heart ached from how much he wanted that touch. Wanted to accept it and lean into it and be taken in by it. And the fact that his own damn body wouldn't let him—

He bit back something that he didn't want to admit was a sob, hiding his face behind his hands. Where was that damned gala mask when he needed one? "I'm sorry," he repeated.

"It's okay." Shane sighed and wrapped his arms tighter to his chest. He glanced away, then back, and when his gaze met Andres's again, he held it there. "But you did this at the boardwalk, and the next morning, and now... You hurt me."

"I'm so sorry. I didn't mean to." Andres would not keep crying. He could not. They had work to do here, and he was ruining it, turning his eyes puffy and smearing his makeup and making a spectacle of them both. But the more effort he put into keeping his calm, the harder it became. "I know I keep *reacting,* but I promise I've never wanted to."

"Sometimes when I go to touch you, I swear you flinch?" It wasn't an accusation the way Shane said it, but a question, his voice soft and his brow tight. "Has something happened to you, Andres? Did someone…"

"No? No!" Andres laughed, a bitter, choked sound that only made him feel worse. "Why would you ask that?"

Shane curled his arms across his chest, his hands creeping toward his neck. "It's just that after the blood bank, I looked up more about physical reactions to past events— PTSD and stuff." His tone softened, and he edged closer, just a hair, but enough to make Andres want to pull him all the way in, hold onto him and never let go. "I know I implied then that you got over Maul's assault easily, but I was upset and I jumped to conclusions. If the way you're reacting now is because of Maul, you could tell me, you know that right?"

It was sweet and honest and wrong. Shane was wrong. Andres couldn't even fathom it, his mind glancing off the idea with a fit of panic. "It's not like that!" It came out sharper than he meant it; as sharp as the truth. "As you'd said, what Maul did doesn't bother me that way."

"And there's nothing else?" Shane asked, curling a little tighter.

"I think I'd know if someone fucked me up enough to cause this." He would, he'd know. He'd remember it. Something that big and traumatic—he'd be like Shane, covering his weaknesses. The thought made him drag his hands back through his hair. They didn't shake. So where the hell were his tears still coming from?

Shane didn't meet his gaze as he whispered, "Then is it me?"

"No!" Andres responded instantly, throwing all his resolve into the word. He forced himself to breathe after. "I don't know. I mean, I know it's *not* you. But I don't *know* what it is. It's like something takes over my body and I'm aware, in my head, that you would never show me anything but affection. In that moment, I don't see you, though. I just see an invader."

"An invader?"

"I know how that sounds, okay. But I..." He swallowed around the lump in his throat, wiping back another tear. All he wanted was to stop talking about this, to pull Shane into his arms and let everything just stop. He trusted Shane. With his love, with his life. Maybe with his past too. Perhaps they could understand together. Andres ran both hands through his hair, wishing it were Shane's dirty-blonde waves under his fingers, bringing with them the instinct to nurture and not to yank out. "To tell you the truth, I've been like this long before Maul. The reaction was just weaker, or maybe because I was weaker, it wasn't so obvious the way it is now. If someone grabbed me back then, it wasn't like I could do anything about it."

Shane looked no less distressed and worried, but he nodded comfortingly, watching Andres with a gaze like a very specific kind of prey-thing; large and dangerous and prepared to fuck up the world for his family. "Who was grabbing you, my love?"

"Everyone?" Andres said, half an assumption and half a memory. "But no one was abusive," he clarified. "I was just a small, distractable kid and I hit all my growth spurts late. People pulled me around. And sometimes my friends or partners, if I wouldn't leave my sewing or I was caught up cleaning or reading or something. And I didn't yank away back then. At least, not very hard. It would get a laugh most of the time—I was a joke to them anyway, the sad little neat-freak twink—and you know how parents and aunts and uncles are." It was beginning to sound like a string of excuses, so he shut up.

"Andres." Shane spoke tenderly. "I mean this with all my love, but I'm not sure if your opinion on what is and isn't abusive is entirely accurate."

"Oh," was all Andres could think to say in response. "Well," he added, and rubbed his wrists. Then another, softer, "Oh." He finally managed something a lot like, "But I—" and then shut up again.

Maybe Shane was... right.

Andres didn't want to admit that. The idea felt large and terrifying and awful and it meant... it meant... he didn't even know. That he'd been a victim for the first half of his life? That he should have done something, changed something? His family wasn't malicious, he knew that, and his friends had just been cruel in the same way that many boys were allowed, even encouraged, to be, and while he'd always been pretty sure the couple of partners he'd had before turning hadn't liked *him* as much as they'd like the idea of a pretty twink they could fuck at their leisure, they'd never actually forced him into anything he hadn't wanted. Just latched onto him, made it clear what they wanted, and that they *could* take it.

It didn't feel like enough to fall apart over. Yet the memories crawled up Andres's spine all the same, begging him to look away. Forget it all. Go back to the life where none of them could take from him any longer.

"Ah," Andres said finally. "I guess that could be it."

Shane was quiet for so long that Andres's stomach began to hurt. He wiped away another awful tear. When his little swan spoke again, it was so gentle and so firm, he felt like the vulnerable one, being unfurled for a lover. "And Maul?"

"I haven't thought about that night in years." Andres couldn't bring himself to do it now, either. He didn't want to, he realized. Because it *had* hurt. Of course it had hurt. He'd been turned into a vampire. But there was a far worse part of it than that even: what Maul did to him had felt... normal.

Not right or good, but accurate, somehow. Like that was just how things were for human Andres; his plans and desires falling to the wayside because someone stronger wanted something from him. Even if it hurt him. Even if it drove fangs into the already mutilated flesh of his soul and fucked it up in a darker and more terrifying way than ever before.

Andres's throat caught and slowly, terribly, he began to sob.

Shane didn't reach for him, but he extended his wrists, vein-side up, calm but defiant. "Would you like to hold me?" he asked, a lifeline in a storm.

Andres grabbed onto him, pulling him close, wrapping him up like a security blanket. He cried softly in Shane's hair, and it felt a little better, somehow, than standing there alone. People still glanced their way—he could feel their gazes, their unsubtle whispers—but it mattered less now, and that was a revelation. "Thank you."

Shane kissed his temple in response.

They lingered there, Andres's chest slowly turning from havoc to a post-cry emptiness, a feeling that said the world was supposed to get better, but offering no actual improvement yet. His contacts blurred across his eyes as he opened them, and he had to blink and twitch his gaze around to finally get the damn things back into place. By then, something almost like reassurance had settled in him.

There was a reason he was like this. And if there was a reason, at least he could understand it, predict it, work through it.

Andres ran his fingers through Shane's hair, cradling his head tenderly. "I'm sorry I hurt you."

"It's not your fault." And the way Shane said it made it true somehow. "What was it you told me—*you can't brute-force your body into accepting something that's hurt it in the past?* You were right, at least according to therapists on the internet. These instincts of yours are just trying to protect you from what it knows hurt you in the past—things you should never have needed to protect yourself from in the first place."

Andres sniffled, and it was all he could do to press his forehead to Shane's, and not lose himself. "Thank you."

Shane drew his hands soothingly up and down Andres's back, and it felt like being known. "Whatever happens, I will keep being here, with you." His smile was contagious. "I'll protect you too, for a change."

The idea of his Cygnus standing between him and Maul made Andres panic just a little. He hugged Shane tighter. "I like the thought of that, but I don't know if it'll work."

"Someday it will." Shane seemed so certain. And so willing. "For now, we'll take it slow. You've been gentle with me. I can be gentle with you too, my love."

That, Andres could believe, and it made his heart feel whole in a way he hadn't known it could. A few fresh tears slipped from the corners of his eyes, and he laugh-sobbed, wiping them away. God, he had to look a mess.

Yet his boyfriend was watching him like he was the most magnificent thing in the whole world: a treasure. Someone to be gentle with. "Would it help if I asked before I touched you?" Shane asked.

"Not all touches matter. It's mostly when you have to reach for me. Especially if you're moving toward my wrists." He paused, then whimpered. "I... I've been fucked up. *God.*"

"That's *not* your fault," Shane repeated, putting emphasis on each word like he was prepared to crawl into Andres's brain and slay his guilt single-handed. "And fuck them— fuck everyone who contributed to what you're feeling now. You've gotten the better of them all, because you're happy and you're loved and you know that *you* are *not* your body's impulses, even while they continue to happen. Isn't that right?"

"Yes." Andres *was* loved, and he *was* happy, and he could not deny that for a moment. "And when we're home, I think I might... maybe we can talk about this more? About Maul and my past, and everything. After we're done here."

"Of course." As Shane stepped back, he kept his hand near his side, merely widening his fingers, palm angled toward Andres, and his lips turning in a little smug quirk as he asked, "For now, my love, would you hold my hand? We have a mission to finish."

Andres took it, fingers twining through Shane's, and even there, puffy-eyed and surrounded by his enemies, he had never felt safer.

ANDRES

Natalie and Anthony were now chatting with a group of what Andres could only assume were scientists by their fashion sense—or lack thereof—and that suited Andres fine, his eyes still red and his makeup a disaster. He kissed Shane's hair and excused himself to the bathroom with a request that his boyfriend actually find them something to drink; he was probably going to need it in order to retrieve his sorely decimated confidence for the night. He dabbed his eyes as best he could and managed to at least smear the makeup into some semblance of normalcy, even if the silver and gold were now irreversibly mixed together, before heading back into the night.

The party atmosphere was in full swing, loud and bright and perfect for the start of a morally upright crime, if the criminal himself could only pull his shit together.

He was still on edge though, particularly now that Shane's comforting presence was somewhere across the patio. While his partner's attention had momentarily abated Andres's recurring panic, it was already shooting warning shots up Andres's spine. His fingers ached to be dragged through his hair once more. The tunnel vision of his contacts made the colorful outfits of the guests twist and blur in his periphery. It was amazing that he spotted Dr. Blood at all.

She wore a grey and white pant suit—so simple and clean it should have been illegal how perfectly she pulled it off—with her long, dark hair pinned back and a thick rope of gold at her throat that matched the gleaming line along the outside rim of her delicate glasses. Andres had expected to see her here—she'd been at the October costume gala, dressed just as simply, with the idea of a Frankenstein's monster painted in silver threads across her fine features, accenting the angles of her face.

What he could barely process was the sight of a tooth-smiling Frederick Maul whispering in her ear.

Andres's heart thrummed and his throat went dry as Maul clapped her on the shoulder like they were... not old friends, certainly, but at least estranged associates. Dr. Blood scowled. She didn't push him off, though, didn't call her security over. Maul stepped away with a casual wave and she just stared stiffly after him for a moment, before turning her attention to the next guest.

A horrified *what* echoed in Andres's head, followed by a *why* he almost didn't want to answer. He had to slink back into the crowd, to figure out what this meant—for him, for Shane's article, for the blood trade, but too quickly Maul's gaze slid over Andres. His expression turned stormy. He redirected himself toward Andres, his strides lengthening.

Andres fought down the instinctive fear that rose in his chest. He forced himself to keep his fangs concealed, straightening his shoulders and glaring. When he opened his mouth, though, Maul beat him to his own question.

"What the hell are you doing here?"

Andres could have laughed if he hadn't felt so broken inside. "I'm following your orders? You wanted dirt, I'm getting dirt."

"You *got* dirt," Maul snapped, too close for comfort. But Andres could not let himself take a step back. This was still just his boss; aggressive and cruel and responsible for compounding Andres's trauma into what it was now, perhaps, but also the grouchy vampire who'd been pushing Andres around for years now, and all that time, Andres had not let himself be cowed. He thought. "And it worked. You did your part;you can return to stealing me blood."

It worked. The words rang in Andres's head, a siren drowning everything else out. Far more calmly than he felt, he asked, "What do you mean, it *worked*?"

"Thanks to that specimen list you scrounged up, I convinced Blood to strike a deal with us. We continue to keep her lab's *secrets* a secret, and she gives us a say in what her people do while they're on our streets."

The way Maul said *specimen list*, like they weren't murdered vampires, sent a shudder up Andres's spine.

"Don't look at me like that." Maul snorted. "You know if this information got out, it could ruin Vitalis-Barron, but it could hurt *us* too. Do-gooders will flock to vampire charities once activists get involved, flood the market with free blood."

Of course Maul's *us* wouldn't be the same *us* that Andres used; it didn't mean their community, but rather the two of them. The business. The blood trade. "Holding it over their heads is better than releasing it upfront. This *helps* us. Now we get to choose who they take and who they leave, and if they step out of line, they know we can defend ourselves."

"Who they take..."

Maul must have thought the flatness of his voice was consideration, because he brightened, clearly self-satisfied. "Those damn blood bank mosquitos for starts. Whoever can't pay us, or won't pay us? We give Vitalis-Barron their names, make their disappearance look like vamp-on-vamp crime—the media loves that, makes them feel so safe and justified—and in exchange, they leave *our* customers alone. It won't be viable forever, but in the meantime, we knock out our competition and renew our customer's dedication to us."

The horror of it all descended on Andres so fast that his brain clung to the little ironies at the edges—that they were having this conversation here, at a gala of the richest humans in the city, and none of the dozen people around them had noticed. And if they had noticed... they wouldn't care. Because, Andres realized with a dawning sense of absurd hilarity, most of these people probably didn't *hate* vampires. In fact, in many ways, they actually liked vampires. Liked how much money and power they could gain at their fanged population's expense, and how easy it was to push them into these corners where they traded each other's lives away for the chance to be *almost* as free as the humans.

And they had made Andres an unwitting accomplice in it.

He felt sick. The work he and Shane had done for this— their plans to expose Vitalis-Barron's experimentation and murder to the whole city in a plea for compassion—and Maul was going to use it to put more vampires in those cells and help cover up how it happened. And he expected Andres to assist him; would demand it.

"It's what's best for us," Maul said. "Once we get going, you'll see that." From behind the subtle parting of his lips Andres could just make out his fangs.

They were *meant* for Andres to see. Meant to… to remind him…

He felt like the moment Shane had looked him in the eyes and put a word to his pain all over again, the creeping realization that Maul had known what he was to Andres all this time. The reason Andres had always felt on edge with him, defensive and hostile regardless of the mood or their conversation. Andres had forced himself to forget what Maul had done to him, but Maul had kept it just beneath the surface, ensured that it festered. And it had—it had turned to this, panic taut in his muscles, screaming at him that he was too weak to truly defy Maul.

He needed Shane suddenly—to protect him or be protected by him, Andres wasn't sure—but the instinct was so strong that his attention shifted automatically through the crowd, toward the bar Shane had been waiting in line at. He was there still, accepting a cocktail with one hand, a water in his other.

Maul followed the look.

"*Why* is he here?" This interrogation had none of the grouchy roughness that Maul used to question Andres's attendance, but that was worse somehow. The quiet, deadly tension in his tone made Andres want to scoop Shane into his arms and run with him.

He focused on his own breathing, and the softness of Shane's smile as he chatted with the bartender, seemingly unaware that their lives were being torn down a dozen yards away. "He's here," Andres said, irrationally calm, "because I brought him."

"You brought your plaything to work," Maul replied, just as flat, but he flashed that hint of fangs again. "If you give me this *he obeys me* crap—"

"He *does*," Andres said, but amidst his fear and fury, his mind snapped to the comfort of Shane's touch, the thoughtfulness of his care, the way he'd so genuinely meant it as he promised to be Andres's protection. He couldn't do this. He couldn't look at the vampire who spent his life making those around him less than himself and pretend that Shane was anything but magnificent. "He listens to me," Andres restated, "but not because he's my pet or my toy. Our respect goes both ways. He's here because he wanted to be and I wanted him with me. Because I love him. And because he's my boyfriend."

It was that moment that Shane finally turned away from the bar, looking back through the crowd. He must not have seen Maul—or else despite all the photos Andres had given him to memorize, he still couldn't pick out Maul's face in the crowd—because his gaze settled purely on Andres and his expression lit up. He gave a half-wave around the drink he held and pointed towards the food. Andres lifted his hand in return, hoping Shane took the signal as *I'll join you in a minute*, and not *I might have gotten us both killed*.

Shane's shoulders bobbed, and he disappeared toward the appetizers.

Maul snarled. "You fool. He's fucking with you! He's a goddamned journalist, and he's landed in the juiciest story he could possibly have imagined. Of course he's going to try to worm himself into your good graces, where he can uncover all our dirty secrets and pull the bones out of our closets. You're not his *boyfriend*, you're *his* goddamned *plaything*."

Andres heard the words, but all he could think was that Shane had left his insulin in the car. He'd gone to pick up appetizers he couldn't even eat.

His phone buzzed gently in his pocket.

He didn't have time to reach for it though, because Maul was in his space suddenly, a hair from his chest, and he couldn't move. Couldn't breathe. His skull tingled, his jaw and his neck felt as though they were shattering, and he could do nothing.

"You've been my greatest asset, Andres. But you've gone soft again—let your weak fucking heart get the better of you. If you don't do something, that'll kill you just as surely as your pathetic human body would have."

Maul didn't have to reveal his fangs any further than the tiny tips that only Andres could see—the way his attention bore down on Andres, he could almost feel their sharpness. Those fangs weren't the exact pair that had dug into his flesh and ripped his old life away from him, but it might as well have been with how Maul had given the order, looking on unconcerned while it happened.

Maul pressed his palm to the front of Andres's shirt and twisted his fingers. Strands of the thin fabric ripped. All of Andres's muscles screamed to pull away, but he felt himself go dead inside; dead and cold, locked in the festering place Maul had cultivated.

"If you want to keep the life I've given you, then you'll put your *boyfriend* in a cage," Maul growled, "or I will put you in one instead."

He gave a shove as he let go, and with his legs stiff and wobbly, Andres nearly ended up on the ground for the second time that night. He caught himself, just barely. His hands lifted toward his hair, brushing back the loosed strands, and the chill along his skin quieted. It felt better to have his arms up, he realized. To have them in front of his neck. Perhaps he'd been protecting himself for a lot longer than he'd known.

Maul stepped back with the same suddenness that he'd come in. "Do it *now*, Andres. So long as you're compromised by that pest, you're too much of a liability to have any use to me."

Then, he left.

Andres's body didn't seem to recognize it—his own mind could barely track the place where Maul had wandered back off into the crowd, his heart thudding and his vision tunneling like his boss was still there, just waiting to jump back out at him and finish the job. Whatever that job was.

Somehow, he managed to retrieve his phone. He clicked right past Shane's text to a call. His hands didn't shake. His voice didn't stutter. It felt like the universe was laughing at him. "Are you safe?"

"I think so. I'm hiding near the entrance," Shane replied. "Why is Maul here?"

"He made a deal with Blood in exchange for the information we got from Wesley and Vincent, for keeping it buried, I guess. I'm sorry—I didn't know he'd—"

"It's fine. We'll release the list ourselves, and then whatever deal he's made will be void."

Oh, obviously, part of Andres responded, while the other part droned, *if we live that long*. He couldn't help but remember Maul's accusations about Shane, and he was sure this wasn't the time or the place, but it felt better to say the question out loud than hold its poison tucked against his heart. "You're not just with me because you're trying to get the Vitalis-Barron story, right?"

Shane went quiet. The sound of his side of the party collided with Andres's. His final reply was gentle, but firm. "Would you let me have that story, even if I no longer wished to be yours?"

Andres didn't even have to think about it. "Yes. Of course."

"Then that's your answer," Shane replied. The sound that came through after was breathless and lovely. "You do know I was obsessed with *you* first, right? You were why I started investigating vampires. You're why I'd keep doing what I could to help them, even if we weren't together, because I—" His voice broke, and the rustle that came over the speaker had Andres's heart in his chest until Shane hissed, "Shit, I see Anthony Hilker walking toward the elevators."

"Shane!"

"We came here for a reason." Shane panted softly. Fuck, he was running.

"Wait for me, then." Andres ran too, trying to dodge through the mingling guests with all the vampiric agility and speed that his anxiety-ridden legs were objecting to.

"He can't know you're a vampire."

"I don't—" *care*, he wanted to say. But he did care about that, the thought of losing Natalie, regardless of whatever horrors she'd committed, too unbearable to fathom. "Please, wait for me. I'm almost there."

"It's too late," Shane said.

Andres side-stepped a couple just entering the party and charged into the roof's lobby in time to watch the elevator door close, Shane and Anthony behind it.

29

SHANE

Shane was doing this. It would help if he knew exactly what *this* was, but he'd stolen the longest, sharpest looking knife from behind the appetizer table—which, admittedly, wasn't *very* long or *very* sharp, but neither were vampire fangs and they could still slit a vein just fine—and Anthony had no reason to anticipate Shane was here to threaten him.

He looked surprised to see his girlfriend's online bestie dart into the elevator, taking a step back as Shane approached. Shane hit the button to pause the elevator's descent and hoped it didn't automatically release an alarm. He didn't think too hard, not about the look on Anthony's face or how much taller he was this close to Shane. Anthony was just a human—a single, unarmed human who had used his knowledge of science and his access to holy silver to bully his vampiric coworker in the past, but a human nonetheless.

Gathering his courage, Shane shoved the knife against Anthony's neck.

The skin puckered around Shane's knife tip, and Anthony's eyes widened. His lips parted and closed again. He slid his palms against the elevator's shiny railing.

"You have my attention," he said, finally.

"Perfect." Shane tried to imitate the inflection Andres would say it with, and found it was easy. If all this took was confidence... He bared his teeth. "Here's the deal. I want access to Dr. Blood's office, and you're going to help me get it. I trust that you can do me this simple favor, since you've wormed your way into this place so deeply that no one's noticed your *customized* activities yet." Customized activities, like the custom drugs he'd been using Vitalis-Barron technology and resources to create for years.

Clementine hadn't been *certain* that would translate into an ability to get them the files they wanted, but he'd been hopeful enough to suggest it. And the way Anthony's expression shifted, every line going tight from withheld breath, Shane expected he was right.

"So, what do you say?" Shane asked.

"I'd say you don't know how to hold a knife."

He swore he didn't see Anthony move, but the ground shifted out from under Shane as his wrist twisted. He hit the elevator floor with a painful thud that radiated up his hip, then a rush of panic that felt like fangs in his neck, in his wrists, Maul's voice echoing in his head. But Maul wasn't the one standing over him, carefully balancing the knife between two fingers.

Anthony snorted and shoved it into his belt. "You can tell your dear Dr. Hughes that Nat's been teaching me a thing or two. Just in case."

Then he leaned forward and offered his hand like he was going to help Shane up. It felt so absurd against the adrenaline still flooding Shane's body that he hesitated.

Anthony snorted. "You should be aware that I'm not a man of any particular honor. If I was going to hurt you, I'd do it while you're down."

As ridiculous as this whole situation had turned, Shane couldn't think of a reason Anthony would lie about that. In fact, he seemed incredibly calm, watching Shane with an amused congeniality. Shane had to remind himself that this was the same person who'd nearly ruined Clementine's life for no reason other than that his then-coworker was conveniently in the way. Whether that was before or after he'd developed the alleged crush on Clementine, Shane had no idea.

But maybe that very lack of morals and loyalty was his saving grace: Anthony was probably just as likely to turn on Dr. Blood as he was on the person who'd held a knife to his throat.

Shane accepted his hand and stood. He gave Anthony a hard look after, lifting one eyebrow. "So?"

Anthony raised his own eyebrow right back. "You really don't take no for an answer."

"Because that's not the answer you're intending to give me," Shane countered. "You're not a man of any particular honor, after all, yet you helped me up."

Anthony laughed at that, and the sparkle in his eye sent a chill down Shane's spine. "My allegiance is to the science I can do with Vitalis-Barron's resources, not to this place and certainly not to Dr. Blood. And you've intrigued me. So, what do you want from Blood's office? Be honest with me, please. It'll be very inconvenient for both of us if you aren't."

Shane doubted that *inconvenient* would be the right word for whatever might happen to him if Anthony discovered he'd lied. He suspected, though, that in this case the truth might convince a competitive scientist like Anthony better than any alternative Shane could think up on the spot. "Blood has a new project, something outside the regular bounds of the vampire research she's conducting in the basement."

"How do you know this?"

"She offered Dr. Clementine Hughes a job on its research team after Vitalis-Barron fired him." Shane held his breath, hoping that the revelation aimed Anthony's fury in the right direction.

"Well, that—" He seemed to search for a word and then fail to find a suitable option, merely gritting his teeth in something that would almost be a smile if it wasn't so deadly. "They'd fired him. And she still—"

Bingo. Shane breathed out.

Anthony scowled. "You think there might be some hint in her office as to what this project is?"

That was a start, and a better one than Shane could have ever expected. "It's the only lead we have."

With a flash of his badge against the elevator reader, Anthony punched a decisive number into the pad, his lips curling. "Then I think it's time we do a little digging."

"A little *digging*?" Shane complained as Anthony unlocked Dr. Blood's office door with what he assumed had to be a stolen key. He'd already used his phone in the elevator to do something he assured Shane would loop the cameras. "Are we criminals or archeologists?"

The office was exactly what Shane had expected from the head of Vitalis-Barron's research department: polished wood and big windows, stately cabinets, a personal printer, and a computer system with three separate monitors that each looked more cutting edge than the last. Her only pieces of décor were a small line of awards and a single picture that showed a young, pale man who looked like a ghostly version of Dr. Blood herself: the only living member of her immediate family. As far as Shane's research could tell, she loved him in a distant, proud way.

Anthony snorted, closing the door behind them. "I don't think any proper criminal threatens someone with the world's fanciest butter knife."

Shane felt his cheeks prickle with a flush. "It was *not*."

In response, Anthony pulled the knife back out and prodded him in the shoulder, one eyebrow raised.

"Well, fuck."

Anthony scoffed, taking a seat behind Dr. Blood's computer. "I'm beginning to wonder if everyone who breaks into this place is incompetent."

Shane began checking the cabinets. "My partner—"

"Ah, yes, the one you left uselessly in the lobby." He plugged something into the computer's port. It was probably not true hacking, but Shane knew so little on the topic that it certainly looked like hacking to him. He glanced at Shane after a moment. "You should text him back. The buzzing is annoying."

He'd done so once in the elevator while Anthony was distracted—a simple confirmation of success—but he still felt relieved when he retrieved his phone. Andres's messages had grown no less panicked since his first one, but slightly more supportive and slightly *less* like he was considering chaining Shane to his bed after all. Shane replied quickly and moved back to his searching.

He could still feel the occasional vibration of Andres's texts, each one warming his heart. Anthony continued typing and clicking, and Shane glanced over at him what he felt was the appropriate amount for a bastard he was putting just enough trust in to get use out of. Somehow, Nat had fallen in love with this man. Was heartbroken over him. And as much as Shane thought his friend's best option was probably to run far and fast in the other direction, he'd noticed the way Anthony had smiled whenever she did, a more genuine and happy expression than any of his others.

"You know," he said, closing yet another cabinet full of signed regulatory paperwork, "Nat's worried you're losing interest in her." The computer clicking paused, and Shane forced himself not to look.

"We haven't seen each other as much since she was fired." Anthony cleared his throat. "Is she… all right?"

"That's a question you should ask her yourself."

Anthony made a noise, soft and thoughtful and a little melancholic, and then the clicking resumed. After a while, he muttered, "I don't see anything immediately useful. You don't have a name or a term I can search for? Otherwise we might be here a while..."

"Did you try the date ranges yet? A special projects folder?"

"I'm not an amateur. But neither is Blood, unfortunately."

"VR Study." It was an impulse, nothing more. "Look that up. It's not the name, but it might get us closer."

"Give me a minute…"

Shane was going to need a lot more than a single minute by the looks of Dr. Blood's filing system. He stumbled across the research proposal hard copies by sheer accident, but the drawer barely opened, its filed folders propped unreasonably high. He jiggled it, sticking in his arm to shove the unhappy thing into place. Something at the bottom clicked.

Shane froze.

Numbly, he began pulling out the files, clearing away the drawer until he could make out the compartment hidden in the bottom. A single folder sat within. It was too old to be their new secret project, but as Shane removed it, he recognized the title instantly. The VR Study. VR for *Vampirism Reversal.*

A flutter of butterflies seemed to burst through his stomach, but as he delved into the first page, then the second, his gut twisted. He googled the name of the key patient to verify, and there it was: twins, one announced dead at age seventeen after a freak accident, and the other...

Shane glanced at the photo of Vitalis-Barron's head of research and her son, the poised, pale imitation of her.

Earlier, when he'd sensed how close they were to their plans falling apart, Shane had managed to catch Dr. Blood as soon as she'd left Maul's line of sight. *"Would you like to make a comment on your inclusion of vampires in your research studies?"* he'd asked.

The glaze that had come over her eyes felt different in retrospect, hostile in a way he only now understood. The Vampirism Reversal study hadn't just been her first as Vitalis-Barron's department head. It had been her most personal.

This new information was everything—a scandal even the rich would respond to, a break of ethical protocol outside any matters of vampirism, perhaps even enough of a threat to keep Dr. Blood off Vincent and Wesley's backs regardless of the article—but it was also just a piece in a much larger puzzle. One Shane suspected the new special project played a role in, as well. As he flipped to the final page, Anthony glanced back at him.

"Something interesting?"

Shane could deny it, but the way Anthony was looking at him, all languid scrutiny, made him choose honesty. "It's an old one, but it's... well, here."

He handed Anthony the folder. The look on his face, shifting from awe to confusion, then an indecipherable stare as his gaze moved from the study's purpose to the main patient, confirmed everything Shane had just looked up. "Huh," was all he said, in the end, before handing the packet back.

Shane copied the front page, folding the originals and tucking them into his outfit's inner pocket. By the time he'd finished, Anthony was on the camera station app on his phone, frantically adjusting which screens looped. "Blood's in the left elevator."

"Is she—"

"Out. Now." Anthony began turning the computer off.

Shane scribbled across the front of the copy's first page: *We know* with a pair of fangs after. He left it on her keyboard.

Maybe it would be enough to keep Vincent and Wesley safe, and maybe it wouldn't. It was better than nothing.

They locked the office after them and ran. Anthony led the way, going right, then left, and tore through a door that Shane only realized was the emergency stairwell when he nearly toppled down the first step. The exit clicked into place, cutting off the sounds from beyond, but on the display of Anthony's phone, Shane could see Dr. Blood pausing in the elevator's open door and glancing down the hall the way they'd escaped. After a painfully long moment, she seemed to second guess herself and started toward her office.

Anthony looked at Shane, and Shane shrugged. In silence, they descended the stairs a level. Anthony led the way to that floor's elevators. Shane pressed the lobby button, no ID swipe required, but Anthony didn't step inside with him.

"I'm going up to get Nat," he explained, and watched, quietly, as the doors began to close. At the last moment, though, he shoved his hand between them. "Does she like me?"

It was not at all what Shane expected. "She's in love with you."

"Yes, I do know that. I'm not an imbecile. But does she *like* me? If we had met in different circumstances, would she be my friend?"

"Would you go to LARP-con with her?"

"If it would make her happy."

Shane just smiled in response and clicked the button to close the doors.

The lobby was no more crowded or chaotic than it had been—less so, in fact—yet it seemed suddenly that every eye was on him, the stolen paper weighing heavy in his pocket. He swore the chandeliers were sharper than before, and the air staler. The noise of chatter and electricity left a faint hum in his skull.

He sent Andres another text, *done; meet me in front of the left-most ground level doors*, but the nerves bundling under his skin only grew. Trying not to look any more suspicious than he already did, Shane stepped from the hot, loud room into the cool of the outside.

After the brightness of the lobby, the plant-lined border of the parking lot walkway seemed to go from the hazy orange glow of the streetlamps to the deep shadows of monsters and mayhem in a single step. The dark filled his lungs. He waited for it to soothe the lingering panic in his bones.

They had come, they'd done what they meant to, and whether or not Shane could include the information they'd uncovered in his larger article, it was still an ace they hadn't had before.

He closed his eyes, and breathed in. He breathed out again. The uncomfortable sensation remained. When Shane opened his eyes once more, a pair of fangs shone from the shadows.

"What do you know? A lonely pet," the vampire hummed. "Are you in need of a cage, little plaything?"

30

ANDRES

Andres was out front in what felt like a matter of heartbeats, time eaten up by his anxiety and desire to see Shane in the flesh—to run his hands over his Cygnus's shoulders and up his neck and hold him close and tell him how he was never allowed to be so reckless ever again, interspersed with admissions of how much Andres loved him.

Andres loved him.

He loved Shane enough that between seeing him vanish into the elevator and receiving his latest text, he'd decided in no uncertain terms that if they had to flee the city together to keep him safe from Maul, then Andres would.

As he left the building, though, he found that Shane hadn't arrived yet. His worry tried to urge him back inside, but that would just take him further away from the place Shane was ultimately coming to. He sent a text instead, a simple *I'm here*, and leaned against the wall between the two left-most doors. A few people came and went from the farther entrances.

When the door beside him finally opened, he jerked upright, but it was only a woman dressed like a modernist interpretation of an upside-down triangle, who did her best to ignore him. Behind her came someone he knew, at least.

"Hey, gender thief."

"Hey, Natalie." He didn't have the energy for banter. Even the smile he gave her felt weak. "Have you seen Shane?"

"You lost your partner too, huh?" She grumbled, though Andres thought, uncomfortably, that her partner hadn't just been threatened by a vampire who'd already tried to kill him once.

Not that Maul would do anything to Shane, yet. Probably. Just how little he found himself believing that once-certainty made him feel sick.

"What's up? Your makeup is different..." She reached for the glitter around Andres's eyes.

Andres flinched away. The panic settled protective and fierce at the top of his spine, and he breathed through it, letting it ease back into himself.

Natalie was still watching him, looking even more worried now. "Are you okay?"

Andres thought of Shane's arms around him, his offer of protection, and shook his head. "I'm not, really." He said it, and it didn't hurt. Instead, it made the hurt that was already there unravel, let his chest loosen and tempered his body's lingering panic. "Our childhood fucked me up a lot more than I'd realized, and now that I have someone close to me again, it's all coming out. But I'll be okay, I think. I'm just a little on edge right now."

Natalie groaned sympathetically, bumping into his shoulder as she leaned against the wall at his side. "I went to therapy in college, you know? I don't really talk about it, but it helped. I realized our family didn't mean to be shit, but that didn't stop it from happening. Didn't stop it from hurting me. And you, I guess." She pecked his cheek softly. "I'm sorry."

Andres wrapped an arm around her back, squeezing her gently. "You think it was just us, the black sheep?"

"I don't know. Our siblings seem fine, but... I also thought you got out unscathed. Like I was the only one who it fucked up because I was just weaker or something." She laughed. The sound was less bitter than he expected, especially from her: a child who'd been all rage and recklessness, grown into someone just as sharp, with far more ways to weaponize it. "Though my therapist always said that was unfair to myself. And they were right."

"Do you still go?" Andres asked.

Natalie shrugged and shook her head at the same time, an expression of confusion more than anything. "Not really. Not since Matthew was murdered—my mentor, you remember I mentioned him?"

He did remember, but the context of the night put what he knew into a more sickly light. Murdered was perhaps not the word Natalie should have been using, though by the look on her face, she clearly felt it was. "He worked with Vitalis-Barron too?"

"Yeah," Natalie replied, like it was of little importance. "Well, after what happened to him, I tried to go back, and I just—I don't know, they didn't get it. But maybe *I* was the one who didn't get it."

He wanted to hug her, to hug her and strangle her all at once, to ask her where he went wrong with her—whether this was his fault. If he hadn't pulled away so much after he'd turned, or he'd told her way back then, when she was still a teenager, maybe she wouldn't have become this. He swallowed instead, swallowed through the lump in his throat. "What was he like?"

"He was funny and thoughtful and he treated me like I was worth his time, right from the beginning. I had no one, except the rare occasion of you, and then Vitalis-Barron assigned me to him and he... he cared. Not just about our work—though he believed in me there, made me feel like I could actually do something important for once in my stupid, floundering life—but about me, as a person. And then some criminal with fangs bashed in his head, and Vitalis-Barron won't even admit it happened. I was so angry when he died." She drew in a sharp breath that seemed half sadness and half rage. "I'm *still* angry he died, I just can't seem to do a goddamn thing about it on my own."

"Life sucks sometimes," Andres concluded, his voice rough, "and emotions are little bastards."

Life had sucked for them both, giving them similar painful childhoods and vastly different adult losses. Natalie's pain wasn't any less real than his. Hers, though, could get innocent people hurt—could get himself hurt, if she knew what he was—and Andres had no idea what to do about that, except hug her, and hope that was enough to keep the worst of her demons from lashing out.

And maybe go to therapy.

Natalie returned the hug like she was afraid it was the last one she'd get, her arms tight around him and her face buried in his shoulder. She didn't let go until Anthony strolled out the farther doors and called for her, and even then she gave a quiet, *I love you*, as she disengaged. Anthony extended a hand to her. She smiled and took it, squeezing gently.

And, god, Andres still loved her too. Without his cousin at his side though, the space felt increasingly emptier, his earlier fears creeping back in.

"Was Shane with you?" he asked Anthony.

"I left him in the elevator to the lobby. He should have been here ten minutes ago."

That was when Andres had first gotten the text, though. He could feel his heart beating in his ears like a rush, his knees going weak. He leaned against the wall and heard himself say goodbye to Natalie and her boyfriend without really processing it.

They walked away, hand in hand, and Andres was alone.

He pulled his phone out, nearly missing the buttons as he quickly reopened his message thread with Shane. Still no reply.

Andres

Are you here? I'm worried.

A read sign appeared. No response bubbles. Andres felt like the ground had been swept out from under him, and he didn't know what else to do but charge onward and try not to think of Maul's fangs.

Andres sprinted through the darkness, checking under bushes and around corners, moving so far out from the building's main entrance that a security guard around the back attempted to stop him. His distress must have come through as he explained, though—or else they were just as worried by the thought of a diabetic guest accidentally wandering their property at night—because the guard radioed in Shane's description. It took them half an hour to confirm that he was no longer on the premises.

All that time, Andres panicked. He stared at the last text he'd sent, typing and untyping into the chat box, confessions and pleas. But deep down, he knew the truth. He'd known it since the moment his boss had proclaimed Shane a manipulator and a liar.

As he dragged himself into his car—passenger seat empty of all but the packet of the nutrition bar Shane had eaten at exactly six-fifteen pm that night—he finally sent another text.

Andres
Maul, what have you done with him?

Shane
You'll know in the morning.

31

SHANE

Andres wasn't coming.

Shane didn't hold that against him—Andres was one vampire and this was a city of secret spaces just like the desolate, unfamiliar courtyard Shane had been brought to. Dozens of those locations belonged to Maul. Shane knew; he'd wandered into enough of them himself in his search for vampires. For his vampire.

Andres had already found him in a situation far worse than this literal cage, saved him and cherished him for over four incredible weeks. That miracle wasn't likely to happen a second time.

No one had bitten Shane yet, pricked him with any needles, pressed any blades to his skin, but part of Shane wished they had, that they'd just get it over with. The wait was killing him. His body was so tight that it felt like if he just curled a little more, he could pull himself into a secret place, a safe place between the shadows. Every tiny sound made him flinch.

"We're saving him for later." Maul had nearly smiled when he'd said it, the barest turn of his lips and a twinkle in his eye like a cat on the prowl.

Shane felt that look so deep in his bones that it had blurred everything else out—the trip here, bound and gagged, being unloaded from the van like a sack of blood, nails digging into his arms. His outfit had torn. That moment kept coming back to him now, lying curled on his side beneath the cage bars and the distant starlight, like an irrational part of him was just as sad that Andres would have to mend it. As though when his vampire found his body— and he was sure that was the plan, the way Maul skirted his name with a sneer—Andres would see the rip first, and the corpse second.

The early morning air chilled Shane through, leaving him to cycle between the trembles of fear and those of cold. He could no longer feel his fingers beneath the tightness of the bonds, and the glucose monitor on the back of his arm pinched against the hard ground beneath him. He was certain his blood sugar was all kinds of off, and he kept reminding himself it didn't matter. Andres wasn't coming, at least not in time. Everything else would be redundant soon.

He could not make himself feel the wonder or acceptance he had when he'd spoken of death with Andres, couldn't push through the horror enough to find any beauty in a demise like this. It would have been better if his atoms ceased to exist rather than go on to be a part of Maul's terrible system. His lungs caught, the base of his throat burning, and he tried to picture the shallow grave he was sure they'd toss him in after, the little spring flowers that would soon grow up from it, but he could only see the way Andres's face would crack when they finally stumbled upon it. That image seemed more certain now than anything he'd seen in his life.

Purple streaked across the sky, then a brilliant orange highlighted the undersides of the fluffy clouds. It signaled the coming of Cygnus's lover, Phaethon, flying his sun chariot too high, then too low, his reckless ambition blazing across the face of the earth. Maybe this was their fault, naming themselves after a Greek tragedy. They'd just gotten their roles wrong, was all.

Maul waited until the light had begun to stream into the courtyard, creeping its way closer and closer to the boxy, six-foot tall cage the vampires had initially thrown Shane into. It looked built for a mastiff, or a tiger, perhaps, positioned in the courtyard's center, where the low, tired walls and shadowed openings that surrounded it wouldn't block out the sun for long. It seemed wrong for what Shane was—pale, but human. He didn't think Maul's intention was to give him a sunburn.

Unless he meant to turn Shane, like he had Andres. Leave him to die there one way or another, in agony.

That was a new thought, and it tore over Shane with a fresh wave of terror, so deep and smothering that he barely saw Maul's goons opening the door. They plunked down a chair just outside it, and Maul straddled it as he stared at Shane. His eyes narrowed.

"Do you like him, really?" He sounded curious, but skeptical, like the answer wouldn't change anything.

I love him, Shane couldn't say through the gag, but he ground his teeth into it and nodded. For the first time since Maul's goons had grabbed him, he felt his eyes moisten. *I love him,* he wanted to scream, *I love him so much that he's what I cry over, not fucking you.*

Maul shrugged. "That's a pity."

His goons pulled Shane up by his arms, and Maul thrust the chair into the cage. When they shoved Shane into it, he swore it was the same one he'd been strapped to before. He could almost feel the way he'd thrashed and screamed when they'd bound him then. This time his hands were too numb and prickling and his throat raw from breathing in the sickening strap of fabric pressed halfway into his mouth all night, his lungs too tight to scream and his muscles too cold to fight, but the memory melded into the reliving of it, nothing in his mind but terror and abhorrence. And Andres. *Andres.*

Maul slapped his hand on the cage door a few times. "Take what you want," he sneered to his goons. "I just need him alive in the end. Alive and bleeding."

Shane managed to whimper something that sounded like a protest before one of the vampire's hands fisted into his hair, holding him as the other three pressed up the layers of his sleeves and pulled down the fabric around his shoulders.

His choker came away with a searing tug, leaving his neck bare and stinging for mere moments before the fangs sank in. Through the gag, he sobbed.

He didn't know if they gave him any venom—didn't think he'd feel it beneath the pain and the panic. His body, so sluggish and hollow, still fought the touch with everything it had, trembling jerks that grew smaller and smaller with each bite and rip.

Alive and bleeding, Maul had said.

They were feeding, all right, but with every fresh bite their fangs dragged along his skin, no gentle brush of tongue following, leaving the fresh cut to drip. They were tearing him open.

Shane choked, his head spinning, and he could feel himself slip like he had in the blood bank, darkness crashing in around him that could have been blood loss or sheer anxiety.

"That's enough," Maul barked.

The vampires let go. It barely helped. The sting of their fangs and the ire of their touch still flared across his skin, ground into his soul. Shane could barely see through the tunneled fog of his fear, Maul's face floating behind the bars of the cage as it clicked shut.

"I should have told him no, bagged the rest of your blood and been fucking done with you. But then, this is what happens when you give your playthings too much freedom." He shook his head. "It has to stop somewhere."

Playthings. It took Shane a moment to understand him through the haze, and then all he could see was Andres's face crumbling as they'd admitted that Maul had hurt them, that after escaping a childhood of bullying and quiet insidiousness, Maul had taken advantage of Andres's attempts to downplay the pain in their life and used them like a toy to be manipulated or discarded.

Find me again, my love, Shane wanted to hope, to pray even, though what he'd be praying to he didn't know. But as the sun slid across the courtyard, the drip-drip-drip of his bites turning the white of his outfit to red, Maul's goons dropped mirrors into place along the courtyard's edges, one by one by one, until every bit of light in the space was angled at the cage. A vampire's death sentence. Shane could see the nail-marks on the cement floor beneath him now, dried blood in the cracks, the deep, near-black color of a vampire's, and he could wish for nothing but this: *Forget me, Andres.*

Don't let the gods throw your body to the stars.

32

ANDRES

Somehow, amidst the total collapse of his mental and emotional state, Andres had managed to contact Wesley and Vincent and warn them of Maul's treachery. Then he'd collected Shane's insulin in a little freezer bag, and fed his cat, and stood in his apartment like a goldfish out of water, his tears slipping into his mouth for what felt like the hundredth time that night. He barely noticed them anymore.

Do something.

He had to do something.

But what.

He didn't know anyone but Natalie who he could trust to help him in this, and if he had to share all the details with her—no, that wasn't even a question. It would be worth a stake through the heart, so long as she helped rescue Shane first. Hands shaking, Andres made a list of all the places he could possibly think for Maul to go: van lots and storage centers and their range of trading locations. He sent it to Natalie with as vague an explanation as he could, saying merely that someone who didn't want Shane's article to come out had taken him and there might be vampires involved.

She didn't ask questions, except which places he'd be hitting first, and quickly divvied up the rest by who was closest.

Hell Creature Extraordinaire
I'll bring you some of my holy silver. I have a couple pistols too, if you're comfortable.

Cat Mom
No worries, I've got my own stuff.
But thanks.

He bared his fangs in the mirror on his way out.

After a quick stop at his place for the less tooth-based weapons he occasionally brought on more dangerous heists, he systematically set himself to flying through his list. The night wore on. All he could taste was salt—salt that seemed to come from nowhere, because he absolutely refused to think of all the things Maul could be doing to Shane. All the ways he might already have been hurt, or worse.

You'll know in the morning, had been Maul's only text.

Andres almost missed the sun's rising entirely, its first direct rays across his face catching him off guard. It chilled him to the bone. He was down to the second-to-last location on his list, near the north-west outskirts of the city, just finishing another pointless check in with Natalie, when the text finally came through.

Shane
If you want him, come get him.

It was followed by a map location, one that hadn't been on Andres's list in the first place. He felt so sick and hollow at the sight of it that he was certain his insides had turned to a black hole, the dread in his gut slowly consuming what little hope and strength remained. He forwarded the whole thing to Natalie, but based on her last check in, by the time she arrived he'd either have rescued Shane or died trying. With the sun streaming through his windshield as he pulled onto the street, he was sure it would eventually lead to the latter. But sun-poisoning hit slowly, and it had always come for him with pain more than shakes. If he was fast enough… if he could free Shane before his suffering truly set in…

The building was an old Spanish-style place on the last wide lot of the rundown residential neighborhood that clung to the edge of the warehouse district like it was dying from infection. It had fallen into the same disarray and ruin that tainted most of Maul's properties, its foreclosure sign half buried in the dirt and weeds. A single decrepit tree loomed over the south side, leafless and melancholic.

It looked as ominous as it felt.

Andres abandoned his attempts at stealth, strolling through the open front door with all the confidence he'd learned to feign over the years. The burnt-orange ceramic tile cracked under his feet. No one emerged to stop him. He poked from one room to the next, but it took little searching to find the trap Maul had set for him: the building's courtyard, Shane encaged in the middle.

His head lolled, his lashes fluttering, but he was clearly alive from the way the blood still dripped from the jagged bites that littered his arms, shoulders, and neck, painting streaks of red across his skin and smearing down the front of his torn white outfit. For all the adrenaline and rage that had already ripped through Andres in waves that night, all the terrible fates he'd expected to find his little swan trapped in, the sight still struck him like a physical blow.

"You'll put your boyfriend in a cage," Maul had said, *"or I will put you in one instead."*

One of them was clearly meant to end up dead within those bars.

"Maul!" Andres shouted his boss's name into the depths of the house with a growl so deep it rattled. "I know you're here."

Frederick Maul emerged in one of the open windows on the far side of the courtyard, his elbows on the ledge and his face in the shadows. Andres burned at the mere sight of him, his rage and terror coalescing into a painful fire.

"Lately," Maul called, "when one of my subordinates grows too accustomed to pushing their luck with me, I give them fifteen minutes in the cage. Many of them even live through it. But your defiance is... peculiar. I thought this would be more fitting. Save yourself, or risk the sun to save your little pet. It's your choice." The satisfaction that dripped from his voice was a horrifying thing all on its own. He pulled away from the window with a final announcement. "The keys are in his lap."

Maul had timed it too perfectly: the blood seeping down Shane's skin in awful rivulets, his consciousness too far gone to even notice Andres's approach. He might last another half hour. Or another ten minutes. Or maybe he'd die in the time it took Andres to gather his courage at the edge of the sunlight as his whole body screamed at him that this wasn't his natural territory anymore.

Andres plunged forward.

It was so bright, beams of blazing sunshine streaming into him from the mirrors on all sides, but he kept his attention fixed on Shane. He could face whatever came after, so long as he knew his little swan was safe. The chains around the cage's door were so thickly wound, the locks so many, that Andres had the impulse to rattle the thing first. But if other vampires hadn't broken out that way, he wasn't breaking in. Maul had designed this as a taunt and a game— one he'd bet on Andres nearly solving, pushing himself to his limit as each lock came away. Locks, like the very first one of Maul's he'd broken, the night he'd been turned.

If he had the time, he'd have searched for a way around the obvious trap—kill Maul and whoever he'd surely brought to back him up, break the mirrors, return with a blanket and a pole to fish the keys from between Shane's thighs. But those thighs were already spotted in the dribbles of red from his bleeding arms.

Andres had no time. He had one thing Maul wouldn't expect, though. The sun-poisoning would make Andres suffer—kill him quick as any—but unlike most vampires, he wouldn't shake uncontrollably while it ravaged him. At least, not at first.

He could feel the start of the pain as he slid the lightweight tools he carried on all his cons into the first lock, but it was still a subtle ache, a warning that he'd been in the sun too often since it rose. Whatever toxins were forming in his body now, those would need time to take effect. If his hands were sure enough, he could get Shane out before it fully consumed him.

The first chain fell with a rattle.

Shane blinked, his gaze drifting lazily before fixing on Andres.

"I'm here, my love," Andres said, soft and sweet as anything he'd ever muttered in the dead of night, his arms wrapped around Shane's sleeping body.

"No." Shane's voice was hoarse, and Andres could make out the raw edges of his mouth, the lines where too-tight fabric had rubbed against his cheeks. Amidst his rage, he barely recognized the word Shane spoke. "No," he whispered again. "The light..."

"I know." Andres kept working.

He didn't think about the sun, or the way Shane's blood kept spreading, seeping across his white fabric until the streams met and darkened, or the bob of his head as he slipped in and out of consciousness, occasional whispers that sounded like, "Leave."

Andres was not leaving. He was doing his job, setting his love free one chain after the next, calmly dropping each to the ground until the final lock came away gracefully in his hands. He gritted through the pain that tore along his bones and the spears that had begun shooting through his muscles three or four locks ago, and swung open the cage gate as though its solid form wasn't holding him up.

He was vaguely aware of Maul watching from the courtyard's entrance, aware too that he wouldn't be stepping aside to let them pass. But one way or another, Shane was getting out of here alive.

Andres nearly stumbled into him as he hastily knelt, one eye on the cage's gate and one foot propping it open. Shane's blood still pumped, sluggish in his veins. Andres licked what seemed to be the worst of his wounds, barely tasting his blood as he gave Shane the tiniest doses of venom, scared to push so far it might turn him instead of saving him. It was the little sounds that Shane made that wrenched Andres's heart back open: not cries or moans but something in between, like his body was fighting to flee and his soul to stay.

"I'm here, my love." In pain, and in pieces, but he was here.

He pulled Shane into his arms the moment he was free, lugging them both out of the cage. Beneath the plastered red, he could sense Shane's smaller cuts still weeping, and he wrapped him up, kissing his wounds with each grueling step they took toward the shaded entrance. His body urged him to bite, as though it knew the hell that would come for him as the rest of the sun-poisoning set in, but he held back.

They made it halfway before Maul clapped. He stood at the edge of the shade, his fangs bared. "I see you've made your choice then."

"I have," Andres replied and drew his pistol.

As he aimed, the sun-pain flared through his arm, jerking his grip. Maul crashed into him. The weapon slipped from Andres's grasp, and it was all he could do to let Shane go as he and Maul fell backward through the blinding courtyard in a tussle of limbs and fangs. They punched and clawed, hissing like feral animals, and for the first instant of adrenaline, Andres thrilled at his own strength compared to Maul's. Then the aching of his body set back in.

Maul shoved him at the cage, one hand buried in the torn sheer fabric of Andres's shirt. Andres didn't react with the fear of being grabbed—he was fear already, fear and rage and fermented pain. As Maul threw him past the gate of the cage, Andres wrestled for the chair they'd tied Shane to, swinging it back before Maul could lock him in. It split over Maul's head and shoulders, wood coming apart in pieces.

Maul snarled. A streak of thick, dark vampire blood oozed down the side of his forehead, but when he grabbed for Andres again, he seemed stronger than ever. He shoved Andres against the front of the cage, his teeth bared, a fresh light in his eyes. "I never sank my fangs into you myself. Maybe that was my mistake."

Andres flinched from the spittle that flew with his words, struggling against his grip, but his former boss felt unmovable now, Andres's limbs all but numb from overuse and pain. The brilliant sunlight gleamed off Maul's fangs as he bared them, a bead of venom already dripping from the tips. For a human, the toxin was made to calm and gratify, but plunged into another vampire…

The horror of it caught Andres in the chest, strung together from the rumors and legends. What was real and what was myth, he didn't know. But Maul must have. And Maul was going to bite him; invade him the way he'd ordered his goons to so many years ago, a punishment and a subjugation and a death sentence.

Andres gave one last panicked thrash, but the fear could no longer drive his muscles the way it had moments before. Maul rammed him a final time against the cage. Andres was flooded by memories he thought he'd lost—teeth burying into his skin, hands gripping his shirt and hair, a palm over his mouth, the life slowly draining out of him, his whole world turning to days of misery as his body rewrote itself into something new.

Two sharp points touched his neck, bringing a hint of pain.

And then it was gone.

Maul slumped slowly against him, fangs retracted and a look of horror on his face. From the center of his chest poked the tip of something wooden, black blood spreading around it. A stake.

Shane's shoulders heaved, and he stumbled, dropping the other end of the chair's broken arm where he'd plunged it through Maul's back. Andres let the dead vampire fall to the side and staggered to catch Shane—to catch them both on each other's bodies, holding each other up with sheer force of will.

"Pet," Andres murmured, and what he meant was *I love you.*

Shane managed the weakest of smiles, but to Andres it was so bright that it almost cast the searing ache now taking over his body in shadow. "We're going home, love."

But as they trekked back across the courtyard, Andres could hear Maul's subordinates circling through the house with shouts and hisses. Shane picked up Andres's fallen pistol, and Andres let him have it—he couldn't hold the weapon and support them both at the same time.

As they stepped into the shade, his Cygnus—angry and red and littered with their half-closed bite marks—aimed the weapon with steady hands at the first of the vampires who emerged, but another appeared to their right, and then to their left, fangs bared like they would kill for another bite, perhaps for loyalty to the corpse cooling in the courtyard but more likely because they believed Andres, as his right hand, was the only thing standing between them and taking Maul's place at the top of the blood trade. They weren't entirely wrong in that either.

Andres repositioned his hold on Shane.

Maul's successors lunged toward them only to stumble, cowering. Andres felt the force that had slammed into them moments after, the sharp sun-like searing of holy silver intersecting with his already building agony. He slumped against Shane to keep from crumpling to the floor as Natalie stepped through the door to the building's front room. She held a pistol in one hand, and a long baton of holy silver in the other, wielding it like a torch against the night.

As her eyes adjusted to the room, her gaze locked on Andres. He could see her taking him in, like each millisecond was a millennium, her focus jumping from his fangs to his poisoned body, his skin already sweltering red in the presence of that much holy silver. The hurt and fury that followed wasn't unexpected, but that didn't make it any less agonizing. She aimed her pistol at him.

"Hellbeast." Andres murmured the words, affectionate even now.

"Vampire," she stated back.

And he felt his heart seize as she pulled the trigger.

33

SHANE

The shot rang like it was the only sound for miles, blasting through Shane's head in an unending flurry. Andres swayed against him—his Andres, his Andres who'd come for him, who'd risked everything and more for him, whose suffering Shane would have given anything to stop. Shane screamed as he held to him, and behind them, someone else shrieked too.

Only then did he notice the shift in Natalie's aim, up and a little to the right—straight across the courtyard behind them to an open window where a rifle lay abandoned in the gap.

Shane didn't know how to say thank you, except to move, pulling Andres with him as they stumbled toward the house's front door. After a moment of hesitation, Natalie stepped to the side. Andres hissed at the holy silver weapon still gleaming in her hand, shying away from it, and she tucked it behind her back. She seemed barely able to bring herself to look at him now, her face contorted into shades of disgust and pain, but as the first true enemy bullet rang through the space, she leapt into action, silver waving before her once again as she charged the vampires still lingering in the hallways to either side.

"Nat," Shane shouted, almost tripping over the front door's threshold in his haste.

She shook her head. The look on her face was inconsolable. "Don't—" she snarled. "Don't let me see him again, understand?" Her expression twisted. The tears that blurred along her lower lashes slipped in angry torrents that reminded Shane so much of Andres he wanted to cry for them both. "Just keep him safe, okay? I love him."

"So do I," Shane replied and staggered from the building.

He could hear her screams of attack behind him as she charged in the opposite direction, and he could do nothing but guide Andres the rest of the way to the car. His vampire was quickly looking like the weaker of them, his body slowly tearing itself apart from sun exposure while Shane's had started rejuvenating, ever so slightly, under the power of Andres's venom.

Shane helped him collapse into the back, shaking as he covered Andres with the blanket folded on the floor, and climbed into the driver seat. He felt sick as he turned on the engine, his head light and consciousness attached by a thread. From inside the house came another scream, another series of gunshots. Then nothing.

Shane hit the gas, tearing out of the front yard.

He could hear Andres making agonizing moans that seemed ripped from his soul itself, but the periods where all noise stopped were the hardest to bear.

"How are you doing, love? Andres? Stay with me?" He'd ask it like he was waking his vampire up after a long night of work and not hoping with everything in himself that he wouldn't arrive to the townhouse with a corpse in place of his partner.

But each time, came a weak response. "I'm fine."

They were both *so far* from *fine* that Shane could hardly remember what that looked like on either of them, as he half carried, half dragged Andres out of the car and up the stairs.

"Your insulin," Andres mumbled. "In the passenger seat."

"I'll get it in a moment." He could feel that his body was dangerously off, between the blood loss and the lack of his nightly dose and the hormonal upheaval of every nasty emotion he'd experienced. But he, at least, could mostly walk if he really put his mind to it. And Andres no longer could.

Shane deposited him into bed as carefully as he could, propping the pillows behind him and pulling the blackout curtains shut. His clothes would have to be changed later, but Shane drew off his shoes and unbuttoned the top of his high-waisted pants to let him breathe.

"Your contacts?"

Andres groaned. He lifted a hand sluggishly toward his eyes, but it shook with such ferocity that he couldn't make it half the distance. He seemed to notice the trembling and his breath caught in a sob. "Ah," he said, dropping his hand.

Shane kissed his forehead. "Relax."

411

He found the little bottle of Andres's eyedrops, and, gently as he could, he held open Andres's eyes. His hands shook still too, but he managed to keep himself still long enough to slide the little pieces of plastic free. Andres barely flinched, his lids immediately falling shut after. It was such a small thing, but Shane swore he looked more at ease after.

It seemed to take Shane a thousand years to get back to the car for his insulin and return again, though the time on his phone read one minute. He sent off a text—to Clementine, Vincent, Tara, and Valentine all at once—and received three immediate responses, all echoing what he already knew.

Blood.

But it's not a cure.

Shane didn't know how much he could give in his present stage, but he had to try. He could not watch his vampire die in his arms while he lived. He refused to be the Cygnus of their story.

Clementine and Tara were typing still, but Shane slid the phone onto Andres's nightstand and, peeling off his ruined outfit, he climbed into bed with his vampire. It was awkward at first, Andres unconscious and shivering, and Shane trying his best to maneuver them both. He pressed soft kisses to Andres's skin whenever he could, subtle *apologies* and *thank yous* and a thousand other things he couldn't say. Might never get the chance to say again.

His chest caught, but he breathed through it, and focused on Andres.

Placing his pale, marred wrist in Andres's mouth didn't seem like enough to Shane, and in the end he managed to lay, cradling Andres from a little higher up, and pressed the crook of his elbow to Andres's lips. Beneath the smeared blood, it was the one place that hadn't been bitten—by sheer accident, he bet—and from it, Shane could no longer feel the memory of Maul's first puncturing needle, only the brush of Andres's fingers, the touch of his mouth, the gleam in his smirk, the way he said *you're mine*, and meant it to the ends of the earth and back.

Shane pressed his skin into Andres's fangs. The pain tingled up his elbow, no venom to temper it, and turned to a gentle sting as his blood flowed. Compared to the bites Maul's goons had inflicted on him, this felt blissful. Shane brushed his free fingers through Andres's hair, kissing the top of his head and he murmured, "Drink for me, my love."

Slowly, Andres did, taking shallow, instinctive drags that pushed his fangs a little deeper into Shane's flesh, locking them together. Shane never wanted them to come apart again. He held Andres as he drank, and when his partner had taken all he could, Shane drifted off with him, dizzy and lightheaded, Andres still wrapped tightly in his arms.

Shane woke with his vampire still warm and shivering against his side, the world an aching blur beyond them, and a steady hand on his shoulder.

"Easy," Valentine whispered, and life did feel easier suddenly, like he and Andres were both going to be okay. "We brought Andres blood. I'd also like to give you venom, if you'll allow? And we should get you fed something too."

Shane wasn't sure if he'd responded verbally, but his expression must have shown his gratitude, because the vampire—not his, but still one he knew he could trust—had scooped up his hand, and the next thing he knew, he was fading into a lovely dream.

It was the only peace he seemed to get for the next twenty-four hours.

Clementine and his boyfriend showed up with another bag of fresh blood, Tara with their doctor, and Valentine called in both Maddox and their second vampiric spouse, all three of whom seemed there for the sole purpose of becoming Andres and Shane's unsolicited surrogate parents, taking over the tiny house like they were permanently moving in, while Vincent and Wesley texted constantly from the place they'd gone to hide in case Vitalis-Barron chose to take immediate action against them. Shane recovered quickly with another few doses of venom and a constant eye on his glucose levels, but Andres's health remained touch and go as he fought to return to consciousness long enough to feed before slipping back into painful throes. The doctor reassured them that they were doing everything they were capable of with their current level of medical knowledge. It was hellish—between his worries over Andres and the chaos invading Shane's normally solitary life.

But it was wonderful too.

Everyone cared so goddamned much, because Andres and Shane had tried to do something good perhaps, but also because they were in need and these people—these vampires and their humans—saw that as an opportunity and not a burden. They watched Andres each time Shane showered and slept and gave him all the venom he could possibly have needed to keep him capable of safely feeding Andres. Food appeared for him at such regular intervals that it became the only way Shane could manage to track time.

As Shane's messages to Nat went unanswered, he debated asking Clementine for Anthony's contact information, but in the end, it was Anthony who reached out.

Anthony Hilker
Natalie has returned none of my communications since the gala and she appears not to be home. This is unlike her, and it scares me. If you know where she is, or whether she is safe, I would be grateful for whatever information you can provide. Thank you.

Shane had no information he could safely give him but the confirmation that Nat wasn't responding to his messages either, and the address he'd last seen her at. He felt nauseous sending it, and for the next few hours he could do nothing but curl up against Andres's side and remind himself that she'd made this choice too.

"*Keep him safe.*"

If that was her final wish, it was one Shane knew he'd uphold to his grave.

He would keep Andres safe, and he would do what he could to keep every other vampire in the city safe as well. That it involved bringing down the workplace who'd fired Natalie, and treated their human employee's deaths with little more regard then they did their vampiric test subjects, made him pretty sure at this point she'd have been happy for that too.

So between feeding Andres and feeding himself, Shane began spending his hours curled at his sleeping vampire's side with his laptop propped between them, every little pained whimper Andres made spurring him on.

It was on the fifth day of this, Shane's emotions running dry from the constant highs and lows of love and fear, that Andres finally turned a corner. The tension and trembling that had radiated through their body in alternating waves broke, and Shane was stroking their hair tenderly when they burst awake with a shout.

"Shane!"

"I'm here." Shane drew Andres's hand to his lips, kissing them first on their knuckles before leaning in to press his lips to their temple, wrapping them up as slowly and gently as he could.

The flinch he expected never came. Andres slumped into his arms, holding onto him like he was life itself, and every tear they cried seemed to wash away the horrors, leaving both of them shining in the starlight.

34

ANDRES

The pain was made real only when it finally split, casting Andres from a hellish realm of nightmares into a tattered body in a bed, aching all the way through his bones. His head pounded and his thoughts moved slowly, tugged in and out of the darkness. They had coalesced finally on one image: his Shane, bleeding. *Dying.*

But then Shane had been there, holding him, whispering to him, so alive that Andres could do nothing but cry into his shoulder with relief. They were together, and they'd made it through. This time, Phaethon and Cygnus both lived. Andres managed to hold that thought as he drifted back off, falling into a sleep that felt, for once, restful.

When he woke again, his head a little clearer and his stomach growling softly, he managed to prop himself up on his pillows while Shane went for food. It was loud downstairs, but he recognized at least two of the voices as Maddox and Valentine. How long had they been here?

The thought of them in his house while he recovered brought a wave of nausea and anxiety, so like his reactions to being reached for that he had to force himself to breathe and sit with the feeling, turning it over from all directions. These people—the caring, jovial people who'd come to show their support—had power over him, he realized; power he hadn't given them, an inherent authority that came from staying in his house while he hovered between life and death.

Shane had taken that power too, donned it like a piece of his own soul.

Andres felt himself recoil from that as well, and he gave the reaction the hugest, ugliest middle finger he could. Shane was incredible. What he'd done for Andres—what everyone who'd come through his doors as he'd lain helpless had done for him—was born of love. There had been people in Andres's past whom he should have let himself yank back from, yank straight out of their lives the moment he could, but they were not *these* people.

These were people who would be gentle with him.

Shane returned with a plate of tortilla casserole, setting it on Andres's nightstand and climbing onto the bed like he knew just how much he belonged there. "How are you feeling?"

"As though I've been turned into a vampire all over again." Andres's voice came out so hoarse that he had to clear it in the middle. "I don't think I know my own body anymore." It was like a void had opened between the shell of his skin and the hollow of his soul, empty nerves and a deep ache that wasn't exactly pain, but it wasn't *not* pain either, a liminal thing that screamed constantly in the back of his mind. But he was alive, and Shane was sitting with him, facing him, their thighs pressed together and Shane's hand on his knee, stroking so tenderly that it made Andres almost feel like he existed.

Shane looked concerned, but his smile was still bright, overflowing with love. "We can relearn your body together."

It could have been a statement of lust, but instead there was a sweetness to it, so soft and romantic that it filled Andres with a warmth like the sunshine of Shane's blood-scent. He fiddled with the sleeve of Shane's shirt, tracing his fingers along the back of Shane's hand. "When I have the strength again…"

The little smirk that twisted into Shane's lips was delicious, somehow both submissive and insistent all at once. "Your physical prowess is not what makes me yours. Besides, you need only command me to please you, and I'll obey."

That *was* deliberately sensual, but beneath the careful words, Andres could see what else Shane was offering him: to relax and have his needs tended to, even if he couldn't reciprocate or take control. And as much as he loved the control, the dominance, the way Shane would shudder under his touch and whimper for him, he thought he might grow to love *this* too.

"I know you will, pet," he whispered. His hands were still unsteady, but he managed to trail his fingers over Shane's jaw and onto his throat, following his vein not for the need of blood—he could feel how utterly sated Shane had kept Andres while he was unconscious—but because he could.

As his fingers drew over Shane's neck though, they caught a faint ridge he hadn't expected. Andres leaned in curiously, trying to get close enough that his terrible vision righted itself, but as he did, Shane pulled back.

He pressed his palm to the place Andres had touched.

"Shane? What's wrong?" Andres asked the question, but his mind had already caught up, reason supplying him with the only logical answer. It settled like a weight in his stomach.

His little swan made a sound, pained and frustrated. "I know you won't love me less—I know that. I just..." Shane's voice broke, and when it returned, there was a broken longing in it that Andres hadn't expected. "If I were to be marked in this way, it should have been *your* fangs."

"Oh, love," Andres whispered. For all the pain he'd undergone over the last hours—days? He wasn't sure— Andres thought the feeling in his chest right then was worse. He lifted his hand once more, not reaching, just holding it out as best he could with the weakness still plaguing his muscles. "Can I see?"

Quietly, Shane handed him his glasses. The hazy edges of the room turned sharp, Shane's freckles and lashes popping back into existence from the blur of his face, and there, where Andres's fingers had brushed, lay the small, raised line of a ragged, improperly healed bitemark. Gently, he drew aside the collar of the shirt Shane had borrowed from him, pushing it over his shoulder as he traced scar after scar, a constellation of tragedies that wound their way down Shane's arm, spanning neck to wrist on either side.

Andres could almost smell the scent of the blood that had dripped from each rushed and ragged bite, not the bright and bold sunshine but a terrified void of fear and misery. The crust of that red life had been washed clean now, and what wounds had remained after Andres's hasty job at closing the bigger ones were knit into soft pink lines.

"This is my fault." The words caught in Andres's chest like a knife. "I should have healed them better. If I hadn't been so sloppy—"

"You were dying," Shane interrupted him, the blunt power in his words enough that it seemed he might rewrite the past. "We were both dying, and you still saved me. I'd rather have the scars *and* you, than even conceive of losing the person I love most in all the world."

The person Shane loved most: that was Andres, absurdly and beautifully. "I love you, too," Andres replied. He ran his hands along the small lines. So many of them. "You know, I think they are mine, and not because I feel guilty—though I do, and I imagine I will for a while. They're my marks because *you're* my partner. You were there for me and I was there for you. When you see them, when you touch them, let them remind you of how much you're worth to me."

The softness of Shane's smile was a delicacy. His brow knotted, though, and he hesitated before reaching for Andres's neck, slow and open-palmed.

At first Andres thought the reluctance was simply giving him space in case his body felt the need for it, but with the way Shane focused, the precision with which his fingers brushed skin, the sorrow of the motion...

Shane's thumb rolled over a line of flesh that felt wrong under the pressure, then a second just below it. "Is this how much I'm worth to you as well?"

Andres's blood went cold. He found the spot on instinct, two scars, thin and long, as the memory of Maul's fangs tore back through him. They hadn't pierced him properly—hadn't bitten into him to inflict their venom—but that hadn't stopped the damage from being done. Shane's hand came over his, though, skin on skin, and Andres closed his eyes, focusing on the present. And, just a little, the look on Shane's face as he'd held the stake in Maul's back. Andres smiled. "This is the reminder that I have a partner who would kill for me."

Shane gave the smallest, sharpest laugh. "God, I did that, didn't I?" He shook his head. "I don't condone the death penalty, but he deserved it."

"He really did."

Without him, the black-market blood trade would likely descend into chaos, those more loyal to the money than the community all fighting among themselves to become the new Maul. Whether the vampires who came out on top would have the infrastructure to support the giant customer base that Maul had lorded over was another question, and one that would need solving sooner than later. Which meant Andres would have to do it.

He was done with Maul, but he wasn't done with the blood trade—no vampire ever truly was.

That would have to wait until he could get out of bed, though.

"I think I'll give that casserole a try now?" His stomach made a sound in agreement.

Shane helped him sit up a little straighter. Once he seemed sure that Andres was capable of eating, he dipped across the room to pull a set of papers off the dresser. "Oh, one more thing, while you eat." His cheeks brightened as he handed the little stack over. "It needs a final edit, but I... I hope you're not too disappointed. I couldn't just leave it at Vitalis-Barron. It needed the whole story."

Andres's stomach twisted as his gaze swept over the title: *The War on Blood.* Beneath it read, *Vitalis-Barron, the Black-Market, and the Artificial Scarcity of Life.* It was so much more than he'd said he was comfortable with Shane publishing, than he'd believed would do the vampiric community any good.

As Andres skimmed the first page, Shane kept speaking. "Some pointed internet searches show that Vitalis-Barron has been undermining attempts to create vampire blood donation charities and biting centers for years now. It has the direct effect of driving hungry vampires to volunteer for research in the hopes of getting blood or money out of it, while conveniently adding fuel to the system that keeps them trapped in cycles of illegal dealings and poverty. The horror of the black-market blood trade was Maul's fault, but it was their fault too, and all of ours. The world needs to know it. And, we conveniently get ten pages on how *exactly* Vitalis-Barron has been utilizing their power over the vampire community."

The more Andres read of it, the more he realized: it wasn't about Vitalis-Barron at all. It was about their victims; their pain and desperation, their personhood, their strength. Between the quotes from Tara were those from friends and family and lovers—both human and vampire—who'd lost someone to Vitalis-Barron's labs. It shouted the names of the murdered like they would go down in history. And then—only then—did it come for Vitalis-Barron, and it came hard.

By the end, Andres had set his food to the side and given up wiping back his tears, fat, salty drops splattering the paper.

"Is it...?" Shane's voice quavered and cut out.

"It's *perfect.*" With what little strength he had, Andres pulled Shane close.

His partner melted into him, laughing, and then he was kissing Andres, not the quiet, obedient kisses of their role play or the soft, lingering workday ones, but something altogether different and magnificent, a force of affection and desperation to be reckoned with. Andres returned the kiss, weaker but with just as much longing, opening himself up to Shane and letting the taste and feel fill him to bursting. Even the tang of his tears seemed right in that moment, a perfect, beautiful thing shared between their lips and hanging in their common breath.

As Shane finally pulled away, Andres smiled. "I mean it, you did an incredible job. Of course you did."

"It wasn't just me, though. I had all the vampires read it—even Vincent left notes in a copy I emailed. I had to be sure it was telling the *right* story."

Andres kissed him again. It was slower, sweeter this time, and he heeded his worn body's urging to relax by settling back into the pillows after. He eyed the rest of his food but didn't reach for it. "Natalie...?" He hadn't wanted to ask. Between his choppy, pained memories, he thought he already knew.

Shane shook his head. "There was nothing when the police went looking. Anthony hasn't seen her. They probably..."

He seemed unable to find the strength to finish that thought, and Andres didn't push him. Maybe once he had a therapist to help him process. Perhaps the Starlight Club knew someone.

"She loved you," Shane added, looking utterly miserable.

Andres squeezed his hand. "I had been a terrible cousin to her in recent years. I'm glad she had you for a bit."

That seemed all there was to say, at least for now. Shane pressed his lips to Andres's fingers and set both his hand and his plate into his lap. "Now finish eating. And rest. I have a final edit to do, but when I'm done... I could pick up my collar from the apartment, and then you could lay there like you own my world and guide my head between your legs, and order my mouth to good use?"

"Well, now I *certainly* won't be resting," Andres grumbled and smirked.

Shane sent out the article and received an immediate offer for a permanent position at The Star—not the ordinary way these things flowed, Andres learned, but Shane's exposé was far from ordinary. Then they just had to wait.

Most of the vampires came back for that evening, everyone alight with anticipation for the morning's release. It was still an odd feeling to have so many people in his home, so many hands constantly trying to help him around, bring him things, dote on him like he was about to die instead of steadily recovering. The middle-aged Starlight polycule were the worst about it, forcing their love on him like they'd realized his own parental relationships were abysmal and were determined to make up for it.

It was odd, watching them together—odd in a beautiful way, their relationships so deep and complex that Andres thought they could spend years in his living room and he still wouldn't fully grasp it.

It seemed Maddox was Valentine's human in a far softer sense than Andres had first imagined, their relationship composed of lingering touches and cuddles. That, too, was so different than the sharp, aggressive thing Maddox had with his other vampiric spouse, Diego. He approached their relationship like a man prepared to cut out his own heart for his lover at a moment's notice, yet still one who knew every curve and edge of their love and used it to keep them both safe. When he was gone, Diego and Valentine bickered like an old married couple whose attraction had vanished to leave a deep platonic love behind. The three came together to interweave their affection perfectly, a vibrant family unit so tight it seemed destined.

Andres could see hints of himself and Shane in all three relationships, and places where they were in the process of becoming their own thing. And he loved it. He and Shane had started with their obsession and turned that into love, and with time, they could keep growing it. They could be old together, and this fiercely into each other, and this deep and knowledgeable of who the other was.

They had so much to look forward to.

And with the release of Shane's article, they could both hope the future they were entering would be a little brighter in other ways as well.

35

SHANE

Change that lasted was often a slow but steady thing, a constant push forward. Shane reminded himself of that every day as the media cycle churned and the uproar blistered.

Vitalis-Barron was everywhere now—on TV, in every newspaper, plastered across social media. Just as Andres had feared, some people had used Shane's exposé to platform their own hatred, with factless fearmongering responses a dime a dozen. But there was real, honest investigative work being done as well, some of it Shane's own as he continued to track down more of the friends and families of the vampires Vitalis-Barron had murdered.

Everything had changed, and yet nothing had. What Vitalis-Barron was doing was not technically illegal—not when their lawyers could argue that regulations on the ethics of research were written about humans, not vampires—but the right court case could change that. And there were plenty in the works.

Still, the article had done *something* imminently important: it had told the vampires of the world, and everyone who loved them, exactly what to expect from within Vitalis-Barron's walls. Volunteering flyers were shredded and physical ads vandalized. Safety systems sprang up across the city, and a list of everyone who worked for the lab's vampire hunting acquisition's team was plastered across the internet. If a few hunters went missing because of it, well, Shane certainly wouldn't shed any more tears than the few he'd cried quietly in the bathroom for Natalie.

Whatever became of Vitalis-Barron's legal battle, they would have to work ten times as hard for every vampire they wanted to hurt, and any time they succeeded, the world would know. It wasn't enough change—not nearly enough—but it was a useful first step.

And Shane's exposé wasn't the only progress the vampiric community was experiencing either. Andres was seeing to that. Piece by piece, he was pulling Maul's city-wide blood trade territory back into place, wielding the strength and aggression of his vampiric persona like a weapon against anyone who threatened to turn the selling of blood into a system for profit.

With both their jobs in hyper-mode, it meant he was with Shane a bit less, but that just made Shane savor every moment they had together, from lazy afternoons exchanging poetic theories and soft kisses in the townhouse kitchen, to early mornings in bed, where Andres's mouth would take on a very different purpose, rose gold gleaming at Shane's wrists and little ornamental chains draped across his bare skin.

He fiddled with the one on his right wrist now, repositioning the fabric of his Starlight Club outfit beneath it. Tonight's event had been a small one, an artistic, unstructured gathering held in the secluded warehouse-style brewery owned by one of the wealthier human members. Dark silk curtains were strung through the space, creating a whimsical labyrinth that let patrons appear and vanish like sparkling ghosts. It was so different from the gothic parlor setting of the first event Shane had attended, yet somehow every bit as beautiful and magical.

It also happened to land on the three-month anniversary of the night Andres had bought Shane's life from Maul, though Shane couldn't imagine the Starlight Club owners were aware of that. *Shane* certainly hadn't told them.

At the beginning of the night, he'd worried that interacting with their family in such a sensual setting would be awkward now, but the moment they strode in, Valentine smiled at them like he was on the hunt for a half-clothed delicacy and Shane forgot for a moment that the older aro-ace vampire had openly admitted his sensual prowess here was all an act.

His gaze lingered across Shane's body, one edge of his lips quirking over the point of his fangs. "I see you brought your little swan; just as beautiful as ever," he murmured, reaching casually for Shane's jawline.

The shiver that ran through Shane was so different from their first time—not a fear of what Valentine might want from him, but a thrill of how Andres would react. How he'd protect Shane, as he always did, claiming him body and blood and soul.

A snarl rose in Andres's throat as he caught Valentine's wrist with two fingers, a clear message despite the lack of pressure. His other arm tightened around Shane's waist, slipping beneath the fabric, trailing possessively. "I think you'd know by now that he bleeds only for me."

That was true, both in the game and out—at least, it would be until Shane was ready to start donating to Jose's blood bank again. With the amount of time he volunteered there, he could feel his body moving slowly but surely towards acceptance once more. Any week now, he hoped his blood bags would be waiting for a vampire in need, though he was determined—as he assured Andres and Clementine and Valentine and Vincent and Diego and every other goddamned fanged creature of the night who'd decided they cared for him—that he wouldn't push himself toward anything he wasn't ready for.

As the night winded down, Shane stepped onto the balcony overlooking a now empty patio. The lights were turned low, the sky awash with stars. A soft breeze swirled through the blossoming trees, twirling up a few of the fallen flower petals and sending them dancing around his sandaled feet. Shane closed his eyes and just breathed. It smelled of the arriving summer.

Perhaps change did come slowly, but they'd get there. And every step along the way—bright or bloody, quiet or chaotic—would be worth it. In the moments between, they had to find the time just to live.

Shane didn't hear the door open or close behind him, but he could feel the approaching presence in the tingle that ran up his spine, the hairs lifting on the back of his neck. He tensed, the fear and the thrill both holding taut in his chest. The heat of a breath came at his neck, gusting between the chains and plates of his collar, and his stalker's finger traced over his hip, slipping just beneath the fabric of his outfit to caress the delicate skin. Their other hand trailed between Shane's collarbones and up his throat to fiddle with the collar's clasp.

"Master?" Shane breathed.

His vampire made a sound, soft and predatory. "You have such a lovely neck, my swan," they murmured, their voice as dark as the night and perfectly velvety. "Lean back your head."

Shane obeyed with a fierce joy that made the world shine and left fire in the wake of Andres's fingers as they slipped between Shane's legs. Their fondling brought a soft cry from Shane's lips. He let himself be touched, be taken, pinned there against the dark balcony in the quiet, empty night, his vampire's mouth on his neck, gently kissing him between nips of fangs. The orgasm came like a firecracker, bright and sparkling, and Andres gentled their stroking after, bringing Shane down slowly as they finished feeding.

When Andres closed the bite with a series of long, lingering drags of their tongue and squeezed gently between Shane's legs a final time, he was almost disappointed his vampire hadn't pushed him harder—held him tight to the railing and made him come a second time with his body bucking against it. But then Andres hummed, kissing him beneath the ear, and said, "I'm thinking of putting you in a new outfit next time. One with a little pocket just the right size for that vibrator you connected to my phone."

The shudder that worked through Shane's body was a beautiful thing, all lust and anticipation.

Andres must have felt it, Shane's back pressed to their chest, because they laughed softly and dragged their thumb along Shane's lower lip. "Would you like that, little swan?"

"I'll like whatever you want from me, master."

Andres wrapped one arm around Shane's waist, folding their free hand against the front of Shane's throat with such care that it felt like a shield instead of a noose. "I want you to know your place, my pet. To know that I can take what I want of you, when I want you, and you will always submit."

Shane couldn't have faked the whimper of desire that escaped him even if he'd tried. "I'm yours," he whispered.

And his vampire replied, "I love you."

The pressure of Andres's arms turned warmer somehow, less sensual but more affectionate as he continued to hold Shane, burying his lips in Shane's hair and snuggling against him. Shane relaxed into the hold, turning his head to kiss his vampire on the cheek. Shane the blood slave would never have dared, but Shane the boyfriend received a little happy noise from his partner and a tug of teeth on his lower lip.

"Was that nice?" Andres asked, sounding proud but a little hesitant.

"It was lovely," Shane reassured them, snuggling against their chest. "You could have pushed me even more, though. And I like the vibrator idea. For the right event, anyway."

Andres beamed. "Diego mentioned one in July that sounded like it would fit. They're really leaning into kink for it. Sexual torment, or something? Maddox is planning the subordinate side of things."

"That sounds delightful." Shane pressed his lips to the two little fang scars on Andres's neck. He could feel his partner's fingers circling a line along his shoulder, so soft and slow Shane didn't think Andres realized he was doing it. "How was your last meeting with Dr. Ivey?"

The two of them were taking some sessions together and some apart, and Shane was still not quite sure whether to push Andres for details or wait to see whether he shared them naturally. The question didn't seem to bother him, though, his posture perking up but his body just as relaxed. "It went well, I think. We spoke a lot about my family. And... Natalie."

Her name still felt like a curveball every time it came up. But Dr. Ivey had told Shane that was normal. She was complicated, and her death was complicated, and Shane and Andres were allowed to feel complicated things for it, and to keep feeling them as long as they needed to. "Do you miss her?"

"Every day." Andres held Shane tighter. "I used to get a text or two, a meme, or a picture—just something little. Maybe I'd pulled back, but she was still there."

"And now she's not," Shane concluded.

"And now she's not."

"I miss her too. You haven't found anyone who knows…?" Shane couldn't bring himself to say, *where her body went.* Of course the vampires who'd attacked her had taken it for the blood, if they could, but where they dumped her after was still a mystery.

Andres shook his head, then buried his chin against Shane's shoulder. "That part of Maul's old group is still running in two or three separate but impenetrable blood-dealing gangs. I'll have to start pushing at the one on the East side of the inner city if they keep edging up against Ala Santa, but I don't want to turn it into a thing until I have to." He fiddled with Shane's hair—a distraction, Shane knew, from all the ways his body wished it could hide itself. "How can they not understand that we still have too much trouble with Vitalis-Barron to fight among ourselves?"

Shane ran his thumb along the side of Andres's neck, offering him a measure of protection, no matter how metaphorical or unnecessary. "Perhaps it's easier to pretend you hold some power, than to admit you have none at all."

A little shudder went through Andres, but he leaned into Shane's touch, holding tighter to him. "I told myself he wasn't in control of me. I planned the heists. I took his paychecks. I bared my teeth, and every now and then he'd half-listen to what I had to say. It was easier to be his employee, even if that meant my community suffered, than to accept that I was his plaything."

"You're making the blood trade better *now*. And people are noticing."

"I wish I could give all the bags away."

Shane had reminded Andres enough times that he and his new team of infiltrators and distributors did still need money to survive; not everyone could run a charity funded by their rich human family. Instead, he kissed his good, kind-hearted vampire and said, "When we tear down capitalism, then you can."

Andres hummed and kissed him back. He kept kissing, turning Shane in his arms until they were chest to chest. Gripping under Shane's thighs and behind his back, he picked him up, spinning him once before setting him on the railing, their lips still locked in a soft but hungry union. Shane wrapped his legs around Andres's waist and lost himself in it: the softness of Andres's skin, the way his hair felt beneath Shane's fingers, the curves of his face in the backlight of the brewery's upper windows. His life, his being. He was everything and more.

A part of Shane had known all of that the moment they'd locked eyes at the Halloween gala, but even then he could never have fathomed just how much Andres was capable of meaning to him. His vampire had been his obsession, but now he was Shane's life in an entirely different way, and he knew he was not alone in that.

Andres cupped the side of Shane's head as he kissed tenderly down his jaw and along his neck, but he paused at the edge of Shane's collar. After a moment of hesitation, he straightened just a little, reaching into his pocket.

"I um, have something to give you," he said, and Shane swore he was *blushing*.

Shane lifted his brow, trying to act nonchalant despite the sudden pounding in his chest. Andres was definitely blushing. Oh god, Shane was probably blushing now too, he could feel the heat spreading across his cheeks. "What is it?"

He could not fathom the answer, even when Andres withdrew a small velvet bag from his pocket. Andres cleared his throat, nearly handing Shane the bag before seeming to think better of it and pulling open the drawstrings on it himself. "Mercer made it to fit into the base of your collar, but you can wear it anywhere." As he spoke, he drew out a delicate rose gold choker. It caught the light of the windows above them, and its single dangling ruby gleamed. Andres spread it between his fingers. "No one else will know what it means, but I will. And so will you."

Shane's already thrumming heart caught, a force like wind and fire rushing beneath his skin. He whispered the words, as though anything stronger would break the magic of the moment. "Put it on me."

Andres's fingers slid along Shane's skin, trailing ever so gently. He wrapped the beautiful piece around Shane's neck, his gaze fixed on Shane's like he was taking in perfection. As the lock clicked into place, it sent a shiver along Shane's skin.

He touched the hanging ruby, the stone still warm from Andres's skin. "Tell me again," he asked, "who do I belong to?"

"You, Shane Cowley, are *mine*." His vampire growled, his hands gentle around Shane's neck and his face bright with love and delight. "And *I* am *yours*."

For more of Shane and Andres, check out the free short story *His Glorious Monster* for their first meeting and the exclusive post-book bonus scenes only **available through my newsletter**!

THE STORY CONTINUES...

The villains may be unmasked, but they aren't finished yet. Stay tuned for another *Guides for Dating Vampires book*, where the husky blacksmith who made Shane's collar hides a vampire tangled in his work shed as Vitalis-Barron's new star scientist comes calling...

HAVE YOU read the OTHER BOOKS?

Find out how Wesley and his now fiancé fall in love in their cute, steamy, and heart-tugging friends-to-lovers romance, followed by the slowburn push-and-pull romance of Clementine and human who first agrees to sell him blood.

Or catch MADDOX, DIEGO, and VALENTINE in their own role play club prequel adventure!

CONTENT DETAILS

Two primary scenes in which the main character is bitten nonconsensually by the villains, one in which he is then drained of blood through phlebotomy until passing out, and a second character describing similar events in conversation, as well as the memories and sensations of these scenarios emerging during PTSD at multiple points throughout the book, including one incident after volunteering for a blood draw and multiple incidents of bodily reactions resulting in minor harm to their partner.

Multiple scenes in which one of the main character's boundaries are pushed by the other, in which this character consents but has complex feelings about doing so. The situation involves discussions of consent and culminates in both characters learning to navigate each other's boundaries with healthy communication.

Consensual kinky role play involving obedience and servitude, including one extensive sex scene and another minor sexual occurrence.

A character vaguely describing being (nonconsensually) experimented on.

A run-in with the police that results in a character fleeing (successfully).

General genre-appropriate violence and drama.

OTHER BOOKS BY D.N. BRYN

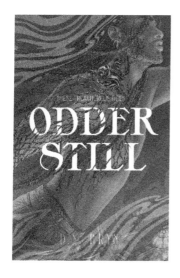

ODDER STILL

A lonely eccentric navigates an anti-capitalist revolution where both sides want to dissect him for the sentient parasite latched to his brainstem.

This slow burn, M/M romance features murderous intrigue and a Marvel's Venom-style parasite-human friendship in an underwater steampunk city.

OUR BLOODY PEARL

After a year of voiceless captivity, a blood-thirsty siren fights to return home while avoiding the lure of a suspiciously friendly and eccentric pirate captain.

This adult fantasy novel is a voyage of laughter and danger where friendships and love abound and sirens are sure to steal—or eat—your heart.

D.N. Bryn is part of The Kraken Collective—an indie author alliance of queer speculative fiction committed to building an inclusive publishing space.

If you're interested in more queer vampires, check out *Stake Sauce Arc 1: The Secret Ingredient is Love. No, Really.*

Once a firefighter, now a mall cop, Jude is obsessed with the incident that cost him his leg and his friend, five years ago. He is convinced a terrifying vampire was involved, and that they haunt Portland's streets. Every night he searches for proof and is about ready to give up... until he runs into one—a fuzzy, pink-haired vampire named Pixie. Cuddly, not-at-all scary, Pixie needs his help against his much deadlier kin. Stake Sauce is a perfect blend of dark and amusing, while giving a wide space to trauma healing and found families.

Made in the USA
Monee, IL
12 May 2024

58373318R00267